D1528317

The Kronos Interference

POP CULTURE ZOO PRESS

Superlative Speculative Fiction and Beyond!

First Edition, June 2012

Printed in the United States of America

ISBN-13: 978-0615651620
ISBN-10: 0615651623

Pop Culture Zoo Press
info@PopCultureZooPress.com
www.PopCultureZooPress.com
(503) 523-9308

First Printing: June 2012

The Kronos Interference

Edward Miller and J. B. Manas

Pop Culture Zoo Press
2012

Praise for *The Kronos Interference*

"In this time-travel thriller, debut authors Miller and Manas spin a clever, original variation on a classic alternative history premise...The prose is unfussy, the pacing appropriately brisk, and the past and future sequences show the authors' admirable imaginative gifts...

[A] tour de force...impressively original."

—*Kirkus Reviews (starred review)*

"With The Kronos Interference, Miller and Manas have produced a high-concept thriller that will keep you on the edge of your seat. Through twists and turns galore, the authors take you on a wild ride that is physically and emotionally dangerous, morally challenging, and visually stunning."

—*Paula Berinstein,*
The Writing Show podcast

"This only is denied even to God: the power to undo the past."

- Agathon

Acknowledgements

First, we would like to thank our editor extraordinaire, Paula Berinstein, for being a true partner throughout the creative process. Like any great coach, Paula challenged us to reach down deep and keep fine tuning, rewrite after rewrite. Also thanks to Brian Thompson, veteran film actor and valued friend, for his keen insights and enduring support. Thanks also to our publisher and marketing agent, Joseph Dilworth of Pop Culture Zoo Press, for believing in our book and partnering with us to bring it to the public. We also must thank our brilliant cover designer, Kirk DouPonce, of DogEared Design. Kirk is one of the great masters of cover design and we were excited to have him design our cover. He exceeded our expectations. And we can't forget our photographer, Ann Beth Goldblum.

Special thanks to Eric Manas for validating our physics references. Thanks also to our test readers for their candid and helpful feedback: Bob and Jennifer Abrahamson, Ralph Posmontier, Julie Gromer, Paul Monasevitch, Maggie Mullen, Graham McHardy, Ruth Rogers, Mary Keaser, Phil Fisher, Nancy Cutler, Robin Goldblum, Melanie Olsen, Cassandra Denton, and Jonas Sosa, Jr. We'd also like to thank friend and screenwriter Lee Kushner for his insightful advice, as well as Tom Goldblum and Bill Apter for their unending support.

We particularly owe a debt of gratitude to our wives, Heidi Miller and Sharon Manas, for putting up with us as we wrote and talked incessantly about characters and plot elements from the books. To Sid and Barbara Manas, Norm and Sallie Olson, Alfie and Geri Myers, Carl Miller, Stuart Goldstein, Nicole Gordon, Becki and Ben Gomez, and the next generation, Sophia, Gabe, and Alicia Gomez. And to Elizabeth Manas, for allowing her dad a few hours here and there to write.

It's occurred to us that we've thanked everyone but our dogs, so we may as well do that too with an acknowledgment to two of the calmest dogs on the face of the earth, Lady and Kayla.

PART 1
KRONOS

Chapter 1

Paris

The way Jacob figured it, by the end of today, he would either be the most hated man in the world, or the most loved. At least that's how the media was playing it. But for now, between the interrupted sleep and the jetlag from the twelve-hour flight to Paris, he could barely keep awake in the taxi. He'd been spoiled by all those years living in London, when Paris was only a two-hour ride on the Eurostar. Flying from San Diego was a different story. Still, it was good to be back. He hadn't visited the City of Light in at least five years.

The taxi made its way through the familiar Place Des Vosges with its antique shops, cafés, and street musicians, then to the grand, tree-lined Champs-Élysées, and on to the Hotel Concorde La Fayette, where the conference was being held. As they progressed slowly toward the hotel, Jacob looked at the conference welcome letter he'd printed out for the trip.

> Welcome to the World Conference on NBIC Convergence and Human Performance, a gathering of thought leaders in nano-technology, biotechnology, information technology, and cognitive science.

His eyes traveled down to his photo. Next to it was the writeup about his keynote presentation: *Memory Recovery and Transmission from Intracranial Nanobotic Networks in Severe BI Candidates*, which seemed an overly fancy way of saying "recovering and transmitting memories from a dead or damaged brain using microscopic robots." Some of the other topics included transhumanism and cyborg development; brain-machine interfaces; and human cognitive and physical performance enhancement in warfare. He thought about the incredible advancements in his field in the last five years. But those presentations were about works-in-progress—things to come in the near future. His break-through was already here. And people were now going to see it in living color.

As he looked up, he could see that the taxi was finally approaching the hotel. And there they stood out front, just as he had expected: the swarms of protesters. Not surprising, given the news coverage recently.

The driver pulled just ahead of the mob, and Jacob stepped out to pay him. As the taxi drove off, he tried to make his way through the crowd. It wasn't easy, as everyone was pushing and shoving. Protest signs were everywhere, and in all different languages. As he forced his way through the sea of people, an angry bald guy started yelling at him in what sounded like Italian, making the sign of the cross on his chest and forehead.

Jacob shook his head and continued on.

Goddamn lunatics would rather see us usher in the dark ages.

Out of the corner of his eye, to his left, he noticed a little girl crying. She couldn't have been more than four or five. There was no sign of her parents anywhere. Worse yet, this girl was going to be trampled on, and damn soon. He reached out his hand and led her through the masses and into the hotel lobby. He knelt in front of her. The poor girl looked scared to death.

"What's your name?"

She looked at him like a deer in the headlights.

"Tu es française?" he asked. "Tu comprends?"

She nodded her head as she sobbed. At least she understood French.

He asked her name again, this time in her language.

"Kat," she said, still sniffling.

"Ta maman? Ton papa?" Her parents had to be here somewhere.

Just then, as if someone had hit a switch, her face lit up and she yelled, "Maman!"

Jacob looked up to see the girl's mother approaching, a stocky blonde-haired woman carrying a protest sign. The woman gave him a nasty look and pulled her daughter away as if he were a kidnapper, then disappeared back into the crowd. Nice woman, bringing her daughter to a protest.

Jacob proceeded to the spacious, modern lobby. As he was looking around for the reception desk among the maze of palm trees and seating areas, an elderly man in an expensive suit approached him.

"Doctor Newman?" the man said in a slight German accent. "Jacob Newman?"

"Yes, and you are—?"

"You will excuse me, please; I recognized you from the photograph." He held up the brochure. "My father was a good friend of your grandfather. I met your grandfather once when I was a child. He was a great man—a brilliant man."

"Thank you. I'll have to agree with you."

"Our families were neighbors in Germany in the old days. Before, well…." His voice tailed off. Then he added, "He would be proud."

"Thank you. Are you here for the conference?"

"Yes, of course. I serve on the ethics committee. When I saw you were coming here, I wanted to be sure to meet you."

"Why, thank you very mu—"

"Tell me, Jacob. Did your grandfather ever talk to you of Landsberg?"

Landsberg? What did this man know of Landsberg?

Jacob wanted to probe further, but thought better of it. He wasn't about to reveal a family secret to a stranger.

"No, I can't say he did. Did your father meet him there?"

"No, nothing like that," said the old man. "It is not important. Just idle curiosity."

The old man was looking at him oddly. Then he said, "This project of yours—you seem to have hit a nerve. The protesters—"

"I'm a scientist. It's our duty to advance humanity, is it not?"

"Yes. It is."

"Well, then I'm glad we agree, Doctor...or is it Mister...?"

Jacob was fishing for a name, but the man just smiled as if he'd gotten the answer he was looking for and said, "I think we will get along quite well."

Before Jacob could say anything, the old man held out his hand. "I must be going," he said, "but I will see you this evening no doubt. It was a pleasure to meet you."

"Likewise."

Jacob shook the man's hand and watched as he walked past the lobby desk where a well-decorated military officer—American, judging from the uniform—was waiting for him. The old man whispered something to the American, and they both looked in Jacob's direction. Then the two men walked off together.

***

Jacob stood at the podium and looked out at what seemed to be a tense audience. He had never been comfortable speaking to large crowds, and this time he was more nervous than usual. He wiped the sweat from his forehead, cleared his throat, and switched on the podium microphone.

Showtime.

"What you are about to see," he began, "is the culmination of twenty years of research, and the beginning of a new era in human knowledge and capability."

He stepped back for dramatic effect and waited for the lights to dim. The room hushed. "This video," he said, "captures the perspective of a young German soldier during World War II."

The crowd murmured. Jacob pressed the play button and returned to his seat in the first row to watch with them.

The widescreen video image began projecting, showing the title, *NBIC—Program 4233, File Q1240 Sample #12.* Then it cut to a prisoner running away toward an open field. He was wearing a tattered striped uniform and an armband that signified him as a Jew.

"Shoot him," said an offscreen voice in German just to the right, the words translated into English and French underneath the picture. The camera panned to the young soldier's trembling hand holding a gun. He hesitated, aiming but not shooting.

"Shoot him!" the voice next to him repeated.

The prisoner reached a row of trees in the distance, pulled off several pieces of fruit, and started heading back.

"Look," said the soldier. "He was only going for fruit. He's coming back."

The man offscreen grabbed the gun out of the soldier's hand and shot the prisoner in the head. The prisoner stumbled and fell, the fruit spilling onto the grass. The crowd gasped.

Jacob rose from his seat and the lights came on. His blood still boiled every time he watched the scene. The noise in the room escalated as he returned to the podium. He raised a hand to quiet the crowd.

"The video you have just seen," he said, "was extracted from a dying man's brain. The man was a German soldier and later an American citizen." The crowd got loud again, and he raised a hand to quiet them. "This is the first time a human memory has been captured in a transmittable format."

With that, most people in the audience stood and applauded. Some appeared shocked.

"The possibilities," he continued, then decided to wait for the applause to stop. "The possibilities of this research are endless, from solving crimes to learning about our past. We've only begun to explore the applications. The report in your folders explains the technology. And now I'll take questions. We've got five minutes left in this segment, so I can only take a few, I'm afraid."

"How did this soldier come to volunteer his brain?" said a man in the first row.

"Ten years ago," said Jacob, "he was on his deathbed, a ninety-year-old former scientist. In fact, he'd been an advisor on our program well into his eighties. He was one of several volunteers; he knew he'd be ideal for a variety of reasons, and we agreed."

"Can this work with a living brain?" another person asked. "I mean a healthy one?"

"Why, would you like to volunteer?"

A smattering of laughter came from the audience. Then a middle-aged woman in the back rose.

"Why did you select such a horrible memory?" she asked.

"Because those are the strongest and easiest to extract."

People began shouting other questions all at once—Jacob's cue to make an exit. He excused himself and made his way from the podium to the stairs at the end of the stage.

A loud voice emerged from the crowd. "Is it true, Dr. Newman—" Jacob turned to see a man standing in the middle of the audience. He was German, judging from the accent, and had a scar running down the side of his face to his neck. A tall man with short blond hair, he appeared to be in his thirties. "Is it true that you hand selected this image because of your family past, and that you are using it for your own political agenda, thus proving very clearly the danger of this research?"

Who the hell was this guy?

Jacob wanted to ignore the man, but thought that might not be a good idea. "It was a random memory," he said. "It emerged because of its strength. Your information is wrong."

A million people started firing questions again, but Jacob said, "I'm afraid it's time for the next speaker" and left the room.

As he proceeded into the lobby, a group of people from the audience followed him, including a few relentless reporters who were still shouting questions as he walked. The protesters were still out front. Off to the left outside, he could see the taxi he'd ordered waiting for him. Now the trick would be to make it through the crowd again. He exited the front door and elbowed his way through the mob. It was denser than before, and he felt himself being pushed back. Out of nowhere, he felt a hand pull him through the crowd. He could make out an arm, but he couldn't tell who was attached. When he finally emerged from the hordes, he looked around. Whoever had helped him through the mob was gone.

He stepped into the taxi and directed the driver to take him to Charles De Gaulle airport. As soon as the taxi pulled off, he heard the three beeps on his cell phone that indicated a call was coming in from a secure line. Malcolm, no doubt. Jacob picked it up.

"Malcolm?"

"Jake, I hear things went well."

"It depends who you talk to."

"Listen, I know this is out of left field, but we need to pull you off the program."

"Pull me off? I know there's controversy, there always is, but isn't that—"

"Jake, it's not that. Something's happened. Something big was found in the South Pacific. We believe it's foreign."

There was silence on the line for a few seconds.

"What do you mean foreign, like Russian?"

"No, not Russian. We're not sure what it is."

Malcolm wasn't usually cryptic like this. It felt like they were playing a game of 20 questions.

"Is it some kind of sub?"

"No, not a sub. Nothing like that."

Jacob was trying to imagine what Malcolm was talking about. A big, foreign, not-Russian thing that wasn't anything like a sub. Alive? Dead? Technology? A hidden terrorist camp?

"What else can you tell me then?"

"Jake, I can't tell you any more at this point. I can only say it has major significance. We're talking level four SCI classification. Once I get the code word clearance for you, I'll send more information encrypted to your email. But we'll need you in Santiago Chile by tomorrow night."

Jacob wasn't sure how to react. With a simple phone call, his whole world was being turned on its head. He had to continue his research. His whole future depended on this project, especially since Kim was so ill. Still, the scientist in him thought the discovery sounded intriguing, but the timing was all wrong.

"Malcolm, Kim's undergoing chemo. You know that, right? I was planning on a short trip for family matters in the morning, and then I was planning on being home the next few weeks after that. It's why I couldn't even stay for the rest of the conference. You've got to have someone else you can call in the meantime, right?"

"I can give you a day, Jake. Once you see what I'm talking about, you'll understand why you're the only one who can help us. I'm sorry. I know you know the drill."

"I do, Malcolm. Understood."

After ending the call, Jacob leaned back in the taxi and stared out the window. He'd known Malcolm most of his life. He trusted him implicitly. And if there was one thing he knew about Malcolm, it's that he never panicked and never exaggerated. If he said it was urgent, it was urgent. More important, Malcolm was compassionate. If there were a way to avoid bringing him in, Malcolm would have found it.

On one hand, Jacob couldn't wait to learn more about the discovery. On the other, he wasn't looking forward to telling Kim he'd be running off again. But when you're doing top secret work for the CIA, duty calls, and you have no choice but to answer.

Chapter 2

Monsters

Jessica's face was red from screaming and crying. "There's a monster in there!"

"Where, honey? There's nothing here."

"There!" She pointed toward a shadow in the corner of her bedroom.

"There's nothing there. Look." Jacob turned the light on. "See, only your stuffed animals."

She looked at the pile of toys as if she didn't believe him. "Will you sit with me?" she asked.

"Only for a few minutes, then you have to get to bed. You have school in the morning."

Jessica was seven now, but she still had the occasional nightmare. Jacob decided to give her the usual speech.

"Jess, honey, there are no such things as monsters. Do you know how I know there are no monsters?"

"No." She was still sobbing.

"Because I'm a scientist. And I study real things and I learn how they work. There's nothing scary in this world that can't be explained by science."

"Are there ghosts?"

"No, there are no ghosts and no vampires either. Those are all just stories people make up to scare each other. Tell me, when your light is on, your room isn't scary, is it?"

"No."

"Well, when I turn out the light it's the same room. Nothing's different." He turned out the light to illustrate. "See, there are no monsters in the light and none in the dark."

"Ohhhkayyy." Jessica yawned, and he could see she was about to fall asleep. It occurred to him that there's much more evil to fear in the world than make-believe creatures, but he didn't want to get into that with a seven-year old.

After a few minutes, he thought she was sound asleep, but then her little head popped up again. "Daddy?"

"Yes I'm still here."

"Is God real?"

"Of course, honey. Now try to get some sleep."

"Why is God real and monsters aren't?"

He chuckled to himself. "Go to bed, Jess. We can talk more to-morrow."

As he watched Jessica doze off, he thought about their little conversation. The truth was, he didn't know what kind of God would allow the things to happen that had happened in his life—terrible things that he wouldn't wish on anyone. And now Kim was sick. He may as well believe in monsters. Yes indeed, the only real thing in this world, the only thing that made any sense at all, was science—cold, hard, and with visible evidence, even if it was sometimes unexplainable. When all else failed, it was something he could bank on, something he could control.

Jessica was fast asleep, so he went into the bedroom. Kim was getting into her night clothes and puttering. She looked tired from the chemo.

"Monsters again?" she said.

"I think she needs to cut down on the sugar." Kim was always giving Jessica ice cream.

"Ethan called," she said. "He needs money."

"What else is new?"

Jacob went to the kitchen to pour a drink and noticed a large unmarked box on the table. It felt heavy.

"What's in the box?"

"Oh yes," she called from the bedroom, "I forgot. A package came for you. There was no return address."

He looked at it again. There were no markings anywhere, not even a postmark. It must have been hand delivered. He couldn't imagine what it could be, as he wasn't expecting a package. He grabbed a knife from the kitchen drawer and cut slowly through the top, then paused. In his line of work, one couldn't be too careful. Could some nut have sent something harmful? Then again, nobody knew where he lived, unless they had followed him.

He was feeling adventurous and was too curious about what was inside to wait, so he decided to continue. He tore the top of the box open and slowly peeked inside. There seemed to be a jumble of papers and documents of some sort. He pried the cardboard boxtop open wider to get a better look and saw a number of clippings and photographs, and a small book—a journal of some kind. It all seemed safe, so he leafed through the papers to see what they were. One of them was a newspaper clipping. He pulled it out of the box.

"What the—"

The clipping was about his parents' death. Who would have sent this? He picked up a few more documents, all write-ups about his grandfather's research. There were also photos of his grandfather that he'd never seen. Rushing now, he pulled out the journal, which was covered in faded brown leather. On the inside cover, in small handwriting, was his grandfather's name—Max Neumann. Interesting. He had always known Pop as Newman. Neumann must have been his name in Germany. He didn't even know Pop had kept a journal. Jacob thought again about who might have sent this but was at a loss. There was nobody left in the family except for Ellen, and she would have called him before sending something like this. He pored through the box looking for a note, but there was nothing.

He opened the journal and flipped through it. A photo was lying loose in one of the pages—a picture of his grandparents standing in front of what looked like a synagogue. He'd never seen the two of them together before, other than in their wedding photo. They looked young here, and happy. He continued flipping through the journal and came to a page that caught his eye. There, resting alone at the top of the page, was a single word—an underlined handwritten heading: *Landsberg.*

He thought back to the words his grandfather had said on his deathbed. Cryptic as they were, he would never forget them. "Landsberg...millions of them...could...have saved...." Then with one long final breath, "—saved...them...all." Jacob had always wondered if his grandfather had been involved in something—maybe some secret mission. The only thing he knew about Landsberg was that it was where Hitler had been imprisoned in the 1920s. But that was long before World War II, so he couldn't make any connection between that and his grandfather's words.

Then Jacob thought of something else. The old man in Paris had asked about Landsberg. Could he have sent this box? Then again, the more he thought about it, that would have been pretty unlikely. His address was about as private as an address could be. The man would have had to go to great lengths to find it. And for what purpose?

Just then the phone rang. It was the secure line. Jacob picked it up.

"Malcolm?"

"I have your code. Write this down."

Jacob grabbed a pen and paper. "Go."

"Alpha, Charlie, Tango, Whiskey, Bravo, Niner, Bravo. You'll need the code to access the encrypted file I'm sending. Then the usual verification prompts."

"Got it."

"Jake, what we found is big."

"I assume it is if it's above top secret."

"No, I mean big, as in several times the size of Yankee Stadium."

Jacob tried to process what he had just heard. "I take it it's not a sunken cruise ship," he said.

"Hardly," said Malcolm, missing the sarcasm. "This is unlike anything you've ever seen."

"It should be pretty damn interesting then," he said.

"No, that's not the interesting part. The interesting part is what we found inside."

"What did you find?"

"I can tell you this, Jake. It's proof that we're being watched. And just as important is what we didn't find."

Before Jacob could respond, Malcolm said, "Listen, I have to run. Check your email. It'll explain more. I'll see you tomorrow night?"

"Sure." Then Jacob remembered something. "Wait, you'll see me the next morning. I need to go to Philadelphia first. Family matters. I'll fly out from there overnight."

"Fair enough."

Maybe not. Just as Jacob was hanging up, he turned to see Kim standing behind him.

"You're leaving again?" she said. She looked angry.

"Well, you knew about my trip to Pop's gravesite. It'll just be a little longer, I promise. Ellen's coming to stay. I'm sure she can extend her trip a few more days."

"It's not your sister we need here, Jake—nothing against her. What happened to 'Family is everything'? Isn't that what your grandfather always said—what *you* keep saying?"

"This is unavoidable. I wish I could say more, but you know I can't talk about my work. But trust me, what Malcolm called me about has an impact on the world. I won't be gone long. Just a few days."

"When does it stop? That's what I want to know."

Jake shook his head. "If this wasn't absolutely necessary, I wouldn't be going. You know that. Malcolm says this trip is imperative for mankind. I have to believe him."

That argument seemed to register with Kim somewhat. She had always respected Malcolm.

"Okay, mankind," she said. "I get that. But what about your family, Jake? What happens when I'm gone? Are you gonna tell Jess you need to go off and save the world?"

"Of course not. Listen, I'm only going to quickly give my assessment. Malcolm says there's nobody else that can do it. Then we'll have all the time in the world."

"We don't have all the time in the world, Jake."

"You don't know that. It's important to stay positive. Will you promise me that? I'll be back in a few days."

He held her shoulders, then pulled her close. At last she gave in and rested her head on his shoulder.

"We need you, Jake," she said. "I need you."

"Just repeat after me," he said. "All the time in the world."

She was quiet for a moment.

"I'll hold up my end of the bargain if you will," she said.

"That's all I can ask."

As he held Kim, Jacob finally had a chance to process what Malcolm had just told him. He tried to imagine how an object several times the size of Yankee Stadium could mysteriously appear out of nowhere—and what could possibly have been found inside it. He kept going over in his head the words Malcolm had said: *proof that we're being watched*.

Chapter 3

Discovery

Jacob wasn't easily shaken, but he couldn't believe what he was looking at. The files didn't do it justice.

As he stood in the center of the cavernous zeppelin-shaped vessel that sat at the bottom of the South Pacific, he looked up at eight huge monitors, which were arranged in a semicircle like some sort of avant-garde Stonehenge. Only they weren't planted on the ground—they were floating in midair. These were no holograms either; they were solid metal. He couldn't even budge them. He couldn't imagine what technology could be responsible, as he was told there had been no magnetic fields detected anywhere. Even stranger was the thought of these huge things floating in the midst of some vast empty cavern that looked more like the inside of a whale's mouth than any kind of spaceship.

He felt pressure in his ears from being so deep, even though the ship had been depressurized. As he shifted his feet on the slimy floor and smelled the musty air, the ship felt alive, as if he were in the belly of a beast. He could even hear an occasional deep rumble coming from the surrounding walls, which were dripping with moisture. For all he knew, this ship *was* alive. The space was dimly lit with a few portable lights, the only source of illumination other than the monitors and a thin glow coming from a corridor off to the left that led to the labs.

He looked up again at the giant floating monoliths. The images on the first seven monitors were so clear and three-dimensional that he felt like he was looking into a window. But it was the images themselves that really knocked him for a loop. All were full color aerial views of what appeared to be particularly violent events in human history, from ancient times to the present day. But how could these shots have been taken? And why? And why these particular images?

As he contemplated these questions, he took note of the surrounding silence and realized how vulnerable he was. He felt as if any moment the ship could disappear or take off. Worse yet—whoever or whatever owned it might return. He should hurry, but he was here to study and assess the images, so he forced himself to slow down and focus.

The first image showed an old city, built mostly in white stone upon a hilly landscape, with a massive complex off to the side and a gathering of people on a hill. According to the files, the historians had been able to identify the city as Jerusalem, and the large complex as King Herod's temple, which they validated against the remains of the Western Wall. The iconic Dome of the Rock was nowhere to be seen in the landscape, as it hadn't been built yet. In its place were what appeared to be acres of rubble. As he looked intently at the people on the hill, he could make out Roman soldiers in the crowd. Looking closer, he realized this was no gathering. It was a bloody clash. Romans slaughtering Jews? He wasn't sure. It just looked like mass chaos. He stared in awe, wondering how on earth there could be a bird's eye view of an event that had taken place thousands of years ago. And in full color, no less. That is, if these images were real. And from what the report in the file said, they were. These were no reproductions.

The next image was horrific. He could see knights riding through a village, fires everywhere, and piles of bodies—men, women and children—thousands of them. People were running through the village, being chased by the knights. According to the files, the scene dated from some time during the Crusades.

The third image was more recent and more easily identifiable, though just as horrible. The files identified it as Gandhi's Salt March on May 21st, 1930, when the British viciously beat thousands of nonviolent protesters in India. Jacob could see the scene clear as day, as if he were hovering just above the action. There was an endless sea of men in long, blood-stained white cloths, some shirtless, being beaten with batons and rifle butts by British soldiers. He shook his head and moved on to the next monitor.

The fourth image showed Adolf Hitler giving a speech to a large crowd inside a massive hall with arched ceilings. The file identified this building as the Hofbräuhaus in Munich. This particular speech, in which Hitler first proposed the National Socialist program, had been given on February 4, 1920. Jacob wondered how alien beings could have captured this image from inside the hall. Then again, how was any of this possible? One thing was clear, though. Whoever had captured these images was making a case. Though this image wasn't violent in itself, it represented a catalyst for later violence. In that respect, it was most intriguing.

As he began contemplating the whereabouts of the ship's owners, Jacob nearly lost his footing. The entire ship was shifting and the ground was now moving under his feet. Barely staying upright, he could hear creaks echoing throughout the darkness. He glanced to his left toward the corridor that led to the labs, where he could still see a faint light but no apparent source of the noises. Then, as quickly as it had begun, the movement stopped.

He took a breath. It was dead quiet. Behind him to his right, he heard a shuffle. He turned quickly and thought he saw a shadow disappear into the dark recesses of the ship. He couldn't be sure though. He kept watching but then heard nothing else. He called out. "Anyone there?"

Nothing.

Once again, the ship shifted, and he tried to keep his balance. As the creaks returned, he wondered if this whole contraption could break apart. Then the shaking stopped again. He wasn't sure whether to head to the labs, but after a brief internal debate, decided to stay a few more minutes. Nobody from the labs had come running for him, so this occasional shifting may have been normal activity. Besides, he was determined to absorb all he could from the images. He might never get this chance again.

Keeping his senses alert for movement, he looked up at the fifth image. This one was perhaps the most appalling of all, which was saying quite a bit. It looked like something out of one of Bosch's paintings of Hell, except this scene was real. He could see thousands of women running toward a lake. Many had children with them. To his horror, some looked like they were drowning their children. Who would do something like that? Then, as he looked to the left, he got his answer. He could see soldiers raping and torturing many of the women. He could barely look. He couldn't make out where the soldiers were from, and the historians' report was inconclusive. He figured the people had to be either German or Eastern European, given the fact that the images seemed to be arranged pretty much chronologically, and the soldiers and villagers were white.

Aware of the need to hurry, he moved on to the sixth image, which had been taken beside the Enola Gay as the bomb fell on Hiroshima. Through the window of the plane, he could almost make out the back of the pilot's head as the mushroom cloud formed below. He could clearly see the number 82 marked on the side of the famous B-29 bomber. He could have stared at it forever, but he felt the floor shifting again and quickly moved to the next image.

The seventh image showed two planes headed toward the World Trade Center. The fact that this was an aerial view taken from above the two planes before the event happened was most intriguing, not to mention that the image served as proof that whoever was observing us was still at it in this century.

Whatever he was dealing with here was almost beyond comprehension—an intelligent species that had been watching humanity for thousands of years. At least he hoped they were merely watching. It was almost hard to believe that the same entity that had observed events from thousands of years ago was still watching us today.

He glanced at the eighth monitor. That was the one that puzzled him more than anything.

It was blank.

He thought about the implications. If the other images weren't random, but instead represented milestones or turning points in our history, was there some major event yet to happen? And why were there only eight monitors? What would happen after the next major event? As he thought about the situation, it all seemed so surreal, as if it were part of a movie or a bad dream.

He wondered if whatever species or entity that owned all this had died somehow, or had gone on some other temporary mission. Could this ship have crashed and landed in the ocean? Or had it been here all along for thousands of years?

Footsteps echoing to his left jarred him back to reality. He couldn't make out anything in that direction; it was too dark. He could only hear the squishing of footsteps on the wet ground. Every step seemed to echo throughout the ship. Finally, a figure started to emerge into the dim light.

It was Malcolm, coming to greet him.

"Malcolm!"

"Jake, it's been much too long."

"Yes, six months at least."

"Just be glad for technology," said Malcolm, smiling.

As Jacob shook Malcolm's hand, he smiled back at the old friend who had not only been his boss on the NBIC program, but also his mentor since childhood. Malcolm was in his mid-seventies, but he still looked as vibrant as ever—though with his grey hair, he was starting to resemble Nelson Mandela. Malcolm patted Jacob's arm and looked at him with that familiar "cat that ate the canary" smirk that usually meant there was some heavy information coming.

"Come walk with me."

As they exited the ship into the adjacent underwater research facility that had been built around it, Jacob followed Malcolm down the long corridor that led to the labs. The corridor was lined with oversized glass windows, and he could see sharks swimming just outside the window.

"Nice view," he said. He was trying to appear calm, though the whole situation was unlike anything he'd ever experienced. Just being here was unsettling.

"After a few days you won't even notice it," said Malcolm. "I take it you had no trouble getting here?"

"Submersibles are a wonderful thing." In reality, Jacob was more than a little relieved. Not being a fan of scuba diving, he had been wondering how he'd get onboard. Fortunately, DARPA's new submersible plane had been able to take him directly into the facility.

After the usual small talk about Kim and the kids, Malcolm briefed him on the project and the activities ahead. Somehow, focusing on the work had a calming effect.

"Informally, we've been calling this the Kronos Project," said Malcolm. The official code name is the one you saw in the brief."

"Yes, Kronos 13. I understand the Kronos part. God of time and all that. I assume the 13 isn't random."

"That's right. It's the thirteenth project we've had in Special Programs dealing with temporal phenomena. Of course, this one puts the others to shame."

"So, do we have any evidence that this ship could be used for time travel, or do we think it's just for observation?"

"That's one of the things I'm hoping you can tell us. There are a number of—let's say, peculiar elements that could support either conclusion."

"Peculiar elements." Jacob shook his head and chuckled at the understatement. "Well if what I saw wasn't weird enough, I'll be curious to see the rest. How large is the ship anyway—minus the research facility?"

"About three hundred yards," said Malcolm. "Quite a monster, isn't it? And to think we had a hard time finding it."

Before Jacob could process the idea of something that large and yet so empty, they had reached a large set of double doors on the left. He followed Malcolm inside.

"Our cafeteria. We also have a separate dining room and chef. All the comforts of home."

Malcolm grabbed two bottles of water out of a small refrigerator and they took a seat at one of the tables. The room was modern, with sleek furniture in metallic silver and black. The external wall was mostly thick glass overlooking the blue sea.

"I take it you want to know how we found the ship," Malcolm said as he opened his bottle.

"Yes, I was wondering about that." It was a question he'd been waiting to ask ever since he'd seen the file—or at least the part he'd been privy to.

"It started in '97. SOSUS picked up some unusual sounds about fifteen hundred miles off the coast of Chile. We knew it wasn't a geological event. And it wasn't a sub. Everything—all the frequency patterns, the sounds, the chirps and clicks buried in the mix—said it was biological. Only it was ten times the size of any biological entity we've ever seen."

"This thing isn't biological, is it?" That would certainly explain why the ship had felt alive to him.

"We're not sure yet, but we believe it may be. Our organic chemists are analyzing it. We didn't find it right away, either. We had helicopters with divers, DPVs, wet subs—and we didn't find anything. Same thing happened several more times that year. Anyway, five years later the sound waves were leaked to the media, along with the code name we gave it—in this case Bloop. And then, everyone forgot about it."

"But I take it you really did find something."

"No, we really didn't for a change—at least not for a few more decades. It wasn't until a few years ago that we picked up the same sounds again. But this time we found something."

"Interesting. I figured it must have taken some time to build all this. So you've known about this for a while."

"It took over three years. We had to secure the area, put the right team together, and then, of course, build the lab. Plus we had to penetrate and secure the ship. That's another unusual part. The outer shell was tough to penetrate, and it was more like skin than anything manmade, almost like a whale. But when we did get inside, which was only recently—against my recommendation I might add—it was dry, like being in a huge sub—except there was no sign of a crew, no buttons, dials, displays, seats, periscopes. Nothing to indicate it was a ship. Only the monitors you saw and a few other objects you'll hear about. Oh, and a small closet-like alcove on the far end of the ship, but nothing was in it."

"Maybe it's not a ship then," said Jacob. He thought he might be stating the obvious, but what else could it be?

"You could very well be right—we don't know. These are all things you can discuss with Lauren and Beeze at dinner tonight. We have a bunch of other folks—biologists, computational chemists, astrophysicists, you name it—but the three of you will make up the core team. I want to keep this wrapped tight until we know what we're dealing with."

"Beeze. That's some name. What's his first name?"

"Just Beeze. Don't ask." Malcolm smiled. "He had a tough upbringing, but he found a way to rise above it. Oh, he's still a wiseass all right and doesn't look anything at all like the academic type, but he's a whiz when it comes to history. He's helping us analyze the images."

Jacob could see why Malcolm probably identified with Beeze, having survived his own ordeals. Malcolm once talked about having had a severe speech impediment as a child. He overcame it with flying colors to eventually become a great speaker and professor in the scientific community. He even received the prestigious Spingarn Medal for his essays on science and religion.

"Come, let's go to my office. You can bring your bottle."

He followed Malcolm out of the cafeteria and back to the long corridor.

"What can you tell me about Lauren?"

"Lauren Fox. She's our resident space-time expert. She's a real hot shot, like Beeze. You'll be impressed with both of them. They're young, and brilliant."

As they continued along the corridor past a large conference room, they approached an office on the right. Malcolm motioned him in.

"Jake, the monitors were only part of what we found. There's more to this—much more—and you'll see why we needed you to lead the research on this. Put simply, we can't get any further without your help. It's good to have you here, Jake."

Chapter 4

Toast

After meeting in Malcolm's office for several hours, Jacob freshened up in his cabin and arrived at the dining room at six, right on time. Beeze and Lauren were sitting at a large round table, which was in a semi-private area separate from the main dining room. As he noticed the bartenders and servers, it occurred to him that it looked more like a cruise ship than a government project, but Malcolm had explained that the agency spared no expense to keep the best and brightest here long term.

Beeze was just as Malcolm described, a young skinny black man with dreadlocks who was dressed like he was still living on the streets of Detroit. Beeze stood up to shake Jacob's hand. "What's up, Doc," Beeze said, with an ear-to-ear grin. Then he turned to Lauren, "Get, it? 'What's up, Doc?' Bugs Bunny? He never gets old."

Lauren didn't seem to have the same sense of humor and rolled her eyes.

"Jacob, you'll excuse my insane colleague here," said Lauren. "I'm the normal one." She was beautiful, with light blue eyes and long straight dirty blonde hair. As she stood up to shake his hand he could see that she was tall, at least 5'11", he guessed. In her thin black jumpsuit she looked more like a dominatrix than a scientist, let alone a top expert in space-time theory. If Kim were here, she'd call him a sexist and tell him not to stereotype people.

"Well, you both seem normal to me," Jacob said, as they all sat down. He was trying to be polite.

"Yeah, well, don't let her fool you," said Beeze. "She's really the bitch from hell. I'm not lyin', man."

Lauren stared daggers at Beeze, then turned to Jacob and smiled as if to tune Beeze out.

"So...Malcolm's running late," she said. "He should be here any minute. How was your trip?"

"Good," said Jacob. The waiter came over for his drink order. He ordered a vodka with lemon on the rocks.

"I'm glad you're here," she said. "If you're as good as they say, maybe we can all get out of here in a few weeks."

"Actually, I don't expect to be here that long," he said. "A few days maybe. Long enough to offer my perspective."

Beeze turned to Lauren, laughing. "Doctor Frankenstein here has some more brains to harvest."

Jacob had to laugh, but Lauren didn't join in.

"Here comes Malcolm," she said.

Jacob turned to see Malcolm approaching the table as the waiter brought his drink.

"There's a motley crew," said Malcolm. "I see you've all had a chance to meet." Malcolm turned to the waiter. "Bring me one of those, too."

"Motley," said Beeze. "That doesn't even begin to describe it."

Beeze winced as Lauren elbowed him.

Malcolm turned to Jacob smiling. "See, I told you about him."

During dinner, Beeze entertained everyone with his ideas for a series of comedic short stories, which he called *Loose Shorts*.

"Y'all, get this," Beeze said. "This guy's watching *A Christmas Carol* on TV for the umpteenth time, and he's there eatin' whole pizza by himself. Then he falls dead ass asleep. Lo and behold, he has this crazy dream about being visited by his fat roommate and three ghosts about his eating habits. I call it *A Diet Christmas Carol.*"

Jacob didn't know if it was the stories or the way Beeze told them that made him laugh. Or maybe it was the several rounds of drinks, not to mention the wine with dinner. He looked over at Malcolm, who was once again giving him the "I told you so" look, which made him smile more. He was going to like this group. He was curious to learn more about Lauren too, who at the moment had a forced smile on her face. While Beeze rambled on, Lauren turned her attention to Jacob. She seemed genuinely interested in everything he had to say, and kept asking him about his NBIC research. She sure didn't hide her disdain for Beeze, though. At least now she was doing a better job of ignoring him.

Just as Beeze was about to fill the wine glasses again, the room began to shake. Nobody seemed to panic though. Then it stopped.

"Damn, I hate that," said Beeze.

"What is that?" asked Jacob. "I felt that in the ship too."

"We don't know," said Malcolm. "We've investigated but found nothing usual. It's been doing that off and on since we've been here."

"The nature of the beast," added Beeze, looking at Lauren. She ignored him.

"So what's everyone's thoughts on the images?" Jacob asked.

Beeze answered first. "Well it's obvious that someone or something is watching us—and our wonderful history of violence. If you ask me, I say it's a judgment being made. Or maybe it's already been made."

Malcolm gave Beeze a strange look.

"Of course," said Beeze, "whoever they are, they sure seem to be takin' their good old time. So maybe we have a few thousand more years before we find out."

Jacob wondered if it was his imagination. It seemed that Malcolm had given Beeze a look and Beeze suddenly changed his tune.

"Or maybe we don't," said Lauren. "Maybe we only have days, or not even that. We could be sitting on a time bomb."

"Wait a minute," said Jacob. "What if this isn't a ship at all? What if Lauren's right, and it's some sort of bomb?"

"A bomb?" said Beeze. "She didn't mean a real bomb. It's a figure of speech. You know that, right? Cause you'll be scarin' me if you don't."

"I know, but what if it really is a bomb? We have to consider that option."

"Jake," Malcolm said. "There's no evidence—"

"Exactly," said Jacob. "No evidence. No evidence of any navigational equipment. No evidence of a crew. No evidence of how this thing got here. I'd say it's as likely to be a bomb as anything else. Maybe it's been planted here for thousands of years and if we make one more screw-up, we're history."

"It just means we have to work faster to figure everything out," said Lauren. "And we have to stick with it until we do."

Jacob looked at his phone. He wished he could call Kim to tell her he might be a little longer than he'd hoped, but as the file noted, phone service wasn't an option down here.

"We don't want to jump to any conclusions," said Malcolm. "But of course, we do want to be careful. And yes, we want to work as quickly as possible."

"I agree," said Jacob. "All I'm saying is that we don't really know anything at this point, except that whoever all this belongs to knows a lot more about science than we do. We only need to look at the floating monitors to tell that. If they want to make a bomb without wires, they probably can. And if they want to make a ship that can transport without an engine, they can probably do that too. So, yes, we want to be careful, but we can't discount anything."

"Agreed," said Malcolm.

"In that case," said Beeze, "I have a toast."

Beeze held up his glass.

"My fellow citizens," he said. "To the Kronos Project."

Jacob held up his glass with the others, as they all said together, "To the Kronos Project."

"And to saving the world," Lauren added. He could tell she was getting tipsy—if not by her voice, then by the way she was looking at him.

"To saving the world," they all said.

Suddenly Lauren leaned across the table and grabbed Jacob's arm. "You're staying with us, right Jake?" She was giving him a look he could have sworn was halfway between pleading and seduction. "You can't leave us," she said. "We need you if we're going to put all the pieces together."

She was staring straight into his eyes.

"Sure," he said. "I'll stay."

She sat back in her chair and silently mouthed the words, "Thank you."

Chapter 5

The Box

Though his cabin was more comfortable and spacious than he would have expected for an underwater research facility—it was more a large hotel suite than a cabin—Jacob couldn't sleep. He thought he'd be tired after the long day, not to mention absorbing all the information Malcolm had given him, but now a million thoughts were floating in his head. He could feel the room swaying from the ocean currents as he looked out the huge bubble-like picture window at the blue sea. Watching a school of ghostly white fish with exotic fins swim by, he felt like Captain Nemo. It was hard to believe that only twenty-four hours ago he had been in Philadelphia making his annual visit to the family gravesite.

He glanced over at Kim's photo, which he'd placed on the table next to his bed, along with pictures of Jessica and Ethan. Despite what Kim thought, he hated being away from the family, but it was a necessary part of his job. Not that he got to see Ethan much anymore, even when he was home. At least Jessica had over ten years before she, too, would be off to college.

He picked up his watch to check the time. It was nearly one in the morning. It would be fruitless trying to sleep now. He climbed out of the king-size bed and picked up the new briefcase Kim had gotten him for his birthday. It was the latest biometric model designed by Heys USA; it could be opened only through the retinal scan of its owner. It must have cost a small fortune. He brought the briefcase up to his eye and felt the lock click. He opened the case and lifted up the Kronos 13 folder so he could peek at the other materials he'd brought with him—the contents from the box that had arrived. Glancing with disappointment at the small desk in his cabin, he decided to bring his briefcase to the lounge where he could lay everything out on a table.

He left his cabin, shut the sliding door behind him, and made his way up the long corridor to the lounge. As he entered the empty lounge area, he could see several circular couches with tables—all empty. There wasn't a soul around, no bartender or anyone. Everyone was asleep in their cabins. There was something peaceful about walking around at night, with the primary light coming from the large windows that looked out at the ocean floor, lit by the external lights surrounding the labs.

He took a seat at one of the tables and flicked on the small silver hanging light. He laid out the contents from the briefcase on the table in front of him. The first thing he picked up was a small photo of his grandmother, Anna, in which she was probably about eighteen years old. She looked so vibrant and youthful, with her dark hair in a bob with bangs, and a captivating smile with perfect teeth. She had doe-like eyes that gave her face the innocence of a child, and a beauty mark just below her left cheekbone, which he recognized from his grandparents' wedding photo. It occurred to him that she could have well been a movie star or a model. But he would have settled for knowing her as a grandmother. She had died much too young.

As he put the photo down, he noticed the journal. He had been so focused on the Kronos project that he'd nearly forgotten about it. He picked it up and looked once again for the section about Landsberg. It didn't take him long to find it.

He skimmed over the text, as it was in German and there were a lot of extraneous thoughts and details he couldn't understand. As he perused the pages, certain phrases, which he translated as he read, jumped out at him like daggers.

...As the devil's guardian...Samuel, by the grace of God, has borne witness to Hitler's devious plans.

...No doubt, the monster Hitler must never leave Landsberg alive.

…And we must ask ourselves, to what ends must we go to save our family…to save our way of life?

…We have found our weapon…an undetectable poison.

His heart skipped a beat. So, his grandfather's final words hadn't been just the ramblings of an old dying man. Pop was involved in something, and so was Uncle Samuel. They obviously didn't succeed, and apparently their plot never saw the light of day or they'd have both died way before they did. So that's what Pop meant when he said he could have saved them all. If the plot had succeeded, the Holocaust never would have happened. And Pop wouldn't have lost the love of his life. That was some cross to bear.

As Jacob read further, he saw that they'd planned to have an assassin pose as Hitler's psychiatrist. Samuel had been Hitler's prison guard at Landsberg. That would explain the devil's guardian statement. They also spoke of a lucky break—the perfect opportunity. And they even mentioned a date, April 30th, 1924, which they referred to as the day of reckoning. He wondered what had made them abandon their plan. And then, a few pages later, he got his answer.

It grieves me to write that we must abandon our endeavor and renew our prayers for a better future. For alas, it is much too risky. For to make it work, we require my brother.

So that was it. Samuel must either have refused to participate or hadn't been available for some reason. But one thing was still puzzling. Why would Pop have written all this in a journal—he, of all people, who always spoke of the need to exercise prudence and take the utmost security measures? And how had he let this journal get out of his hands? Who could have gotten hold of it? The only logical explanation was that it had been stolen. And whoever stole it obviously knew about the plan, assuming they were still alive. And chances are they *were*.

The more Jacob thought about it, the less doubt he felt. Whoever had stolen this journal must have sent the box. But why? And why now? The most likely suspect was the old man. Could he have been a German spy?

As Jacob held the journal deep in thought, a photo dropped out of the pages. It was the one with Max and Anna standing in front of the synagogue. He looked at it and speculated about what must have been going on in Pop's mind during that time. *Pop, what were you up to? What were you involved in?*

Just then, a noise startled him. It sounded like it was coming from the far corner of the room behind him, from the corridor—a soft ruffling. He turned around. At first he didn't see anything. Then he heard the noise again. Maybe it was the shuffling of feet, though it didn't sound like footsteps. Finally, a shadow emerged from the corridor, then a figure in the darkness. As the figure approached, he saw the light from the window hit the long blonde hair.

It was Lauren. With the light hitting her full on, he could see she was wearing a short white silk robe. He cleared his throat so as not to startle her.

"Jake, it's you," she said.

Jacob had to laugh. "I guess I'm not the only one who had trouble sleeping."

"I heard someone walk past my door," she said. "I couldn't sleep so I thought I'd see who was up. Mind if I join you?"

"Please." He slid over to make room, putting the journal back into the briefcase.

"Oh, I didn't want to interrupt." She indicated the mess of papers on the table.

"It's nothing. I was just looking over some old family photos. They arrived in the mail. Funny thing is I have no idea who sent them."

Why was he even sharing that with her? He was feeling particularly open for some reason. Maybe he was still jetlagged.

"That's really strange," she said. "Maybe it was a relative." As she looked over his shoulders at the photos and clippings, he could smell the soft fragrance of her hair.

"What's that one?" she said.

"Which?"

"The one in your hand." She put her hand on his to look at the photo.

"Oh," he said. "My grandparents. Probably taken in Germany."

"They look so young," she said. "Did you know them?" He could sense her looking at him so he turned to face her. Even in the dim light, her light blue eyes were striking.

"My grandfather, very well. He raised me. Never met my grandmother though. It's a long story."

"Well I'm not going anywhere," she said. Then she added, "Actually I am," as she slid off the couch and got up. "I'm going to get us something from the bar. Let me remember, vodka and lemon on the rocks."

"You have a good memory."

She looked back at him. "It was only a few hours ago, dummy."

He watched as she went to the bar and made the drinks. He wasn't sure if he wanted to get into his past with Lauren. At least not right away.

When she returned with the drinks and slid back beside him, he thought he'd change the subject.

"So what about you?" he said, as he took his glass from her. "What's your story?"

"Not so fast," she said, smiling. "We're still working on you."

"Working on me, are we? That sounds ominous. What do you want to know?" Again, he was opening his world to her. Definitely the jetlag.

"You said you lived with your grandfather. What happened to your parents?"

He hesitated, then decided to let down his guard. What was it about her that made that so easy?

"I barely knew them," he said. "They were killed by a drunk driver when I was four. My sister was six. My grandfather took us in."

"My God, that's horrible," she said. "I'm sorry."

"It's okay. It's part of who I am, I suppose. The real hell didn't begin till I was 15, when my grandfather died."

"You were alone?"

"I wish I *had* been alone." He took a drink. "I spent three years of hell in foster homes and government institutions. I'd be safer there, they told me. The whole time I had no idea where my sister was. I'll tell you one thing. You won't ever see me in any kind of institution again."

"Jake, I had no idea."

"Well, I don't exactly put it in my bio." He smiled. "It was all a long time ago though."

"I'm almost afraid to ask," she said. "How did you—" She hesitated.

"How did I get into physics?" He laughed. "I guess you can say I was always into physics. My grandfather had a lot to do with it. The ultimate distraction, he called it. Plus it was in my genes, I suppose. Didn't help me any in the institutions, though. To say I was Max Newman's grandson didn't buy me crap. To them, I was just that weird science kid."

"Wait a minute. Max Newman was your grandfather? I've heard of him. He was one of the pioneers of quantum mechanics."

"That's him. Funny thing is, I always thought physics was the one way I could make sense out of life. I guess our little project shoots *that* theory to hell." He couldn't help laughing.

"Let me see the photo again—of your grandparents."

He picked up the photo to show her. She held his hand while she looked more closely. Her hand was warm, almost hot to the touch.

"You look like him," she said. "What happened to your grandmother?"

"She died in the Holocaust. The love of his life, just taken away. I mean, how much loss can one person deal with? But he was a trouper. He used to tell me loss was a part of life. I'm sorry, but I'll never accept that."

He tossed the photo onto the table. Lauren picked it up and looked at the back of it.

"There's something written on the back," she said.

She handed him the photo, and he looked at the handwriting.

Kronenstrasse 15,
Karlsruhe, Germany,
24 Apr 1924, 19:30.

"That's where they lived," he said. "Karlsruhe."

"They were very exact," she said, pointing at the writing. "Location, date time. A time traveler's dream. Wouldn't it be amazing to travel back there and see them in their prime?"

"Keep wishing."

"I do. All the time. In fact, I'm half hoping we find out this ship is used for time travel."

He laughed. "You're kidding, right?"

"No seriously," she said. "Think of all the things you could do. Think how healing it could be. Not that I'd actually do it. But it's a fantasy I think we all have."

"—says the space-time theorist."

"You've never thought about that?" she asked. He could feel her leaning closer into him.

"Sure," he said. "I'm an explorer at heart. The quest for the grail and all that. But you can never go back. Not really. For me, all it would do is remind me of what I never had. Besides, if this thing is used for time travel, we'll have bigger things to worry about."

Just then the room began shaking again—another shifting event. Lauren grabbed onto Jacob's arm as he held onto the table. Each time the shaking started again, he wondered if this time would be the straw that broke the camel's back.

"Come," he said, as he swept the materials from the table into his briefcase. He noticed the small photo of Anna on the couch and tucked it into his pocket. "Speaking of things to worry about, we should get some sleep so we can get to the bottom of this sooner rather than later."

The lab was still shaking as he helped Lauren off the couch and they made their way to the corridor. This time seemed to last longer than the others.

"Yeah, like I'll actually sleep through this," she said, grabbing his hand.

It was hard to keep their balance as they walked.

"Has it lasted this long before?" he asked.

"A few times maybe. Not often."

As they approached his cabin, he motioned to the door. "In here. Just until it stops." He banged the button and the door slid open.

He pulled her into his cabin and tried to hold her upright while the room shifted from side to side. Grasping his arm around her as tight as he could, he looked for something to grab onto. As he heard the loud creaks coming from the walls, he looked at the window hoping it would hold out. She looked at him like a frightened child as he held her tight against him. The room was shifting more violently, and it was getting hard to keep his balance. Finally he lost his footing and fell back on the bed, pulling her down with him. Lauren was giggling, which made him laugh. "I swear," he said, "I didn't arrange that." Then, in an instant, the rumbling stopped.

"The oldest trick in the book," she said, smiling.

"Yes, the 'make the room shake' trick. I learned that in college."

He glanced over at her lying next to him, then stood up and went to the window to check for damage. Luckily everything was still sealed. "I guess we survived the worst of it," he said. When he had turned around, Lauren was standing right in front of him, looking at him. This time, it wasn't a scared look; she had a slight smile on her face, like she wanted to say something. Then, without taking her eyes off him, she undid the tie on her silk robe and in one movement let the robe fall to the floor.

He was transfixed as she stood naked before him, her golden hair barely covering her breasts. His eyes explored her face and body as she moved closer, pressing against him and putting her lips to his ear. She was almost his height. "I have a very good memory," she whispered, "and you said you're an explorer at heart." Her smell was intoxicating. He knew he shouldn't be doing this, but as soon as her breath had hit his ear, he felt paralyzed. He couldn't help running his fingers through her hair and down her spine, feeling the smooth skin of her lower back and hips. She put her lips to his. As they spun around, their tongues exploring, he felt like he was in another world. It was almost as if he were drugged. He backed up into the bed and fell back on it as she fell onto him. Then she was grinding against him and ripping off his shirt. As he threw the shirt off the bed, he heard a loud crash just beside him and glanced over to see his family photos lying on the floor, the glass over Kim's photo cracked in a diagonal line. *What the hell am I doing?*

He grabbed Lauren's arms. "I can't do this. *We* can't do this."

"Jake," she said. "I'm sorry."

"It's okay. It was my fault."

"Can I stay?" She climbed off the bed and put on her robe. "I mean in case those noises come back."

"Not a good idea." He wondered how she had handled the noises before he'd arrived.

"I know your family means a lot," she said. "You won't leave us, will you Jake? We need you for the long haul."

"I'll stay for a while," he said. "But I need to get back to my family sooner rather than later."

Lauren's face turned cold. She walked to the cabin door and stopped. Then she turned to face him. Her eyes narrowed. He could finally start to see the Lauren that Beeze seemed to know. "Jacob," she said. Her voice sounded suddenly harsh. "I need you to hear this. If the world is in danger, so is your family. Remember that. If you leave, you endanger them too. Think about that."

He watched without saying a word as she turned around and left the cabin, the sliding door shutting behind her.

Chapter 6
Entangled

As he stood with Malcolm, Lauren, and Beeze around a long rectangular table in the conference room, Jacob stared at a large metallic silver sphere that was resting on the table like a grand centerpiece. He felt like he was at a séance and everyone was looking at a crystal ball. Except *this* crystal ball was undeniably alien. Next to the sphere was a smaller, disc-shaped object about six inches in diameter that appeared to be made of the same material.

"So, what do we know about these?" he asked no one in particular.

"Well, for one thing," Malcolm said, "try picking up the sphere."

"Is it heavy?"

Malcolm had a smile on his face. "Just go ahead and pick it up."

Jacob tentatively reached for the sphere, which was about three times the size of a large globe. It looked like it was solid metal and incredibly heavy. He half expected to get a shock, so he hesitated, even though Malcolm wasn't the practical joker type. Finally, he put his hands on both sides of the sphere and gently lifted it off its small pedestal.

He couldn't believe it. It was as light as a balloon. He must have thrown it three feet in the air before it landed again in his hands.

He looked at Malcolm. "Is this the sphere you said was impenetrable?"

"Yep. Light as a feather, but we couldn't even scratch the surface—literally."

"Is it hollow?"

"We don't believe it is," said Malcolm.

"Material?"

"Unknown. Nothing we've ever seen, that's for sure."

"So let me get this right," said Beeze. "We got two-ton monitors that float and a damn featherweight sphere that don't. What, did we fall down some freakin' rabbit hole?"

"It doesn't make sense," said Jacob.

"Nothin' here does," added Beeze.

Jacob looked at Lauren, who was holding the smaller disc-shaped object. "What do we know about that?" he asked, motioning at the disc.

Lauren placed the object on the table so he could see it. At least she was acting professional, albeit a bit cold. Good. The last thing he needed in this situation was drama.

"See the three rows of codes on the front?" she said. "That's what we've been focusing on."

He looked at the codes on the face of the device. The symbols weren't from any kind of alphabetic or numbering system he'd seen.

"Have we been able to identify the symbols?" he asked.

"The codes are binary," said Lauren. "Notice there are only two symbols used throughout all the codes. Also, if you look, you'll see that each code has four sections."

"I see," said Jacob. He could see four distinct blocks of symbols on each code.

"We've mapped the four coordinates on the code to altitude, latitude, longitude, and temporal."

"How the hell did you figure that out?" he asked.

"Easy," she said. "One of the codes, the top one, constantly changes to reflect the current space-time location whenever we move the device. Once we made that assumption, it wasn't tough to figure the rest. Besides, the fourth part of the coordinate is always moving, like a clock. That represents the temporal element."

"The what?" said Beeze.

"The time," Jacob said.

"Jake," said Malcolm. "We believe this device—we've been call-ing it the Kronos Device, by the way—is some sort of GPS-like unit. We think it may be tied to the images on the monitors."

Jacob looked again at the three rows of codes. "Okay, so the first code represents the current location. Do we know anything about the other two rows?"

"The second set of codes is frozen," said Lauren. "We think it may represent the last coordinate set by the device. The only puzzling thing is that we discovered the same type of code at the bottom of each image on the large monitors."

"That's great then," said Jacob. "You should just be able to match the frozen set of codes with one of the images."

"Only one problem," she said. "None of the codes on the images match the frozen code on the device."

Jacob thought for a minute. "Strange. What about the third row of codes?"

"That's another puzzle," said Malcolm. "You can change that set just by tapping each digit with your finger. Only, nothing special hap-pens when you do. No lights, sounds, buzzes—nothing. We tried aim-ing it at the monitors, and even at the sphere, but nothing."

"So that leaves us shit out of luck," said Beeze.

"Not necessarily," said Jacob. "There's one more piece—the ship. What else have we discovered about the ship? Anything new?"

"Nope," said Malcolm. "We only know that our scientists said it tested positive for carbon and hydrogen, which would indicate that it's organic, but beyond that, nothing. Oh, and apparently it has self-healing properties. When we first penetrated it, it healed itself within twenty-four hours—that is, until we built the permanent tunnel to the lab."

"So let's assume it's biological," said Jacob. "Let's think about that for a minute. How would a biological entity communicate?"

Beeze scratched his head. "Telepathy. Mathematics. Light. Voo-doo."

"Sound," said Lauren.

"Bingo," said Jacob. "And we first found this entity when we picked up its sonic frequencies in the South Pacific. So that's a hint. Has anyone checked for waves?" He felt he was onto something, but wasn't quite sure how to prove it yet.

Malcolm spoke up. "Jake, our people did check and there was no wireless interference or any other type of waves we could detect. Are you thinking the sphere may be part of the communication mechanism—that all these things talk somehow?"

"I think we have to consider that. Where did you find the sphere and the Kronos device?"

"The sphere was sitting on a small platform under the monitors," said Malcolm. "And the device was found just below it, in a compartment on the side of the platform."

"Did you try using the Kronos device while the sphere was sitting on the platform?"

"We did. We were standing right in front of it, but the results were the same. No difference. In fact it took a lot of debate before we decided to move the sphere to our labs for additional study."

"I was against it," said Lauren. "We won't get anywhere until we put the sphere back. Obviously it's supposed to be on its platform."

"Yeah, obviously," said Beeze, giving Lauren a mocking look.

"Why don't we try that," said Jacob. "Only this time, let's use the Kronos device outside of the ship."

Beeze looked at him like he had two heads. Lauren was smiling. "I know what you're thinking," she said. At least she was smiling now.

"It's a long shot, Jake," said Malcolm, "but it's worth a try. I'll go get one of our men to return the sphere."

"Okay, I'm confused as hell," said Beeze, as Malcolm left the room.

"Beeze," said Jacob, "there are some very strange phenomena in physics, especially at the quantum level. Did you know that microscopic light particles—photons—will act differently if they're being watched versus when they're not being watched?"

"Huh?" said Beeze. "If you're not watchin' it, how do you know?"

"It's a well known physics experiment," said Lauren. "The double slit experiment, right, Jake?"

"Beeze gave her a look. "Now that sounds like something I don't even wanna know about," he said.

"Trust us on this one," said Jacob. "Sometimes things act differently if they're not being watched. I'm not saying that's the case here with the sphere and the ship, but we need to rule it out."

"So let me get this right," Beeze said. "You mean it's like that comic strip where the cows are all standing around talkin' and smokin' cigarettes and then one yells CAR! And they get their asses on all fours and start mooing when the cars go by?"

Jacob laughed. "Something like that," he said.

"That sounds like quite a leap you're making there, Doc," said Beeze.

"Well, I'll make another leap. There's a physics concept we call entanglement. The idea is that paired particles that are split will react to one another instantaneously, even if they're separated by light years. We have technology based on this phenomenon today. It's how we have instantaneous communication across continents."

Lauren added, "I love what Einstein called it—spooky action at a distance."

"Exactly," said Jacob. "Einstein always thought nothing traveled faster than the speed of light. And mostly that's true. But entanglement proves that tiny particles can be paired and will react to one another across continents or even planets—and I'd bet time dimensions too—in a split second."

Beeze shook his head. "See, I agree with Mister Einstein. That sounds like voodoo magic right there."

"Well, entanglement has been proven and tested," said Jacob, "but here are my other thoughts, and this is where we get into the real voodoo. If we're talking time travel, or even time *observation*, then we're probably talking wormholes—shortcuts through time. And if we're talking wormholes, then we're talking black holes, because that's where wormholes theoretically exist, near black holes. And the only way we know of to avoid surviving the pull of a black hole is by either traveling near the speed of light or with dark matter, or so we believe. My hunch is that if this Kronos device is truly used for time travel somehow, the ship and the sphere might—just might—be working together to either create a wormhole or tap into one. And somewhere, dark matter could be involved too."

"You could be onto something," said Lauren. "So far, it's the only thing that makes sense."

"I'm glad someone thinks so," said Beeze. "It still doesn't explain why you'd need to be in another room with the GPS device."

"We really don't know," said Jacob, "At this point, we can only take educated guesses and try different things. All I know is that whatever it is, the sphere must be holding something pretty powerful or it wouldn't be impenetrable. Maybe it's holding dark matter, or even a condensed black hole. Anything is possible. These beings know a lot more about physics than we do, so all we can do is rule things out one by one."

Just then, the door opened and Malcolm entered with two scientists in lab coats. He directed them to take the sphere.

"Jake," said Malcolm, "I think it's time to test your theory."

Chapter 7

Trees

With the sphere on its way to the ship, Jacob walked with Malcolm to the lab. Lauren and Beeze had gone ahead.

"So what is it with those two?" Jacob asked. "For people who can't stand each other, they sure follow each other around a lot."

Malcolm smiled. "It's a long story, Jake." Then he looked ahead, which meant he had no intention of revealing more.

When they got to the lab, Lauren was holding the Kronos device in her hand, staring at it with wide eyes. "Look," she said, holding the device up to show them. "It's incredible!"

Jacob looked intently at the device. A crystal clear three-dimensional image of trees now appeared on the face of the disc, just above the codes, where before there had been only silver. Strange. The image didn't match any of the ones on the monitors. It was just a view of trees, from above.

"What the hell *is* that?" Beeze asked.

Jacob was too engrossed to give a sensible answer.

"Trees," he said.

"I know it's trees, but damn, where'd that image come from? And what location is that?"

Jacob just shook his head, still mesmerized.

Lauren appeared to be fiddling around with the device.

"I think I've discovered how the controls work, too," she said.

Slowly, she waved a finger over the image and the view began to move, hovering over the trees. The more she waved her finger the faster it moved. Almost instinctively, she pulled her hand back and the view pulled to a higher altitude, away from the trees. Then she pushed her hand forward and the view moved closer toward the ground.

"Damn," Beeze said. "Does this mean those Google guys were aliens?"

Jacob gave Beeze a quick look, and for a moment actually tried to process that.

"You were right, Jake." said Lauren, ignoring Beeze. "We're getting somewhere. It must use some sort of energy-based gesture technology."

"Look," Jacob said, returning his attention to the device, "the target codes are also moving when you do that. Try setting them to match the frozen codes and see if the image changes to match one of the monitors."

She did as he suggested, but the image was still showing the same old trees.

Jacob heard Malcolm talking quietly behind him and turned around to see him talking on his mobile communicator. After a few seconds, he said thanks and hung up.

"Well folks," said Malcolm, now directing his attention to the group, "the images on the monitors haven't changed."

Jacob was really perplexed now.

"There has to be something we're missing," he said. "Something we're not thinking of."

He tried to think about all the pieces—the ship, the sphere, the Kronos device. What could possibly be needed to make the device and monitors work together?

"Malcolm." Lauren interrupted Jacob's thoughts. "I think Jake and I need to go over a few calculations and compare notes. Can we maybe take a break?"

Malcolm glanced over at Beeze, then at Lauren. "Not a bad idea," he said. "I suggest we all take a break and think on it for a bit. Let's meet up again for lunch at one."

As Malcolm and Beeze left the room, Jacob felt Lauren's hand on his arm holding him back. She motioned for him to wait with her.

"Jake, I need to tell you something," she said.

"Look, if it's about the other—"

"No, it's not about that. I want to share something that I'm not ready to tell the others yet."

"And you're comfortable telling me." That seemed a bit odd, but she was looking at him like she wasn't sure what to do. "Okay," he said. "What is it?" He couldn't imagine what she was about to tell him.

"I felt something in the ship the other day," she said, "when I was carrying the device. I can't describe it. I thought maybe it was my imagination."

"This could be important. What was it?"

"I don't know. It was like a mild electric current running through my body. It was when I went into the far corner of the ship. I was scared, so I turned around and headed back to the lab."

"My God, why didn't you say anything? I think it's something pretty relevant to what we're trying to do."

"Jake, I wasn't even sure if it happened. I just had a strange feeling, that's all."

Jacob thought for a moment. It was probably the same reason he hadn't told anyone about the feeling he had of being watched.

"We should probably tell Malcolm about this," he said.

"No, not yet." She looked nervous. "Look, it's just that I'm wondering if there's something there—something in the ship. I don't know, maybe even something that could have to do with the device. Will you check it out with me?"

Jacob hesitated. It wasn't that he didn't trust her. He just felt better being unencumbered. That way, he could make a quick escape from the ship if he had to.

"Lauren, listen, "he said, "I'd rather you'd wait here. If you let me take the device, I'll go check it out."

"I can't ask you to do that."

"It's okay. I'll just walk through the ship holding the device and see if anything responds. Then I'll come back. Trust me."

"Are you sure?"

"Of course not, but I'll do it anyway."

As she handed him the device, she put her hands on his.

"Be careful, Jake."

It was hard to ignore the feeling he got from her touch, especially when she looked into his eyes. It occurred to him that if anything was going to send electrical currents through his body, it would be her, but he couldn't go there. Better to take his chances with the ship.

He put the Kronos device in his pocket and headed down the corridor toward the ship.

Chapter 8
An Unexpected Trip

Jacob felt bad declining Lauren's offer to join him but he wanted to explore a bit on his own. He made his way up the corridor and approached the double sliding doors that led to the ship. The keypad was on the wall to the right. He entered the passcode Malcolm had given him. With a whooshing sound, the doors slid open. He passed through the entrance into the cavernous vessel and walked slowly in the direction of the monitors, his footsteps echoing in the large chamber. His eyes had to adjust to the darkness. He felt like he was in some big slimy tunnel, only much larger than any tunnel he'd ever seen. He heard another whoosh behind him as the doors sealed shut behind him.

He hadn't given the walls much notice before, but as he approached the side wall, he followed the network of tubing with his eyes. The tubing didn't appear to be man-made. He wasn't sure what it was. He moved closer and reached out to touch it. It was soft and moist to the touch, almost like skin. He felt as if he were inside a human body, like in *Fantastic Voyage*, where scientists, shrunk to microscopic size, journeyed through networks of arterial walls. He looked up at the ceiling and noticed a series of small protruding bumps all along the surface, almost like little showerheads. He could barely make them out in the darkness. The ship was musty and damp, and he wondered what it must have been like depressurizing it. It must have been quite a chore.

As he walked farther, following along the wall, he saw the light from the floating monitors travel toward the center of the ship. He glanced again at the giant images. What beings could have created both this organic, slimy monstrosity and the sleek modern objects found inside? And why were they watching us? What was their goal? The more he thought about it, this couldn't have been a ship. If it were, it would probably have been made of the same sleek material as the other objects, or at least something similar. And if there were codes and controls on the Kronos device, certainly there'd be ten times as many of them on a spaceship. But if it wasn't a ship, what was it?

He took the Kronos device out of his pocket and glanced at it. Nothing had changed yet. The image of trees was still there. He made his way into the darkness toward the far end of the ship. He hadn't ventured into this area yet. As he left the ambient light from the monitors, he used the Kronos device to illuminate his path. The farther in he went, the darker it got. The only sound was the echoing of his footsteps on the wet ground, so he stopped for a moment to listen for other noises. All he could hear was the occasional drop of water or slime dripping from the walls. As he aimed the light around, the emptiness spoke volumes. What could the purpose be of something this large with no controls or equipment? He walked closer toward the wall to his right. There he'd be better able to keep his bearings.

So far, he hadn't felt any electrical currents, nor had he sensed any shadowy figures or heard any shuffling. The whole place gave him the creeps though. The farther he got from the monitors and the labs, the more vulnerable he felt. He continued along the wall until he came to a small closet-like recess. This must have been the alcove Malcolm was referring to.

He held up the Kronos device and looked inside. It was empty, except for a small square platform. He knelt down and felt the platform. It was smooth. Against the light of the device he could see that it was made of a material similar to that of the sphere and the device— some sort of metal. He stood up and stepped on the platform.

Immediately he felt the device in his hands begin to vibrate. Maybe this was the electrical current Lauren had spoken of. He was tempted to throw the object to the ground, but he held on a few more seconds. The device was now illuminated around the perimeter in a bright blue ring. It was mesmerizing. A vertical bar appeared superimposed over the left side of the image of the trees. It looked like a meter of some sort, with three distinct sections in progressive shades of grey. The device was vibrating more strongly now. He noticed that the target coordinates still matched the frozen set of codes. He tried waving his hand over the image. Nothing. He tapped the screen and a round icon immediately flashed on in the center of the image. Could the alcove have been the missing ingredient needed to activate the device?

He thought for a moment. Maybe he shouldn't press the icon. What if this *was* some sort of time travel device? It certainly seemed like it could be, what with the GPS-like coordinates on the Kronos device, the images on the monitors, and now this alcove where apparently all the magic happened. He envisioned himself stuck somewhere in the past—or the future—unable to return. He was curious, but not *that* curious. No, he had taken his investigation as far as he wanted to at this point. At least now he could report the breakthrough.

Just then, before he could process his thoughts, something jolted him—strong vibrations through his whole body. He tried to move—to leave the platform—but couldn't. He was frozen in place. He couldn't even move his arms now, or a finger. His pulse quickened as he waited for whatever was coming next. The vibrations kept getting stronger and stronger, and then...nothing. He felt his body rise, weightless, as if he were floating. He wasn't sure if he actually was floating; he was too afraid to look. But it felt like his arms were being lifted like wings. No sooner had he started to adjust to this new feeling than a field of blinding light surrounded him, and he felt heavy as a brick. He could feel himself falling rapidly, as if down an elevator shaft, pulse quickening again. Now lights, colored lights, everywhere...spinning. He felt himself losing consciousness, losing all control, falling and spinning at dizzying speed.

And then it stopped.

He was afraid to open his eyes, but he knew he was no longer inside the ship. He was outside somewhere. He could smell the fresh air. He was kneeling on one knee. He could feel the ground at his feet and under his hands. Birds were chirping in the distance. He opened his eyes slowly and looked up. In front of him were trees, the same trees from the image!

He stood up slowly, still feeling unsteady on his feet. He was both surprised and relieved to see that he was still holding the Kronos device. It was still illuminated around the edges, the round icon in the center of the frozen image.

"Bet Google can't do *that*!" he muttered to himself.

Where was he? He looked around to the left, then to his right. It looked like an endless row of trees in both directions. He shook the cobwebs off and turned to his right slowly.

At first, as though his senses weren't fully working, it didn't hit him. He saw a set of railroad tracks extending out to the horizon. Then, as he turned around further, he began to see the back of a wooden slatted boxcar that was directly behind him, stalled on the tracks. Turning further, facing the train, he could make out some painted numbers. And then, as he turned fully and his vision cleared, he saw it.

It was a sight he had seen so often in old photos, but nothing could prepare him for what it would be like in person. Nothing. There was no doubt where he was, though he wasn't sure of the exact location or day.

He lurched back as he felt his heart beating through his chest. Because there in front of him, pouring out from the open doors of the boxcar and onto the ground, was a pile of dead, emaciated bodies. There must have been hundreds of them. As he approached, the smell made him sick to his stomach. They were dressed in tattered, muddy prisoner outfits. A few were naked, their clothes perhaps torn off in the panic. All were just flesh and bones—it was obvious they had been deliberately starved. As he looked down the line of cars to his right, there were other piles of bodies extending from the adjacent cars.

He leaned forward and put his hands on his knees and took a few deep breaths to calm down, as the shock of where he was finally began to take hold. How could he be here, of all places? This wasn't even on any of the monitor images. What alien beings might have been here before, observing this or doing who knows what?

He stared again at the bodies in front of him, scanning their faces. He was horrified but couldn't take his eyes away. All those stories his grandfather had told him. He looked at the faces, each one telling a story, each one a member of a family, each with their own dreams and desires. How horrifying to have all died alone, every damn one of them—away from their loved ones, their children.

As he looked at each of their faces one by one, the dead eyes of a young woman met his. He stared at her face, her familiar features. It almost looked like—

No, it couldn't be! God, no!

He stumbled back in disbelief, then made his way closer, toward the boxcar in front of him, trying not to step on any of the bodies. She was sprawled on her back on top of the pile to his right—her arms spread out over her head toward him as she hung practically upside down. Her head was bent back in a grotesque way. It looked like she was staring right at him, right into his eyes, as if beckoning, or pleading.

He got closer, his heart pounding. Praying.

She was rail thin. But, the eyes, the cheekbones, the beauty mark. It was unmistakable.

It was Anna. Pop's beloved Anna.

He knelt down in front of her and stared at her face. Dammit, Pop was a young man—a family man with a young child and a wife. She had been torn from his arms, and he had suffered not knowing where she was or how she was being treated. And here she was in the flesh, tortured and beaten, left like a rag doll. What if this were Kim, lying here alone, thinking of him and Jess and Ethan as she took her last breaths—alone? Nobody should have to die this way. He thought back to how he had felt when he no longer had Pop to consult, and as a young child knowing he'd never see his parents again.

As he studied Anna's cold, stone-like face, he reached into his pocket for his wallet and took out the old photo of her. He gazed at the picture and then at the face in front of him. It was her all right. The hair had been cut off, the body was emaciated, and the face was pale and drawn, but every last feature matched. What a stark contrast between the youthful, vibrant girl in the photo and the tortured soul in front of him. He wondered where he was. What year was this?

Now he understood why Pop would cry while staring at Anna's picture—usually on her birthday or their anniversary, and why he never remarried. And it made sense that he could never bring himself to look at books on the Holocaust.

As he looked at Anna's frozen expression of sadness, Jacob felt his hands turning into fists. He forced himself to rise as he looked up and down the railcars at the countless bodies—each one representing someone's lost hope, their dying thoughts of a loved one, the longing for the touch of their child's hand. How can one group of human beings do this to another?

Then he thought of Kim. He had to get back to her. But first he had to get back to the ship and warn the others. Someone or something had been traveling through time, and God knows what they'd been up to.

As he took one last look up and down at the masses of bodies, he took a deep breath. He couldn't help thinking of his grandfather's last words.

I could have saved them all.

Chapter 9

Missing

Malcolm entered the lab, thinking he might find Jacob and Lauren there poring over notes or testing the Kronos device. It wasn't lunchtime yet, but he was hoping they might have made some progress. Maybe they were in the ship. Besides, he was a little concerned about leaving the two of them together. He knew Lauren and he knew Jake. Oil and fire were always a dangerous combination. Still, it was a necessary evil that they work together.

He made his way down the corridor to the familiar double doors, pressed the passcode, and walked into the darkness toward the monitors.

He listened intently to the silence, hoping to hear footsteps or perhaps Jake and Lauren talking.

"Jake!" His voice echoed over and over.

No response.

He walked past the monitors toward the far end of the ship, but soon it became obvious nobody was here.

Just then he heard the whoosh of the double doors.

"Jake?"

"No," a female voice called out from the distance. "It's Lauren."

He walked toward the lab and saw Lauren emerge toward the light of the monitors.

"Where's Jake? I thought you two were together," he said.

"We were. Jake borrowed the device. He said he wanted to try something. I thought he might be in here."

Malcolm shook his head. "No such luck. Maybe he's in his cabin. I guess we'll see him at one."

"His loss," she said.

"What do you mean?"

She smiled. "Only that I think I found something."

"You're kidding."

"Meet me at the lab," she said, "and bring Beeze. Jake too, if you see him. I think I cracked it."

"Cracked what?"

"The code. I think I cracked the code."

Chapter 10
Silence

As Jacob stared at the Kronos device through the glare of the sun, he tried to create shade with his hands. He breathed a sigh of relief when he saw that the device was still illuminated. Thankfully, it looked like the round icon was still on the screen. He was almost afraid to press it. He dreaded the trip and that dizzying free fall rollercoaster feeling, but it would be his only way back. That was, if it worked.

A sudden noise in the distance startled him. Gunfire! It sounded like it was coming from ahead of the boxcars. Then airplanes—he couldn't tell how many—coming from the same direction. It was hard to tell how far away they were, but they appeared to be getting closer. He had to get out of there, and fast—before the planes or anyone else arrived. There was only one thing he wanted to do first. He just prayed he could do it quickly.

He hastily reached for his cell phone on his belt holster. Somehow, the phone had actually survived the trip. He was hoping its camera would still work. There was no signal, which wasn't surprising. He aimed the camera at Anna's face and snapped two photos. He took a quick look at the last image on his phone as another bomb went off in the distance. Looking at the distorted, frail face in the image, it was hard to believe this was once a young, cheerful woman with her whole life ahead of her.

As the noise got closer, he fumbled to put the phone back in its holster. Just then, he heard the sound of leaves crunching in the trees behind him. He could barely hear it against the distant roar of the planes, but he was sure it was the sound of people approaching—most likely soldiers. His hands were shaking as he looked at the Kronos device and struggled to see the screen.

He had to hold it steady. They were getting closer, and so were the bombs. He could now hear the soldiers' voices coming from just behind the trees, but he couldn't make out the language. The crackling of leaves grew more intense, and he could now hear the sound of feet shuffling faster. The soldiers were running. He didn't have much time. At that instant, a tremendous explosion just to his left made him jump. He dropped the device and juggled it as he tried to pick it up. Then he heard planes approaching from behind him—fast. They seemed to come out of nowhere, and were almost on top of him in an instant. He crouched down among the bodies and prayed he could blend in. He looked up to see a single plane coming directly toward him, swooping down from the sky, its silver nose pointed right at him. Its noise was deafening, and his ears buzzed as he cupped his hands over them. Just then, three other planes emerged. He thought they were all going to crash right into him until the first plane abruptly swooped upward into the sky, the others following suit. He kept his hands on his ears and felt the wind blowing hard against him. As the planes flew off, he noticed the stars on the three pursuing planes. They were Americans; chasing a German plane, no doubt.

Before he could breathe a sigh of relief, he heard soldiers behind him, about to emerge from the trees.

His fingers shook as he pressed the round icon on the Kronos device's small screen. Nothing.

He pressed it again.

Still, nothing.

Shit.

He couldn't wait here any longer. He had to hide behind the train before the soldiers emerged. He kept touching the icon as he climbed through to the other side of the train between the two boxcars. Still no response. No vibrations. Nothing.

Come on, damn it.

Just as he was climbing through, one of the soldiers yelled, "There! I saw something."

They were American.

Still, he couldn't get caught here. Not with a cell phone, an alien device, and a driver's license from 2024.

Finally, as if he had willed it to happen, the device began vibrating again. This was a good sign. A great sign! He could hear the soldiers approaching the train now, just in front of him. Someone shouted, "Oh my God!"

They must have seen the bodies. The device was buzzing and he looked around anxiously, praying for something to happen before they arrived. He was startled again by an explosion ahead of the train and turned to see a fireball in the sky off in the distance. Beyond the fireball, he could see three planes flying away in formation. They must have shot down the German plane.

The soldiers were approaching his boxcar now. At that instant, he began to feel the now familiar tingling in his body as the vibrations took hold. Finally! He was frozen in place and hoped something would happen before they saw him. Just like before, he couldn't move his arms or legs. He couldn't even turn his head to look around.

Then the weightlessness came, and he felt his body floating, his arms involuntarily rising, even despite his fear, his nervousness. As if watching a movie, he could see an American soldier emerge from the end of the next boxcar and point to him in horror. Then he saw the soldier being pulled back by another one, who covered the first man's eyes. Before he could process any of this, the intense heaviness took over, the world began to spin, and he lost all control, falling rapidly. Falling and spinning. Magnificent colored lights that he could barely register as he fell.

When it all stopped, he sensed the cool dampness of the alien ship. He opened his eyes slowly and exhaled. He was back in the closet-like room where his journey had begun, kneeling on the floor and drenched in sweat.

It had been silent for only a few seconds when he heard footsteps echoing. He forced himself up and stepped out into the ship, struggling to gain his balance. It was Lauren.

She had a curious look on her face.

"Jake, what was that noise?"

He wasn't quite ready to share anything yet.

"I heard it too," he said. "What do you suppose it was?" He was trying to look nonchalant, which wasn't easy given what he had just been through, not to mention that he was still trying to catch his breath.

She just shrugged and shook her head, as if she had bigger things on her mind.

"Dunno. Anyway, I was trying to find you."

Then she paused. "Jake." She was staring at him as if trying to read his face.

He looked at her, afraid she might have noticed something. Then she broke into a sly smile.

"We did it," she said. "We really did it!"

"Did what?"

"We mapped the codes. We were actually able to pinpoint some of the images. Even better, we mapped the coordinates of the frozen code. Are you ready for this? Jake, it's a Nazi concentration camp. Listen, I know—"

"Which one?" He grabbed her arm.

"Dachau, in Bavaria. April 29th, 1945, to be exact."

How could that be? She couldn't have still been alive. How the hell did she end up at Dachau?

He had to gather himself together and process all this.

"Jake, listen, I remember what you said about your grandmother. I'm sorry. I can imagine—"

"You can't imagine," he said. He felt every muscle in his body tighten. Then he saw the disappointed look on Lauren's face and eased his stance.

"I'm sorry," he said. "It just took me by surprise when you said Dachau. My grandmother was at that camp." Then he added under his breath, "Apparently."

He was trying to work out the timing. This was five years after Pop believed Anna to be dead, and in a different camp. The incident he had always thought had led to her death had happened in 1940 at Ravensbrück, where Anna was last seen.

Lauren interrupted his thoughts.

"Beeze said this must have been just before the Americans arrived at Dachau to find rail cars full of bodies."

Jacob just shook his head, trying not to let on what he had just witnessed.

"Anyway, Jake," she said, "I'd like the device back for a bit if you're done with it for now. I want to validate my numbers, just to be sure."

He barely registered her words, but handed her the device and gave her a polite smile as he walked beside her toward the corridor.

"Of course, if you come with me," she said, "I can make it worth your while."

He looked at her. Not again.

"Relax," she said. "I can show you how to set the coordinates."

He smiled and nodded his head.

As he walked down the long corridor with Lauren, his thoughts turned to Anna. He'd never forget the look of horror and despair on her face, like she was beckoning him to help her see her husband and child again. What a difference from her happy smile in the synagogue photo. She and Pop both looked like they hadn't a care in the world. Little did they know how life can change on a dime.

He wondered what it would be like to see them in their prime, to remember them that way instead of old and depressed, or in Anna's case, lying dead, an emaciated pile of flesh and bones. Maybe Lauren was right. Maybe going back and seeing them alive would be healing in a way. The strange thing was, now he could actually do it. As Lauren had pointed out, the photo had the date, the location, everything he'd need. All he'd lacked was the means. And now he had that too.

He chuckled at the thought. It felt strangely good—powerful even—to be able to travel somewhere in history and return unscathed. The possibilities were endless. But then again, so were the risks.

He thought back to the soldiers he'd seen. Why had the one covered the other one's eyes? Would they investigate? Then again, how could they? What they thought they'd seen was just one soldier's stressed out hallucination, or even two. Who would listen to them? He was lucky to have escaped. The more he thought about it, the more he realized he could have easily been discovered, or even killed. He wasn't sure which would have been worse in the grand scheme of things.

Despite all that, he was feeling less afraid, especially now that he knew how the device worked. Besides, if he could escape World War II surrounded by bombs, planes, and soldiers, he could escape pretty much anything. Still, he couldn't risk doing something—even inadvertently—that could alter the past. He had to admit, though, that it would be nice to have just a quick look—a brief glimpse he could carry with him forever. For just one moment, he could be whole again. And maybe that would be enough to last him the rest of his life.

Chapter 11

Images

Malcolm entered the graphics room to find Beeze staring at a giant LED screen, intently studying photographs of the monitor images. Beeze was deftly moving the images around with his hands, apparently trying to look for a pattern of some sort.

"Grab a seat," said Beeze, without turning his head from the screen, his hands still flying back and forth.

"Find anything yet?" said Malcolm.

If anyone could find commonalities in all this—beyond the obvious—Beeze could.

"Oh, a few tidbits here and there."

Something told Malcolm that was an understatement.

Beeze brought the first image to the forefront, the one that showed a violent clash in ancient Jerusalem.

"This is during the rebellion of the Judean province again Rome," said Beeze. "70 CE to be exact, just before the fall of the Second Temple."

"Romans slaughtering Jews."

"Hell no. Jews slaughtering Jews. The Zealots were fanatics, hated by their fellow Jews and Romans alike. If it hadn't been for them, the Romans probably would have left well enough alone."

"Is there a link to the other images?"

"Let's just say there's a pattern," said Beeze.

Beeze put up the next image.

"This one's from July 22nd, 1209, during the Crusades," he said. "A town called Beziers in southeast France. Hell of a day. Seventy thousand unarmed men, women, and children, slaughtered like lambs in a single freakin' day. And that's just in this little village. That's a shitload of people."

Malcolm shook his head. "About the same number of people killed at Hiroshima. So, it looks like a case is definitely being made here."

"Sure as hell seems like it. All the images deal with massacres. Except maybe the Hitler one, but that's the beginning of a massacre. Maybe the message is that humans are a violent species. Period."

"Could be. Or it could go deeper than that. Do we know if there's a religious statement being made?"

"Doubt it," said Beeze. "If there's a common theme, I'd say it's that nobody's innocent. Now, we already identified Gandhi's Salt March, when the damn Brits beat the hell out of them, and Hitler's speech in Munich. Same with 9-11 and the bomb falling on Hiroshima. But let's look at this one, too."

Malcolm watched as the next image flashed up on the screen. It was the one with women and children running to the lake. They were fleeing in horror from hundreds of soldiers who were torturing and raping anyone they could get hold of.

"This one's in Berlin," said Beeze. "The Soviet Red Army going badass on German villagers after World War II. The war was over, but for these guys the fun was just beginning. Not so much fun for those moms and kids though."

Malcolm shook his head.

"Like I said," said Beeze, "nobody's hands are clean. We got Jews killing Jews, soldiers killing civilians, Christians killing everyone, Russians killing Germans. We got Americans, Muslims, everyone's in on the act. It's all about the damn violence, no matter what side of the fence you're sitting on."

"No," said Malcolm, "not violence."

Beeze looked at him.

"Arrogance."

"Arrogance," Beeze echoed. He appeared to be thinking it over. "Maybe. I might give you that. Explains the Hitler speech. I guess it's kind of ironic when you see what else I found."

"You found something else?" Leave it to Beeze to save the best for last.

Beeze smiled. "Check this out. I ran the images though a comparative analysis. Part of my routine. You never know what you'll find."

Malcolm watched as Beeze zoomed in on the image and zeroed in on one of the soldiers' hands—specifically the man's right index finger. And even more specifically, the ring on the finger.

Malcolm looked at the silver ring getting larger and larger. He could now make out the symbol on the ring's face, resembling a tiny three-rung ladder.

"Now look at this," said Beeze, as he put up the image from Judea again.

Beeze zoomed in on one of the clashes going on and then brought the focus in on one of the robed fighters.

"This is one of the Zealots," said Beeze. "You can't see his face, but he looks like he's shouting orders at some of the other men. Now watch as I zoom in closer."

As Beeze zoomed in on the man's hand, Malcolm's eyes widened.

"Tell me that ain't the same symbol on that ring," said Beeze.

"Yes, it sure looks like it," said Malcolm. He didn't want to say anything, but ideas were already forming in his head.

"That's not all, either," said Beeze. "There's one person in each of the seven images with the same...exact...ring. Even the co-pilot in the Hiroshima image has a damn ring. I can't quite make out the symbol as clearly, but I'd bet anything it's the same. Kind of a coincidence, don't you think?"

"Are the faces visible in any of them?"

"No siree. But this is some weird shit. I mean, something's been going on for millennia right under our noses, right? Some kind of secret society?"

"Not sure. How about the symbol? Do we know anything about it?"

"I knew you'd ask that. So I did some research. Had to do a bit of digging but I found a match. Well, a few variations, but all the same general shape. It's damn old. Latin in origin. And when I—"

"Beeze, what does the symbol mean?"

"I was getting to that. As it turns out, it's an ancient symbol signifying doomsday."

Malcolm thought about it for a moment. "Interesting," he said.

"That's all you got to say? Interesting? Don't you think 'Holy shit' might be more in order?"

Malcolm barely heard Beeze's words. He was deep in thought trying to put the pieces together.

"Well, you may find this even more interesting," said Beeze.

Beeze switched over to the image of Hitler. "Look here next to our friend Adolf, the third person to the right. Just behind him you can make out an arm with the ring, right?"

Malcolm watched as Beeze zoomed in on the ring.

"Now, let's look to Hitler's left," said Beeze, "two people over. I'm gonna zoom in on the face."

As the magnified image cleared, Malcolm recognized the face immediately. He felt his blood boiling, but knew he had to remain calm.

"Interesting enough for ya?" said Beeze.

Malcolm was formulating theories in his head, but wasn't ready to disclose his thoughts to Beeze yet. He turned to Beeze.

"Not a word of this."

"Agreed," said Beeze. "But what do we do now? What do you think all this means?"

"I'm not sure yet," he said. "But I know one thing. Jacob can't know about this. Not yet anyway."

"All right," said Beeze. "You're the boss."

As Malcolm turned to leave, he stopped and turned around again.

"Oh, and Beeze," he said.

Beeze looked up.

Malcolm tried to force a smile. "You did well."

He felt bad about not sharing more, but he needed to think further about the implications at play. There were still pieces to fit together, but this little finding changed everything. And worse yet, he knew this discovery only scratched the surface. There was much more to figure out.

One thing was certain though. The stakes on this project had just gotten exponentially higher.

Chapter 12
Decisions, Decisions

After meeting with Lauren, Jacob decided to take one more walk through the ship. He took his notebook containing Lauren's calculations with him. Now that he understood how the codes worked, he wanted to have another look at the images. He had never actually seen the codes below the images, though he didn't doubt that they were there. He just wanted to see for himself. He was also curious about the angle the images were taken from. All were aerial views, and even the one of Hitler, to his recollection, looked like it had been shot from the ceiling.

As he entered the darkness and saw the light of the monitors ahead, he approached slowly. The ship seemed slightly brighter now, though maybe he was imagining things. As he got closer, he could see why. The eighth monitor was now illuminated!

He rushed forward to look. When he saw the image, his heart started pounding.

No! How could this be?

It was an aerial view of the boxcars, dead bodies piled up next to it.

He got closer to see if he was in the image. His eyes scanned up and down. He looked everywhere he remembered running, on both sides of the train.

Scanning...scanning.

He was in luck. He wasn't in the image.

When could this picture have been taken? Was he being watched? Most likely it had been taken just before or after he had been there, probably after. The image wasn't there when he'd returned from the ship with Lauren.

He stepped back to take in all the images. He thought back to when he had first arrived. Seven of the eight monitors had displayed images of human violence, or in Hitler's case, the seeds of violence. The eighth one had been blank. Now it, too, contained an image of violence. But why now? Why only after he had visited the place did the image appear? Had he disrupted "them" in the middle of their case building? This couldn't have been a coincidence. And with Anna right there at that very time?

He thought back to the package that had arrived. Photos from his family's past. One of the photos with a date and location on the back. Now, by some twist of fate, he'd ended up in Dachau and seen Anna, who was supposed to have died five years earlier at Ravensbrück. It was as if someone were messing with his head. But here he was, in a strange alien ship at the bottom of the sea.

Somehow, it seemed obvious that they were trying to make a case against humanity. Could there be some judgment day coming based on these images? Why else would extraterrestrial beings gather images of human violence?

He had never been one to believe in the paranormal. The physical world was fascinating enough without throwing in voodoo thinking about the metaphysical world. But it was as if Pop or someone was trying to send him a message. Thanks to the journal, he was now privy to inside information that could bring down Hitler before he even came to power. And thanks to his little trip to Dachau, and, of course, Lauren's calculations, he now had the ability to travel through time.

The message was becoming clearer. Only he, with his inside knowledge and newfound power, could undo Hitler, and thus prevent an episode that would tip the scales toward a judgment against humanity. The more he thought about it, his role in this began to make more sense, though who or what was driving him to it was a mystery. The alien beings must have been making their case, and someone or something was feeding him the information he needed to fight against it—to go back and influence the Hitler plot.

Then again, what if he was wrong? After all, he was just speculating. What if he found a way to influence the plot to kill Hitler, and that led to other catastrophes?

Unfortunately, he didn't have a crystal ball. He couldn't ask the aliens if they were really planning on wiping out humanity.

The more he thought about it, this was a risk he was going to have to take. There was too much at stake, and there was no time to wait for more information. He certainly couldn't share his ideas with anyone or they'd think he was crazy. And maybe they'd be right.

Nobody ever said saving the world would be easy.

Chapter 13
Pain and Suffering

Malcolm returned to his office at the lab to think things through. The images were most certainly being used to make a case. That much was clear. But everything else he was seeing indicated that historic events were being manipulated. To what extent, and exactly by whom, he wasn't sure yet. And there was still a major piece of the puzzle missing.

He was deep in thought, reclining by the oversized porthole, when Jacob entered and sat in one of the visitor chairs. Without saying anything, Jacob handed him an old black and white photo of a young well-dressed couple standing in front of what looked like an old synagogue.

After perusing the photo, he looked up at Jacob. "I don't understand."

"Turn it over."

Malcolm turned the picture over to see a handwritten date: April 26th, 1924. The location was there too. Strange.

"Your grandparents?"

"Max and Anna Newman—or Neumann as they were called at the time. I know I've talked to you about them before. This was taken after a Friday night service in front of their synagogue in Karlsruhe, Germany."

"I see. I'm sure this Dachau discovery has brought up a lot of stuff for you, Jake. Your grandfather was an amazing man. And it's tragic what happened to your grandmother."

"Malcolm, you know me better than anyone. But I've never told even *you* the full story about my grandparents."

"Only that your grandmother died in the concentration camps."

He could see that Jacob needed to get this off his chest.

"Well, you remember that my grandfather was one of the pioneers of quantum physics back in Germany in the thirties. Did I ever tell you he was forced to work for the Germans?"

"No, I don't remember you telling me that."

"It was right around the beginning of modern physics, and people like my grandfather, Einstein, and others were prized by the Germans, especially during the arms race. The Germans called their research *Jüdische Physik,* or Jewish physics. As Hitler rose to power, most of the scientists could see the handwriting on the wall, so there was a big push to leave the country."

"Yes, Einstein managed to get out early."

"Well, my grandfather wasn't so lucky. The German government convinced him and a number of others to stay. They offered a guaranteed job and promises of safety for all the Jews. Of course, he hated Hitler even then, but it was too risky to leave at the time. Besides, the so-called promises were worded more like threats. Anyway, before long, it became apparent that Jews were being harassed everywhere, despite whatever promises the Germans were making. And so, my grandfather eventually joined some other scientists in a plot to leave Germany. Except he never left with them. His wife, Anna—my grandmother— wanted to visit her mother first in Poland before they left for America."

"And did she ever get there?"

"Oh, she made it to Poland all right, but then she couldn't return because the Germans denied all Jews entrance into the country. And, to her surprise, Poland wouldn't let them back in either. And so, there she was, stuck in no-man's land with a bunch of other unfortunate outcasts."

"Jake, that's dreadful. Nobody should have to live like that. I'm assuming that's when she was captured."

"Yes, but only after days of trying to survive out in the cold with no food or water. Anyway, before long she was rounded up with the others and sent to the Lichtenburg concentration camp in eastern Germany. This was in 1938. My father was only a year old at the time and had stayed with my grandfather and their nanny."

"Is that where she died, at Lichtenburg?"

"No, she was there for a year. Then she was transferred north to the Ravensbrück camp for women. The Germans kept stringing my grandfather along, promising to locate her. This went on for several years. Then, in 1943, he had an opportunity to leave for America with another group of scientists. Of course he also had his six-year-old son—my father—to think of, so he had to consider his actions especially carefully. Like my grandfather, some of the scientists were Freemasons, who were forced to meet in secret when the Nazis banned Freemasonry in the thirties. But the network still existed, and they were able to arrange an escape plan. He didn't know when he'd get the opportunity again, so he made the tough decision to leave."

"I can imagine how difficult a decision that must have been."

"Yes, it tortured him for years, not knowing whether Anna was dead or alive. It wasn't until years later that he ran into an old family friend, a Holocaust survivor, who told him she had seen Anna being pulled along by Nazi guards. Apparently Anna was captured trying to help a group of women flee the camp. The other women got away."

"And when was that?"

"1940."

Malcolm could see that Jacob looked uneasy. He took a cigar out of his humidor and offered one. Jacob politely declined, so he just lit one for himself.

"Jake, you should at least take comfort that your grandmother was a hero. She saved those women's lives."

"I tried to tell my grandfather that. Didn't help much. But there was something else. There were some words he mumbled as he was dying. Something about how he could have saved them all. I never knew what he meant. Then, just before I left to come here, an unmarked packaged arrived at my house with photos from my family's past. That's where this photo came from. There was also a journal in the package. That's when I found out about the plot."

Now Malcolm was curious. He looked at Jacob silently, waiting for him to continue.

"Malcolm, apparently, my grandfather was involved in a plot to poison Hitler in Landsberg prison in 1924. The plot was never carried out, but all the plans were in place."

"And you learned about this from the journal?"

"Yes."

"Any idea who sent it?"

"Not a clue. Though there was an old man who approached me at the conference in Paris who said his family knew my grandfather in Germany. I didn't get his name, though. He seemed to know something about Landsberg, but he was very cryptic."

"Interesting. Did the journal say any more?"

"Yes. It mentioned that my uncle Samuel, Max's older brother, was assigned as Hitler's guard at Landsberg during his time in prison there. Supposedly, they had an assassin all set to pose as a doctor and kill Hitler, but Samuel called off the plan. He felt it was too risky and didn't want to implicate anyone in the family. According to the journal, my grandfather resented Samuel for that."

"That's some burden he carried."

Malcolm paused for a moment to consider his next words, as he put his cigar out in the ashtray.

"Jake," he said, "I know this is all heavy stuff, and I don't think anyone could argue that the impact on your family, and the millions of others, was absolutely tremendous. Beyond anything anyone should have to deal with. But, like I know we've talked about over the years, we have to make do with the cards we're given, and then we have to look forward. Isn't it a Jewish proverb that says it's better to light one candle than curse the darkness?"

He could see Jacob mulling over his words.

"I suppose you're right," said Jacob. "But Malcolm, let's think hypothetically for a minute. What if, somehow, this equipment we found would allow us to travel back in time? Would you change anything?"

"Like killing Hitler?"

"No, no," said Jacob, "I mean smaller than that. If you could just help an old friend solve a problem, or scare away a childhood bully, would you do it?"

"Jake, any little thing we do, no matter how innocent or well-meaning, could have tremendous implications, beyond our comprehension. So, no, I wouldn't."

"What about something good for humankind, like a cure for cancer?"

"That would be even worse, Jake. What if we cured cancer, and some horrible demon of a person, ten times worse than Hitler, lived as a result? I'd never do it, not in a million years, even if I had the chance. The risks would be too great. Now, I don't know if this technology is used for time travel or not, but if it is, it's in the hands of an intelligence far greater than ours, or so I hope."

"Okay, what if it were to save humanity? Like maybe you had to go back and fix something that would have led to global devastation?"

"This is hypothetical, right?"

"Yes, of course."

"Even then, Jake. How would you know you weren't causing an even bigger problem? It's not for us to question the natural course of things."

"And what if the course of things led us into a rat hole?"

He looked at Jacob. Something didn't seem quite right.

"Just asking," said Jacob. "Anyway, it's just hypothetical. I guess all this mystery is making me philosophical. Who'da thought, right?"

"Are you okay, Jake? Is there anything else you need to talk about?"

"I'm fine. Really. Thanks, Malcolm. I mean it. You're a good friend."

Malcolm handed Jacob back his photo and patted his arm.

"Any time. Just remember, look forward. Don't regret the past."

"Thanks, my friend."

When Jacob had left, Malcolm thought about their conversation. Something was amiss here, and not just Jacob's demeanor. Something in the story didn't add up. About the package, the journal, the old man. He needed some quiet time to think, so he got up to shut his door. Then he noticed it.

Ordinarily he wouldn't have given this kind of thing a second thought. Some mud on the floor. So what? He was about to just kick it aside, but something made him bend down to touch it. He felt it in his hand. It was moist. The mud was fresh! He wondered how Jacob could possibly have had fresh mud on his feet down here in the middle of the ocean. Then he began to think about their conversation: time traveling back to the past; the date on the photo, from April 1924; Hitler in prison in 1924; Jacob's grandfather's plot to kill Hitler in 1924; fixing a mistake.

Somehow, Jacob had found out how to time travel! But where? And what now? Could he actually be planning to influence the plot to kill Hitler? Had he done something already?

Malcolm knew Jacob well. Jacob was too intelligent to do anything that would dramatically alter the past, like tipping off an assassin about the future. And he certainly wouldn't risk his life to do anything dangerous, not with a loving family right here. Not to save a grandmother he had never met. And most important, not after all these years of learning to control his anger. He hoped Jacob had taken to heart all those conversations about opportunities and choices they'd had over the years.

God gives us opportunities, and it's up to us to make the right choices—our destiny in this world is not guaranteed. Hopefully, that message had sunk in somehow.

Either way, he had to find Jacob now. Because somehow, some way, he'd already been to the past and back. And who knows what hell he'd unleashed or was about to unleash that would have implications beyond his wildest dreams?

There was no doubt about it. It was time to tell Jake about the rings.

Chapter 14
Karlsruhe

Jacob held tight to the tree's branches as he slid down low enough to jump to the ground. From watching Lauren, he had figured out how to hover his hand over the image and fine tune the altitude of his arrival location. Unfortunately, he had estimated about seven feet too high and ended up in a tree. But now, here he stood, in Karlsruhe, Germany on Friday, April 26th, 1924. He had chosen a target where he could arrive unseen among the trees—just opposite Kronenstrasse 15, where his grandparents' synagogue was located. Before the trip, he had familiarized himself with the city, which wasn't too difficult. Almost anything in Karlsruhe could be located using the center of the town as a base.

The synagogue was southeast of the Karlsruhe Palace, which sat at the center of town. He was surprised to learn during his research that Washington DC's circular design was, in fact, partly modeled after Karlsruhe, with everything fanning out from the center. In the case of Washington, house numbers were assigned based on their distance in blocks from the Capitol building, with the Capitol marking the axis of the city's four quadrants. Here, it was the palace that defined the city's quadrants, with thirty-two streets radiating out from the center like spokes on a wheel.

He knew from Max that Karlsruhe had a thriving Jewish community in the 1920s, and housed the renowned Institute of Technology, where Max had attended college. He had to get used to thinking of him as Max now. He certainly couldn't call him Pop.

Glancing around to make sure he was well hidden, Jacob unlocked his briefcase using the retinal scanner and placed the open case on the ground. He took out the clothes he had packed—a white dress shirt and dark slacks, so as to blend in—and quickly changed. He had also brought the trench coat Kim had packed for him, and put that on as well.

Then he tucked the cell phone and the Kronos device in the briefcase, as he couldn't afford to be seen with either of those in 1924. He put his watch in, too, just to be safe. Before closing the briefcase, he looked at the Kronos device one last time and noticed the meter was a third shorter than before. Where before there had been three sections, now there were only two. It must have been a power meter of some sort, perhaps limiting the number of trips. He'd have to keep an eye on that.

He closed and locked the briefcase and made his way toward the street, which he could see in the distance through the trees. If all was right, it should be the early evening, and so it seemed to be. As Lauren had suggested, he used Coordinated Universal Time, or UTC, which accounted for leap seconds, for his calculations.

As he approached a clearing, he glanced through the trees and saw people walking back and forth on the street. It seemed strangely surreal seeing old fashions and hairstyles, especially as an outsider from the future in a foreign city he'd never been to. He could hear the clip clop of horses, and in the distance the faint sound of voices singing in unison. As he got closer to the street, he could see that the music was coming from a partially open window in the building across the road. It was the synagogue. At least now he knew he was in the right place at reasonably the right time.

The synagogue was a grand building, almost gothic, with a large circular stained glass window above the two oversized wooden doors. The intricate carvings that adorned the doors were magnificent. He noticed a bench facing the synagogue on his side of the street, just beyond the clearing. After waiting and watching for a while, he finally got up the courage to emerge into the open and enter German society.

He nonchalantly walked to the bench, where there was nothing to do but sit, observe his surroundings, and wait for the moment when he would finally see his grandparents in their youth.

Chapter 15

Gone

Malcolm found Lauren sitting in the lab making notes.

"Please tell me you have the Kronos device."

She looked up at him confused. "No, Jake has it. Something about more experiments."

"When did you last see him?"

"A few hours ago, why?"

"Does he know the algorithms to the codes?"

"Yes, I showed them to him. Is there something wrong?"

Malcolm was trying to read her face.

"I need to find him," he said. He was about to leave when Lauren called him back.

"Wait," she said. "Before he left—" She paused.

"Before he left, what?" said Malcolm.

"Before he left, he was asking lots of questions about wormholes and dark matter. Something about creating a wormhole out of thin air instead of finding one that already existed."

"What'd you tell him?"

"I told him it's impossible, given today's knowledge."

"Today's knowledge." He shook his head.

He made his way to the door.

"Is Jake okay?" she said.

"He's fine."

"I'm coming with you."

"No stay here. I need to see Jake alone."

Malcolm thought hard as he walked. The ship—he had to be in the ship. He moved faster, racing down the long corridor that led to the ship.

Jake, please don't do it. Whatever you're thinking, don't do it.

As he entered through the double doors into the darkness, Malcolm looked around. He walked quickly toward the floating monitors, scanning in every direction for Jacob.

"Jake! Are you in here?"

He could hear nothing but his own voice echoing.

Then he saw it. The eighth monitor. It was now showing an image of boxcars with dead bodies. Dachau! It had to be. It was the same location that was frozen on the Kronos device. But when did this appear, and why now? Had Jake traveled there? His grandmother had died at a different camp, so why there? Something was definitely amiss here. Unless Jake had seen this image first and thought he could fix it. That was more likely than anything. And if that were the case, his going back there could be disastrous.

Malcolm hurried to the far end of the ship, using a pocket flashlight to illuminate his way. With any luck, maybe Jake was still here. Then he noticed what looked like footprints. He bent down and felt the ground. Fresh mud again, the same mud that was on the floor in his office. There was no doubt that Jacob had been here recently; whether he still was remained to be seen.

The footprints seemed to be going toward the far end of the ship. Malcolm continued on through the darkness, following the trail until he reached the alcove at the farthest end. The mud stopped just outside the alcove.

Wherever and however it was that Jacob had travelled through time, there was something special about this alcove.

Malcolm shined his light on the platform inside.

Footprints.

So this was the point of departure. It had to be.

At that moment, Malcolm heard footsteps behind him and turned around just as a hand touched his shoulder.

"I hear you're looking for a missing person," said the familiar voice. It was Beeze.

"Yes," said Malcolm. "We may have a little problem on our hands."

"You mean besides a celestial judgment day looming and a possible conspiracy to help bring it about? 'Cause I thought that was a problem too. Or did I miss something?"

"I believe Jacob has found a way to travel back in time. And based on some personal things he shared with me, I suspect he went to Germany. Karlsruhe to be precise, to see his grandparents in 1924."

"Holy shit!" Beeze was shaking his head in disbelief. "I could think of ten million places I'd want to go first. But what if he did. So what? Long as he doesn't touch nothing."

"Well, these weren't your everyday grandparents. They were involved in a plot to kill Adolf Hitler in prison. And, as you know, Jake has certain opinions on Hitler. Not to mention he now has an incentive to help them, given the new monitor image."

"There's a new image?"

"Dachau. You ran right past it."

"You don't think he'd actually go that far, do you? Kill Hitler? I mean we're talking major shit."

"Well, the logical Jake, no. But the emotional Jake? If he actually ends up meeting his grandparents? And he ends up getting hooked in? Not to mention, he might think he's saving the world in the process. I don't know. Stranger things have happened."

"Stranger things?" said Beeze. "Oh I don't think so! What the hell could be stranger than a mild-mannered scientist time travelin' back to kill Hitler? That gets my vote on the strange list."

"Well, the old Jake isn't so mild-mannered. And if the old Jake comes out and decides to act on his emotions, he just might tip the scales and bring about the very thing he's trying to stop: Armageddon."

"Wait a minute," said Beeze. "What do you mean, the old Jake?"

Malcolm looked around in the darkness aiming his flashlight. He thought he had heard a noise, but now he didn't hear anything. Content that nobody was there, he continued.

"When Jake's grandfather died, Jake ended up in a foster home, where he was abused and beaten for over a year. Apparently the foster father was an alcoholic and the mother was weak. One night, Jake ran away. I guess he figured he'd take his chances on the streets. It wasn't too long, though, before he was caught, and, with a fake name and no identity, he was thrown in a detention center. Anyway, as it turned out, that was no picnic either, as you can imagine. Here he was, some quiet kid, no family, abused, with only one thing to keep him sane—physics. He got that from his grandfather, and I guess it reminded him of happier times. And so he kept to himself and immersed himself in his studies."

"I bet that made him Mister Popular there."

"You can guess what comes next. Here he was, the weird kid—the mad scientist that didn't talk to anyone or hang with anyone. Except one day, one of the bullies had the misfortune of being the one to break the proverbial straw on the camel's back. He kept whacking Jake in the back of the head with a book, waiting for a response. Well, he got a response all right. All the rage Jake was carrying was let loose on that one kid. The kid ended up in the hospital for weeks and nearly died. Nobody messed with Jake after that."

"Dammnnn, so our little mad scientist has a bit of badass in him."

"Which doesn't bode well for us right now if it comes back."

"How'd you find out about this anyway? This detention center stuff. Did he tell you?"

"No, I saw it."

"You saw it?"

"I was volunteering at the detention center right around the time Jake got there. When I saw what he'd been through, I sort of became his mentor. I was one of the few people he trusted. I guided him through some rough times, but I like to think I got through to him. I could see that he had a good heart, and he had his grandfather's talent for science. When he turned eighteen, he gained access to his inheritance, so I helped him get started with his career. He got into college, and, as I suspected, emerged as one of the world's great scientists. I also helped him channel his emotions."

"Yeah, well, let's hope he remembers how to do that."

"Let's hope."

"So what do we do now?"

"We wait."

Chapter 16
Max and Anna

Jacob was watching the environment in awe as people passed him along the sidewalk. Occasionally he'd see a horse and carriage go by, and one or two old-time cars that appeared to be taxis. Even though he didn't look that much different from anyone else, he felt oddly out of place. He was taking in the atmosphere when suddenly he noticed that the singing had stopped. He watched the doors of the synagogue intently, waiting for something to happen.

Finally, after ten or fifteen minutes, the doors burst open. First a few people trickled out onto the sidewalk, then more. He began to wonder if he'd even be able to pick his grandparents out among the crowd. People stopped to converse. Some seemed in a hurry to leave. Then he saw a young couple that almost certainly was Max and Anna. They walked slowly, looking around, as if they weren't sure where to go next. He felt his pulse beating faster as he sat back on the bench, frozen. They were turning to cross the street directly in front of him!

As they reached the middle of the street, he could make out their faces. Could it be?

No, it wasn't them.

Just then, out of the corner of his eye, across the street against the stone wall of the synagogue, he saw them. It had to be them. A young man in his twenties was posing them against the wall for a photo—the very same photo Jacob now had in his briefcase. Jacob sat and watched quietly, breathing deeply to calm his nerves.

After a few photos, they were on the move, walking to the left with the photographer, who apparently was a friend of theirs. Jacob got up and followed along from a distance, remaining on his side of the street so he'd be less likely to lose track. He followed for a few blocks until they stopped. He watched as they stood at the head of an alley outside a jewelry store, having a conversation. The photographer shook hands with Max, gave Anna a kiss on each cheek, and turned up the alley. Max and Anna continued straight ahead, holding hands.

He almost couldn't believe this was Pop, a spritely 24-year-old with a full head of dark brown hair, not much older than Ethan. And Anna was only 21. How strange it was that they reminded him of his own kids. He hadn't even met them yet, but he already felt protective of them, especially given what he knew about their future.

He continued to follow them for several more blocks until they turned right at the corner. He crossed the street and saw them disappear into a side street on their right, so he ran ahead. He turned the corner just in time to see them entering a doorway.

He noticed a bench across the street on the left, opposite what seemed to be their apartment. Once again, he took a seat. He would have to think through his strategy.

He knew he needed to do something fast, but he had to be careful. He wondered when the owners of the ship would return, whoever or whatever they were. He thought about Kim and the family. Kim must have been on pins and needles waiting to hear from him. There was no phone service on the ship, and he sure as hell couldn't call her from here. As excited as he was to meet his grandparents in their youth, and most of all, to see Pop one last time, he longed to be home. But he had a mission to complete. Only when it was over could he return and hopefully have some semblance of a normal life—if that was even possible after all this.

Chapter 17
Conspiracy Theory

Beeze returned to the graphics room to examine the photos again. He put up the images, including the new boxcar image, which he had captured on his way back from talking with Malcolm. As he looked at the boxcar image, he began thinking about the possible scenarios that could result from Jacob going back in time. He decided to write them up.

> **Scenario #1:** *Jacob looks at grandparents. Sniffs. Comes right back.*——-à <u>Probability:</u> Damn low; <u>Impact:</u> Maybe some fallout from sighting or contamination.

> **Scenario #2:** *Jacob influences plot. Succeeds. Hitler dead.*——-à <u>Probability:</u> Low; <u>Impact:</u> Domino effect probable, results unknown.

> **Scenario #3:** *Jacob influences plot. Fails like all the other attempts to kill Hitler. Jacob and/or Grandpa captured or killed. Hitler alive and well.*——-à <u>Probability:</u> High; <u>Impact:</u> Grandpa used by the Nazis for nukes; Nazis steal technology or info from Jacob. Game over.

There were too many variables here to figure out what the hell would happen. But no matter how you sliced the pie, it still smelled like shit.

He thought back to the rings. What was Malcolm not telling him? Malcolm sure seemed cool about everything, almost like he knew more than he was letting on. Probably one of those top secret things.

One other person here might know something, though. And it was time everyone stopped babying her.

He grabbed printouts of the images and left to go see Lauren. She had to know something about this.

As he entered the lab, Lauren was buried in her notes, running calculations.

"Find him?" she said without looking up.

Beeze threw the images on the table in front of her.

"I don't get it," she said finally looking up. "Is there supposed to be something I'm looking at?"

"Recognize this symbol?" said Beeze pointing to a blown up image of one of the rings.

"Should I?"

"I thought you might know something about it. This same ring is in every one of the images."

"First of all," she said, "why would I know about this? And second of all, how can you be sure it's the same symbol? That doesn't make any sense."

"Actually it makes lots of sense if there's some sort of conspiracy going on."

"Conspiracy for what? That's ridiculous."

Beeze put another image in front of her. "Tell me that's not the same ring."

"You don't know that. I'm sure there are hundreds of rings with similar markings. Did you actually do any research on this?"

"Actually, I did."

"Listen, I'm busy here, so unless you find Jacob, I don't have time for your crazy conspiracy theories."

He tossed the blown-up Hitler image on the table in front of her and pointed out the second person to Hitler's left.

"Yeah," he said, "well maybe *that's* part of the conspiracy too. "Look familiar?"

He was sure he was seeing a look of visible shock on her face. Either shock or anger, he wasn't sure. He decided to press further.

"Who's that with Hitler?" he said.

"I have no idea."

"Care to guess?"

"I never guess. It's a bad career move. It could be anybody. Lots of people look alike."

"Where's Jake?" he said.

He could see her anger rising.

"I don't know," she said. "Listen, I'm busy here, so if—"

"So it seems you know more than anyone about all this hi-tech stuff. And the last person Jake was with was you."

"That means nothing and you know it. What Jake does is his business. I just showed him how it worked. He's probably in his cabin. Did you even think to look there?"

"He's not in his cabin, and he's not anywhere else we looked either. He's nowhere. You don't just disappear when you're at the bottom of the damn ocean. He time traveled somewhere and you had to help him."

"I told you I didn't help him. I just showed him how it worked. And if he's really missing, I'm sure he'll be back. If he's not, well then there's nothing we can do, is there? He obviously made his own choice."

"Yeah, sure he did."

"When are you going to get it through your thick skull? I am not Jake's keeper."

"No, Lauren, obviously you're not."

He realized he wasn't getting anywhere with Lauren. He should have known better, but it felt good to try anyway. He felt her eyes staring daggers at him as he left. If there was one thing he hated, it was being made a fool of.

But if Lauren really didn't know anything about the rings—or about Jake's whereabouts—then just what the hell was going on here?

Chapter 18
The Visitor

"And so, Mister Gratz, you claim you have followed me here?"

It was incredibly unsettling to hear Pop talk as a stranger. Jacob couldn't help staring at his face as they sat opposite each other in the living room. All the features and mannerisms were there, but in a much younger person. He felt almost as if he were talking to some stranger and not the beloved family member who had raised him. It was only minutes ago that he had made the decision to knock on Max's door. He had explained that he was an American scientist, Joseph Gratz, stopping in Karlsruhe en route to visiting family in Strasbourg. Fortunately, Max was gracious, inviting him in and offering to continue in English, much to his relief.

"Joseph," said Jacob. "You can call me Joseph. Yes, if you'll pardon me, I did follow you. You see, I recently read your student research paper on probability factors in electrons with great fascination. I noticed it came from the Institute of Technology at Karlsruhe, the Fridericiana, as I believe you call it."

"Yes," said Max, "after the Grand Duke Frederick of Baden." Jacob could see that he was mildly surprised at his foreign visitor's knowledge of the local culture.

"Well, I must say it was my great fortune that Karlsruhe was directly on my route. And once I arrived here, it didn't take much to find you—just a matter of asking around. I hope I'm not disturbing you."

"How, may I ask, did you come upon my paper, Joseph?"

Max looked curious, but cautious.

"Well I'm a research scientist myself, so of course I make it my habit to keep up with university publications and journals, especially in the area of quantum mechanics, as Max Born has come to call it."

"You know Born?" Now Max's interest appeared to be piqued.

"I haven't met him, but I have a particular interest in his work. I've done a bit of research in this area myself, and I thought we may be of some help to one another."

Before Max could respond, Anna entered with a tray of assorted teas and cakes.

"Max," she said, "we can't let our guest starve."

Jacob turned to face her. She was even more beautiful than her photo, and her smile lit up the room. It was hard to believe she was the same person he had seen less than twenty-four hours ago as a tortured, emaciated soul lying dead in the boxcar at Dachau.

The rest of the evening went like a blur. Jacob watched Max listen intently as he shared insights about waves and particles, borrowing slightly from modern theory without giving away too much. Jacob knew that modern quantum mechanics wouldn't begin until 1927 with the acceptance of the Copenhagen Interpretation. Max didn't realize how close he was.

They spoke of other topics as well, from music to film to religion. While Jacob wasn't up on the films of the time, there was at least one he had seen and could discuss: *The Thief of Bagdad*, with Douglas Fairbanks.

Anna's questions took on a more personal note, asking about his family and whether he had any children. He shared that he had a wife and two children: a seven-year-old daughter and an older boy in law school. It was soon after, however, that Anna seemed to appear withdrawn. He was sure it wasn't his imagination.

"You'll have to excuse her, my friend." Max looked toward Anna and back at him. Jacob wasn't quite sure what was going on, but he had an idea something he'd said had touched a nerve.

"You see, Anna's doctor believes a child is not in our future. It's sad, yes, but we are dealing with it. Every so often the issue comes up. It's unavoidable I suppose."

"It's okay, really," added Anna. She grasped Max's hand and smiled.

Jacob wished he could tell them that he was living proof that their doctor was wrong, but he dared not. He couldn't help imagining the joy they must have felt when they eventually did have a child. And then he thought of the terrible, gut-wrenching pain Max must have felt when Anna was torn from his life without warning. He realized he was clenching his fists again, angry that such innocence, such love, had fallen prey to the brainwashed regime of a lunatic.

Max's eyes suddenly lit up. "Your ring!" The comment, probably meant to change the subject, snapped him back to reality.

Jacob looked down at the Masonic ring he wore with pride.

"Yes, I'm a Freemason. So was my father." He dared not mention his *grandfather.* "I see you wear one too."

Max smiled. "Then it appears we are brothers."

Jacob extended his hand, smiling back as they exchanged the Masonic handshake that had spanned generations.

"Then, as a brother," he said, leaning in toward Max, "you must be aware of the dangers we are facing today, not only as Freemasons, but as Jews."

He wasn't sure what made him say that, but he felt compelled to bring up the subject of Hitler. After all, in four days, on April 30th, 1924, a psychiatrist would be visiting Adolf Hitler in prison, a psychiatrist who would hopefully be replaced by an assassin. Jacob wondered if the decision to cancel the plot had been made yet.

"My friend, there have long been threats to us, in both areas, but somehow we survive."

Max wasn't taking the bait, so he'd have to clarify.

"I'm speaking of a certain Adolf Hitler. Do you know of him?"

The smile vanished from Max's face, and the man he had once known as his loving grandfather had turned ice cold.

"I know of him, but I have no opinion on the subject."

Just then, Max abruptly stood up.

"Joseph," he said, "you are more than welcome to stay the night. We have a spare bedroom that I'm sure you'll find comfortable. It's getting late, I'm sure you understand."

As Max walked toward the stairs, Jacob looked over at Anna, who was watching uncomfortably. She excused herself to prepare his room.

As he sat in the living room sipping his tea, Jacob began to think about the possibilities, and of course the dangers, of influencing Max and Samuel's decision to proceed with their plot. He'd been dead set on his decision, but now the thought was nagging at him.

If he chose to change the future by killing Hitler, the effects, though mostly positive, would be dramatic. But what unforeseen consequences might occur? He'd heard Malcolm's warnings, but Malcolm wasn't aware of the full situation. Is it possible the aliens weren't building a case after all, but were instead about to give us a warning—a last chance to set things right? Who could say for sure? Sometimes you have to go with the data you have, especially when you can't wait to find out. And besides, in any case, undoing Hitler's actions would seem to put us a level down on the violence scale.

No matter how he looked at it, with the opportunity four days away, there just wasn't time to wait and see.

Then he thought of the Talmudic saying that Max had shared with him shortly before he died.

Whoever destroys a soul, it is considered as if he destroyed an entire world. And whoever saves a life, it is considered as if he saved an entire world.

He thought about that. Destroying Hitler versus saving millions of lives. That seemed like a fair trade no matter how you cut it. When he looked at it that way, it became clearer that he was doing the right thing.

Just then, a creaking noise startled him.

"He's awfully stubborn, you know." It was Anna coming down the steps.

"Don't I know it." It was an automatic response, but he caught himself before she could react. "I mean strong-willed people in general are like that," he said. "But I'm sure he has his reasons."

"So what do you know of him?" She sat on the chair opposite him.

"Max? I've only just met him, but he seems—"

"No, I mean Hitler."

"I know he's in prison. But more than that, I've heard about his senseless accusations. He thinks the Jews and the Freemasons are colluding to take over the world, and he's using a bogus document he's discovered to make his case. At least that's the word in America. What worries me is what might happen if he comes to power."

"But I don't see how he could. For one, he's in prison."

"Circumstances could change."

"You sound like my husband."

He realized he was getting testy, probably because he knew there'd be little time to act if he didn't decide something soon. He also wondered if she even knew about the plot. Max certainly did. His reaction had made that obvious.

The more he thought about it, with time being of the essence, he knew he couldn't wait any longer. He'd have to go upstairs now and confront Max with the truth.

Chapter 19
Proof

After distracting Anna by spilling his tea and saying he was going up to change, Jacob tapped on Max's door. Fortunately, Anna was busy cleaning up downstairs. The door opened slowly, and Max, clearly still suspicious, waved him in. He entered as Max turned to walk toward his dresser.

"Max," he said, "there's something I failed to tell you earlier. I promise you'll find it interesting, even more so than our little physics discussion." He thought that was probably the understatement of the century.

Max turned to face him. He didn't look amused.

"Joseph, I just want to make it clear that I do not wish to discuss Adolf Hitler. I know of him. Let's leave it at that. The man is a lunatic who should remain behind bars, and that's all I can offer on the matter."

Max returned his attention to the dresser, where he appeared to be arranging items in a valet box.

"I'm afraid there's much more you can offer, Max." Jacob paused before continuing, trying to find the right words. "You see," he said, "I know about your plan."

Max stopped arranging and slowly turned to face him again. He had a look of horror on his face, like he was seeing a ghost.

"Don't worry, Max, your secret's safe with me. I know that four days from now, there will be an opportunity to kill Hitler in prison. I'm here to provide information that I believe will be helpful. That's all."

Max's face turned from pale to red. "I don't know who you really are or what you're after, but there is no plan. You've received bad information. If you wish to kill Hitler, I wish you the best of luck, and I'll even applaud, but I want no part of it."

This was going to be harder than he'd thought.

"I'm afraid there is a plan, Max. And I know Samuel has convinced you not to go forward with it. Please, I'm on your side. Please hear me out."

"There is no plan! Who are you? How do you know my brother?"

Before he could answer, a noise on the stairway startled him. Anna had probably heard the yelling. Jacob turned around briefly, and then faced Max to respond. Only now Max was pointing a gun straight at him. This was certainly unexpected. Pop had never mentioned anything about owning a gun.

"Max, please," he said. "I'm not who you think I am."

"That, I'm aware of, Herr Gratz, if that is your name. Now tell me who you are. Sit in the chair first." Jacob moved slowly as Max pointed to an armchair with the gun.

As he sat, he heard the door open behind him. It was Anna.

"Stay out!" yelled Max. "Back away!" Max was definitely agitated, so he remained perfectly still on the chair.

"But wha—" Anna looked as confused by the gun as Jacob was. "Out!"

Max kept the gun pointed at him as Anna backed out of the room. Jacob felt he was running out of options, save for the one he was hoping to avoid. But now all bets were off.

"Max, can I show you something from my briefcase? I can explain who I am."

"I'm afraid not."

"Max, I am a fellow Mason—that much you can see. And I am a Jew. And a scientist. You know that from our conversation."

"You can be all that and a spy. I don't know what you're after. As I told you there is no plan, and I will not have my family put in danger."

"I am not a spy. Max, I know that you love Anna more than anything in the world; that you adore the music of Gershwin, though your tastes usually run more toward Sibelius; and that you have a scar just below your knee that you got as a child when you fell on a toy soldier, or at least that's what you told me."

Jacob stared at Max to see his reaction. At first his words didn't seem to register. Max was still pointing the gun at him, only now his hands were beginning to shake. Then, finally, Max stepped back, almost stumbling as he sat on the bed, still pointing the gun his way.

Then the gun lowered, and Max's expression changed from anger to confused shock.

"By God, how do you know this? Have we met?"

"We have, and if you'll please allow me access to my briefcase, I can explain further. I need you to trust me."

Looking totally bewildered, Max waved Jacob on to get the briefcase. As he crossed the hallway to his room, Jacob looked down to see Anna on the steps staring up at him. He motioned to her that everything was okay, and she immediately ascended the stairs to go into the room with Max.

When Jacob returned to Max's room with the briefcase, Max and Anna were sitting side by side on the bed. Max had the gun pointed his way again, apparently just to be safe. At least the anger had gone from his face.

Jacob opened the briefcase with the retinal scanner, watching the shocked look on their faces as he placed it on his lap. Max lowered the gun.

"I'm going to show you something," said Jacob. "You may not understand at first, and what I tell you may come as a shock, but I assure you every word of it is true."

He reached into the briefcase and took out the photo of Max and Anna posing in front of the synagogue. He handed it to Max.

Max and Anna studied the photo. As expected, they looked confused, as if they didn't believe what they were seeing.

Anna looked up at Jacob. "But how did you get this? This photo was taken only this evening. Are you a friend of Robert?"

"The photographer, I assume? No, I don't know him."

Now Max looked up. "It looks old and tattered. I don't understand."

He thought maybe it would be easier if they discovered the answer on their own. "There's only one way I could have gotten this," he said. "Can either of you guess how?"

They both stood there staring at him, shaking their heads. He decided his only option was to just blurt it out and explain afterwards.

"Max, Anna, as hard as this will be to comprehend, I'm from your future. Max, it was you yourself who told me about the plan, and of course the other things I mentioned."

They looked at each other in disbelief, and then at him. Max picked up the gun again. "Now I *know* you're crazy."

"Listen, I know it sounds impossible, but how else can you explain the things I know, or how I had the photo that was just taken?"

Max still stared at him with the gun pointed. "That's what I aim to find out. I don't know w—"

"I can prove it."

He thought of one more way to ease their doubts. He took his cell phone out of the briefcase and aimed the camera at them. He pressed the camcorder icon and touched the record button.

"What is that?" Max looked concerned.

"Don't worry, it's safe. It's a camera. It takes moving pictures."

"Impossible."

"See for yourself."

He pressed the stop button and played the video for them. He watched as Max and Anna viewed it with their mouths open.

"I also have materials with me that show what will happen if Hitler comes to power. Or, should I say, *when* he comes to power."

He handed them a small book on the Holocaust, as Max placed the gun on the bed.

As they turned the pages, he watched the horror on their faces. At one point, Anna gasped and closed the book. She had tears in her eyes as she looked up.

Jacob spent the next hour explaining to them about Hitler's legacy, and how six million Jews and countless other so-called undesirables lost their lives.

"And you say he commits suicide?" Max seemed hopeful and more than a trifle relieved.

"Yes, but only after the damage has been done. So you understand why I must learn more about your plan and ask you to carry it out."

"And how is it that you have come to find us? How do I come to know you in the future to share such things? Are you a relative? A friend?"

At least Max seemed to be opening up finally.

"You might say I'm a relative."

Jacob thought about how much he should share. Then he decided it was best to be honest.

"I can assure you of one thing. Your fears about having a child are unwarranted."

Anna looked up, her eyes red, tears running down her cheeks.

"Are you—our son?"

Jacob shook his head and sighed.

"I'm your grandson. I've come here from the year 2024. And of course, my name is not Joseph Gratz. It's Jacob Newman."

He watched as Max and Anna broke down and held each other. He wasn't about to tell them about Anna's future. Certainly not now, and hopefully not at all. He felt he'd already opened Pandora's Box. He was sure they'd have a million questions. He decided to head that off by insisting he'd be unable to answer questions about their own future.

Once everyone had calmed down, he explained further, merely offering that they were both a huge influence on his life. That seemed to pacify them for the time being. He told them how Max would later go to MIT, and eventually would teach there. He dared not share anything about the car accident that had killed his parents. He did tell them, however, that it was Max's teachings that had fascinated him as a teen and led him to study quantum science. He told them about the Kronos discovery, and how he had arrived here. And, finally, he explained that Max had told him of the plan to kill Hitler using an assassin to pose as Hitler's psychiatrist. He left out the part about the journal for now. He couldn't help also mentioning the ultimate irony of the planned April 30th date for the poisoning, considering that Hitler would later commit suicide on that very date in 1945.

"So, as you can see," he said, "it's imperative that you convince Samuel to go ahead with the plan. If you need, I can stay a little longer to help you convince him. I only hope there's still time to arrange for the assassin."

Max looked confused.

"Jacob, I'm afraid your information is missing quite a few details. For one, there is no assassin. I'm not sure why I would have told you that, but there never has been any assassin."

"No assassin? How were you planning on carrying out the killing?"

Max and Anna looked at each other.

"There *is* a plot, isn't there?" He knew Pop wouldn't have made this up.

Silence. This wasn't good.

Chapter 20
Change of Plans

Jacob held his head in his hands, hoping and praying that either Max or Anna would say something to ease his fears. He was also growing concerned about how long he'd been here. Who knows how much time there was before the aliens or whoever they were would make their judgment? And besides, Malcolm and Lauren and the team must be searching all over for him by now. If the Hitler plot was bogus, he was going to have to get back, and fast. He glanced down at the Kronos device in the open briefcase and was relieved to see that the meter was still at two-thirds and the icon was there ready to be pressed at any time.

Finally, Max broke the silence. "Jacob," he said, "I will share our secret with you."

Jacob looked up at Max and listened intently.

"Yes," said Max, "there was a plot. But I hope from my story you will see that, as bad as this monster is, as horrible the actions he will take, we are powerless to help."

Max stood up and put the gun away behind his valet as he continued on.

"My brother Samuel—your great uncle, I suppose—is a prison guard in the Fortress of Landsberg. His assignment? To guard none other than Adolf Hitler. Oh, they say Hitler is there for trying to overthrow the government, but the fact is, he is treated like royalty. He has many friends in high places who are more than sympathetic to his views. Samuel has had the misfortune of getting to see Hitler on a daily basis, watching him pace back and forth in his study, dictating his thoughts to his fellow inmate, a man named Rudolf Hess, who takes notes for him."

Jacob knew all about Hess. "Hess became Hitler's deputy," he explained to Max. "I'm sure the dictation was for Hitler's book, *Mein Kampf*, which I understand he wrote in prison. You mentioned his study. He's not in a cell?"

"Like I said, he is treated like royalty. You are aware, no doubt, of the Protocols?"

"Yes, *The Protocols of the Elders of Zion,* a fabricated piece of garbage. You taught me about that."

"Yes, and a gross forgery too, but still very dangerous. Hitler preaches it like gospel. So does his friend Henry Ford in America. Imagine! Jews and Freemasons working together to take over the world. We can barely run our own businesses! I can't imagine the German public buying into it, though."

"Max, trust me. Hitler will end up rising to power based on those claims. The economic problems Germany is having now will get even worse. Soon the whole world will suffer a great economic depression. And Hitler will use that opportunity to create a country of extreme nationalists—a country led by fear. He'll paint himself as the savior of Germany, and a big part of his strategy will be spreading a message that they have to take Germany back from the Jews. And the Jews? Well, they'll become the symbol of all that's wrong with Germany. I already told you about the six million of them, brutally exterminated in the camps like they were pieces of meat. But I haven't mentioned the millions of others—or the fifty million when you consider the war and the decades of copycats."

Max appeared to be giving this information some thought.

"Now that you mention it, Jacob, Hitler's speeches have already been riling people up in some circles. Others see him as a harmless loudmouth, an extremist. But his views are gaining popularity with larger and larger audiences, not to mention those in high places. Samuel has witnessed his passionate rants firsthand, for months now—and also his plans for manipulating the masses. The problem with Hitler is that he's crazy like a fox. There is nothing more dangerous than a man with an utter lack of humanity, a distorted view of the Bible, and an absolute genius for manipulation."

"Then we agree that something must be done about it. After all, there's a unique opportunity coming up."

"And so we thought too, Jacob. You see, Samuel has a good friend who's a bartender in Munich. His name is Joseph, ironically. A few weeks ago, Joseph wrote to Samuel to tell him about a conversation he had with a regular customer, a certain Otto Müller."

"I remember the name. You told me about Müller years ago, or rather you will years from now. He's a psychiatrist, right?"

Jacob remembered Pop talking about Müller after a well publicized arrest.

"Yes, quite right. And one who enjoys a drink. He also enjoys the company of loose women. Joseph frequently sets up dates for him with the local prostitutes. Müller tips him quite well for it, of course. And he has another habit. He's quite loose-lipped when drunk, and from time to time even shares stories of his patients. Recently he spoke of one who interested Joseph very much."

"Hitler?"

"Yes, it seems that Hitler, despite his delusions of grandeur, suffers from severe anxiety and depression. And so, he receives regular visits from his psychiatrist. But on April 30th, the psychiatrist will be out of the country and is sending none other than Otto Müller in his place. And that choice was not a random one, I might add. Müller, it turns out, is a Hitler sympathizer. Of course, Müller was excited by the opportunity and shared this news with Joseph. But what Müller doesn't know, nor does anyone else in the pub, is that Joseph is a Jew. And a Jew who knows Hitler's prison guard."

"So, let me get this right," said Jacob. "Joseph told Samuel about Müller coming to visit Hitler."

"Yes, exactly."

"So I assume the plan is to have someone replace Müller, just as you told me."

"Yes, yes," said Max, "but that someone is not a paid assassin. It's much more complicated than that, Jacob."

"You don't mean—"

"The plan was to delay Müller while I took his place. With Samuel as the guard, it would be quite easy to administer a dose of untraceable poison that would take effect hours later, and would appear as a heart attack. There were only a few problems with this plan. One, I am twenty-four years of age, and Hitler asks very pointed questions. It's unlikely I'd be convincing enough. And if anyone saw Samuel and me together after that, it would put both of us at risk."

"Yes, I agree. How were you planning to delay Müller?" He felt as if he were addressing his kids, as opposed to his grandparents. It was a feeling he didn't expect.

"That's an even bigger problem. The only sure way to delay Müller would be to have a prostitute drug him or kill him. But who could we trust? We certainly weren't about to send Anna. Who else then? There was nobody. It was a nice plan, Jacob, but the risks were just too great. Do you see now?"

"I do see. But there are a few other things to consider—and maybe even another solution."

He watched as Max and Anna looked at each other. He didn't want to have to tell them about Anna, but there was no way they'd understand the real cost of their decision otherwise. On the other hand, without a paid assassin, this plan was extremely risky. He couldn't ask them to risk their lives *now* on the small chance of extending Anna's life later. That could be disastrous. But there was another way. A way that involved much less risk. Still, they deserved to know what was at stake. He owed them that much.

They were still looking at him with confused expressions, so he explained.

"We can take care of Hitler," he said, "without you getting involved."

After a few seconds, Anna's eyes got wider as if she had just made the connection.

"No!" she said. "Are you thinking that you'd do it? No, we cannot ask you to do that. Max is right. It's awful what that horrible man caused, but it's too dangerous."

"We cannot let you do this, Jacob," Max added.

"Max, we don't have a choice."

"Why do you say that?" said Max. "We always have a choice."

"Because Anna will die if we don't!"

Max's face sank as Anna's eyes filled with tears again. He gently put his arm around her.

"When?" said Max.

"In Hitler's concentration camps in the mid 1940s, is all I know. Max, you spent the rest of your life regretting your decision not to kill Hitler. That's why I'm here."

Max turned to Anna, and back to Jacob. "Well, we could leave the country now, couldn't we? Then Anna would be safe."

Jacob stopped to think. If it were only Anna he was trying to save, that could very well be an option. But, unfortunately, it wasn't just about Anna. The entire planet was at risk.

"Max," he said. "I know that sounds like the easy way out, but if what you told me as an old man was correct, you don't have the resources to do that now. You can barely afford this apartment. And money will be scarce over the next decade or so everywhere, even in America. Besides, it's the work you're yet to do in Karlsruhe that will lead to your professorship in Boston, whether the Nazis come to power or not."

"But I don't care about any of that," said Max. "I only want to see Anna safe. And she's more likely to stay alive in America."

"The problem is, it's not just Anna's life that's at stake here."

"Jacob, that's not—"

Anna held her hand on Max's to stop him.

"Jacob," Max continued. "I understand there are many others who will die, but our chances of succeeding are small. And if what you say is true and you're from our future, do you understand what could happen by changing history?"

"I do, but there's more I haven't told you. And you probably won't believe me."

"What is it?" said Anna.

"I told you about the ship we found and the images," said Jacob. "Whoever or whatever owns this ship is making a case about human violence, and we believe a judgment day is imminent. I mean think about it. Big alien ship appears suddenly in the South Pacific. Giant monitors showing images of major massacres in human history. It doesn't take much to guess what's coming next. All I'm trying to say is that undoing Hitler could be our last hope. For my family. For your great grandchildren. For everyone."

Max and Anna just had blank stares on their faces, and Max was shaking his head. Jacob thought he'd better explain what he was thinking.

"Listen, I know it sounds far-fetched. I know it sounds like I'm making some pretty big assumptions. Just hear me out. I came here with a time travel device. Nobody knows me here. I'm a complete stranger with no identity. I can impersonate the psychiatrist."

"Are you crazy?" said Max.

"I did psychiatric work in graduate school, and my work spans both physics and neuroscience. Once the drug is administered, I can go back to my time with nobody the wiser. And I can go back even sooner if anything goes wrong. If everything goes as planned, great. And if someone does make the connection later that I wasn't Müller, so what? I could have been some spy, or part of some political plot. You and Anna won't be implicated at all."

Max seemed to be contemplating this logic.

"But your German," said Max. "Is it good enough?"

He had a point.

"Don't worry," said Jacob. "I can make up something about my American accent. Let that be the least of our worries. The bigger issue is what to do about Müller."

"I'll do it." Anna stood up. "I'll take care of Müller."

Max's face turned red. "Absolutely not! We already—"

"I *want* to do it," she said. "If I can save our future and help all those people, I insist. There's nobody else to trust. I'll die anyway if this fails—only alone and far away. And Jacob is right. You'd be sacrificing too much if we went to America. I won't have it."

Max hung his head and appeared to be processing what she'd said. Jacob could now see the Anna that Max had always bragged about—the Anna who led the daring escape that saved those women's lives, who sacrificed herself for their freedom. And she was right. There really was nobody else.

He watched as Max sat there silently. After several seconds, Max looked up at Anna.

"I'll contact Samuel," he said. "We'll meet him in Munich tomorrow. I will try to explain the best I can."

Anna sat back on the bed with Max and put a reassuring arm around him. "It will be all right. I promise."

Jacob liked seeing them like that. It was just as he had imagined it when Pop used to talk about her. He would describe her voice as soothing whenever times got tough. Jacob could now see what he'd meant.

Max then turned his attention to him.

"We will need to hire a taxi to Frankfurt first thing. It'll take us at least half a day to get there. From there we can take the train. The Deutsche Reichsbahn is completed now, so it can get us to Munich in a matter of hours. The Fortress of Landsberg is less than an hour west of there. We can do our planning in Munich with Samuel."

Jacob began packing up his briefcase. "We're doing the right thing," he said.

"I pray you're right," said Max. "Oh, and Jacob…"

"Yes?"

"If you think it was difficult convincing us, wait until you meet Samuel."

Chapter 21
Timecode

Malcolm was sitting in his favorite chair by the porthole in his office when Beeze came in.

"I can't take this anymore," said Beeze. "I feel like we're sitting ducks."

"Sometimes a sitting duck is just that: a sitting duck."

"What the hell's that supposed to mean?"

Malcolm smiled.

"It means—"

He was interrupted when the whole lab began vibrating heavily. Everything felt like it was shifting. Malcolm held tight, and Beeze fell into the wall. The noise was deafening.

"The monitors," Malcolm shouted to Beeze over the noise. "We have to check the monitors."

Malcolm helped Beeze steady himself as they made their way to the corridor. Lab technicians and crew members all poured out into the hallway wondering what was going on, as this was no doubt the worst they'd experienced to date. The whole facility continued vibrating, with the occasional shift throwing everyone off balance.

Finally, after pushing their way through, Malcolm and Beeze arrived at the double doors, and Malcolm entered the code.

"What do you think is happening?" said Beeze.

"We'll find out soon enough."

The doors slid open and they ran toward the large floating monitors.

"Holy shit!" said Beeze. "Look!"

Malcolm looked up to see the giant monitors slowly inching closer together. What was happening?

He watched with Beeze as the monitors came together and formed one huge rectangular monitor. At that instant, the images all went black, sending the room into darkness. Then everything stopped. All the noises and vibrations. Everything.

"I don't like the looks of this," said Beeze.

Beeze had barely gotten the words out when the giant monitor screen turned bright white. It was almost blinding. Then, gradually forming in the center of the screen was a series of codes, in a single horizontal line. It looked just like the symbols on the Kronos device. Only the codes were all moving quickly.

"It looks like some kind of countdown," said Beeze.

Malcolm looked at him.

"Maybe. Maybe not."

"What do we do, then?" said Beeze. "Just stand here?"

"No," said Malcolm. "I'll wait here. I want to check something out. You go get Lauren. Tell her I need her immediately."

Chapter 22

Munich

The trip to Munich was uneventful except for an unusually yellow sky and freakish electrical storms that began as soon as they left Karlsruhe. As Jacob glanced out the hotel window, he could see that this situation was showing no signs of letting up. He half-wondered if it had anything to do with the ship. Meanwhile, Samuel was pacing back and forth in the hotel suite, ranting and waving his hands around. Samuel was a bear of a man, about 6'3" and stocky. It was no wonder he was a prison guard. Max and Anna sat together on the couch as Max continued his debate with Samuel.

"I don't know what to think," said Samuel. "My own brother and my sister-in-law come here with a stranger—no offense—who claims to be our relative from the future."

"But you've seen the proof," said Max. "He produced a photo of Anna and me that was taken less than an hour before we met him. Yet it was old and tattered. And the books! Surely the books don't lie."

"Books can lie! Anything can be fabricated. I'm not saying this was, but it's possible. It's a lot to consider for what we're risking. My God, we're talking about killing an innocent psychiatrist."

Jacob's alarm bells went off. He turned to Max. "Killing him? I thought Anna just had to delay him." Now he knew why Max was so against her involvement.

"Well, killing him will delay him," said Max.

Samuel looked concerned about the mix-up.

"Max, we've gone through this," he said. "The psychiatrist would have to die. It would put us—and by *us* I mean me—at risk if he lived. And you know our original plan. No traces."

"Yes, yes, I know. I didn't get a chance to share this detail with Jacob. So you're saying you'll help us?"

"I'm not saying anything yet."

Jacob felt he'd better speak up now.

"Müller's not innocent."

"Not innocent? Not innocent?" It appeared Samuel had a flair for the dramatic. "No, the man likes his drink and his women, but then if we considered that, we'd be killing half the men in Germany."

"I'm not talking about his drinking, or his women."

"What then?"

Jacob could see he had everyone's attention.

"The fact is, Otto Müller was, or will be, arrested after the war for conducting horrible psychological experiments on Jews. Along with Ernst Rüdin and other Nazi cohorts, he was a proponent of a concept called *racial hygiene*, which, I might add, led to the Nuremberg Laws, which allowed for official and legal persecution of Jews. That same group spearheaded the Sterilization Act to prevent what he called ge-netically diseased children—that is, those from races and dispositions he didn't like—from being born. It's all in the book there. You can look it up."

He watched as Samuel leafed through the book. He had promised Max he wouldn't bring up anything about the alien judgment day, but he needed to at least exhaust all his other options. Samuel was shaking his head as he read, as if he didn't quite believe what he was seeing. Finally, he stopped at a particular page and appeared to be intently studying whatever he was looking at. After a moment or two, he looked up at Max and Anna, then at Jacob. All of a sudden, his skeptical de-meanor dissipated, replaced by a look of resolve.

"When you come to the prison," said Samuel, "you will announce yourself simply as Otto Müller and ask for Otto Leybold. He's the pris-on's director. He will bring you to me. Max do you have the drug?"

"Yes," said Max. "We can put it in Hitler's food. It's untraceable and will cause death three hours later, which will present as a cardiac arrest."

"And for Müller?"

"It's a powder we can put in his drink. It will cause death within five minutes."

"Good. Lord knows it will be no trouble getting him to drink. Now listen, he has a secluded cottage near Lake Starnberg, not far from here. He frequently brings the ladies there that my friend Joseph sets him up with. Anna, I'll contact Joseph at the pub and have him arrange for Müller to meet a new girl, Nora, who's in the area for one night only. Of course, you'll need to be Nora. We'll get you the outfit and the blonde wig. Are you sure you want to do this?"

"Yes, I'm sure."

"Good. Now, Anna, you will arrive at the pub on the evening of April 29th—that's two days from now, so we have all day tomorrow and most of the next day to rehearse and get anything we need. Joseph will introduce you to Müller. Just make small talk. If all goes as usual, Müller will invite you back to his cottage. You'll have to get him to have a cocktail and find an opportunity to slip the powder into his drink. As Max said, it will kill him within five minutes, so you only have to stall for a little until it takes effect. Max, you'll need to wait near the cottage with a gun and a can of kerosene as per our original plan. Do you have the gun I got for you?"

"Yes, I brought it with us."

"Excellent. Hopefully you won't need to use it. Once Müller's dead, you and Anna will have to wait at the cottage until the next afternoon, let's say around two o'clock. Then burn the cottage. As far as everyone's concerned, Müller died in a tragic house fire after his visit with Hitler. Are we all clear?"

Jacob watched as Max and Anna nodded. He turned to Samuel.

"What about Hitler?" he said. "What can you tell me about him?"

"I was getting to that," said Samuel. "You'll arrive at Landsberg the morning of the 30th at ten o'clock. As I mentioned, Otto Leybold will bring you to me, and I'll take you to Hitler's study. During your visit, I will deliver his lunch on a wheeled cart. The meal will be served in a covered silver platter. You will jump up to get it from me and inject the poison into the meal."

"Do I inject it into the meat, or doesn't it matter where?"

Max answered. "You can put it anywhere. It will dissolve."

"Besides," Samuel added, "there is no meat. Hitler's a strict vegetarian—for ethical reasons no less. Or so I'm told. He's an animal and nature lover. Of course we know that even a man who pets his dog can be a depraved liar and a murderer."

"But he ended up poisoning his dog!" said Jacob. He remembered reading that somewhere.

"I cannot assume to get inside the head of this man, but he will get inside yours, I assure you."

"How so?"

"Well, at first it will seem like a casual discussion. He'll talk about things like the arts and his philosophies on life. He'll want to know about yours too, even as his doctor. He's soft spoken, unlike in his speeches, and will ask your thoughts on a variety of matters. But he'll ask many pointed questions as well. He's very shrewd. If it turns out he's on to you, you'll never know it until it's too late. And be careful of anything he says. He's a habitual liar. I've seen him win over people who were his mortal enemies, lying through his teeth, of course."

"Well he won't win me over, that's for sure. I know his future."

"Yes, let's hope. All I know is he is craftily and methodically planting the seeds of hatred in everyone he meets."

"Well, those seeds will take root when the Depression comes. Does he talk of killing Jews?"

"There is no talk of killing anyone. He is simply calling for the Germans to take back Germany. Privately, of course, he talks about his plans to manipulate the system. And he blames the Jews, of course, for all Germany's problems. And so, we see persecution coming, and possibly even expulsion—as an extreme—but the horrors you have revealed go beyond our wildest nightmares."

"I wouldn't believe any of it myself if I didn't know it to be true. But trust me, it is."

"Then we had better succeed. And speaking of our plan, when you leave the prison, go directly to this hotel suite and wait here for Max and Anna. I'll go over the transportation details with you, and we'll get you some German money. I will call you all here from a private phone in the prison when the drug has taken effect." Then Samuel paused.

"Jacob," he said.

"Yes?"

"You look dejected. Are you having second thoughts?"

Jacob wasn't aware that his concern was that obvious. But the killing Hitler part wasn't what was bothering him.

"Yes, I'm okay. I'm just trying to get my head around the fact..."

He was trying to find the right words as he felt everyone staring at him.

"...well, that I'm about to take part in a plan that involves sending my grandmother out to pose as a prostitute and kill someone!"

He realized he was getting a little too animated, so he settled down again.

"Other than that, I'm fine."

Anna, always the optimist, chimed in. "Jacob, it will all work out. I'm ready to do this. You aren't making me."

Samuel clapped his hands together. "Then we are agreed," he said. "Does anyone have any further questions?"

Max and Anna shook their heads. But Jacob still had one more question to ask. It had been plaguing him this whole time.

"I have only one."

"Go ahead."

"What did you see in the book that made you believe me? What convinced you to do this?"

Samuel's strong, confident face turned suddenly passive. He stood silent for a moment, then spoke solemnly.

"Joseph."

"Your bartender friend? What's his connection?"

"I recognized his face among the dead."

Chapter 23
Müller

Max stood outside watching anxiously, staring at the front doors of the pub across the street on the far corner. Anna was already inside posing as Nora. It was cold and still raining, as it had been for days now. He could still see streaks of lightning in the night sky, though it was quieting down. Strange. He'd never seen electrical storms last this long, even intermittently. He was glad Jacob had agreed to stay back at the hotel, as it was important for them not to be seen together.

It had already been an hour since she'd entered the bar. In a way, that was a good sign, but nonetheless he would feel more relieved when this was all over. He listened intently for any sign of a ruckus. At one point he heard a woman scream, but then the door had flown open and the source—a drunken couple—had staggered out.

By now, Joseph should have introduced Anna to Müller and they should be engaged in conversation. Max had made sure Anna knew to nurse her drink slowly. She couldn't afford to have anything less than a clear head, and she wasn't used to drinking. He was glad they'd had most of the last two days to prepare. He'd scouted out Müller's cottage the night before and buried the kerosene nearby.

Just as he glanced once more at his watch, the doors of the pub flew open again and Anna emerged. She was wearing her wig and out-fit, and was arm in arm with a middle-aged man of average height with a sturdy build, short ash-blond hair, and wire-framed eyeglasses. Max had expected Müller to be an older man, but either way, he'd soon be a dead man.

He followed on the opposite side of the street as the two of them boarded a taxi waiting on the next block. He watched as the motorcar pulled away, and waited a few moments before approaching another taxi. Lake Starnberg was about a half hour away. He asked the driver to take him to the marina. From there he could walk to the cottage, as per the plan. In the dark, nobody would see him.

Chapter 24
The Cottage

Anna clung tightly to her pocketbook as she followed Müller down the hallway toward the bedroom. She was going to have to be careful around him; he seemed sharp and well traveled, more so than she had expected. To say he was intimidating was putting it mildly. He had already drilled her extensively on her hometown, which she'd given as Stuttgart. Fortunately she knew enough from her visits there to bluff adequately.

In the hallway, on the right, she noticed a tall wine cabinet filled with dusty bottles.

"I see you're a connoisseur," she said. "My father used to collect wine." She prayed she could get him to drink before she'd have to sleep with him—something she was hoping to avoid.

As they entered the bedroom, he put his arm around her. She could smell the alcohol on his breath. "I like the finer things," he said. "Now if you don't mind, please wait here and make yourself comfortable." She looked at him, and he pointed to a small antique bistro table with two chairs. "Have a seat, my dear. I'll return in a moment."

Müller's faux debonair attitude made her uncomfortable because she knew what was hiding beneath it. She'd been hoping he'd be a halfwit.

She was too nervous to sit yet, so she placed her pocketbook on the floor by one of the chairs and looked around the room. The bed was straight ahead, facing her, its large mahogany headboard dominating the far wall. While Müller was gone, she decided to snoop around and get familiar with the place.

She walked toward the bed and looked on the nightstand. There was a lamp and a small wooden box. It looked like a gun box, similar to the one Max had. She wondered if this one too held a gun. Or perhaps her mind was running away with her. Maybe the box held cologne. Not that Müller would use a gun on her without cause, and she wasn't going to give him any, but still, he made her nervous. She moved slowly toward the box, listening for sounds coming from the other room. She picked up the box. It felt heavy. She opened it as quietly as she could, but before she could see what was inside, she heard a noise. Müller was coming!

She tried to put the box down, but her hands must have been shaking because in a split second it had fallen from her hand and landed on the floor with a thud. She wanted to scream, but couldn't. There was no time to pick up the box! She ran toward the table and stood there trying to look nonchalant just as Müller entered the room. She was hyperventilating and thought she might pass out.

Though her heart was pounding, she was relieved to see Müller holding two wine glasses and a bottle. If he *had* heard the noise, he wasn't letting on. He pulled out one of the bistro set chairs and Anna took a seat.

"Chateaux Margaux, 1915," he said. "I hope you like it." Still standing, he poured a small amount for her to taste. She prayed he wouldn't look over at the nightstand.

She sipped the wine, trying to keep her hand from shaking.

"It's wonderful," she said. "You really are a connoisseur."

He looked at her with a smile as he sat on the chair opposite her. "I'm a connoisseur of many things, wine being one of them."

She wanted to roll her eyes but caught herself. He was staring at her, too, which made her even more nervous. Had he heard the noise? Either way, he seemed the kind of person who gets immense pleasure out of making other people uncomfortable. She waited for him to pour his glass, but for some reason he didn't.

"Aren't you having any?" she said.

"Why do you ask?" he said. "Are you trying to get me drunk?"

She felt chills as he gave her a suspicious look.

"Relax," he said, a crooked smile forming on his face. "I'm joking. I couldn't very well have you drink alone; that would be quite rude of me." He finally poured his glass and raised it to toast. "To new friends."

"Yes," she said. "To new friends." She raised the glass to toast and took another sip. She thought she saw him glance over at the nightstand, but she wasn't sure. Somehow, and soon, she was going to have to find a way to reach into her pocketbook for the powder and slip it into his drink.

"You know," he said, "this bistro set is from 1814 France. The design is very rare. I'm a collector of all things French. Odd for a German, I know."

She forced a smile.

"I noticed it immediately," she said. "I enjoy rare artifacts myself. My uncle was an antiques dealer."

"You don't say? What was his name?"

"Fritz."

She said the first name that came to her mind. Max always used to talk about a famous scientist named Fritz Haber.

"And did your Uncle Fritz have a last name?"

She paused trying to think of a last name. She felt like she was about to have a panic attack.

"It's funny," she said. "I can't remember his last name. I only knew him as Uncle Fritz."

She knew that sounded ludicrous. She tried to change the subject quickly.

"Do you have others?" she said. "Other artifacts, I mean?"

He smiled politely.

"I do, my dear, and later I will be happy to show you." He was still staring at her as if to test her reaction.

"I would enjoy that," she said. "As you know, I can only stay the evening, so I would very much like to see them while I have the chance." She was praying he'd show them to her sooner rather than later. Anything to get him walking around. As far as she was concerned, the less time here with him, the better.

"Yes," he said, "about that, where are you traveling to that you are only in Munich for an evening, if you don't mind my asking?"

"I'd rather not say. It's...well, it's a private matter." Max had told her to say that, anticipating that Müller might ask. "I can come back another time, though," she added. She hoped he'd accept that answer and move on.

"Pity," he said. "I ask only because I'm away in the morning, but just for a few hours. I could take you wherever it is you're going, and even bring you back. If it's money—"

"Thank you," she said, "but I'm fine. It's gracious of you. Really."

"Perhaps another time, then," he said. "Meanwhile, let's not spoil a lovely evening."

He lifted his glass to toast. He was still staring at her with that fake smile, as if he were examining her, looking for flaws in her story.

"Oh yes," he said, "I almost forgot. You want to see an artifact."

He said it in such a sing-songy tone that she couldn't tell if he was mocking her. Then he stood up. For a moment, it looked like he was heading toward the nightstand. Then he stopped.

"It's occurred to me that I do have another artifact to show you, a curiosity you might enjoy. Wait here while I get it. I won't be long."

He turned and walked in the other direction. As he made his way behind her toward the door, she exhaled a sigh of relief and jumped into action. This would be her one chance. She felt almost as if God Himself had decreed that the man should get up and leave the room. Her hands shook as she reached down into her purse and found the small capsule with the powder. She looked nervously around and quickly opened the capsule, sprinkling the powder into Müller's wine glass. Just as she moved her hand back, she heard a noise behind her and jumped. She turned to see him approaching behind her, carrying a medium-sized oblong velour maroon box; she thought perhaps it was a jewelry box. She prayed he hadn't seen her hand near his glass. Her heart was pounding through her chest as he sat opposite her and placed the box on the table. He didn't appear to have seen anything. And, thankfully, the powder had dissolved quickly.

Müller opened the box, and inside was what looked like a small golden antique dagger with opulent carvings along the handle.

"Is it French?" she said. She wondered if he could sense the nervousness in her voice.

"It's German, actually. But you're partially right. It's French-related. It's from 1796. It was used in the war against Napoleon. It belonged to my grandfather. Do you like it?"

"It's beautiful."

"Yes, it's quite beautiful. And yet it strikes me—the irony—that something so beautiful should be used for such deadly purposes. Don't you think?"

Once again, his smile unnerved her. She wasn't sure whether his double meaning was intentional or not, but he was making her even more uncomfortable now. She couldn't wait for him to sip his wine.

Without warning, he stood up and walked around behind her. She felt his hands on her shoulders, massaging them. This wasn't going well at all. She needed him to drink the wine, yet she didn't want to be overly obvious either. Finally, she couldn't wait any longer.

"Aren't you going to dr—"

She gasped for air as his hands suddenly wrapped something around her neck. Some kind of cloth. Squeezing tighter, tighter.... Frantically, she grabbed at the material around her neck, desperately trying to pry it loose. In an instant his right arm was around her, pulling her up off the chair, his left hand still holding the cloth tight around her neck. She felt herself being pulled up higher, closer to him. As she struggled to breathe, she felt his breath against her ear.

"What's in the wine glass?" he said.

She felt the makeshift noose loosen and she coughed, gasping for air. "I don't...know...what...you're—" She'd just about managed to get the words out, when she felt the noose tighten again.

"Liar!" he yelled. His voice was deafening right there in her ear, making it buzz. She felt the whole room going dark as she struggled to breathe, his hands squeezing the cloth tighter.

"I'll ask again," he said. "What's...in...the wine glass?" His tone was almost mocking. The bastard was enjoying this.

He began dragging her backwards toward the bed, his right arm squeezing her ribs and forcing up under her breasts, his left hand still holding the noose tight around her neck. Her feet were dragging loosely along the floor, and she kicked as hard as she could. Once he had stopped beside the bed, she felt his grip on the cloth loosen just enough for her to breathe again.

Again, she coughed to catch her breath, but this time she screamed as loud as she could for Max. She screamed till she was hoarse. The last thing she wanted was to jeopardize Max, but it was too late now. Almost immediately, she felt Müller's left hand cover her mouth and felt herself being lifted and thrown with force. She went headfirst into the wall behind the bed, her head hitting hard against the wall. Then everything went black.

Chapter 25
Changes

Beeze pushed his way through the crowd, trying to get to the lab. Almost from the minute he entered the corridor, the facility began rumbling again and people were scuffling about trying to figure out what was happening.

Freakin' people. It was like Mardi Gras, but without the beads. As if running around would actually help anything. As he forced himself past a man the size of the Statue of Liberty, he noticed Lauren heading his way. He waited along the side wall until she had caught up.

"What's going on?" she said.

"I'm hoping you can tell me. Malcolm's looking for you. He's back by the monitors. There's some kind of code, a countdown or something."

"A countdown? Where?"

The shifting began getting worse, so Beeze grabbed her arm, more for balance than anything.

"Come with me," he said.

He moved as quickly as he could in the direction he had come from, with Lauren following close behind.

Beeze hurried to enter the passcode and they entered into the cavernous darkness once again. They ran toward the single large monitor, which was still showing the code sequence in the center. Except Malcolm wasn't here.

"Where's Malcolm?" she said.

Beeze looked around.

"I don't know. He said he'd be here. What do you make of that code?"

Beeze watched as Lauren stared at the code.

"Is it a countdown?" he said.

She held her hand up to quiet him.

He waited while she kept looking, apparently making mental notes.

"It's not a countdown," she said. "The codes are moving forward and backward at random."

"At random?" he said. "That doesn't make sense."

"It makes sense if you understand temporal paradoxes and multiverse fluctuations."

"Care to say that in English?"

"I can't be sure," she said, "but if Jake went back in time, he might have already caused a change to the future. It's possible the system is recalculating."

Malcolm's voice suddenly echoed from behind them. "Is this a restart?" he said.

Lauren turned around and looked at Malcolm.

"I said, is—this—a restart?"

Malcolm sounded pretty pissed.

"Not yet," said Lauren.

"Wait a minute," said Beeze. What do you mean a restart? Is this some kind of computer thing? Someone wanna let me in on the joke?"

Nobody answered.

"Your friend Jake," said Lauren, still looking at Malcolm, "must have already changed the past. And if I'm right, something is about to happen in the present. Something we can't do a thing about."

Beeze looked at Malcolm. "Do you know what she's talking about? Cause I sure don't."

Malcolm didn't respond. He was too deep in thought.

Chapter 26

Dead

Max had heard the screams and had run to the bedroom window just in time to see Anna being thrown headfirst into the wall, her limp body sliding down onto the floor. He couldn't see where her body had fallen; the bed was in the way. He smashed the window with his gun and yelled for Anna. He could only watch as Müller ran from the room.

The window was too small to climb through, so he ran as fast as he could to the front door.

He kicked open the front door and entered the cottage with his gun pointed. His shoes were slippery from the wet ground and he almost fell. He looked around carefully in case Müller was hiding to his right or left. The last thing he needed was Müller tackling him and wrestling the gun away.

He walked down the long hallway to the bedroom straight ahead, still looking behind him occasionally, just in case Müller came up behind him.

As he approached the bedroom, he could see Anna lying on the floor by the bed, her arms spread out in a grotesque position, a necktie resting at her feet. She wasn't moving.

He entered the bedroom looking to his right and left, then headed toward Anna to check whether she was alive. He could see blood tricking down her forehead. He reached for her wrist to check her pulse. Just as he grabbed her hand, he was rammed from behind as if he were being hit by a train. It was Müller.

Off balance, Max fell forward, still holding the gun in his right hand. At the same time, Müller jumped on him and grabbed his right arm from behind, pulling it back. Before Max knew it, he was on his knees, his face at Anna's lifeless feet, being forced onto his back by

Müller. He felt his right arm being rammed against the floor, Müller's knee in his face, until the gun came loose. Before Max could react, Müller was standing over him, aiming the gun directly at his chest.

He slid backward until he felt his back press against the wall.

"Who are you," said Müller. "What are the two of you after?"

Max glanced over at Anna, then felt excruciating pain as the butt of the gun hit his face.

"She can't help you answer now," said Müller. "Your whore is dead."

Max had never wanted to kill someone so much in his life, and now here he was, as helpless as a mouse. He was contemplating taking his chances trying to charge Müller anyway.

"She's—not—a—whore," he said. His blood was boiling as he looked directly in Müller's eyes.

To his surprise, Müller smiled.

"That's the first true thing I've heard all night," said Müller. "But what I really want to know is who is she, and who are you?"

"Please," said Max. "Let me tend to her. You can keep me here. Just let her go. She's of no danger to you."

"She's dead! She's of no danger to anyone. And if you want to be with her so much, I can arrange that too. Or you can tell me what you're after. I may even feel generous and send you back where you came from."

Max thought hard about what to say, trying to come up with anything he could to keep stalling.

"Nothing?" said Müller.

Müller cocked the pistol and aimed it at his head now.

"I thought perhaps, just perhaps," said Müller, "that you might save me the trouble of disposing of both your wretched bodies in the lake."

Think, Max, think! Have to buy time.

He looked around, trying to calculate what he might do if he could just surprise Müller.

"You know," said Müller, "Anna—that is her name, right? Anna is a lovely young woman. Or was, anyway. I may just have my way with her after you're dead. The way I see it, she owes me."

Max spit in Müller's face.

Müller slammed the gun against his temple, then aimed it again at his head. Max's ears were ringing from the blow, but he tried to grab Müller's arm. He struggled hard, but he could see it was a losing battle, as Müller was too strong. Müller's hands forced the gun back toward Max's face. He watched helplessly as Müller's finger tightened on the trigger. He closed his eyes and grimaced, trying to move his head out of the way of the shot. He felt the gun press hard against his face.

He felt his final moments coming, but the gun never fired.

After a few seconds, he opened his eyes. Müller had a look of shock on his face, and was staring right at him with an open mouth and a pained expression. It looked as if he either couldn't talk or was having a stroke, and his whole face was shaking. Then Müller fell forward onto him, knocking him back against the wall. As Max fell back, the lifeless body on top of him weighing a ton, he could see over Müller's shoulders.

There was Anna, kneeling, blood running down her face, very much alive.

Max looked down at the pool of blood running down Müller's back, and then he noticed it—the ornate handle of a dagger protruding out.

Anna had plunged a golden dagger into him.

Max heaved Müller's body aside, and Anna crawled over to him to embrace him as he held out his arms. Holding her close, he kissed her and caressed her face, wiping the tears from her eyes, then from his own eyes. He had almost lost her this night. He thought he *had* lost her. Now, more than ever, he was certain that they were doing the right thing, because he wasn't about to lose her again. Not to Hitler. Not to anyone. Not until it was God's time for her to go. He couldn't bear the thought of living without her.

For a time, he just lay there with her, thankful for the moment. Then, as she tended to his wounds and he to hers, he glanced over at Müller and the pool of blood forming on the floor around him. He turned back to Anna, who was still in his arms.

"I guess we wait here until tomorrow afternoon," he said. "Let's pray that our grandson has an easier time than we did."

"And I thought I had the easy job," said Anna.

Max had never been so relieved to hear her voice. Leave it to Anna to crack a joke at a time like this. Her constant good humor was one of the things he loved about her.

"No, you had the tough job. He only has to deal with some Hitler guy."

She looked up at him and elbowed him. And for the first time in days, despite everything that had happened and all the danger that lay ahead, he couldn't help smiling.

Chapter 27
Adolf

As he stood in the entrance to the large stone ivy-covered castle waiting for Otto Leybold, Jacob got the impression he was visiting either a respected university or a stately mansion, and not at all a prison. The white walls were adorned with paintings, and the tables, which were covered in elegant linen tablecloths, were well appointed with large flowerpots, books, and serving trays.

The skies were a strange yellow color again when he'd awakened, with dark clouds and the occasional flash of lightning. He couldn't help thinking this odd weather had something to do with the ship, especially since it had been going on for several days. In a way, the atmosphere and his speculations about it gave even more urgency to what he was about to do.

Before long, a heavyset, balding man who appeared to be in his sixties approached.

"Guten Morgen, Herr Doktor Müller," said the man. It was Leybold. "Willkommen." Leybold extended his hand, and after a brief handshake, motioned for him to follow. "Bitte."

Jacob followed him down a musty corridor past a row of mahogany doors, and then down a hallway to the right. Standing at the end of the hallway was Samuel, who stepped forward to greet them.

"I'll leave you in capable hands, Herr Doktor," said Leybold. "I have a meeting I must return to. This is Samuel. He'll take you to see Herr Hitler."

"Come this way," said Samuel, in his usual gruff tone.

Jacob followed Samuel down another corridor toward Hitler's study. As they walked, Samuel briefed him quietly.

"Be very careful, and don't get into extended conversations. You won't win any mind games, trust me. Hess won't be there. He never is for Hitler's appointments. Just engage in small talk and stick to his psychological issues. And stay away from politics."

"I thought I'm supposed to be a sympathizer," said Jacob.

"Yes, that's correct. If he brings up politics, just agree with whatever he says. Here, we're approaching his study now on the right."

As they entered the open door to Hitler's study, Jacob could see Hitler standing by the window looking out. He was wearing a white shirt, black pants, and black suspenders.

The more Jacob thought about it, the harder it was to believe he was about to have a private consult with Adolf Hitler. The whole situation seemed otherworldly.

And then it dawned on him. It *was* otherworldly.

"Herr Hitler?" said Samuel.

Hitler turned around. His face looked firm and angry, just like in all the photos and newsreels Jacob had seen. It was hard to believe he was face to face with the man who had caused so much hatred and death—the man who had killed Anna.

"Ahh, Herr Doktor. Come. Please be seated." Hitler's voice was quiet and controlled, unlike in his famed rousing speeches. He pointed to the chair opposite the desk, so Jacob took a seat as Samuel left the room. Hitler sat down behind the desk, his hands tapping nervously. "You must excuse me. I recently quit smoking. I don't know what to do with myself."

"You're better off," said Jacob. "It'll kill you." Jacob hoped his German was passable, and spoke in short sentences.

"Otto Müller," said Hitler. "Are you a relation to the artist?"

"Nein. Nein. But my mother is an admirer of his work. I'm not familiar with him myself." He didn't really know what artist Hitler was referring to, but figured that would suffice.

"You should become familiar," said Hitler. "I find his work haunting. My great hope is that one day I will have him paint a portrait of me. He is the only living artist who could capture my soul. Of that much I'm certain."

"And how is your soul these days, Herr Hitler?" Jacob leaned back in his chair, trying to appear relaxed.

"My soul? Only ten days ago, more than forty people were here to celebrate my thirty-fifth birthday. Thirty-five, and yet I feel ancient. I am treated like royalty, and yet anxiety plagues me."

"And what is it that you're anxious about?"

Jacob recalled his days studying psychiatry in graduate school. Always keep the patient talking. Except, instead of answering, Hitler just stared at him. Then finally, he spoke.

"I wonder," said Hitler, "how does it come to be that an American becomes a psychologist in Germany? You are American, correct? Or do my ears deceive me?"

Jacob could see from Hitler's face that the man seemed to take pride in manipulating others.

"I see my accent has yet to improve," said Jacob. "You're partially correct. I was born here, but spent most of my life in America. I was raised there by my uncle. It wasn't until a year ago that I returned to Germany to care for my mother. She's still alive, God bless her, but very ill."

"Ah, I am sorry to hear that indeed. And so it is even more surprising that you are familiar with my work, as I understand you are."

"I have friends who've attended your speeches," said Jacob. "You make quite the impression."

Again, Hitler just looked at him.

"My anxiety, Herr Doktor, is for the future of our country."

Jacob figured Hitler had either bought his story or was playing along.

Hitler took a deep breath.

"The future of our country," continued Hitler, "I carry like a ball and chain around my neck. And as long as I am in here, I can do nothing about it. But it does give me time to think and plan. For that I suppose I should be thankful."

"I must ask then," said Jacob, "what exactly is it you're planning for?" As soon as the words had left his lips, he remembered what Samuel had told him. Don't engage in political discussions.

"Change, Herr Doktor, change. Our economy is in ruins. It will take perseverance and vision to make this a great country once again—fearless, unrelenting vision."

Feelings, Jacob. Stick to his feelings.

"So, does it make you anxious that this vision may not be carried out? Or does the vision itself make you anxious?"

"Neither," said Hitler. "It's the waiting that makes me anxious. The confounded waiting. I know exactly what must be done. And it will be done! I've learned my lesson from this recent detour."

Hitler leaned forward.

"I know," he said, "that they say my political career is over. But I've come to realize that it is not. In fact, it is just beginning."

"And what will be different this time, Herr Hitler? What was it you've learned?"

Hitler leaned back and, for the first time, smiled.

"You know, Herr Doktor," he said, "I was never a religious man. But I read often, and I study. Several years ago, in Vienna, I was introduced to Dr. Karl Lueger and the Christian Social Party. More than any other influence, this chance meeting has affected me deeply. It's only now that I realize it. Yet it wasn't any particular concept that moved me. It was the party's *conviction*—its ability to move masses. And even more, its incredibly brilliant use of propaganda. I tell you as I sit here, if Dr. Lueger had lived in Germany, he would have been considered one of our greatest minds."

"So, conviction and propaganda can turn around public opinion? That's the lesson?" Jacob was dying to know how Hitler would manage to bamboozle an entire country, since none of the reports he'd read seemed to offer a decent explanation.

"What I have learned," said Hitler, "is that the political opinion of the masses represents nothing but the final result of a thorough and complete manipulation of their minds and souls. This happens all the time with newspapers and newsreels, only on a small scale. You see, people do not know what they want. They only know what you tell them they want."

"And what do you plan to tell them they want?"

"What I know they *need.*"

"A new philosophy."

"Philosophy? Herr Doktor, the great masses of people do not consist of philosophers. Any logical appeal would be lost in the wind. Like talking to a dog. And so we reach them instead with something else. We reach them with faith. And the only way to do that is with passion. And by that I mean the passion of the spoken word. If you look at any of the greatest religious and political avalanches in history, it has always been through the power of speech. But there is another crucial ingredient, Herr Doktor."

"And what might that be?"

"Intolerance. People need to be led. And they need to be led firmly."

"Intolerance for what?" This was Hitler at his finest, if you could apply such a word to the man who murdered millions. If there's one thing the bastard knew, it was how to force his will on people. What a legacy.

"For resistance, Herr Doktor. Intolerance for resistance. Do you think for one moment the greatness of Christianity came from negotiations with others, or from compromises? On the contrary, it survives today because of its sheer fanaticism in preaching and fighting for its own doctrine. Do you think scientific fact matters? Or historical research? Not a bit. Facts are just facts. They are overrated. But conviction and intolerance, these things can perform miracles. And that, Herr Doktor, is how to move the masses."

"And what is it that you hope to move them to do?"

Hitler smiled again.

"I will show you."

Hitler stood up and retrieved a whip from a hook where his jacket was hanging on the wall. He sat back down and laid the whip along the table.

"I cannot move the masses unless I address their agenda. No politician in his right mind would attempt to ignore the will of the people. And what is on their mind is jobs, land, and money, and making Germany great again. But we cannot do any of this while we have a cancer in our midst."

"A cancer?"

"Herr Doktor, the financial institutions are slowly but surely robbing our people of jobs and the right to earn a living. And filth floods our theaters and our literature, corrupting our youth in a way that will affect generations to come. This is not how a country achieves greatness. And who is responsible for this? Who runs the financial institutions and the theaters?"

Jacob looked at him, waiting for the answer he already knew Hitler would give.

"The Jew!" said Hitler. "Make no mistake: we can no longer starve while the Jewish bankers get rich. We cannot spend our hard-earned income attending theater and cinema presentations that serve only to keep the Jew employed."

"And what of the people who won't follow this philosophy?" said Jacob, trying his best to keep calm. "Surely, not all Germans will support persecution of an entire people, or is that what the whip is for?"

Jacob thought of all the bodies at Dachau. And of Anna's tortured face. He was tempted to grab the whip and wrap it around Hitler's neck right there, but he had to keep reminding himself that patience would be a virtue.

"Hah!" said Hitler. "The whip is my talisman. When Christ discovered the Jews conducting business in the temple, he drove them out with a whip. And so, I carry it to remind me of my mission. As Christ drove them from God's temple, I will drive them from our temple as well—the temple of our country, and the temple of our blood. I tell you as we sit here, as long as the Jew prospers and infuses our youth with his poison, we shall not be free to fulfill our potential as human beings."

"So your mission is to rid Germany of the Jews."

Hitler smiled.

"No," he said. "My mission is to create opportunities."

Jacob felt his fists tightening as Hitler leaned forward again.

"And now I ask you a question, Herr Doktor. Have you never felt so consumed with a purpose, so sure that what you're doing will set the world on its rightful path, that you know you were born to do it—*meant* to do it?"

Jacob thought this an ironic statement considering what he was here to do. Still, he was losing his patience.

"I've had goals," he said. "But it's the idea of a rightful path that I'm not so sure about. Many people have been killed in the name of religion by those claiming to be on a rightful path."

"Ahh, I could not agree more," said Hitler. "There is nothing worse in this world than the devastation brought about by misuse of religion."

That was a hell of an odd statement coming from Adolf Hitler.

"And yet you claim," said Jacob, "that faith is the only way to reach the masses."

"Yes, but it must be sincere, and passionate. I am nothing if not sincere, Herr Doktor. We are witnessing in our country a physical and intellectual regression, and hence the beginning of a slowly but surely progressing sickness. For this to happen is nothing less than a sin against the will of the eternal creator! I'm doing God's work, Herr Doktor. Do you not see? I was born to do this work. It can only be me. Now you see my anxiety? The burden I bear?"

God's work? Killing millions of people? The man was insane, and shame on the fools who followed him. The more Hitler spoke, the more Jacob was convinced that Hitler was right about one thing, though. It could only be him—Adolf Hitler—who could bring about such change. Before, he hadn't been so sure that killing Hitler would indeed prevent the disasters to come. But now, more than ever, he was entirely convinced.

"Yes, I would say you *were* born for this, Herr Hitler." Jacob stared at Hitler without a hint of irony. "And it is a tremendous burden. One thing troubles me, though."

Now it was time for him to play with Hitler a little bit.

Hitler looked surprised. This was good.

"And what is that?" said Hitler.

"I know many Jews. Most of them are laborers. For every banker, doctor, or lawyer, there are a million tailors and grocers. Surely they couldn't take over Germany, as you've said in your speeches. Or is that just part of the propaganda you were talking about?"

He didn't know why he was even asking this. Probably because he wanted Hitler to admit he didn't believe his own bullshit.

Hitler looked at him with narrow eyes, as if examining him. Then he smiled.

"Herr Doktor, you don't realize it, but you have the classic thinking of a Jew. Ethics, conscience, these are all things the Jew cherishes. But in the same breath they are arrogant to a fault. They believe it is man's duty to overcome nature, and to progress beyond what God has provided us."

"You talk as if they're all the same."

"They *are* all the same! A Jew harbors the same seeds of thought whether he is a banker or a shopkeeper, and whether or not he ever sets foot in a synagogue or has ever recited a Hebrew prayer. It is inherent in them to act superior, and to think themselves above others. I tell you they are the only race that is determined to rule the world. So, yes, I do believe they wish to take over Germany—maybe not with weapons, but with their ideas. And I see it as my duty to defend our Fatherland from their poison."

Now he was starting to sound like the Hitler Jacob knew, even becoming more animated in that old newsreel way. So he did believe his own bullshit after all. And he would use propaganda to sell it.

"So you want to cleanse Germany," said Jacob. "And how do you propose to convince the public to do this?"

Hitler narrowed his eyes again.

"I shall go along with your ruse just a little longer," he said.

Jacob looked at him.

"Ruse?"

Could Hitler have been on to him this whole time?

Hitler stared at him for a few more excruciating seconds. Jacob tried to think about his options.

"I was told that you and I were of like mind," said Hitler. "But I see you enjoy playing devil's advocate, and so I shall go along. It's okay. It's okay. Your methods are unorthodox. I admire that."

Jacob breathed a sigh of relief. He watched as Hitler leaned back in his chair and closed his eyes, his head moving around like a crazed man. Then the would-be dictator's eyes opened, and he continued.

"How do I convince the public?" Hitler said. "As I said, it is simply a matter of passion. That, and a great deal of patience to wait for the right moment, something I lacked before. You asked me, Herr Doktor, what is different this time? *That* is what is different. And *that* is what creates my anxiety. The confounded waiting. Now, if you'll excuse me, Herr Doktor, I will call for the guard."

Jacob tensed up as Hitler reached for an intercom buzzer on his desk.

"Is there a problem?" he said. He wondered if Hitler had been on to him all this time, taunting him intentionally. He gripped the briefcase in case he had to make a run for it.

"Nein, nein," said Hitler. "On the contrary, I wish you to stay for lunch."

"Oh, that won't be necessary, I have another—"

"No, I insist. Please. Our chat has been helping me organize my thoughts."

Jacob was getting anxious as he watched Hitler press the intercom button to order an additional meal. He hadn't anticipated staying through lunch. And the last thing he wanted to do was help Hitler organize his thoughts. Either way, he needed to go find Samuel and deliver the poison.

He stood up with his briefcase and excused himself to use the toilet, but Hitler stopped him.

"Before you go, Herr Doktor, that's a most unusual briefcase. Do you mind if I look at it? I might have to get one for myself."

Shit.

Cautiously, Jacob handed Hitler the briefcase and watched as he examined it. He knew he couldn't leave without it. The medicine bottle with the poison was still inside.

Hitler fumbled with the lock, then looked up.

"How does it open?"

"You just slide the latch."

Jacob knew sliding the latch wouldn't work without the retinal scan to unlock it, but he let Hitler make several feeble attempts. He watched as Hitler tried the latch to no avail, then held out his hand to help.

"It must be jammed. Let me have a look."

Hitler handed him the briefcase and he pretended to fumble with it on his lap.

"I can't get it open either," said Jacob. "I'll bring it with me and maybe in the light of the restroom I'll have better luck. I won't be long."

He got up casually, and Hitler just looked at him. Then he left the room without looking back.

Soon the worst would be over. He only hoped Hitler wasn't becoming suspicious.

Chapter 28

Complications

As he walked down the long hallway to find Samuel, Jacob brought the briefcase to eye level to unlock it using the retinal scanner. Upon turning the corner, he got a whole-body jolt as he slammed into what felt like a pillar and dropped his briefcase, spilling its contents everywhere. He shook off the cobwebs to see what he had run into. Apparently, it wasn't a pillar or a wall, or any other inanimate object. It was a German military officer, a man who was now helping him pick up his belongings, starting with the medicine bottle with the poison.

"I'm sorry," Jacob said. "I should have been looking. That was careless of me." The man remained silent and continued retrieving the items on the floor.

Jacob scrambled to pick up the remaining contents before the German could, but the man had gotten to the medicine bottle first and was looking at it. Rather than apprehending him or getting suspicious though, the soldier just handed him the medicine bottle. Quickly, Jacob tucked the vial into his pocket and stuffed the papers into the briefcase's built-in folder. Then he looked up. This time the man's face was as pale as Hitler's white shirt as he stared in horror at one of the clippings he had picked up from the floor. From the size, Jacob immediately knew which one it was. It was an article about Hitler and the Holocaust.

In a split second, the man was reaching for his gun. No time to think. Jacob barreled into the German, knocking him off balance. Then, before the man could recover, Jacob grabbed him and threw him to the right, toward an open stairwell. The German quickly grabbed Jacob's shirt and forced him into the stairwell with him. Jacob tried to avoid being pulled down the steps as they wrestled for control of the gun. He couldn't afford the sound of gunshots. If they caused a scene, this mission would be over. He pushed his hand over the man's face, trying to force his neck back. Then he felt a sharp pain as the German punched his ribs. In a swift move, he kneed the man in the groin and grabbed the gun with both hands. Running on pure instinct, he wrestled the gun from the German's hands and slammed the butt end into the man's temple, then into the back of his neck. This advantage was short-lived, as the German's iron hands grasped Jacob's neck, squeezing tight. He could hardly breathe. Choking, he tried to pry the man's hands off, but it was no use. Desperate now, he slammed the gun harder against the German's neck and head, again and again until he could hear the sound of muscle and bone crunching.

Finally, he felt the hands loosen around his neck as the German fell forward, the heavy weight knocking him off balance. He stumbled backwards against the hard steps, the German's lifeless body falling on top of him. Exhausted and drenched in sweat, he forced the German's body off and stood up slowly. With great effort, he dragged the dead German downstairs by his feet. Luckily, there appeared to be a vacant storage area at the bottom of the steps, which would be perfect for now. He pushed and pulled the body into the dark storage closet and stood up to catch his breath. His heart was pounding, but there was no time to lose. He straightened his outfit as best he could and climbed the stairs. As he ascended, he could see Samuel waiting at the top of the steps.

"Jacob, where have you been? I've been trying to find you. You look like hell!"

"I *feel* like hell. I'll explain later, but you'll find a German military officer lying dead down there." He noticed Samuel had a food cart with two covered silver platters on top.

"He must be here for the meeting," said Samuel. "I'm sure they'll be looking for him after a while. We don't have much time. Hitler already called once asking where the meal was. He also asked if I had seen you. Hurry! Empty the poison into his meal. It'll be easy to tell the meals apart. Yours is steak. His is vegetarian."

As Samuel uncovered one of the platters, Jacob reached into his pocket for the medicine bottle and used the dropper to inject the contents into what looked like some sort of creamed cabbage. It dissolved instantly.

"What is this stuff anyway?" He couldn't place the smell, though he had to admit, it smelled good.

"The poison?"

"No, the food."

"Ah, *Lauch mit Sahne und Nuessen.* Sautéed Leeks. It's quite good."

Jacob couldn't avoid smiling as Samuel put the cover back on the dish. Not now, it isn't.

"Okay," said Samuel, "now you bring the cart to him. Tell him you ran into me and offered to take it. I'll keep an eye on the stairwell. Now listen, if anyone should go down the stairs and find the body, I'll blow a whistle. It won't look suspicious; I'll do it as a reaction when they yell. You'll be able to hear the whistle while you're in with Hitler. If you hear it, go to the hallway immediately to see what the fuss is. Then walk briskly but casually out the door, like you're leaving the appointment. Do you understand?"

"Got it."

"And go wash up first. You look like you were in a fight."

"Where's the washroom?"

"Down the stairs. It's where you dragged the body. There's a cord you can pull to turn on the light."

Jacob hurried down the stairs while Samuel waited. The German was sprawled out on the floor. He kicked the body just to be sure the man was in fact dead, and felt for the cord. When the light came on, he could see that he was in a washroom, just as Samuel had said. As he looked in the mirror, he could see deep red marks around his neck where the German's hands had been. He pulled his collar up to try to hide them. He had a cut on his forehead that he rinsed off and covered with his hair. Once he was satisfied that he looked presentable enough, he turned off the light and ran back up.

When he emerged from the stairs, he could see Samuel at the far end of the hallway to the right, watching. Nodding at Samuel, he turned left with the food cart and rolled it toward Hitler's study.

When Jacob entered the study, Hitler was standing at the window again. Hitler turned around and stared at him. Jacob figured he'd better explain.

"I saw Samuel and offered to bring the meals."

"And what took you so long?"

"My apologies, Herr Hitler. I ran into someone who recognized me." He couldn't help thinking back to that old saying, *The truth shall set you free.*

"Ah, well let's not delay any further, Herr Doktor. I'm hungry and I'm sure you must be as well."

Hitler motioned to a small pub table with two chairs, so Jacob wheeled the cart over and placed the meals on the table. As they sat and ate silently, he observed Hitler, knowing the man was eating what would hopefully be his last meal.

"Have you always been a vegetarian?"

Hitler looked up at him. "Not always. Today I am. Tomorrow I might be. The next day, I'm not so sure."

Jacob wasn't even going to guess what that was supposed to mean. But then Hitler elaborated.

"My doctor tells me it's necessary for my health. But I don't suppose it'll last."

"So it's not for ethical reasons?"

"Hah! Ethics. There you go again sounding like a Jew. Nein, Herr Doktor. Don't get me wrong; I love animals, more so than people sometimes. They say dogs do not have souls. I disagree. In fact it has occurred to me that I'd sooner have a dog sitting with me for supper than a Jew."

Hitler laughed, but even in the role he was playing, Jacob couldn't bring himself to do likewise. He forced a fake smile that he knew didn't look sincere. He wasn't sure if Hitler was onto him and goading him, but he was very sure that, three hours later, Hitler would much prefer to have eaten with his dog than this particular Jew.

"So," said Jacob, "you are saying that Jews do not have souls?"

"I am saying worse than that. They are of the devil, here to rob our souls—every Jewish man, woman, and child."

"The children, too? Surely—"

"Especially the children!"

Jacob was done discussing anything with Hitler, even under false pretenses. He could no longer bear to sit with a man whose hatred would culminate in a so-called *final solution* to exterminate all Jews, and along with them, anyone else who wasn't a perfect Aryan specimen. He stared at Hitler until his thoughts were interrupted by a shrill sound—the sound of a whistle blowing from the hallway.

He jumped up with his briefcase.

"I'll check and see what's going on."

As he left the room, he looked back at Hitler sitting there watching with a confused expression. Then he did as Samuel had suggested and walked quickly but calmly down the hallway toward the exit. People were running back and forth around him. He heard yelling, but just kept walking straight ahead and out the front doors into the open air. In the hustle and bustle, nobody was paying attention to him, but he couldn't be sure how long it would be before Hitler got suspicious. And if Hitler did get suspicious, he hoped that the investigation wouldn't lead to Müller's lake house while Max and Anna were still there.

Outside, it was silent as the cool air hit his face. The skies looked like they were clearing up as well. It was about time, and quite fitting. He turned around and took one last look at the prison.

"Bon appétit," he said.

As he walked away, he thought of all the lives that would now be spared. No matter what else happened, the man who had caused it all would soon be dead. Nothing could stop that now. And as he rounded the corner toward the taxis, he muttered, "There's your final solution, asshole."

Chapter 29

Zero Hour

Beeze looked down at the hysterical crew member he had to pin to the floor in the corridor.

"They're taking us! They're taking us!"

That's all the man kept repeating.

"Who's taking you? What are you talking about?"

"They're gone!" the man said.

Beeze looked down the corridor. There wasn't a soul there. Strange. There was some weird crazy ass shit going on here. The facility was still vibrating, but the shifting had slowed down.

"If I let you go," said Beeze, "will you stay here?"

"Hell no, man. I'm coming with you."

"Your choice," said Beeze, "but you get nuts and I'm gonna go crazy on your ass, got it?"

The man nodded and Beeze helped him up.

Together, they continued up the corridor toward the labs. Where was everyone? As they approached the first door on the right, Beeze entered first.

"What the—?"

Everyone was crouched down on the floor in silence. Some were hiding under the lab tables.

"Aw, y'all threw me a surprise party," said Beeze.

"They're taking us," said a Latino woman under the table.

"I told you," said the crew member with Beeze. "People are just disappearing."

"What's happening to us?" yelled another man in the distance.

No sooner had the man finished his sentence than everyone starting screaming again. Beeze looked down just in time to see the Latino woman dissolve right before his eyes.

Holy—

"Wait here," he said. He had to tell Malcolm and Lauren, fast.

He heard them all yelling for help, but he left them there and ran as fast as he could back toward the ship. Hopefully, Malcolm and Lauren were still there watching the monitors.

Just as he neared the double doors, the vibrations began getting stronger. He entered the passcode and the doors slid open. He ran inside toward the monitors and could see Malcolm and Lauren still there, standing silently watching the screen.

"You're not gonna believe this," said Beeze. Then he looked up and saw the code on the large monitor. It wasn't moving anymore. "Wait a minute," he said. "What's happening up there?"

"The code stopped," said Malcolm.

"What's that mean?" said Beeze.

Lauren looked at him.

Just then there was a deafening sound as the giant monitor went black, casting the area into near darkness. Everything began shifting again. Beeze looked up to see the monitor breaking up again into multiple monitors. They were moving back into their original positions.

When the monitors were in place, the shifting stopped. So did the vibrations. Faintly, he could see the monitor images lightening.

"It looks like some kind of images are forming," said Beeze. "The same ones?"

"I think you'll find them to be quite different," said Lauren.

"I don't get it," said Beeze. "What's going on?"

"You know the answer to that," said Lauren.

He thought about it for a moment. Then it hit him like a ton of bricks.

"And that's why people are disappearing off the ship?" he said.

"Disappearing?" said Malcolm. "How many?"

"I don't know," said Beeze. "I think just a few. Is it all over?"

"No," said Lauren. "It's just beginning. The process takes time."

No sooner had she said that than the vibrations began again, growing louder and louder until everything was rumbling.

Beeze looked at Malcolm. "How does she know this shit?" he said, over the noise.

"Look," said Malcolm, pointing up at the monitors.

Beeze looked up at the images that were forming. As they started to become recognizable, he couldn't believe his eyes. It was worse than anything he could have imagined.

"How can that be?" he said. "So this is it? This is how the world ends?"

"No," said Malcolm, "Not yet."

Chapter 30
Fire and Water

Max looked at Anna, who was pacing back and forth nervously in the cottage. They had spent the night on the couch in the living room. The bed would have been more comfortable, but sleeping next to a dead body and a pool of blood on the floor wasn't an option that appealed to either of them.

He looked at his watch.

"It's time," he said.

"Thank God," said Anna. "Where do we pour the kerosene?"

"All over. Let's start in the bedroom."

He had brought the cans in the night before, so they each grabbed one and drizzled the kerosene around, leaving a trail through the house. Max made sure a trail led from the bedroom to the front door. Then he called to Anna, who was still in the bedroom.

"Come," he said, "we'd better be going."

She emerged holding the empty can. "Will they be able to smell the kerosene?"

"Probably," he said, "but who cares? By the time anyone gets here, we'll be gone."

"Should we take the cans?"

"Yes, we can throw them in the lake. Wait here, I'll take them."

Max grabbed the cans and ran behind the cottage to the lake. He looked around and didn't see anyone nearby, so he tossed them in. But as he watched to make sure the evidence was destroyed, it wasn't the cans that sunk. As he watched them floating—bobbing up and down in the blue water like swimming pool toys—it was his heart that hit bottom.

Hoping that he was still unseen, he looked around and quickly pulled a branch off a nearby tree and used it to fish the cans back. Angry at himself for not realizing that empty cans wouldn't sink, he pulled each one out of the water. Then he filled one of the cans with water and tossed it back in. For a few agonizing seconds, it appeared to float. Then it disappeared into the water. He filled the second can and tossed it in. Just as it, too, had sunk, a siren startled him.

Police sirens! And they were getting closer.

How could this be? He ran toward the cottage and saw Anna fleeing toward him. Behind her, he could see smoke emerging from the cottage. The smell overtook him immediately. She must have set the fire when she heard the sirens.

She was out of breath. "I...had...to...do...it," she said. "The sirens."

"Don't worry. They couldn't know about the fire already. Let's run for the road. Put your wig on in case anyone sees us leaving the scene."

"What about you?" she said.

"Don't worry about me. Let's just move."

As they ran, he watched Anna put on the blonde wig. When they got to the main road, he could see the police cars approaching.

"Slow down," he said. "Walk normal." He grabbed her hand.

His heart was pounding as they continued walking. He could hear Anna muttering, "Please God, please God, please God."

Within seconds, the cars had arrived, sirens blaring.

"Keep looking straight ahead," he said.

He grasped her hand tightly as the two police cars motored past them and disappeared into the horizon. He watched in relief as Anna burst into tears.

"It's okay." He put a comforting arm around her. "They must be after something else. Look, there's a taxi ahead."

Chapter 31

Goodbyes

Jacob sat in the hotel suite, waiting anxiously. Max and Anna weren't due to arrive yet, but he wanted to be sure they were safe, both from their assignment, and from any investigation into the occurrence at the prison.

Just as he was pouring himself a drink, he heard footsteps in the hall. Then he heard the door latch turn. He put the glass down as the door swung open.

Thank God! It was Max and Anna. They rushed toward him with open arms. As he hugged Max, and then Anna, he felt their tears against his cheek.

They spent the next hour sharing their stories. Jacob was shocked to hear that their brush with death had been even worse than his, and felt an overwhelming surge of guilt. If anything had happened to them, he wouldn't have been able to forgive himself.

He reflected on their story as he sipped his gin.

"Well, it sounds like you've covered all your bases," he said. "Thank God the dagger was there. By the way, what did you do with it?"

Anna looked up. "I cleaned it and put it back in its case."

"Good idea. And the cottage, are you sure the fire took?"

Max looked at Anna. "Yes, we heard the explosion in the distance as our taxi pulled away. We just looked at each other and didn't say a word."

"I think we're in good shape then. At worst, it could be ruled a murder-suicide if anyone connects Hitler's death to Müller's. More than likely it will just be viewed as a strange coincidence. Nothing can point to any of us, and in any case they'll never find Müller—or me."

He looked at Max and Anna, who were now lying back on the couch. They looked exhausted, which was certainly understandable.

"So now," Anna said, "we only need Samuel to call."

After a few more hours of talking, resting, and nervous pacing, the phone finally rang. Max jumped up to get it.

Jacob watched Max's face, trying to get a read on what was happening. Max just listened, occasionally saying "Yes" and "I see." Aside from that, Jacob couldn't tell what was happening. After a few minutes, Max hung up the phone.

"Well?"

Max looked up.

"Adolf Hitler was pronounced dead of an apparent heart attack at 6:14 pm."

Jacob and Anna let out a sigh of relief.

Max continued. "A few hours ago, they also found a dead body in the stairwell, as we know. The man was identified as Oskar von Schleicher, a political army officer who was in the fortress for a meeting. He was presumed to have left the building an hour earlier, and they claim he must have gotten into an altercation before he left. They say it was unlikely that the injuries were sustained from a fall, and the body appeared to have been dragged into a washroom."

"And do they have any suspects?" said Jacob. "Are they connecting the two deaths?"

"They say they're investigating whether the two deaths are connected, and whether the man was involved in a plot to kill Hitler. They also looked into the possibility of poison, but found no obvious traces. Apparently, Hitler had been complaining of severe anxiety and headaches over the last few weeks, so they believe a heart attack is more likely."

"So, that's it?"

"That's it," said Max. "At least until they find out about Müller."

"I wouldn't worry too much about that. They may try to connect the three deaths, but they won't get very far. If anything, Müller's death will complicate their case just enough."

"Agreed," said Max.

Jacob looked at Max and Anna. "Whatever happens," he said, "I know this wasn't easy for any of us, but I want you to know that we did the world a great service today."

"It is because of you that we did," said Max. "And I have you to thank for Anna's life—and for my life as well, because I wouldn't want to think of living without her." Max reached out for Anna's hand.

Goodbyes are always difficult, but this one was especially so. Jacob knew he would never see them again after this. It wasn't until now that he started to think about how his own upbringing might be altered, now that Anna would live. But if anything, it would change for the better.

The three of them embraced. Jacob wished he could bottle the moment. He would soon think about all the lives that would be saved as a result of this day, but for now, all that existed was Max and Anna, and getting back to Kim, Jessica, and Ethan. As he grabbed Max's arms, he reminded him not to mention a word of this day—or his visit—to any family members, and especially to a young grandchild named Jacob.

"God be with you, Jacob," Anna said in her youthful voice. As she held out her arms, he clasped her soft hands one last time and gave her a final hug, grateful to have met her at last. He felt a tap on his shoulder, and he turned around.

"I want you to have this," said Max. "It's not much, but it's a reminder of our time together. Besides, why leave any evidence?"

He took the object from Max and smiled. It was the book of matches they'd used to burn the cottage.

Jacob held it to his heart. "I'll treasure this forever," he said.

"It's a symbol, Jacob. We burnt the horror from our past. What was it Cortez said? Burn the ships."

He smiled back at Max. "Burn the ships."

Then he left the room without looking back. He went into the hallway to use the device, as he didn't want to transport in front of anyone, especially after having seen the soldier shield his eyes near the boxcars at Dachau. As he thought about it, the whole boxcar incident seemed so long ago.

Looking around to make sure he was alone, he took the Kronos device out of his briefcase and pressed the icon. As he waited for the familiar vibrations, he wondered what awaited him in 2024.

Chapter 32

Surprise

As he felt the damp ground around him, Jacob knew he was back in the alien ship. Even though this was his fourth trip through time, the process hadn't gotten any easier. There was just no getting used to the feeling of falling down a spinning elevator shaft. Either way, it was a relief to be back in modern times in familiar territory. It was hard to believe what had transpired over the last several days. Everything seemed so surreal. It was one thing to envision changing the course of history, but he had just done it for real. And if all had gone well, nobody would even know he'd been gone. And if it hadn't? Well, he'd soon find out.

He stepped out onto the damp floor of the ship and looked around. Nobody had come looking for him this time. That was a good sign. He made his way toward the monitors to get to the long corridor that led to the labs. That was odd. Something was different. The images were all blank.

Could he have successfully headed off the judgment? He couldn't wait to find the others to see what was going on. If things had been resolved, he'd soon be able to get home to Kim. He ran toward the doors that led to the labs.

When he exited the ship into the corridor, though, he noticed something else.

Everything looked different. The walls were painted a pale blue, whereas before they had been white. And the corridor itself seemed narrower. What was going on here? It couldn't have been his imagination. He walked toward the lab. When he got there, the lab was in the same place, but it was empty, and none of the furniture was the same. How long had he been gone? Where was everyone?

He left the lab and made his way down the corridor toward Malcolm's office. Except this time, there wasn't an office, just a solid wall. He began to wonder if he had returned to the right time period. At least the ship was still here, and there was a facility built around it. Plus the ship was depressurized like before. But nothing could have explained the smaller corridor, or the missing office. Then he thought of something even more alarming. Was it possible he was now stuck here alone, out in the middle of the ocean?

He checked the Kronos device, and noticed that the image still showed a view of the synagogue, his last destination. More important, the bar was now a third of its original size. If worse came to worst he could make one more trip. He decided to head toward the cabins. Maybe everyone was there sleeping and he had just gotten the time wrong, though that explanation wouldn't account for the reconfigured facility.

Just as he began walking, he heard a door burst open in the distance. The sound had come from the direction of the cabins ahead, around the bend. He heard voices, too. Whoever it was, they were running. In an instant, they emerged. It was a group of military men wearing black uniforms, flying toward him with guns aimed in his direction. There must have been a silent alarm of some sort. He held a hand up and tried to get their attention.

"It's okay! My name is Jacob Newman. I'm here doing research."

They were on him in an instant.

"Hands in the air!"

He did as they asked. In a split second, they had surrounded him and checked his pockets. He felt them take the Kronos device from his coat pocket.

"On the floor. Now! Arms behind your back!"

He put his arms behind him and felt a pair of metal handcuffs fasten onto his wrists. As soon as he had heard the handcuffs snap shut, someone pulled him roughly to his feet. He noticed that one of the soldiers, a tall blond man, had taken his briefcase.

"Where's Malcolm?" Jacob said. "He can explain who I am. What year is this?"

They ignored him and led him down the corridor to the exit. He thought he'd try once more.

"Listen," he said. "I'm an American scientist. I'm supposed to be here, but there was a mistake."

Still, they ignored him. Whoever these men were, they were well trained.

As they arrived at the exit, he recognized the same circular entrance where he had initially arrived at the underwater lab. Only this time, instead of an elevator to take him to the submersible plane, some sort of bright yellow electric monorail awaited. They pushed him into the vehicle and four of the men climbed in after him. The vehicle moved quickly and silently through a network of tunnels until it arrived at an elevator. He figured they must have moved the elevator too, but why? They led him out of the vehicle and into the elevator. His ears popped as it rose quickly.

With a jerk, the elevator stopped, and the doors slid open and he felt a warm breeze hit his face. At first it didn't register, but as they led him out of the elevator, he could see where they were. And what he saw defied all logic.

Where there had once been an arrival pool for the submersible plane, there was now only sand—sand and trees. Somehow, the ship was no longer out in the middle of the ocean. Whatever time period he was in, the alien ship must have been moved close to shore. But how? And who had moved it? Even more important, how did the Kronos device know to adjust his return coordinates to arrive at a different location? Even with all these questions, the only thing that mattered now was finding out where he was and getting the Kronos device back.

As they led him across the deserted beach, he could see a military plane in the grassy field ahead. It bore an emblem he'd never seen before. It wasn't a U.S. flag, yet these soldiers clearly had American accents. They took off his handcuffs and led him onto the plane. He thought of running, but he knew it would be no use. He took a seat, and within minutes the engine was roaring and they were airborne. As he stared out the window, he could see that they appeared to be headed north. Assuming they were still in Santiago, he guessed they were probably going to the United States. He figured the answers would come soon enough.

Then, just as the plane began to ascend into the clouds, one of the soldiers seated behind him tapped him on the shoulder. As he turned to face the man, a cool spray splashed his face. No sooner did he smell the hint of oranges and roses than he began to feel dizzy. Within seconds, everything had gone black.

PART 2
ICARUS

Chapter 33
Bradley

Jacob wasn't quite sure where he was when he opened his eyes. He remembered being captured back at the ship, and had a vague recollection of walking toward a military plane by the beach, but that was all. He was now seated in a folding chair in a large room that was empty, save for a rectangular metal table sitting several yards in front of him. Beyond that was a small window. He tried to move, but realized his torso was strapped to the chair and his legs were tied together. At least his arms were free, which he thought was unusual. It appeared that he was in some sort of interrogation room.

After a few moments, a door opened behind him and he heard footsteps walking in his direction. A man with a crew cut and a black uniform, who appeared to be in his fifties, walked to the metal table and leaned back against it, facing him head on. At first he thought the man looked familiar, but he couldn't place him. He was obviously a military official of some sort, and had a stone face and piercing blue eyes. Jacob recognized the emblem on his uniform from the plane. Now that he was closer, he could see that the emblem bore the letters *GC*.

The man just stared at him, so Jacob decided to open the conversation.

"Can I ask who you are?" he said. "What does the *GC* stand for?"

"Who am I?" The man seemed incensed that he would even ask. "The bigger question is who are you and how did you get on board that ship? And while we're at it, maybe another question is, what's that device you were carrying?"

Jacob wasn't about to respond until he knew who this guy was. He needed some questions answered first.

"Sir," said Jacob, "can you tell me what year this is?"

"I'm the one asking the questions! Now who are you and how did you get on board that ship?"

Jacob figured he'd better provide some information if he was going to get any details out of this guy. Per protocol, he thought he'd drop the highest-ranking name possible.

"I was part of a team commissioned by Admiral Mason Hughes and the CIA to examine the ship," he said. "But something went wrong, and the rest of the team disappeared. Next thing I knew, your soldiers came out of nowhere and attacked me."

"First of all, we have no Admiral Hughes. Second, there's no way you were commissioned by the CIA or anybody else to be on that ship. The only ones authorized to be on that ship are my people, and you're not one of them. Now who are you?"

"Hughes is the head of Naval Operations and the Vice Chair of the Joint Chiefs. You've never heard of him?"

The man just stared daggers at him. This was impossible. Could this time be so far in the future that they didn't know who Hughes was?

"What year is this?" said Jacob.

"What's in the briefcase?"

Obviously he wasn't going to win this battle. But he wasn't about to answer yet. For all he knew, this man was with a foreign spy agency or some rogue terrorist organization.

The man stood up and started to pace.

"We're going to find out either way. We can break it open, or you can tell us what's in it. It's your choice."

"It's just personal items and notes."

"I want to see it."

"And I want to see someone in higher authority before I say anything more," said Jacob.

This time he decided he'd stare back. He was expecting the man to explode, but instead the stone cold face took on an air of confusion. Or maybe it was shock.

"Holy shit. You really don't know who I am, do you?"

The man genuinely seemed to believe that everyone in the world must know him.

"I'm afraid I don't. Should I?"

"Okay, I'll play the game—once." The man sat on the long table, looking a little more relaxed. "I'm General Cole Bradley, the highest authority here, reporting directly to the United States General Councilor. Recognize me now?"

This wasn't making any sense.

"First of all," said Jacob, "I'm not aware of any United States General Councilor, and second of all, where's *here?*"

Bradley just stared at him, as if he couldn't believe what he was hearing. Before Bradley could respond, Jacob decided to test him even more.

"Okay, General Cole Bradley, if you won't tell me where I am, then maybe you'll tell me what organization you're with."

Bradley jumped up and lunged forward.

"Listen, the only thing preventing me from thinking you're a raving lunatic is that you've somehow entered a top secret secure facility from the ocean, with no visible marine craft nearby. Because I know you didn't get through our guards on the beach."

Jacob couldn't imagine what had gone wrong. Could killing Hitler have initiated such a domino effect? Or had he returned to the wrong time period? He sank back in the chair and felt the straps constrict around his chest.

He thought he'd try one more thing.

"Can I call my wife in San Diego?" he said. "She can explain who I am." He wasn't sure even what time period this was, but Bradley's response to this request might give him a hint. He thought of mentioning Malcolm, but if Bradley didn't know Mason Hughes, then he sure wouldn't know Malcolm.

Bradley narrowed his eyes and walked toward the small window behind the table, shaking his head. Then he turned around.

"There *is* no San Diego, and there hasn't been for over sixty years! Whoever your wife is, if you have one, she's not in San Diego!"

Jacob was trying not to panic, even though everything he knew in the world was being turned on its head. How could there be no San Diego? He must have arrived so far in the future that the world had changed drastically. Yet the ship was still there being guarded. He decided he'd better tell Bradley more if he was going to find out anything.

"My name is Jacob Newman," he said. "I'm a quantum physicist working with the CIA. I was born in 1975 to Stuart and Rebecca Newman. My grandfather was Max Newman. I was—"

"You don't mean Max Newman the famous scientist?"

"Yes. You've heard of him?"

Finally, he felt like he was getting somewhere. Max must have gone on to do great things.

Bradley rolled his eyes.

"Everyone has heard of him! He died in that famous helicopter crash during the war—the one that took out JFK."

Jacob couldn't believe what he was hearing. JFK died in a crash? And Pop was on it? He couldn't imagine what could have gone wrong, or what war Bradley was talking about.

"That's crazy," he said. "My grandfather never fought in any war. What war did he die in? When?"

"World War II, Jacob."

How could that be possible? Could there have still been a war without Hitler? Then another possibility dawned on him.

"General, please tell me this one thing. Was the war with the Germans? The Japanese?"

Bradley started walking past Jacob toward the door behind him.

"Neither," he said. "It was with the Russians."

"The Russians?" Now he was really confused.

"Information, Jacob."

Jacob twisted his head around to the right to look at Bradley.

"I don't get it. It doesn't make any sense."

"Information, and then you'll get your history lesson."

Before he could respond, he heard the door shut behind him. Bradley had left the room.

Jacob wracked his brain, trying to figure out how World War II could have involved the Russians but not the Germans or the Japanese. What scenario could have even led to that? Anyway, he still didn't know where he was, or even when, for that matter.

After several more minutes, he heard the door open behind him and watched Bradley walk to the table again and sit on the edge.

"Okay, Jacob," said Bradley. "One more try. How and when did you get on that ship?"

Maybe it was time to stop asking questions and just tell them what he knew.

"I last remember working on the alien ship on March 16th, 2024. I flew there the day before from Philadelphia. I was working with a team of scientists analyzing the objects found on the ship and—"

"Jacob, I have to stop you there. It's not adding up."

"How so?"

"Well for one, *today* is March 16th, 2024, and I can assure you there is no team of scientists on that ship. And I can also tell you there's no way you could have flown there from Philadelphia."

"Don't tell me there's no Philadelphia either!"

Bradley just stared at him with an expression that was a cross between disbelief and disgust.

Jacob's heart sank. How could this be? Today was the very day he had transported from the ship. Only now everything had changed. No team. No San Diego. And God only knows about Philadelphia. He began to feel weak, wondering what he had done. His main thought was of Kim, Jessica, and Ethan. If there was no San Diego, he had to find out if they were somewhere else, if they were safe.

"What objects?" Bradley interrupted his thoughts. Jacob couldn't even think straight enough to comprehend the question. Bradley must have sensed his confusion because he repeated the question more slowly.

"What...objects...did you find...on the ship?"

Jacob took a deep breath, trying to gather himself.

"We found a silver sphere, and eight monitors showing images from our past." He didn't want to mention the Kronos device yet.

"What images were on the monitors?"

Jacob summarized the content of the eight images. He couldn't read Bradley's reaction though. The man would make a great poker player.

Before Jacob could ask any more questions, Bradley interrupted again.

"There wouldn't be additional objects in your briefcase, would there?

"Just newspaper clippings from my family's history, and some random notes from my studies."

Bradley walked around to the side of the table and picked up the briefcase. He placed it on Jacob's lap.

"Show me."

Jacob saw Bradley motion to someone behind him. Then he heard a gun cock. Apparently Bradley wanted to make sure he didn't have a weapon and had called for a guard to observe.

Jacob brought the briefcase up to his eyes to use the retinal scanner, then placed it on his lap and opened it. He pulled out a book on the Holocaust and handed it to Bradley, who grabbed it from him.

He watched as Bradley scanned the pages. Again, Bradley remained poker-faced. After a few moments, Bradley slammed the book down on the table and looked back at him.

"Impossible!"

"General, where I come from, this was a crucial event in history. Adolf Hitler led Germany to kill six million Jews and many other so-called blemishes on society. Not only that, but he inflicted his Fascist aggression all over Europe, invading Poland, France, England, you name it. This was *our* World War II in the forties. And if you add years of copycats, I'd say Hitler was responsible for over fifty million deaths."

"That's all fine except for one thing, Jacob. I don't know where you come from! And where I come from, none of this ever happened! The war in the forties was with the Japanese, not the Germans, and I've never even heard of this Hitler. Whoever wrote this sick shit should see a psychiatrist. I'm not even going to ask where the photos came from, if they're even photos."

"Wait a minute," said Jacob. "I thought you said World War II was with the Russians. Now you're saying it was with the Japanese?"

"World War II *was* with the Russians. The war in the forties was with the Japanese."

Before Jacob could respond, Bradley jumped up and grabbed the open briefcase from his lap and placed it on the table, throwing the book back inside. Then he started toward the door again, but stopped and turned toward Jacob.

"Either this is real and you're involved in something crazy, or you're completely delusional. Except somehow you had the resources to get onto that ship. In either case, Jacob, I need answers now, and more than you're telling me."

Jacob was trying to decide whether to explain further, but before he could say anything, Bradley had opened the door behind him and told the guard to stay. Then he heard Bradley say, "Watch him," and the door slammed shut.

Chapter 34
The Needle

After what seemed like an eternity but was probably about an hour, the door opened again, and Jacob heard several pairs of footsteps. This time, Bradley had brought someone with him, a bald man who looked around seventy, wearing a white lab coat and plastic gloves. The two men circled around in front of Jacob. He noticed that Bradley was holding the Kronos device.

"Jacob, I don't know where you're from or how you got here, but I need to inform you that, in our world, the penalty for spying is death. We can't take any chances. We have a zero tolerance policy. I'm asking you one last time. What is this and how does it work?"

Jacob thought hard. The Kronos device was his only hope, the only way he could possibly set things right again—assuming that was even possible. He couldn't afford them experimenting with it and using up what may be the last remaining trip. He also figured they must be bluffing, because without him, they'd have no hope of learning any more. He decided it would be best to remain silent.

"Jacob, if you won't tell us, we have no use for you, and we'll have to assume you're either a spy or a rogue operative bent on either preventing us from using this equipment or doing something with it yourself. Let me assure you, we will take no chances."

Jacob watched as Bradley motioned to the other man, who now approached him. At the same time he heard someone come up from behind. If only there were time to formulate a plan. But time wasn't an option at this point.

Before he could respond, whoever was behind him—he assumed the guard—grabbed his arms and held them back behind the chair.

"This is your final chance, Jacob. I want to know what that device is and how it works."

He needed to buy time.

"I suppose you're going to torture me."

For the first time, Bradley laughed.

"Jacob, we don't torture people here. That's barbaric."

Funny man.

"No trial, then?" said Jacob.

Bradley shook his head.

He had to find another way to stall.

"I want to talk to the General Councilor."

"That is not an option. You can talk to me."

Before Jacob could think of another stall tactic, Bradley motioned to the doctor.

"Time's up, Jacob."

Jacob watched as the doctor pulled a long needle out of his pocket and approached him. At the same time he felt his arms being pulled tighter behind him. Whoever these people were, they weren't bluffing.

"Okay. Okay. What is it you want to know?"

His only option now would be to tell them the truth and pray he could convince them to give him the device back.

Bradley stared at him. "The problem now is that whatever you tell us is going to be a stall tactic. And time is something I don't have."

"No, I—"

"Goodbye, Jacob."

Before Jacob could say anything, he felt the needle plunge into his arm. He could feel his veins tingling as the fluid from the needle entered his system. Then his whole body began shaking uncontrollably and he felt weak and nauseous. The room started to spin and his heart began to race. He didn't want to let it end like this, with everyone he loved gone, but he had no energy. His last conscious thought was that this must have been how Anna felt.

Then he gave up and his head fell forward.

Chapter 35
New World

The light was the first thing to hit Jacob's senses—daylight shining into his eyes. Every so often he'd feel a tremor through his body, and his legs would kick. He had no sense of being, of where he was or what he had gone through; it was as if he were just being born into the world. Then, gradually, his senses started to return, beginning with the faint smell of cigar smoke. He opened his eyes to see where he was. As he looked down he could see that he was lying back in a recliner. He appeared to be located at the near corner of a large office or meeting room, with a long conference table in the center running the length of the room.

Now it started to come back to him. The needle. It hadn't killed him after all. Or had it? It couldn't have, or he wouldn't be feeling all his senses coming back. But if he wasn't dead, then where was he? And why wasn't he strapped down now?

His mind was still foggy. He felt as if he had just awakened from one of those bad dreams where you can't remember the details, but you know it was bad. He narrowed his eyes to get a better look around, but it was difficult with the glare of the sun beaming toward him through the haze of cigar smoke, or whatever it was.

Then he noticed it. Sitting in front of him on the conference table was a silver helmet of some sort. He leaned forward to pick it up. It was light, but solid, almost like the sphere on the ship. As he looked at it, he could see that it was similar to a motorcycle helmet, except this one apparently covered the eyes and ears. You sure couldn't use it to drive anywhere. He wasn't sure if it had been placed there for him, but out of curiosity he slid it over his head. Almost immediately, he heard a whoosh and felt it fit around the rest of his face, and, if he wasn't mistaken, his body as well. Everything went dark, and he suddenly felt himself rising quickly. Before he knew it, the helmet and body cast, or whatever it was, disappeared. He couldn't believe his eyes, but somehow he was flying through the sky!

He had no control over his body, though he could wave his arms and move his legs. He felt a light breeze, but otherwise, he didn't feel like he was outside. All he could see when he looked below was blue sky. He felt himself moving faster now, picking up more speed by the minute. He was getting dizzy but couldn't stop. He closed his eyes, but still felt as if he were moving. If this was a video game, it was the world's most immersive one.

Then, in an instant, he felt himself drop at incredible speed. He was in a complete free fall, and closed his eyes again. This was awful, even worse than the time travel experience. Was this a cruel joke? He felt sick to his stomach and prayed he wouldn't hit the ground and die. As he was falling, the helmet and body cast sealed again, immersing him in darkness. Then, it all stopped and he felt as if he were floating, suspended in mid-air. He exhaled in relief. After a few seconds of this, the helmet opened again. Jacob was surprised to see that he was standing on solid ground. And he couldn't believe where.

Somehow, by some force of magic, he was standing in a crowded room of cheering people. They didn't even seem to know he was there. Many were carrying American flags. This had to be some kind of political convention.

"Look, there he is!" someone yelled, pointing to a huge multi-level stage.

"Ladies and gentlemen," an announcer said over the public address system. "The new President-elect of the United States of America—Richard Milhous Nixon!"

What the—? What the hell was he doing here during a Nixon acceptance speech?

"He just barely beat Kennedy," a man behind him said to someone. Jacob turned around to see the man carrying a *Win with Nixon* sign. Others were carrying signs that said *Nixon's the One* and *Nixon for President.*

Kennedy? What year was this? It would have to be 1960. Then he looked toward the stage and that confirmed it. On the large wall behind Nixon, who was still waving his hands to the crowd, was a sign that read *1960 Presidential Election.*

How could Nixon have beaten Kennedy?

Before Jacob could even process this scene, the helmet sealed shut again and everything went dark. Then he felt himself being lifted up once again—or more like catapulted—higher and higher, like he was being shot out of a cannon. Suddenly, the helmet opened and he was back in the sky. And once again, he felt himself being hurled forward through the air at dizzying speed. He could again feel the breeze blowing against his face. At this altitude he'd expect to be freezing, but he wasn't.

One thing he was, though, was sick from being tossed around like a rag doll. He shut his eyes again to make the experience easier, though it didn't help much. The whole thing was surreal. He had no idea where he was, who was controlling this, or why. All he knew was that he couldn't take many more of these wild trips.

Just then, he began to fall. Even though he had a pretty good hunch this time that he wouldn't hit the ground with a splat, he still hated the feeling. Now he knew what it was like to skydive. Then the helmet sealed shut and, once again, he felt as if he were floating. The change couldn't have come soon enough.

This time when the helmet opened, he was standing outside on the side of a highway in broad daylight. Cars were zooming past. The highway was lined with palm trees. Was this Florida? It certainly looked like it, but he couldn't be sure. But why was he here, in the middle of a highway?

He looked toward the horizon, but he couldn't see anything. He decided to start walking along the road. Something was strange, though. All the cars were heading in his direction. On the other side of the highway, there was virtually no traffic. He tried to wave down some of the cars, but nobody was stopping. He wasn't even sure they could see him. And he wasn't about to jump in front of one of them to find out.

He kept walking, not sure where he'd end up or what was coming next. For a split second, he thought he might be having a bad dream. Perhaps they had drugged him. He felt wide awake though, and alert. Then he thought maybe he was dead, but that didn't feel right either. He thought about Bradley, and the strange uniforms the soldiers were wearing. He thought about the box that had been mysteriously delivered to his house, and his impromptu and improbable trip to Dachau. None of the pieces were connecting, though.

He watched as the traffic zoomed toward him and whizzed by. Occasionally, horns would honk. People sure seemed in a hurry to be going somewhere. Or away from somewhere. Then he noticed that there were cars in the opposing lanes now. Except they, too, were going in the same direction. Whatever was happening, everyone was in a rush. He wondered if maybe he should turn around and go where the cars were headed.

He was suddenly shaken by a blinding light up ahead. It was everywhere—blinding, immersive, incredible light. He shut his eyes tightly, and within seconds, a deafening noise had thrown him back, like nothing he'd ever heard. His senses were knocked out as he fell to the ground. He couldn't hear a thing, other than a loud buzzing in his ear. He opened his eyes, and gradually his sight returned. That was when he saw it—a huge mushroom cloud up ahead, towering up into the sky. His ears were still ringing as he stared into the horizon. Then he noticed something else. Cars in the distance were being tossed in the air like dolls. Many were on fire. He could hear a loud rumble getting closer. Then he realized, it was a shock wave, and it was coming his way, fast!

He crouched down and braced himself for the worst. Burning cars flew into the air, getting closer now. The wave was almost upon him, the noise growing louder and louder. Then a large, fiery truck was thrown into the air and headed right toward him. He wasn't going to be able to avoid it. He shielded his head and got low to the ground and prayed.

He felt something tugging at his head, pulling hard. He realized that the helmet must have sealed shut. Just then, he felt the helmet lift off his head. Everything was spinning and he could barely see. Smoke was everywhere.

Slowly, his senses began to return and he smelled a faint smell of cigar smoke. His eyesight started to clear. He wasn't outside anymore. He was back in the conference room! He shook his head to loosen the cobwebs, and noticed that someone was standing right in front of him. First he saw the grey slacks. Then, as he looked higher, he could see that the man was wearing a grey suit. He leaned back so he could see who it was that was holding the silver helmet now above his head.

As the man moved the helmet out of the way, Jacob could finally see his face. For a second, he thought he was imagining things.

It couldn't be.

He had to look twice because he couldn't trust his own eyes. Then he felt a combination of relief, confusion, and a hundred other emotions.

Because standing in front of him, looking down with that familiar comforting expression, was Malcolm Hoover.

Chapter 36
Consequences

"Youuuuringiiiibaaaa."

Jacob shook his head trying to figure out what Malcolm was saying. Finally, after a few more tries, his hearing started to return.

"Your hearing," said Malcolm. "Is it back?"

"Malcolm?" said Jacob. He was still disoriented.

Malcolm smiled that same old reassuring smile that Jacob had come to appreciate for over thirty years.

"Well, most strangers address me as General Councilor or Dr. Hoover, but it seems you know me on a first name basis, Jacob."

"You're the General Councilor?" Jacob wondered how this situation could have come to be, but he was sure grateful it had.

"I'm almost afraid to ask who you were expecting," said Malcolm. "Do I know you?"

What was going on here? How could Malcolm not know who he was?

"I know it's hard to believe," said Jacob, "but I worked for you. And we were good friends, too. Do you know of the NBIC program? Nanotech, Biotech, Infotech, and Cognitive Science? Convergence? Any of this ring a bell?"

He felt like he was back talking with Pop as a stranger in 1924.

"Jacob, I'm not familiar with any NBIC program or convergence or anything like that, nor have I ever seen you before, but we're obviously in unique territory here. We need to get to the bottom of just what is going on. And to do that, I'll need your full cooperation. Now, you've been interrogated under medication and it seems you're telling us the truth. But we have many other questions."

"I'll do what I can," said Jacob, "but you're not the only one with questions."

As Jacob thought about how to explain everything, Malcolm took a wrapped cigar out of his pocket and offered it to him. He politely declined, and Malcolm put out his own cigar. Jacob thought if he could be candid with anyone, it was Malcolm, who was always the voice of reason.

"Before I go on," said Jacob, "maybe you can tell me where we are, and what that helmet is all about."

"That's not critical right now. But what is critical—very critical—is your answer to some suspicions we have, based on what you've shared, and some things you said when you were under. Specifically, I need to know whether or not you played God, and what exactly you did."

As Jacob thought hard about what to say, Malcolm repeated the question, more sternly this time.

"Jacob, did you play God and change history? And if so, why? What led you to it?"

"Malcolm, I've known you for years—you'll have to believe me on that—but I need to know I can trust you now. I need to know you won't do anything rash."

"We're way beyond trust here," said Malcolm. "This is a matter of human survival. It's beyond both of us."

"I just need to know you won't destroy the device. That's all I ask."

"Destroy the device?" said Malcolm, as he leaned against the table. "You're planning to use it again?"

Jacob couldn't think of an answer.

"We won't destroy it," said Malcolm. "You won't have access to it, but I can assure you it won't be destroyed. So, do we have a deal?"

Jacob nodded his head. As long as the device existed, he'd at least have some hope of gaining access to it again. That made it worth cooperating with Malcolm.

For the next hour, Jacob told Malcolm everything. He told him about the unmarked box that had come in the mail; his surprise trip to Dachau; his grandfather's journal; and the ship's images that had led him to believe the world was about to face an alien judgment day—a judgment day he could quite possibly head off by undoing Hitler's evil.

When he was finished talking, he could see Malcolm massaging his face in deep thought, as he had seen him do so many times when he was working on an especially difficult problem.

"An alien judgment day," said Malcolm, looking at Jacob with a dead straight face. "Jacob, I believe you felt this assassination was a noble act, but there's something you need to understand. You have no idea—"

Malcolm's voice tailed off.

"Tell me."

Malcolm paused, as if he were carefully selecting his next words.

"In trying to save millions," said Malcolm, "you just may have caused the deaths of nearly four billion people."

What?! What could have gone wrong? And where were Kim, Jessica and Ethan? Rather than having saved all those people, could he possibly have brought on an even bigger disaster—and wiped out his own family in the process?

"Tell me what happened," he said.

Malcolm hesitated.

"Please, Malcolm. I need to know."

"You saw what happened. Well, part of it anyway. I was hoping to have a chance to show you the right way, but you decided to try the helmet on for yourself, never mind the controls."

"Controls?"

"We had an idea you'd decide to jump right in and take the scenic route," said Malcolm. "So we put in a little something extra as a lesson."

"You mean the flying," said Jacob. "I could have avoided that?"

"I'm afraid so."

Jacob sighed, shaking his head.

192 EDWARD MILLER AND J. B. MANAS

"So, how did Nixon beat Kennedy? And what was that nuclear blast? In my timeline, Kennedy won the election."

"And why was that?" said Malcolm.

"Well, he was a war hero, for one thing. His actions in the South Pacific on the PT-109 were legendary. Historians say that had a lot to do with it. But I don't understand how that could have changed. What would that have to do with the Germans, or getting rid of Hitler?"

"Well let's find out," said Malcolm. "In this timeline, Kennedy never fought in the war at all. He worked his way up in the Office of Naval Intelligence in Washington. One thing led to another, and—"

"Wait a minute," said Jacob. He was starting to get a sense of what might have happened. "I remember my grandfather telling me something. Kennedy volunteered for PT boat duty because he was stuck in a desk job in South Carolina. He lost the big Washington assignment."

"And why was that?"

Malcolm had a look on his face like a teacher who already knew the answer and was waiting for the student to get it.

"An affair, "said Jacob. "He had affair with a Danish woman who was linked to high-ranking Nazi officials. It's one of the reasons my grandfather never trusted Kennedy. He didn't trust Nixon either, for that matter."

"Well there's your answer. The Nazis didn't exist. So, no scandal, no desk job, and no war record. It's the small details that always get you, Jacob. In this case, that small detail had a huge impact."

Jacob shook his head. He could hardly believe what he was hearing.

"What happened next?" he said. "What was that bomb?"

"That was Florida," said Malcolm. "The first area hit."

"Hit by who? When?"

"That was 1962," said Malcolm. "The Russians."

"The Russians? But—"

Then Jacob got it. He began to understand exactly what had happened.

"Wait a minute," he said, "the Cuban Missile Crisis. Nixon decided to attack Cuba? That's what started all this?"

"He followed his advisors' recommendation," said Malcolm. "The experts said it was necessary, including the Joint Chiefs of Staff."

"So what!" said Jacob. "They told Kennedy the same thing, but he didn't listen. He offered Khrushchev a deal; they remove their missiles, and we don't attack Cuba."

Malcolm shook his head.

"Not in this timeline."

"So what the hell happened? How did billions of people die?" Jacob couldn't believe what he was hearing. Worse, he couldn't believe he had been the cause of it all.

"Everything happened," said Malcolm.

Malcolm picked up a remote and turned on a large electronic world map that appeared in holographic form over the conference table. He demonstrated by drawing lines on the image as he spoke.

"First," said Malcolm, "we launched our invasion of Cuba. The Russians answered by sending the first round of tactical nuclear missiles into the continental U.S. The bomb you saw was the first site hit. It was in Cocoa Beach, Florida, the Air Force Technical Applications Center, AFTAC, based out of Patrick Air Force Base."

"Why there?"

"Well, the center's purpose was to detect nuclear activity from anywhere in the world, so naturally it was a primary target. They also targeted the Nevada Proving Grounds, north of Vegas. Also, NORAD, our North American air Defense site in Colorado. Strategic Air Command Headquarters in Omaha was another big target, plus naval and nuclear developmental sites in San Diego."

"So, pretty much all over the country," said Jacob. "It's hard to fathom they even had that capability."

"And it wasn't just contained to the U.S.," Malcolm said. He continued drawing lines on the map as he spoke.

"They also launched missiles from Russia at our bases in Turkey, Italy, and the UK, and even at our allies in Europe and Saudi Arabia. And of course, we responded in kind with our own nukes, both overseas and long-range from the States."

"So this was global."

"Yep. All over the world, missiles were flying past each other like deadly ships in the night. Pretty much everyone with nuclear capability was getting into the act."

"So how did it all end?"

"Well, eventually, cooler heads prevailed after countries became overwhelmed with their own recovery efforts. But the damage had been done. Jacob, you mentioned World War II being in the forties. Well this was *our* World War II. And a world war it was."

Looking at the jumbled lines on the map, Jacob was speechless. He couldn't find words to describe his shock at the destruction he had inadvertently caused. He could only keep repeating, "I didn't know. I didn't know."

Malcolm seemed unfazed, but then again, this was the only world he knew, and these events had occurred more than sixty years ago. He would have been a child at the time. But with Malcolm, it was always hard to tell. He had an uncanny ability to stay calm no matter what the situation, something Jacob had always envied.

Then Jacob thought of something else. What if this was some kind of trick? What if none of what he had just seen was real? He decided to test Malcolm's reaction.

"Malcolm, no disrespect, but how do I know any of this is real? How do I know you guys aren't just a bunch of aliens messing with my head? I mean, for all I know, you may not even be Malcolm."

Malcolm's face grew even more serious. He stood up and reached beside the table to grab something. It was the briefcase.

"Come with me," he said.

"Where?"

"You'll see."

Jacob stood up. "What do you mean, I'll see?"

"I mean you'll see."

Malcolm walked out of the room into a long hallway, and Jacob followed him. "Here," said Malcolm," handing Jacob the briefcase. "You'll need this."

"What for?"

"You'll see," said Malcolm.

"I was afraid you'd say that."

Jacob walked with Malcolm through a labyrinth of hallways, wondering where they were going. As they walked, Malcolm pulled a mobile intercom out of his pocket.

"Ready the OV-12."

"What's the OV-12?" said Jacob. "Some other kind of mind control device?"

Malcolm was silent.

"I know," said Jacob. "I'll see."

Finally they came to an unmarked white door on the left. Jacob followed Malcolm inside, not knowing what to expect. When they finally entered, he looked around with a combination of awe and relief.

The room was vast. Jacob's first thought was that it looked like an auto showroom, bright and circular. Except this one was filled with a variety of military helicopters and planes, each one unusual-looking in its own way. Malcolm approached two soldiers, who were both dressed in the same black uniforms: a young black man who couldn't have been any older than twenty, and a huge albino who looked like he wrestled alligators for a living. Jacob couldn't hear what they were saying, but then Malcolm returned with the two of them at his side.

"Jacob, this is Reggie. He'll be our pilot."

The young man reached out his hand.

"And this is my bodyguard, Armand," said Malcolm. "It's regulation that he fly with us."

Jacob felt like a child as he shook the giant's hand. He had to be at least 6'6".

Reggie led them toward a sleek silver plane at the far end of the room. Judging by the manta ray shape, it looked to be a stealth fighter. As they approached, Jacob could see it had a single large window that wrapped around the front and sides. Through the window, he could see that half the plane was taken up by the cockpit, with room for about six seats behind it. This was no fighter jet.

Malcolm turned to face him while Reggie went to get the boarding platform that was standing nearby.

"This is the OV-12," said Malcolm. "The OV stands for Observation Vehicle. It's the latest technology from Yamaha. It's got vertical takeoff and landing, and can hover like a helicopter. But unlike a helicopter, it travels at Mach 3."

"Mach 3? My God, you could travel the whole East Coast in under an hour. It doesn't look like a fighter jet."

"No, it's used strictly for observation, which is a huge priority these days. It has all the expected satellite equipment, of course. It's based on their RMAX technology, which about twenty years ago was used in small unmanned helicopters for agricultural replenishment. I'll explain that later. There's a lot that's happened that you'll need to see for yourself. By the way, she also has autonomous flight control. If the pilot leaves the controls for any reason, she hovers in place."

"And how do you get her down in that case?"

"We can do it remotely. The Japanese have excelled in technology, thanks to our reparations after the war in the forties."

"Well, at least that hasn't changed," said Jacob.

Reggie interrupted them. "We're all set."

Jacob was about to follow Reggie and Malcolm, but Armand held his huge arm in the way and went up first. Apparently, he either couldn't speak or didn't wish to. Jacob followed Armand into the plane and saw Malcolm give the albino a gentle pat on the back as if to say that everything was okay. Armand followed Reggie to the right into the cockpit, so Jacob turned left toward the passenger aisle to sit with Malcolm.

"Where are we headed?"

"Florida. Where everything started. I'd brace yourself."

Malcolm looked at Jacob with a slight smile as the plane ascended vertically. Apparently the roof of the building had opened to let the plane through. Once the plane reached its cruising altitude, it charged forward like a rocket.

"I've had enough thrill rides for one day," said Jacob. "Where did you get that helmet technology, anyway?"

"Neuro-triggers, said Malcolm. "That, combined with recorded and simulated material. It interacts with the brain in terms of sight, smell, sound, touch. It's based on Kessler's work."

"Kessler?"

"You've never heard of him?" said Malcolm.

"Can't say I have."

"Maybe he died in your Holocaust."

Jacob leaned back in his seat and thought about the implications of his actions. Somehow, he had to get the Kronos device back. There had to be a way to go back and undo the assassination.

"The facility we just left was in Gettysburg," said Malcolm.

"Gettysburg?"

"I'll explain later. Meanwhile, open your briefcase."

Jacob wasn't sure what Malcolm was getting at, but he did as he'd asked.

"Can I see that journal you mentioned?" said Malcolm.

"Sure." Jacob handed Malcolm the journal and watched as he flipped through the pages studying it. At one point, he put the journal down and stared straight ahead as if he were trying to work something out. Then he handed the journal back to Jacob.

"Jacob," said Malcolm, "I want you to look at the book you have in your briefcase, the one about the Holocaust. Just leaf through it and look at the photos."

Jacob looked through it. His mind wandered back to seeing Anna at Dachau. It seemed so long ago.

"Now look out the window and down," said Malcolm.

Jacob looked out the window. He couldn't believe the devastation. There were no houses anywhere, just charred rubble, barren fields, and giant craters.

"Where are we?" he asked.

"We're making our way down the East Coast. That's Charlotte, North Carolina, but it's like that in much of the country. Floods, fires, you name it, and much of it long after the bombs hit. Many cities are still standing, but the downwind fallout decimated the population. The radiation and the destruction affected people from all walks of life: men, women, children of all races and colors. Many of them had their whole lives ahead of them. Take a good look, Jacob. This is your world, the one you created."

Jacob couldn't find the words to express how he was feeling. He never dreamt his actions would lead to this. He meant to save the world, not destroy it. But still, all he could think of was his family. Exhausted, he closed his eyes and tried to get some rest while he could.

After a little while, he opened his eyes and looked out the window to see a small beach surrounded by more devastation. There was ocean to the left and straight ahead.

"What's that beach down there?"

"That's where we're landing," said Malcolm. "Jacksonville Beach."

Jacob looked again. As the plane slowed to a near stop and began to descend vertically, he couldn't believe what he was seeing. He knew Jacksonville was located on the northern tip of Florida. Yet, he could see nothing south of it but ocean and the tops of buildings occasionally rearing their heads out of the blue sea. And Jacksonville itself, which he remembered as a modern city and a bustling tourist spot, was now nothing but a deserted beach mixed with rubble, ash, and collapsed buildings.

As the plane quietly lowered straight down toward the beach, Jacob felt as if he were in an elevator. Within minutes, he felt a soft jolt as the plane touched down. He couldn't help thinking of Kim's friend Bonnie as he stared at the desolate beach.

"My wife's friend lived just south of here," he said. "She and her husband ran a cruise company."

"Not anymore," said Malcolm. "There hasn't been a cruise operation in over sixty years."

The cockpit door swung open, and Reggie emerged to open the exit doors. Jacob followed Malcolm down the steps. Armand and Reggie waited on board. As Jacob stepped down onto the soft sand, he watched Malcolm staring out at the calm ocean.

"Welcome to Jacksonville Beach, Jacob—the southernmost point in the United States. I wanted you to see this for yourself. To experience it."

Jacob stood next to Malcolm in disbelief. He couldn't fathom that Florida was pretty much wiped off the map, and probably most of Texas as well.

"What the hell happened here? Could one blast have sunk the whole state?"

Malcolm shook his head.

"The nuclear blast caused a lot of problems for sure. And a lot of deaths. But it wasn't until a few years later that we started seeing severe weather changes. The tides began rising, and the storms got much worse. Then came the tidal waves. You can imagine the mess."

"Talk about adding insult to injury. Did you have a nuclear winter, too?"

"Nope. Scientists predicted that, but it never came. We had intense heat in the summers, and fires and storms like you wouldn't believe. It's settled down since, but it took a good twenty years. What really did us in was the impact on agriculture, and the distribution ability. More people died from starvation than were killed in the blasts or from fallout, or even the floods."

"What about the west coast? Did they get impacted as much?"

"Unfortunately, yes. And also a massive earthquake that hit Northern California two years after the bombs. Whether the bombs caused it, we'll never know. Needless to say, there's not much left of California."

Jacob couldn't believe the global catastrophe, all because of one man's death. He wondered where Kim's parents would have been then, or even how he'd find her if she was still alive. But even so, in this world, Jessica and Ethan were gone. And that wasn't something he was about to accept.

Chapter 37

The Doomsday Blueprints

As the plane ascended, Jacob stared out the window at a large white square platform hovering in mid-air. It looked about the size of those dance platforms he remembered seeing on the beach back home; he guessed it was probably about 100 square feet. It had four large horizontal propellers built into it, one at each corner, keeping it airborne. He noticed several other similar platforms in the distance.

"I didn't see those before. They must have been on the other side of the plane. What are those things?"

"ETOPs," said Malcolm. "Electric Tethered Observation Platforms. Built by the Israelis years ago, but they've turned out to be very useful worldwide. They can be launched from the ground or from a plane, and they hover anywhere from 300 to a thousand feet. They used to need a power source from the ground, so they were tethered, but now they're solar powered. We still call them ETOPs though. They can carry about fifty pounds of equipment if needed. You'll see them everywhere."

"Incredible. Speaking of Israel, how is it they came to exist? In my world, it wasn't until after our war with Germany that the State of Israel was founded."

"Interesting. In ours, it wasn't until after the catastrophic events of the sixties, when the world's focus turned from war to relief efforts. That's about the time when Jewish, Arab, and Christian leaders met at a series of summits. It took a global tragedy to get them to finally get past their differences."

"And how did they resolve them?" Jacob couldn't wait to hear this one. With all the destruction he'd caused, he needed to hear something positive.

"Well, to start with," said Malcolm, "they agreed in principle to take a stand against extremism in all its forms. They created a set of guidelines called the Finkel Doctrine that they would all follow."

"And who was Finkel?"

"Abraham Finkel. He was instrumental in facilitating agreements when things got difficult. And because of those summits, we've enjoyed religious and cultural cooperation like the world hasn't seen in thousands of years. In fact, these floating platforms you see are used jointly by Jews and Arabs in the Middle East to monitor activities for peacekeeping purposes."

Jacob was trying to take it all in. Peace in the Middle East. And it had taken a global meltdown to bring it about.

"It's funny," he said, "I've never heard of Finkel either. In my world, he probably never had the opportunity to make a difference."

Jacob stared out the window as his thoughts returned to Kim, Jessica, and Ethan. He had to try to set things right. He thought again about what he could do if he had the Kronos device back. He was starting to formulate a plan when Malcolm tapped his shoulder and pointed out the window.

"This is Berryville, Virginia. See that mountain? That's Mount Weather, code-named High Point. There's a 61,000-square-foot bunker hidden inside it. It's where we relocated the president and his cabinet when notification of the missiles went out. Have you ever heard of the Doomsday Blueprints, Jacob?"

He shook his head. "Can't say I have."

"They were plans originated in the fifties for how to respond to a nuclear threat—or any other catastrophic event, for that matter. Among other things, they called for the creation of a ring of emergency sites, called the Federal Arc. The Pentagon would be relocated to Raven Rock, a massive underground complex near Gettysburg."

"So that would explain Gettysburg. That was the Pentagon we were at?"

"Exactly. Congress was relocated to Casper, where there was another complex. That one was buried under an elegant resort in West Virginia. There were other facilities too. Together, they formed an underground ring around the capital."

Jacob took one last look at the mountain as it disappeared behind them.

"So the full Doomsday Blueprint was enacted?" said Jacob.

"Yes, but there was more. The Blueprint called for the U.S. to be run like one giant regimented camp. So we had food rations, curfews, and censorship of all communication. See those white rectangular buildings down there?"

Jacob looked down at the endless rows of plain white buildings.

"Those are barracks. Everyone in the country who survived lived in those for years; many still do. The ironic thing is, we relocated the government, but Washington DC was never hit. I suppose the Russians wanted to be sure they had someone to negotiate with in the end."

"Incredible," said Jacob.

As the plane soared on and he looked out the window at the devastation, his mind wandered back to San Diego. Then a thought occurred to him.

"I wonder," he said out loud.

Malcolm gave him a curious look.

"San Diego was my home in recent years," said Jacob. "If it was wiped out in the sixties, then I wonder in this world where I ended up moving to, or if my parents even survived."

Malcolm took a deep breath.

"Jacob, there's something you need to know. When word came about the missiles coming, the federal government began executing their plans to secure those vital to national security. Anyone else would have to rely on their own shelters, or public shelters run by the states."

"How did the government decide who to bring?"

"Well, mostly it was a matter of need. Health workers, people with special skills. You might find it surprising that celebrities were also considered vital. After all, if the government's operational and you can still see Bob Hope and Johnny Carson on TV, then there must be some sanity in the world."

"So, my parents—could they have been on the list? After all, if my grandfather was so well known—"

"Jacob—" Malcolm took another deep breath. "If your grandfather was Max Newman, he was on the list, all right. But there was a crash, a helicopter crash bringing him to the holding center in anticipation of the bombs arriving. It was in '62. Nobody knows what actually happened. They were chaotic times. The whole nation mourned his loss. His wife had died about ten years earlier of cancer. And—"

"Cancer? Anna?"

"Yes, that was her name. I'm sorry."

"My father, did he survive? Max's son? He would have been in his mid-twenties about then. Or my mother? They would have been just married or close to it."

"Jacob, by the time the government went looking for Max's next of kin, the bombs had hit. They were never found and were presumed dead. In any case, they weren't among the census of the living." He paused and then added, "Of course, you know what this means. If what you're telling me is true and you're Max Newman's grandson, then, in this world, you were never born."

Jacob was in a daze, trying to digest the news Malcolm had just given him. How could he even be here if he had wiped out his own birth? What had he done? After all that, Max's life ended far earlier than it would have. And Anna had survived only to die of cancer in less than a decade. Now he was stuck here in a world in which he'd never been born. No family. No children. Nothing. He had to fix this somehow. And there was only one way he could think of to do it.

Malcolm gave him a reassuring pat on leg. "I know that's some heavy stuff I laid on you."

"Where are we headed now?" said Jacob.

"Washington, DC. To see Abraham Finkel."

"To see him? The guy who brokered the Middle East peace? He's still alive?"

"Yes," said Malcolm. "Very much so. And he's anxious to see you."

Chapter 38
The Cost of Freedom

As the plane continued up the East Coast, Jacob contemplated a number of things. He wondered why Finkel would want to meet him. Sheer curiosity perhaps. He also thought about the alien ship. Was there still any danger of an alien judgment, or had he headed that off? Could it be possible that he actually had saved the world from a judgment, albeit still sacrificing billions of people? In any case, none of this speculation would bring Kim back, nor Jessica or Ethan. This wasn't the way it was supposed to be. He was sure of that. At least, as sure as he was of anything, which wasn't much these days.

His thoughts were disrupted when Malcolm directed Reggie to head further north and loop around New York City en route to DC. Then Malcolm turned back to Jacob.

"That's another area you'll want to see. The GC decided not to even try rebuilding New York."

"The GC?" said Jacob.

"After the wars," said Malcolm, "it was decided that each nation would have a General Councilor as part of a worldwide Global Council. No nation would be excluded. The GC would set international policy and be the ultimate authority in any disputes."

"Well, I can't imagine that working too well for very long."

Hell, it sounded like the United Nations, but with more power and a more inclusive membership. A recipe for disaster, as far as he was concerned.

"Jacob, since the war, there's been unprecedented cooperation. No weapons, especially nuclear; only defensive measures in case some rogue country gets their own ideas. Let's just say the world has become a more spiritual place, open and tolerant of different peoples and religions."

"You mentioned rogue countries," said Jacob. "I'm sure there's terrorism, right?"

"None whatsoever. No need. There's also no one starving, and no homeless. That's something we couldn't say before the war."

Jacob had to laugh.

"You make it sound like utopia," he said.

"It's far from utopia, but it's working, and that's all we can hope for."

Malcolm paused to point out the window. "There's New York coming up."

Jacob couldn't believe his eyes. The entire city was in ruins. No skyscrapers, just endless fields of debris.

"I guess 9-11 never happened?" he said.

"9-11?" said Malcolm.

Jacob couldn't even answer. He just stared out the window in awe at the sheer magnitude of the destruction. After a few more minutes, the OV-12 circled around and headed south. As the plane sped on, he thought about his plan. And the more he thought about it, the more he realized that he needed to take a chance and share his idea with Malcolm. It was the only hope he had of getting the Kronos device back.

"I can fix this," he said.

He blurted this out so matter-of-factly that he wasn't sure if Malcolm had heard him.

Malcolm had, and gave him a strange look. "Fix it? You don't mean—" He paused for a few seconds before continuing. "Jacob, you played God once and are seeing the results. I can tell you that the world we live in now isn't pretty. But it's our world, and we've worked hard to rebuild it. And more important, it's a peaceful world."

"Please, just hear me out," said Jacob. "That's all I ask."

"Jacob, whatever it is, once you bite from the apple, you can't just put it back. Everything is connected. You should know that more than anyone by now."

"Listen, I can stop my other self, the one that caused all this. I know how to do it."

"Your other self? How would you do that? And more important, *why* would you do that?"

"Okay," said Jacob, "let's say Jacob A has arrived in 1924 and is about to visit his grandfather Max and set the plan in motion." He felt weird referring to himself in the third person. "I can travel there and stop him before he does it. All I have to do is tell him about the catastrophic results. I can use the Kronos device—the one I told you about that your men are holding now. There's at least one more trip left in it before the power is gone. I could undo all this."

"Undo it?"

Malcolm stared at him.

"Jacob, I'm not saying technology is a bad thing. Through it, we can heal the sick, and we can evolve our species. I firmly believe that if we weren't meant to advance, we wouldn't be gifted with such extraordinary knowledge. But the good Lord gave us something else, too. I'm talking about free will. And it's up to us to use it wisely."

"But don't you see?" said Jacob. "That's exactly what I'm trying to do now. This is a chance to set things right." He thought that argument might resonate with Malcolm.

"Then tell me this. By changing the past the first time, how can you be sure you didn't interfere with what was meant to happen? Now you want to do it again?"

"I just find it hard to believe that genocide was meant to happen."

"Maybe not, but it did, and as a result, good or bad, an intricate web of events followed—one so complex, you couldn't even begin to track them all. And when we tamper with that web...well, you see the results. Besides, where do you draw the line? What if you went back and helped the Native Americans fend off their enemies by giving them automatic weapons?"

"This is different."

"I know it is. But I suppose what I'm trying to say is that we're not ready to play God. At least not in our lifetime."

"But that's exactly how it's different. I caused all this, and now what I'm trying to say is that I need to undo it. I know I can fix it."

He looked at Malcolm, who finally seemed to be thinking this idea over. He felt like he might be getting through. After a moment, Malcolm looked up at him.

"What if it goes wrong?"

"The truth is," said Jacob, "I don't know for sure. But this is a chance I have to take. My whole family is gone. Billions of people have lost their lives. The whole future is different—all because of my actions. The way I look at it, what is there to lose?"

Malcolm gave him a look that he couldn't quite read.

"I'll *show* you what there is to lose."

In a matter of seconds, Jacob felt the OV-12 begin its vertical drop. He looked out the window and could see that they were descending over the National Mall in Washington, DC. Before he knew it, the plane had settled upon a grassy field just behind the Lincoln Memorial. As he looked out, he could see people walking around, but they seemed oblivious to the plane, as if military landings near a national monument were a daily occurrence. And maybe in this age they were.

After they had disembarked, he followed Malcolm around to the front of the Lincoln Memorial, and they ascended the steps toward the imposing statue of Abraham Lincoln, who was seated in contemplation as if presiding over the world.

"Jacob," said Malcolm, "this statue gave our nation great hope after the dust settled and we began to finally emerge from our shelters. On the south wall you can see the Gettysburg address. I don't think anyone fully embraced those words before, except maybe when it was first delivered. But they embrace them now."

Malcolm recited the final words out loud, seemingly from memory.

That we here highly resolve…that these dead shall not have died in vain…that this nation under God shall have a new birth of freedom…and that government of the people, by the people, for the people, shall not perish from the earth.

Jacob looked at the words on the wall, and Malcolm continued.

"These words are what kept our country together. They still do as we learn to balance the cost of freedom. After all, a new birth is exactly what we're working to accomplish. I suppose it's only fitting that our General Council facility is located in Gettysburg."

He paused, as if to think, and then continued.

"Jacob, Lincoln said something else that I think is very relevant here. *Nearly all men can stand adversity, but if you want to test a man's character, give him power.* You went back to the past and saw that you could change the world. And now you want to do it again, with the same good intentions. Let's say you can do that, and set everything back to the way it was meant to be. I just want you to think about this for a minute. One thing you can ask yourself: Is the world better now, or was it better before? Don't try to answer right away. Ponder it for a bit."

Jacob didn't have to ponder it. He had been pondering this question for the last hour.

"I'll think on that, I promise. Now can you think on something as well?"

"Fair enough. Shoot."

"Doesn't the world deserve a chance to pursue its own fate, as God would have it, and not because of an act of interference? Think about it. I tried to save millions, but I ended up killing billions. And there's only one opportunity to reverse that, and this is it. Do you think for a minute I want to sacrifice the woman I just risked my life to save? Or the millions of others? But it's the right thing to do. It's what she would want me to do. I know it in my heart. And more important, it's what the Malcolm I knew would want me to do."

Malcolm took a deep breath.

"Jacob, I hear you, I really do. There's nobody who cares more about doing the right thing than I do. But look around you. This is life now. For better or for worse, this is reality."

As Malcolm waved his arm, pointing out the people walking around the National Mall, Jacob wasn't quite sure what else to say. He only knew that whatever he had said so far wasn't getting through.

"Come," said Malcolm. "We'll be late for the meeting."

"Meeting?"

"Dr. Finkel has called a meeting at the National Academy of Sciences. He serves as Special Advisor to the U.S. Government. The agenda is to discuss and prepare a statement to the Global Council. We need to advise them on an urgent matter of international security."

"And it's okay that I attend?"

"Of course," said Malcolm. "He insisted that I bring you."

"And what's the issue being discussed?"

Malcolm smiled.

"*You.*"

Chapter 39

Finkel

As they entered the grounds of the National Academy of Sciences, which was only a few blocks away, Jacob noticed a sign pointing to the Albert Einstein Memorial. He recalled having seen it once before, a huge bronze statue of Einstein reclining on a stone bench, holding a paper with engravings of his most well known mathematical equations.

There was no time for sightseeing though. Jacob followed Malcolm down the long tree-lined walkway toward the building's main entrance on Constitution Avenue. The Academy building resembled an ancient Greek stone temple, with its stressed, white, rectangular neoclassic design. Large oak trees and elm trees stood guard throughout the grounds.

"The National Academy," said Malcolm, "or NAS as we call it, was appointed by Abraham Lincoln to advise the government on matters of science and military endeavors. As you can imagine, after all the devastation we faced, the Academy rose to great importance. It was through the NAS that Finkel established the Global Council."

"He's the one who established it?"

"Yes, indeed."

Jacob and Malcolm continued up the stone steps to a set of huge bronze doors adorned with carvings of famous icons of science, philosophy, and mythology.

As they entered past the main foyer, Jacob's jaw dropped at seeing the magnificence and grandeur of the Great Hall. As he looked up at the arched dome that towered above—it had to be at least fifty feet high—he noticed, among the many paintings, emblems, and tiles, an inscription on the wall.

214 MILLER AND J. B. MANAS

To science, pilot of industry, conqueror of disease, multiplier of the harvest, explorer of the universe, revealer of nature's laws, eternal guide to truth.

"Those are great words," said Malcolm. "And quite fitting for our meeting. Come. Let's go to the boardroom."

Jacob followed Malcolm past a room titled The Lecture Room to a large set of ornate doors.

"This is where we'll be meeting," said Malcolm.

As they entered the walnut-paneled room, Jacob's eyes were drawn to a marble fireplace on the side wall, and above it, a painting of Abraham Lincoln with a group of other men, probably the Academy founders, signing what looked like a charter.

Then, as he looked around at the men in the boardroom, all standing around talking, he couldn't believe his eyes. Walking directly toward him was an old man. Not just any old man. His face was instantly recognizable. There was no mistaking it.

"Jacob," said Malcolm. "I'd like to introduce you to Doctor Abraham Finkel."

Jacob was dumbfounded. Abraham Finkel, the man who had brokered Middle East peace in this new world, and the man who had created the Global Council, was the very same man from Paris, the one whose family knew Pop, and the one who just may have sent the mysterious box. Maybe he'd have some answers. Jacob wondered if Finkel knew about Landsberg in this timeline.

"Jacob Newman," said Finkel, as he approached, "our guest of honor. What a pleasure it is to meet you."

Jacob shook Finkel's hand. "This isn't the first time we've met," he said. "Apparently your family knew my grandfather. He was Max Newman."

"And so I understand," said Finkel, in his thick, Eastern European accent. "It is why I wanted to meet you, the grandson of one of our most brilliant human beings."

"So your family did know him," said Jacob.

"I am sorry to say, I never met your grandfather personally," said Finkel, "nor has anyone in my family to my knowledge. But I can tell you he is a revered man. In fact, we have a permanent exhibit of his work in the rotunda. I must show you when the guests have gone."

"Yes, I'd like to see it."

Jacob wondered if perhaps Finkel's family had known Pop after the war in his timeline. In that case, the two families being neighbors might have not have happened in this timeline—if Max and Anna had left Germany sooner.

Jacob thought he would test Finkel once more.

"Doctor Finkel, does the name Landsberg mean anything to you?"

Finkel looked surprised that Jacob would even ask such a question.

"Why, yes, of course," said Finkel. "It's the reason you're here."

Jacob looked over at Malcolm.

Just then, another familiar face appeared behind Malcolm.

"Ah, General Bradley," said Finkel. "I believe you know our esteemed guest."

Bradley extended his hand. "Jacob," he said.

As Jacob shook the hand of the man who had interrogated him just a few hours ago, something dawned on him. Now he remembered why Bradley had looked familiar when he had first seen him. He was the military official with Finkel at the conference in Paris.

Finkel patted Jacob's arm. "Come," he said. "Let us begin."

Almost instinctively, as Finkel, Bradley, Malcolm and Jacob made their way to the large oval walnut table, all the others in the room followed suit. Jacob sat next to Malcolm, opposite Finkel and Bradley. All in all, there looked to be about twenty people, mostly men. Some were wearing military uniforms, others suits or sport jackets. All three women were Asian. Hanging above the table in the center was an antique light fixture with an illuminated globe inside.

"That's the electrolier," said Malcolm. "The map is based on Da Vinci's design in the sixteenth century."

Just then, the room quieted down, as Finkel stood.

"I have called this meeting," said Finkel, "in response to a matter that came to my attention earlier today. As you, by now, have all been briefed, a man claiming to be the grandson of Max Newman, who is now sitting opposite me, arrived in the top secret and secured facility we call Seawatch."

Jacob looked around as everyone stared at him like he was a space alien.

"Jacob Newman," said Finkel, "claims to have taken part in a plot in 1924 Karlsruhe, Germany to kill a German prisoner named Adolf Hitler—a man who, had he lived, allegedly would have gone on to commit great atrocities to the Jewish population, and many others."

The room filled with chatter, and Finkel raised a hand to quiet everyone. Then he sat down and continued.

"We do have records of an outspoken German politician named Adolf Hitler who was imprisoned during the Beer Hall Putsch in Munich, but it seems he died of a heart attack while incarcerated. Now, our esteemed guest claims to have used artifacts found in our facility to travel back in time to poison Hitler, and that if he had not done so, Hitler would have caused—and in fact *did* cause—mass destruction."

"That's preposterous," said a man at the far end of the table. "He's crazy," said another. Suddenly the room filled with chatter again, and some of the attendees began laughing.

"We have evidence," said Finkel, "that he is telling the truth."

The room grew quiet again. Dead quiet.

"Jacob," said Finkel. "Why don't you pass around your little book? The one with the evidence of Hitler's destruction."

Jacob glanced over at Malcolm, who nodded. He opened the briefcase, took out the book on the Holocaust, and handed it to Malcolm, who passed it around the table. Jacob sat quietly as each person leafed through the pages. He could hear murmurs and gasps coming from the far end of the table.

"We also have in our hands," said Finkel, "the device Jacob used to travel through time—a device that, for whatever reason, we had not encountered at Seawatch, though he claims to have discovered it there. It is now secured at our facility in Gettysburg. And so, it is our difficult mission to decide how to handle such an unprecedented situation. On one hand, we have just learned that the present state of our entire world has potentially been altered because of the man who sits at our table. On the other, here he is, and here we are. So what do we do?"

Finkel held up his hands, as Jacob looked around at the blank stares around the table.

"Jacob," said Finkel, leaning forward, "I care not whether you murdered a madman to avoid a global catastrophe. And this, even despite the damage you have caused by doing so. But I care very much what you intend to do now."

"I'm not sure what you mean," said Jacob.

"I mean," said Finkel, "I am suggesting that we might offer you an opportunity. Do you want to work for our Academy doing great things for the world? You are the grandson of Max Newman; there is no mistake. You even have his features. Think of it. To have the grandson of Max Newman, and, as I understand it, a physicist who was already working with the United States government in a top secret facility; this would be a wonderful thing."

Finkel looked around the room.

"Are we prepared to offer this man the chance to work with us?"

Jacob glanced again at Malcolm, who once again nodded. Everyone around the table nodded in silence, though Jacob sensed that they didn't have much choice.

"I have cleared it," said Finkel to Jacob, "with the proper authorities."

Jacob took a deep breath.

"Thank you," he said. "I appreciate your offer, Dr. Finkel, I truly do. But I'm afraid I must decline."

"Decline?" said Finkel. He didn't look happy. "What will you do? You have nowhere to go, no family to speak of. This is a prestigious, and I might say, given the situation, a very generous offer."

"Let's just say I have some restitution to make. Things I need to do."

Finkel stared at him with a grave expression.

"What...kind...of restitution?" Finkel was practically growling.

Jacob didn't answer.

"Look around you," said Finkel. "We have spent our lives trying to bring about peace in the world. And besides, how do you know it was not God's plan for you to do the very thing you did—to change the world and bring about this peace?"

Jacob tried to think of a response, but couldn't.

"Might I suggest," said Malcolm, "that we take a recess. I think it might be best if I speak with Jacob alone."

A few people gave Malcolm a concerned look, including Bradley.

"He and I have had a chance to chat a little," said Malcolm. "I think we can resolve this."

"Very well," said Finkel. He stared at Jacob for a few long seconds, and then stood up. "We will resume in twenty minutes."

Jacob thought about Finkel's assertion, that this so-called peaceful world was meant to be. Maybe the world was now some kind of Garden of Eden to them, but it wasn't his idea of a Garden of Eden, not with a fraction of the population left and the world in the hands of a select few.

He followed Malcolm out of the boardroom. As soon as they got into the hallway, Malcolm grabbed his arm.

"Jacob, listen," said Malcolm. "I need you to come with me. Don't ask any questions, just follow me."

Jacob wasn't sure what Malcolm was getting at, but he followed him down the hallway toward the Great Hall. As they passed through the grand, domed room, Malcolm hurried him along.

"Quickly, he said.

"Where are we going?" said Jacob.

"We need to leave this place."

"What?"

Jacob was flabbergasted.

"Won't they be looking for us?"

"Not for another twenty minutes or so," said Malcolm. "We should have enough time to get to the plane."

"To the plane? What the hell is going on here?"

"No time," said Malcolm. I'll explain later."

They exited through the huge bronze doors and down the steps. Jacob was surprised at how fast Malcolm was moving for a man of his age. They made their way out of the grounds and toward the Lincoln Memorial.

"This way," said Malcolm.

Jacob kept looking back to see if anyone was following.

Just as he could see the Lincoln Memorial, he heard the roar of planes. He followed Malcolm behind the Memorial where he could see the OV-12 still on the lawn.

Just then, the roar got louder as the planes began lowering vertically all around them. Jacob counted four of them. Malcolm looked alarmed.

"They must have had us watched," said Malcolm. "Finkel knew."

"Knew what?"

Within seconds, Bradley had emerged from one of the planes with a group of other uniformed men. Then, more uniformed men descended from the other planes.

Malcolm grabbed Jacob's arm. "Get in the plane," he said. "Now!"

Jacob trusted Malcolm more than the others, so he ran for his life toward the plane. As he looked back, he could see that Malcolm was following him. Bradley and the other soldiers just stood there, then began running to their respective planes. He wasn't sure why Bradley and the others had hesitated, but he was glad they had. They could have shot him with ease.

Jacob climbed onto the plane, with Malcolm right behind him.

"Reggie, take off," said Malcolm. "Change of plans."

Change of what plans?

As they settled into their seats, the plane ascended vertically. Jacob turned to Malcolm.

"Mind telling me what the hell's going on here?"

"No time now."

Malcolm picked up the intercom. "Evasive maneuvers, Reggie. Whatever is necessary. Head west."

"I thought Bradley works for you," said Jacob.

"It's complicated."

Jacob was startled by loud tapping behind him, like a cork popping, only much louder.

"Are they firing at us?"

"Appears so," said Malcolm.

So much for hesitation.

Just then, Jacob was thrown back against his seat as the plane jerked forward. First, the plane was pointed straight up, like a rocket. Then it leveled out and looped to the right. Jacob felt like a rag doll as he was thrown hard against the side window. It was impossible to hold on or sit straight. Without warning, the plane dropped rapidly. Jacob could feel butterflies in his stomach, like on those rollercoaster rides with a straight drop. This was worse than that damn helmet ride.

He glanced out the window and saw that the other planes were catching up. One was right beside them.

More shots were fired. They sounded like they were coming from above now. He tried to duck down in his seat, as if that would make a difference.

The plane darted forward again, then rose quickly. Jacob wished he could see what the other planes were doing. He felt helpless. Never in his wildest dreams had he expected to end up in a dogfight, especially on a plane with the General Councilor. None of this made sense.

Just then a huge explosion in the rear of the plane made Jacob nearly jump out of his seat.

"We've been hit," said Malcolm.

Jacob looked out the window just in time to see shots hitting the wing, one after the other. The OV-12 began shifting and bucking out of control. He feared for his life as he was thrown from side to side. Then, suddenly, the plane was dropping, nose down, and he was thrown upward.

This was it. They were going down!

He braced himself, praying that the plane would right itself. He glanced quickly over at Malcolm.

What the——?

Malcolm had the Kronos device in his hands. His hands were flying on the controls like he'd used the device all his life. He must have had it with him the whole time.

In a split second, Malcolm grabbed Jacob, and he felt the familiar vibrations take hold. Thank God there was no delay this time. Jacob's whole body froze, and he prayed the device would work before they crashed. Suddenly, with the plane still in a nosedive, he felt that floating feeling. He was light as a feather. Then, as if he were transparent, the plane passed right through him, leaving him floating in mid-air. He couldn't even look over to see what was going on with Malcolm. He began to feel that heavy feeling coming on. He knew what that meant. Just as he braced himself to take the wild ride through time—to who knows where or when—he glanced down to see the OV-12 going down in flames.

Chapter 40

Opportunities and Choices

When he finally got his senses back, Jacob knelt down to feel the ground. Although he couldn't see very well in the dark—his eyes were still adjusting—he knew exactly where he was. He could tell by the musty air and the echoing droplets of moisture. He was back on the ship—not in the alcove, but just outside it. What time period was this?

He stood up and noticed Malcolm standing there next to him, holding the briefcase up.

"Are you okay?" said Malcolm.

"I guess that's all relative, isn't it?" said Jacob. He took the briefcase and laid it on the ground. "Would you mind telling me now what the hell is going on? How did you know how to use that device?"

Malcolm looked at him, apparently contemplating whether or how to answer.

"Okay," said Jacob. "Then can you tell me what time period this is? Or is that also a secret?"

"Same time," said Malcolm. "Different place."

Jacob shook his head. He was getting more discouraged by the minute. And more confused.

"Jacob, listen," said Malcolm. "There isn't much time. The others will be here soon. I need you to listen to me. I believe you have the ability now, and the determination, to accomplish what you need to do. And you're right. It's the right thing to do. But more important, I saw what I needed to see."

"And what was that?"

Malcolm paused for a moment.

"Jacob," he said, "how do I put this? You see, we think we're closer to God because we understand science. But when science understands love—when it understands humility—then maybe we'll understand God."

"I still don't get it."

"Let me put it another way. You're willing to have faith that whatever destiny God has for the world will be better than the one you set in motion. And you're willing to sacrifice everything, even yourself, for the sake of your family and to set things right again. Answer me this, Jacob. Do you consider yourself a man of science or a man of God?"

Jacob thought about the question. A few days ago he knew what his answer would be: a man of science, pure and simple. But it was no longer a few days ago. "Both," he said.

Malcolm smiled.

"Are you familiar with your Biblical namesake, Jacob?"

"To a degree—though I couldn't tell you any of the stories."

Jacob wasn't sure where Malcolm was going with this. He watched quietly as the general councilor began pacing around the ship, his voice echoing as if in a grand cathedral.

"In the Bible, Jacob did a great wrong. He didn't change history or anything like that. But he did trick his father into blessing him instead of his brother Esau. And in doing so, he claimed Esau's birthright. But then as he matured and learned the error of his ways, he tried to redeem himself, much like you're trying to do."

"I see your point," said Jacob.

"That's not my point yet. Anyway, with Esau vowing to kill him, their mother sent Jacob to stay with his uncle. Years later, he decided it was time to set things right. So, he set out for home to patch things up with Esau. On his way back, he sent ahead messages of peace. But the only message he received was one saying that Esau was marching to meet him with 400 men. So much for good intentions."

"And that's the lesson? The dangers of good intentions?"

"No, that's not the lesson either," said Malcolm. "I'm getting to it." He continued to walk around as he spoke. "So, our Biblical friend Jacob, ready to face the consequences, sent everyone away and set up camp alone, waiting for the worst. He prayed all night for God to forgive him. That night, he was visited by a stranger, an angel who, instead of helping him, spent the time reminding him of his sins. Jacob was determined to make things right though, so he pleaded with the angel, and wouldn't let him leave until the angel blessed him. They ended up wrestling throughout the night and into daybreak. Finally, the angel told Jacob that he had just wrestled with God, and from then on, he would be blessed and given a new name—Israel, which meant 'struggles with God.' And because of his persistence—and his determination to undo a great wrong—Jacob was redeemed. Of course, as it turned out, everything went fine with Esau too."

"So the analogy is you're the angel, right? And I've gotten through? I won the struggle?"

Jacob looked around for Malcolm, but he seemed to have vanished. Then he heard footsteps and saw him emerge from the shadows.

"It's not your struggle, Jacob. Not anymore. It's *our* struggle."

"I'm not sure I'm following."

"Let me put it this way, then. I said before, you can't just put the apple back. Well, there's another belief I have, and that's that God gives us opportunities—"

"I know...and the free will to decide."

Malcolm smiled. "I've given you this lecture before. Well, it seems I have an opportunity now, and a choice to make. May God help me if I'm wrong."

Just then, Jacob heard the double doors at the far end of the ship open.

"They're here," said Malcolm.

"What will you do?" said Jacob.

"I'll hold them off."

"How?"

Jacob heard footsteps echoing in the vast cavern. They were getting closer.

"Jacob, listen," said Malcolm. "Finkel and Bradley are not who they seem. That's all I can tell you for now. Finkel is a wolf in sheep's clothing. I realize that now. I'm only now beginning to understand how devious his plans are. Something he said at the meeting confirmed my suspicions. Jacob, this is bigger than you could possibly imagine."

Malcolm handed Jacob the Kronos device. "Here," he said. "When you go, trust no one, not even yourself. And take this." Jacob looked at the small pistol Malcolm was holding out. "Take it!" repeated Malcolm.

Before Jacob could think, Finkel emerged from the shadows.

Malcolm turned to Jacob. "Go!"

Jacob grabbed the gun from Malcolm, picked up the briefcase, and ran to the alcove with the Kronos device in his pocket.

Once in the alcove, he took the Kronos device out to use it for light, and fished through the briefcase for the codes to set for Karlsruhe. He could hear Finkel talking.

"You would go against the Ring of Seven?" said Finkel. "You would defy us all?"

What was he talking about? Ring of Seven?

"It's over, Malcolm," said a familiar voice. It was Bradley.

Just as Jacob found the slip of paper and began frantically setting the code on the Kronos device, he saw a bright light coming from outside the alcove and heard a deep humming sound. It sounded electronic. He poked his head out and couldn't believe what he was seeing. Malcolm and Finkel were aiming some sort of light beams at each other. The lights were so bright, he couldn't tell if they were weapons or something else. Then the massive light in the center reached a blinding intensity, and several other shadowy figures emerged beside Finkel and Bradley.

It looked like Malcolm was being overpowered as he tried to hold off all of them.

Jacob looked down and noticed that the Kronos device was illuminated around the edges now. He was just about to duck back into the alcove when he heard a loud noise, almost like glass shattering. He looked up, and—

No!!!!

Right before his eyes, Malcolm, the kindest, most insightful man he'd ever known, exploded into what looked like a thousand tiny sparkles of light. They killed him! Those bastards killed him!

With no time to think about what he had just witnessed, Jacob jumped back into the alcove, his heart pounding. He could hear them running toward him.

Thankfully, the device had begun vibrating. He stared at it, trying to will it to do something. He tapped the screen and the round icon appeared. The vibrations grew stronger. He kept pressing the icon, even though he didn't need to press it the other times he was in the alcove.

Finally, he began to feel the vibrations extend throughout his body. He was frozen in place, but he could hear their voices. They were here.

Just as they arrived, he started to feel his body lift up, his arms rising involuntarily. Two hands—he couldn't tell whose—reached in to grab him.

At that instant, he felt his body sink fast, spinning and falling, and he saw dizzying colored lights everywhere. He hated this feeling.

When it finally stopped, the cool air hit his face and he fell several feet to the ground, landing with a thud on his rear end. At least this time he wasn't stuck in a tree. He'd forgotten that one flaw in Lauren's calculations. But he couldn't fault her for anything. For here he was, once again, in 1924 Karlsruhe, hidden among the now familiar trees.

As he sat there looking around, he thought about what had just happened. It was hard to believe that Malcolm was gone. Then again, so was everyone else in the world who was dear to him. Kim, Jessica, Ethan, his sister, Ellen. Everyone. Lauren and Beeze were probably gone, too. But the future—all of their futures—was now in his hands. With any luck, he might be able to give all of them their lives back. Whether he could return and be a part of it remained to be seen.

Unfortunately, this course of action would mean giving Anna and Pop their futures back too. And the millions who suffered under Hitler. Still, he knew now that this was the right thing to do. He was sure of it. And if the world had to face its judgment day, then so be it.

As Malcolm always said, opportunities and choices, Jacob.

PART 3
ERRATUM

Chapter 41

Face to Face

Jacob hid among the trees, waiting. If all had gone well, he was at least fifty yards from where Jacob A would soon arrive. He was guessing that would happen in anywhere from a half hour to an hour if his calculations were correct.

He opened his briefcase and took out the cell phone that was still in the hidden side pocket from his previous trip to Karlsruhe. Fortunately, Bradley hadn't noticed it. He turned it on and brought up the image of Anna—the one he had taken by the boxcars. He could barely look at her emaciated face. What had happened to her was even more horrifying now that he'd met her. "I'm sorry, Anna," he said quietly. "You too, Pop." And as he looked one last time at the image that would be etched in his mind forever, he pressed *Delete*.

He put the phone back, locked the briefcase, and decided to move a little closer to the area where he remembered arriving the first time. He was more than a little anxious about seeing his own alter ego. Could some weird time paradox occur, where the two of them couldn't exist in the same location and time? Either way, this mission was a chance he'd have to take. There wasn't any alternative.

As he walked further, he was relieved to hear the synagogue service going on in the distance—proof his calculations were at least reasonably accurate.

He was as close as he wanted to get now, so he sat on the ground, partially hidden by the trunk of a large maple tree, and waited.

The time seemed to drag on forever as he watched two squirrels chasing each other up a tree. It occurred to him that these could very well be his last few moments alive.

Then, finally, after about a half hour, a blinding light coming from the trees ahead grabbed his attention. This had to be it—the moment he was waiting for. His heart pounded as he wondered if this would be his defining moment, or his last. As he shielded his eyes, he recalled the soldiers at Dachau, the one soldier covering the other's eyes by the boxcars. Within seconds, the light vanished, and he could now hear the crackle of branches as he watched his alter ego slide down from the tree in the distance. He called out to get his attention.

"Jacob!"

He could see Jacob A look around nervously and then run toward the street. Dammit. He had been afraid that would happen. He ran to catch up, calling out again to no avail. At least he knew the two of them could coexist now. Still, it was bizarre to see his alter ego and not have any control over his actions. Nothing could have prepared him for the strangeness of watching himself helplessly.

He ran faster, following as quickly as he could. He thought of that old Pogo cartoon Pop had shown him. *Son, we've met the enemy, and he is us.*

He doubted Jacob A even had a chance to see who it was chasing him. Would he have even recognized his own voice coming from outside his body? Jacob tried to keep up, weaving around tree after tree. He could see Jacob A just ahead now.

"Jacob! I need to speak with you about your plan! Please trust me!"

It was no use. Jacob A was still running as if his life depended on it. Jacob was losing ground now. He tried to imagine himself in the same position—what might he have been thinking? Just then, he lost Jacob A in the distance, past a row of trees.

Shit, where was he?

Jacob kept running in the same direction, but didn't see him. Then, a few seconds later, Jacob A reappeared and ran to the right. Jacob tried to follow, but lost sight of him again.

Jacob stopped briefly and stood silently to listen for any sound of movement. But there was nothing. Nothing but the sound of trees blowing in the soft breeze. It dawned on him that Jacob A was probably hiding behind a tree somewhere trying to figure out what to do next. Then, out of the blue, he heard grass rustling and turned to see Jacob A running again, the Kronos device in his hand.

As Jacob resumed his pursuit, he wondered whether Jacob A would simply transport back and abandon the plan, or if he would try to come back later. He thought back to the way he was feeling at the time. Would he have abandoned the plan? Or would he have felt desperate enough to make another attempt, even if it meant a slightly different time or place? It was such an unusual situation that he couldn't be sure. And this was one time he couldn't take any chances. He called out again as he ran.

"Jacob, don't use the Kronos device! Please! I just want to talk!"

It was getting harder to keep up as he watched his alter ego dart to the left and run toward the street again.

"Jacob, I'm you! Please trust me! Turn around!"

As he watched Jacob A get closer to the clearing, he wondered if his alter ego could even hear what he was saying. At least now, he was gaining ground.

Just as Jacob A approached the open street, a horse and carriage was making its way past. At the same time, the synagogue doors burst open and people started to pour out onto the sidewalk. Jacob A darted in front of the horse and carriage and ran across the street toward them. Jacob stopped and went behind the carriage to cross. As he ran to catch up, he saw his alter ego grabbed by a hefty man with a bushy mustache, just in front of the synagogue. Max and Anna hadn't come out yet, but at least Jacob had already changed that part of his alter ego's plan.

The minute Jacob reached the other side of the street, Jacob A broke free and ran ahead, weaving through the baffled congregants. Jacob chased after in hot pursuit, only to be grabbed by the same man—a man who was now looking at him with bewilderment.

"Please," said Jacob. "I need to catch up with my brother."

The confused man let him go, and he took off again to catch up.

It didn't take long to realize, though, that Jacob A was nowhere in sight.

He looked around in all directions, but no luck. He was praying he hadn't transported back already.

Just then, out of the corner of his eye he saw Jacob A practically flying back across the street toward the trees. Why hadn't he transported back yet? And where the hell was he getting all his energy? He must have been running on pure adrenaline.

Jacob was getting winded and could barely feel his legs, but he forced himself to run across the street after his alter ego, following him into the woods. He continued to call, but it was no use, as Jacob A was breaking ahead. He was beginning to see that the only option left was one he was hoping to avoid—and one that Malcolm no doubt had foreseen might be necessary. There was simply too much at stake to risk anything.

In the distance, he saw Jacob A slowing down to operate the Kronos device. He was too far ahead to be stopped, though.

There was no time left. No other options.

As Jacob ran to catch up, finally getting closer, he took Malcolm's gun out of his pocket and aimed it at his alter ego.

Jacob, please don't force me to do this.

One last time he called out as he ran.

"Jacob, please! Listen to me!"

His hand was trembling now as he held the gun, still running, unsure of what the results of his next action would be. He thought of Max and Anna; of the nuclear destruction he had seen; and of Anna's face, as she lay motionless by the boxcars. He thought of Kim, Jessica, and Ethan. He was still running as he aimed for the most gut-wrenching target anyone could imagine. Then he saw the blinding light.

He aimed and fired. He kept firing, his hand shaking and his heart pounding.

God forgive me.

As the light dissipated, he tried to make out whether he was successful. Then he could see it. The body was sprawled out in the grass. He approached closer, glad to be alive, but afraid to look. When he'd fired the gun, he thought perhaps he might have erased his own existence, but he was undoubtedly still here. He felt weak, though, and stopped to rest. He knelt down on the ground to digest the enormity of what he had just done. After a moment, he rose up and stumbled toward the lifeless body.

Just then, he was startled by a noise to his right. He looked over and froze. A man in a black hooded mask was staring straight at him, pointing a gun. Even through the mask, he could tell the man was confused, his eyes darting back and forth between Jacob and his alter ego lying dead on the ground.

Jacob was going to ask the man who he was, but knew there was no time. Without hesitating any further, he aimed his gun at the hooded man and shot. He watched as the man fell backwards. Jacob ran over to the man and began to lift the mask. He was almost afraid to look. As he peeled the fabric up, he was both relieved and confused. The face wasn't familiar. Whoever he was, he was dead. What strange circumstances could possibly have brought a masked man to the middle of the forest to shoot one of them? And which one did the man intend to kill: Jacob or his alter ego? More important, who had sent him? It would have to be someone who knew he'd be here. But how?

A million questions were floating in Jacob's mind, but he had no time to digest any of them. Others must have heard the shots and would no doubt be here soon. Still in a daze, he approached the body of his alter ego, which was lying face down, arms out at the sides. He felt chills as he turned the body over—his own body. But the creepiness of doing that paled in comparison to what he saw next.

He looked down at his own face, lying dead, eyes wide open in a grotesque look of pain. The face and body almost looked like a wax figure of himself. Only, this wasn't wax. It was real—flesh and blood.

It was an image he now wished with all his heart he'd never seen—and one that he knew would be with him for the rest of his life, wherever and however long that might be.

He took a deep breath. He was still alive somehow, but would he be able to return to his own time? He looked down at the briefcase—an exact duplicate of his own—lying on the ground, next to his alter ego's sprawled-out arm. About a foot away was the other Kronos device—the one that belonged to Jacob A. He wondered if it might have enough power to get him back if his own device couldn't. Then he remembered something Max had told him years ago.

If something seemed too good to be true, it usually was.

No sooner had that thought entered his mind than he heard the sound of people in the street, near the entrance to the woods. They must have heard the gunshots.

Chapter 42

Dead Man Running

The last thing Jacob wanted to do was get caught by an angry crowd next to a dead ringer for himself—literally—with two alien devices and two briefcases full of material from the future. He was far enough into the woods that it would take a few minutes for them to catch up if they decided to enter, but still he had to think fast.

He grabbed the extra Kronos device and tucked it into his coat pocket with the gun. Hurriedly, he placed both briefcases on top of the body and pulled it by the feet, looking to make sure nobody was approaching yet. It soon became apparent, however, that this approach wasn't going to work. The briefcases kept sliding off, and he didn't see any lakes or bodies of water nearby to throw them into. They'd catch him in no time.

Then it dawned on him. He could just leave the body and teleport out of there. Nobody would recognize it anyway. He took out his original Kronos device. It was no longer illuminated and, as he feared, the image and power meter were gone. Quickly, he grabbed the other device out of his pocket. He was elated to see that it was illuminated and the meter two-thirds full, the round icon waiting to be pressed. He touched the icon and waited.

At least a minute went by. He kept pressing. Then he heard the voices again. They were heading into the woods. It was no use. It was already past the time it should have taken for the vibrations to take effect. Somehow the device must have to be paired with the person using it, even though he shared the same DNA and fingerprints with Jacob A. There was no time even to speculate. He had to think fast.

Then he remembered.

He still had the book of matches Max had given him. He could burn the evidence and run—at least the papers. As he heard the voices getting closer, he emptied the contents of both briefcases onto the body—papers, books, notes, anything incriminating—and more important, anything flammable. Then he noticed two small bottles of hand sanitizer on the ground, one from each briefcase. That would have to do. Quickly, he pulled some branches off a nearby tree and laid them over the body. He picked up the two cell phones and watches and tucked them into his pocket, then sprinkled the hand sanitizer over the papers and the body. He lit one of the matches and set the papers and the body on fire. He held one of the burning branches near each of the hands, trying to burn the fingerprints. Just as he was about to do the same to his alter ego's face, he heard people behind him, yelling. He couldn't hear what they were saying but they were yelling in his direction for sure. And now they appeared to be running his way.

He left the empty briefcases there and ran as fast as his legs could carry him, weaving in and out of the trees, the occasional low-hanging branch hitting his face. He smacked the branches aside, running through the woods frantically. He stopped briefly to look back through a clearing. It was a good thing he did, as he could now see people approaching the burning body. He fired his gun in the air to distract them. The last thing he could afford was their pulling any materials from the fire before they were fully burnt. His ploy worked, and the pursuers immediately ran his way.

He took off again, running past tree after tree. Then he heard shots being fired. He was out of breath but forced himself to run. Another shot rang out, followed by a piercing pain in his right shoulder that almost knocked him over. He didn't have time to stop and check. He just kept running, seemingly forever, until he could run no more. Exhausted, he finally collapsed onto the soft grass until his breathing and heart rate had returned to normal. He lifted his head to look around.

Strange. Nothing but silence. Either he had lost them or they had given up. But he was sure they'd be back, either with the police or dogs.

He stood up slowly, looking around for signs of anyone following, and then examined the top of his right shoulder where he'd been hit. At first, the blood concerned him. The last thing he needed was to end up in some German hospital, the spitting image of a dead man found in the forest. But then, after he peeled off his trench coat, he breathed a sigh of relief. The bullet had only grazed him. He ripped a piece off the bottom of his shirt and wrapped it around his shoulder, then put his coat back on and made his way toward the street. Judging by how far he had run, he estimated he'd emerge at least a mile from the synagogue.

As he approached the street, he could see that it looked empty, save for a few people casually strolling. Then he saw a few people running to the left, back toward the fire. He could smell the smoke now. He walked casually across the street to an adjacent alley, and continued walking as far as his legs would take him. Then he turned right up another alley that looked like it led to a residential area. He saw a bench and sat down to catch his breath.

It wasn't until now that it really hit him. He was stuck here in 1924 with no identity—in a country he was barely familiar with. But he dared not approach Max or Anna or interfere with history in any way. The bastard Hitler would have to live this time around. He thought of Kim and the kids, and wondered if they were looking for him by now. They must have been. What he wouldn't give for five minutes with them again. And Malcolm must have been beside himself. This, of course, assumed that the past was now set back exactly as it had been—from the point he had left it. But either way, at least they would all have a chance at life now. And that was the thought that was keeping him sane at the moment.

Meanwhile, he would need to figure out how to survive and stay out of history's way. He looked down at his wedding ring. It would forever keep him going, a permanent sign of his love for Kim and the kids—and a reminder of why he had to make this sacrifice. It killed him to think of Kim suffering with her illness alone, not knowing where he had disappeared to. And Malcolm probably would have had to make something up. A drowning accident or something.

He also hated to think of Jessica growing up an orphan if Kim didn't make it—an orphan just as he had been. That was a fate he didn't wish on anyone, least of all Jessica. At least Ethan was of college age, and Ellen would be there for them. It was too disturbing a prospect to think about, so he decided to keep up the hope that Kim would be okay, at least for a number of years. He never should have left her. But what choice had there been?

Then, as he looked again at his wedding ring, something dawned on him. Right there on his other hand, now staring him in the face, as if it were a sign from God Himself, was his answer. The one place he could turn to that would help him without a doubt. For, on the ring finger of his right hand was his Masonic ring. And a brother in need was never left behind.

He sat and thought. Although he remembered that there was a St. John's Masonic Lodge right in Karlsruhe—the one Max had always spoken of—he needed to get as far away from Max and Anna as possible. Plus, he didn't want to take the chance of anyone connecting him with the dead body. He had to leave Karlsruhe—the faster the better. He remembered a Grand Lodge in Frankfurt, which he'd visited years ago when he was in Germany for a conference. He still had some money left that Samuel had given him. All he'd need to do was get to the lodge and say he's a brother in need. That, and hope the Masons hadn't seen any newspapers with his face in them. He wished he'd had more time to burn his alter ego's face.

Assuming they didn't recognize him at the lodge, the big question then would be whether they could help him get to America. At least in the U.S., he'd have a better chance of surviving on his own; he could make his way to the Masonic Temple in Philadelphia and seek help there. But first, he had to make it to a taxi and get out of Karlsruhe without being noticed. That would be a feat in itself.

Chapter 43
Friends and Enemies

Jacob tried to keep an eye out for people as he continued up the alley to the next intersection. As he rounded the corner to his right, back toward the main street, he breathed a sigh of relief. There was a taxi parked right at the corner. He approached the taxi, trying to look nonchalant. As he got closer, he could see that there was another taxi behind it. The two drivers were standing and talking. One looked to be in his thirties; the other was an old man.

As Jacob approached them, they both stared at him as if he had come from outer space. Then he realized what they were staring at. The blood on his shoulder was seeping through the thin material of his trench coat.

"Ah," he said, laughing. "Those low-hanging signs will get you every time." He hoped that translated well in German. They were still looking at him nervously. The younger driver shook his head and waved him off, as if to say he wasn't available.

"Can you tell me," said Jacob, "are there any drivers who will take me to Frankfurt?"

The driver who'd waved him off was now laughing. "Frankfurt?" the man said, as if Jacob were insane to even ask. It wasn't surprising. After all, Frankfurt was hours from here.

"How much money?" said the older man.

Jacob took out half the money Samuel had left him and held it out. He had no idea what it would have been worth in 1924, let alone in Deutsche Marks. The man just looked at him, while the younger driver muttered something in German. Jacob took out the rest of his money and held it out.

"Take all of it," said Jacob. "It's all I have."

The old man looked at the money and then nodded, waving Jacob into the second taxi. Then he said something to the younger driver, though Jacob couldn't hear what he said.

Jacob climbed into the back seat of the antique motorcar and waited as the old man got into the driver's seat.

Finally, they were off, making their way out of Karlsruhe.

"I have family in Frankfurt," said the old man, who had to be in his eighties. "I will visit my brothers."

"That's funny," said Jacob. "That's exactly what I'm doing."

Tired, he closed his eyes and rested, trying to put all the worries and sadness out of his mind.

They hadn't gone more than twenty minutes when he was awoken by a strange horn. It sounded like a bicycle. He looked out the window to see a police motorcycle with a sidecar pulling beside them, waving them over. This wasn't good.

The taxi driver pulled onto the side of the road, muttering something to himself. Jacob watched anxiously as two policemen approached the driver's window and peered inside the car. He tried to remain calm as one of them looked in the rear side window directly at him. The old man was arguing with the other officer about something; Jacob couldn't make out the words.

Next thing he knew, the policeman was making the driver get out of the car. Just his luck to get a driver the German police were after. A knock on the side window startled him. They wanted him to get out too. What was this about?

Slowly, he stepped out of the car. The old man was still arguing with the other officer, a heavyset, red-faced man.

The thinner policeman turned to Jacob.

"Ihre papiere," he said.

They wanted his identification, and he had none whatsoever. He reached into his pants pockets to stall, hoping they wouldn't frisk him and find the gun in his coat pocket, not to mention the Kronos devices, the cell phones, and the watches.

As if to read his mind, the officer pointed to his bulging coat pocket.

"Was ist das?" said the officer.

Shit.

Jacob reached slowly into his right coat pocket. He felt the gun, half-wondering whether he should do something stupid. Instead, he grabbed one of the Kronos devices and started to hold it out slowly.

Immediately, the cop yelled "Halt!" and pulled his gun out, aiming it right at him. The other policeman, the red-faced one, sensing danger, did the same. Jacob held both his hands up.

"It's a toy," he said. He tried to remember the German word. "Spielzeug," he added. "Spielzeug."

Either these guys were way paranoid or they suspected something about him. He wondered if they'd seen the dead bodies yet. He tried to think of his options. The only thing he knew for sure was that there was no way he was going with them. Not quietly anyway.

The cop held out his hand for the device. Bitte," he said. "Please." Jacob's accent must have given him away as an American.

Jacob slowly lowered his hand, still debating what his next move would be. He certainly wasn't about to leave the device here in pre-Nazi Germany, even if it didn't work.

He put the device in his left hand and held it out, while discreetly putting his right hand back in the pocket with the gun.

The officer reached out slowly.

"Aha!!" said the taxi driver, interrupting everyone.

Jacob looked over to see the old man holding up some kind of certificate. The red-faced officer grabbed it to examine it, handed it back to him, and then waved the other cop over. Both of them put their guns back in their holsters and began whispering to each other. The thin cop glanced back over at Jacob.

Just then, the red-faced one then nodded to the old man and said something to him; Jacob couldn't hear what. The old man said something back, and then the officers started walking back toward their motorcycle. Jacob could have sworn the thinner one kept looking back at him suspiciously.

The taxi driver patted Jacob's arm and waved him back into the car.

"We go now," he said.

Jacob climbed back into his seat.

"What was that about?" he said, as the driver got in and started the engine.

"Regulations," said the old man. "Bad certificate. It is good that I have it!"

"Yes, extremely," said Jacob. He exhaled a sigh of relief. "What were the two of them talking about?"

"Ah, they say there was a murder. Two murders!" He held up two fingers, as he pulled back onto the main road.

"So that's what all the fuss in town was about," said Jacob.

"Yes. They are now going to the murder scene to investigate. I told them good luck."

"Did they say anything about me?"

"Haha, yes. They said you were a peculiar American and asked where we are going. I told them you are visiting your brothers in Frankfurt."

Jacob's heart sank. The cops knew he was headed to Frankfurt. And they hadn't checked out the crime scene yet, but as soon as they did, they'd see his alter ego, with the same face, the same clothes, the same everything. Still, he needed to get to the lodge in Frankfurt. It would be his only hope of getting out of the country.

He prayed that they wouldn't make the connection in time to catch up. They'd be at least an hour behind, and probably more. Still, they might notify the authorities in Frankfurt. He'd have to be careful.

With all the excitement, despite his worry, he was exhausted, and closed his eyes. Soon he felt himself dozing off.

After a while, he was awoken by the sun glare coming in through the front windshield. He'd fallen asleep; he wasn't sure for how long.

They were now passing through vast expanses of farmland. He wished the Autobahn had been built by now, not to mention Ferraris with V12 engines, as the trip seemed to go on forever. Now, more than ever, in a strange land, without a bit of money, and in hiding, he would be at the mercy of his Masonic brothers.

After another half hour, Jacob could finally see Frankfurt in the distance. It looked different without the expanse of modern skyscrapers and boxy office buildings—much more elegant and picturesque. As they approached the city, he asked the driver to let him off along the Main River before entering the town proper. From there, he knew he could find his way. Plus he could keep an eye out for police.

When the taxi at long last pulled alongside the bank, he parted ways with the old man and walked toward the trail that ran alongside the river, stopping to gather his thoughts. He looked around in all directions, and saw no one but a young couple with children, and an elderly man sitting on a bench. As he stood there, looking out at the blue water, he recalled Malcolm's words. *Once you bite from the apple, you can't just put it back.* He couldn't help thinking that if he managed to get out of Germany and avoid interfering with history any further, he just might accomplish that. But that would be easier said than done. Now the name of the game was survival—that, and anonymity. He realized he probably looked like hell from running through the forest, not to mention the bloody shoulder, but then it dawned on him that his disheveled appearance could work to his advantage, especially the cuts and bruises on his face from the branches.

He made his way into the city, and headed toward Kruppstrasse, where he remembered the Grand Lodge being located. Best of all, it was an English-speaking lodge, from what he could remember, with American ties. Hopefully it was the same back in these days, too.

He didn't see any police cars, but tried to look as inconspicuous as he could and blend in with the other people. Then he noticed a policeman about a block ahead, walking in his direction. He ducked into a jewelry store, and pretended he was looking at watches, glancing out the window every few seconds. Just then, the door opened and the cop walked in. Jacob froze and kept looking down at the watches.

"Herr Frank!" said the cop. Jacob watched as the cop shook hands with a man who appeared to be the store owner. Jacob casually walked out the door, continuing back up the street.

Finally, as he approached Kruppstrasse, he could see the imposing Grand Lodge. It still looked the same, only cleaner—its large, gothic towers resembling Notre Dame in Paris. He opened the huge wooden doors and entered. Immediately, two men wearing white apprentice aprons over their clothes approached him.

"Can we help you, sir?"

They *did* speak English. At least the man on the right did, a tall bald man with black glasses.

Jacob held up his Masonic ring. "Please," he said. "My name is Joseph. I'm a fellow Brother in need." He figured he might as well use the name he had originally given Max.

The two men approached him and he exchanged the secret handshake with them, along with the requisite verbal passcode. The awkward handshake always reminded him of shaking hands with a small child. He noticed that their eyes kept jumping from his face to his shoulder. He must have looked quite a mess.

"What happened to you, Brother Joseph?" said the bald man.

"The truth is," said Jacob, "I don't know what happened. I woke up in a forest, surrounded by nothing but trees. I was left for dead with no money or identification. They must have taken it."

The other man approached him now. "*Who* must have taken it? Who attacked you?" This man spoke with a French accent.

"I don't know. I only remember certain details. I know I came to Germany to visit family in Strasbourg. I was on my way back to Hamburg to leave for America. I had the taxi stop at a small village so I could get something to eat. It's all I remember. I don't even recall how I ended up here in Frankfurt. I only know I need to get home to America and now I can't."

The two men glanced at each other as if trying to figure out whether they believed the story. Then the bald man looked at him.

"We must get you to a hospital."

"No," said Jacob. "Please, I don't need that."

The two Brothers looked surprised.

"I'm not hurt that bad. I dressed the wounds myself. It's not as serious as it looks."

"But you don't remember anything," said the bald man. "You might have a head injury. We should take you."

The Frenchman put his hand on the other man's shoulder, as if to stop him. "I think I understand," he said. Then he turned to face Jacob and motioned for him to follow. "Joseph, come with me. You must be exhausted."

Jacob followed the Frenchman toward an arched hallway as the bald man watched quietly.

As they proceeded down the hall, the Frenchman patted him on the back.

"I'm Jacques," he said. "I will be here only a few days, but there may be ways to help you. Tell me, what is your last name, Joseph?"

"Gratz. Joseph Gratz."

"Ah, a Jew, as I suspected! Don't worry, so am I. It's one of the reasons I'm leaving. Did you know there's another lodge in Frankfurt called L'Aurore Naissant? It was founded by the Grand Orient in Paris. I'm afraid our kind is becoming—how do you say—more alienated in most lodges. And anywhere else for that matter. But there we are welcome. Here, not so much."

"But isn't this an American lodge?"

"Yes, yes," said Jacques. "But it seems the Freemasons are fighting to show that they are not an anti-Christian organization. And now they go to the other extreme to prove it. Besides, American or not, we are in Germany, my friend. I can smell change happening as we speak."

The Frenchman didn't know how right he was. Jacob followed him into a large study. The room was classic Victorian, with four maroon leather armchairs surrounding an oval mahogany coffee table. To the left were at least five aisles of bookshelves that seemed to go on indefinitely. He felt safe in here for now. The police wouldn't think to look here, and any newspaper articles about him wouldn't be out yet.

"This is our library," said Jacques. "Please, have a seat."

Jacob took the armchair closest to him, while the Frenchman sat across from him.

He looked at Jacques' apron.

"Are you an apprentice?"

Jacques smiled. "No, no," he said. "I am a Grand Master. In Germany, we wear the white aprons to remind us that we are all lifelong apprentices. And yet, some of us have already forgotten."

"But it's a noble gesture," said Jacob.

"Yes, I suppose," said Jacques. "And now, let us speak of your predicament."

Just then, a noise came from the far end of the room, from behind the bookshelves. Jacob heard footsteps approaching, and an elderly man emerged from the third aisle. He assumed the man was a librarian. Whoever he was, he waved to Jacques and left the room.

The Frenchman looked concerned. "If he heard us out in the hallway," he said, "we will get no help here."

"We?"

"You are not the only one hoping to go to America. I have been making plans myself. I can get you there, my friend, but it will not be through this lodge. They are too concerned about protecting themselves now. We must go to L'Aurore Naissant. For today, and maybe for a few days after, I hope you will consider my home yours. I live nearby."

It was as if this man were an angel sent to help him. Jacob had never felt such gratitude, though he was still nervous about spending any more time in Germany. He certainly couldn't afford to stay long. He graciously accepted Jacques' offer, and followed him out of the building and across the street to a pub. He explained that he had no money, but the Frenchman insisted.

Jacob hadn't realized just how hungry he was. He practically inhaled his meal—a platter Jacques recommended that included a massive portion of schnitzel with mushroom gravy and a side of spaetzle and green beans. After the meal, they walked to Jacques' apartment, which was less than a mile away.

When they arrived, the Frenchman showed him to his room.

"It's small, but I hope it will meet your needs for a few days."

"It's absolutely perfect," said Jacob. "I can't thank you enough." He meant it—especially since he was expecting to have to camp out somewhere. "When do you think we'll be able to leave for America?"

"My contact with the tickets should arrive in three days," said Jacques. "A ship leaves from Hamburg on Tuesday."

"Tuesday," Jacob said. "Great." He tried to say it in a hopeful way. He didn't want to appear ungrateful, but he was wondering how he'd survive till then without being discovered.

"My friend, I need to tell you something." Jacques must have sensed his concern. "When you told Brother Lawrence that you did not want to go to the hospital, it was obvious to me that you did not want to be recognized here in Germany."

Jacob was about to say something—though he wasn't sure what yet—but Jacques held up a hand to stop him.

"I do not need to know why," said Jacques. "You're an American, you were attacked, and you want to get back to America. That is good enough for me. We take an oath as Freemasons. Short of murder, we ask no questions of a Brother in need. If you need to stay hidden, you can remain here until it is safe to go."

Jacob nodded his head in gratitude.

"Are we good?" said Jacques.

Jacob knew the Frenchman was really asking if he'd committed murder. "We're good," he said. He hated lying to Jacques, but there was no choice. And in a way, he wasn't lying. After all, the only technical murder he'd committed, the hooded man, had been carried out in self-defense.

On one hand, Jacob was relieved to have someone he could trust who didn't press him for answers, not to mention a room with a warm bed. But on the other hand, he wondered what Jacques would do if he found out the truth.

Over the next few days, Jacob made himself at home as Jacques went about his daily routine, running out each day for groceries or doing other errands. Every time Jacques came home, Jacob would check to see if his benevolent host acted strangely toward him. So far, he hadn't. Instead, Jacques shared details about his life, telling Jacob about his involvement in the Great War, and of his struggles making a living in Western Europe. Apparently he had cousins in New York and was making plans for a permanent visit. Jacob wished he could share more with Jacques. It would have been nice to have someone to talk to about what he was going through, and about his family. But he knew he couldn't. And so, he was alone in his thoughts most of the time.

On the third day, Jacques received a call and left in a hurry. He simply said, "Wait here" as he ran out the door. Jacob wondered if perhaps someone had tipped him off. Or perhaps, more likely, it was the call about the tickets. After a few hours had passed, Jacob became concerned. Then, by the early evening, he began to really worry. He knew Jacques wouldn't have ditched him; he would have at least confronted him. Jacob wondered if perhaps something had gone wrong, and Jacques might be in some kind of trouble.

After a half hour, a loud knock startled him. It wasn't Jacques. He had a key, and wouldn't have banged on the door like that. He thought it best not to answer. Then he heard a voice he didn't recognize yell through the door.

"Joseph! I know you're in there. Please open the door."

Shit! Could Jacques have called the police?

The man spoke broken English. Jacob couldn't place the accent.

"Joseph!" The man kept knocking.

Jacob decided to play along and called back through the door. "Who are you?"

"A friend. Please. Open the door. There is little time."

A friend? Something wasn't right here.

"What is it you want?" said Jacob.

There was no answer.

Jacob listened through the door, but couldn't hear anything.

"Are you still there?" said Jacob.

He couldn't tell if the man was still there, or if he'd left. He ran to the front window and looked out. There was a black car out front. He couldn't see anyone, though. Just as he tiptoed back to the front door, he heard a car door open and close. He waited and listened for the engine to start, but there was nothing.

Then a newspaper slid under the door.

Jacob picked it up and froze. His face—or rather a hand-drawn picture of his deceased alter ego, was on the right column of the front page. Jacob mentally translated the headline:

Strange Double Murder in Karlsruhe

"They want to question you," said the man on the other side of the door. "They know you're here in Frankfurt. Jacques sent me. I am to get you to safety."

Jacob looked again at the paper. It was from Saturday. Today was Monday. Could Jacques have just discovered this?

"Where is Jacques?" said Jacob. He wondered if someone had captured Jacques and somehow got information out of him. After all, why would Jacques still help him after seeing this?

"He is in trouble," said the man. "Please! There is little time."

Something about the desperation in the man's voice told Jacob he was sincere. And besides, if he were from the police or the government, they would have broken down the door by now. Jacob unlocked the door and opened it slowly.

The man pushed himself inside. He seemed to be out of breath. He looked to be in his sixties, with grey hair and a mustache. He wore loose-fitting casual slacks and a black sweater.

"I'm sorry to disturb you," said the man. "I am a friend of Jacques."

"Is he okay?"

"I fear he is not. I can explain on the way. You must come with me."

"Come where? What happened?"

"I'm to take you to Hamburg. It's at least a day's drive. The ship leaves tomorrow morning."

"Are you the man with the tickets?"

"No, but I do have a ticket for you. I can explain in the car. Please! We must hurry!"

He followed the man to the black motorcar that was waiting outside. The back door was already open, and Jacob climbed in. He noticed afterward that the front passenger seat was missing. In no time, they were moving.

"This looks like a taxi," said Jacob.

"It *is* a taxi. I'm a taxi driver, but also a fellow Brother."

"What happened to Jacques?"

"Brother Jacques arrived at our lodge in a terrible state. He said he had been spotted on the street and ran. You see, my friend, there are many people looking for Jacques—the same ones that are looking for me. Only they do not know my face. That's my advantage. The government does not like us very much."

"And why is that?"

"They believe we were part of a conspiracy to—how you say—undermine Germany during the war. This is nonsense, of course."

"And where is Jacques now?"

"We are working to get him across the border into France. He left me a ticket for you with instructions to take you to Hamburg."

"Isn't he coming?"

"No, he would never make it."

"There's no way to get the other ticket to him in time?"

"I'm afraid there is no other ticket, my friend. There never was. Always there was only one ticket, never two. He told me about your unfortunate story. He wanted you to have it. He knew he would never make it onto the ship."

Jacob sank back in his seat. He couldn't believe the generosity of the man he had never really known—the man who had stuck his neck out for him, even after learning of his act. And now *this* man was driving him halfway across the country.

"What do I call you?" said Jacob.

"Call me Marco, my friend."

"Well, Marco, I owe my life to you and Jacques. I don't know how I can even thank you."

"There is no need," said Marco. "Jacques has helped me. I help you. You can help someone else. We'll try to get you to safety. We have arranged for a chaperone to meet you in New York."

Jacob picked up the newspaper, which he'd brought with him.

"Did Jacques see this paper?"

"Yes," said Marco. "This man was your brother. Jacques says you tried to protect him, no?"

"Something like that," said Jacob.

"But the bullets," said Marco. "They were the same for both bodies. And very strange bullets, no?"

Jacob tried to think of an answer.

"Marco," he said, "there's something I need to tell you." He paused to gather his thoughts. "I work for a secret branch of the American government. I was here with my brother. We were investigating Adolf Hitler, but our operation was compromised. Like you and Jacques, we had people after us. The whole thing went wrong."

He didn't elaborate any further, and waited for Marco's reaction.

"I know," said Marco.

"You do?" This certainly wasn't the reaction he expected.

"While you slept," said Marco, "Brother Jacques inspected your gun and those other items you carry with you. They are very strange, I must say. Even the watches. And the gun is very unusual. He suspected you were some kind of American spy. He is smart, Brother Jacques. Lucky for you, we like Americans. And now that I know it was Hitler you sought, it is even better."

"Nobody can know about this," said Jacob.

"Do not worry," said Marco. "Jacques does not ask questions, and neither do I. I am sorry for your brother."

"Thank you," said Jacob. "I mean that."

"They are looking for you everywhere for days now. Of course, nobody knew where you were hidden."

"Why?"

"Because of the murders, of course."

"No, I mean why would Jacques continue to risk his life to help me, knowing I'm a spy? He couldn't have known for sure."

"Ah," said Marco, "he says you have an honest face."

"And apparently a very famous face right now. I'll never make it onto that ship."

"Ha! Do not worry," said Marco.

Easy for *him* to say.

Jacob couldn't imagine what Marco had in mind. As he thought about Jacques and Marco, he thought back again to Pop's statement about what happens when things seem too good to be true. But maybe in this case, Pop was wrong. At least he hoped so.

Over the next hour, Marco updated him on all the political events and regional issues over the last several years. In turn, he shared stories of America, taking care to stay in line with the times. Marco seemed particularly interested in the prohibition movement that was going on in the states, marveling at the stupidity of the idea. After a while they both got quiet, and Jacob stared out the window, daydreaming about being back home with Kim. He prayed that he'd soon be in more familiar territory in Philadelphia.

He must have dozed off, but he was awoken when the taxi swerved suddenly to the right.

"We are being followed," said Marco.

"Followed?" said Jacob. "By who?"

"I don't know."

As Marco sped up and switched abruptly to the left lane, Jacob turned around to look. Sure enough, there was a black car following, and another one behind it.

"There are two of them," said Jacob.

"I know. I will try to lose them."

Jacob wondered if they were after him or Marco. Could someone have spotted him getting in the taxi? Either way, if he and Marco were stopped, it wouldn't bode well for him.

Just then, he was thrown across the back seat as Marco pulled off the road to his right and onto a dirt road. As he was being tossed all over, Jacob looked back to see the two cars, still on the main road, slowing down. There was some kind of old-time pickup truck ahead of them, carrying boxes of produce or something. Marco must have used it as a decoy.

"They're not following," said Jacob. "Were they government vehicles?"

"No," said Marco. "Not government and not police. These people I know not."

"Could you see their faces?"

"I'm afraid no."

For a minute, Jacob wondered if maybe these people were in league with the strange hooded man he'd shot, sent by God-knows-who to stop him. Whoever they were, though, they didn't seem to be following.

They continued along the dirt road, and, after about a mile, Jacob noticed a small market on a road just to the right.

"Pull over there," he said, pointing out the grocery shop to Marco.

"Is it a time for shopping?" said Marco.

"Trust me," said Jacob.

Marco said nothing, but did as Jacob asked and drove to the right toward the market. As they pulled into the small lot beside the market, Jacob looked around. There were no other cars in sight. He directed Marco to park behind the building so as not to be seen.

He was about to get out of the car, when Marco said, "Wait!"

He sat still as Marco reached into a box that was sitting on the front passenger side of the car, and pulled out a paper bag.

"You'll need this," said Marco.

Jacob took the bag from Marco. Inside was a pair of glasses, a fake mustache, a tube of glue, and a jar of hair grease. So that's how they planned to get him on the ship!

"My brother is an actor," said Marco.

Jacob put on the mustache and glasses, and greased his hair. He couldn't imagine what he must look like.

After getting a nod of approval from Marco, he stepped out of the car and Marco followed him.

Once inside the shop, Jacob moved quickly. He grabbed a small wooden basket and filled it with any useful items he could find, including sugar, a bottle of vinegar, flour, butter, several bottles of wine, and a container of fuel. He also threw two apples in the basket. He could see Marco in the front of the store, looking at him as if he were crazy.

As Jacob approached the cashier, he looked at Marco.

"You do have money, I hope," he said.

Marco shook his head in disbelief, but paid the cashier.

"What?" said Marco, looking at him. "Are you going to start cooking now?"

Jacob smiled. "Something like that. Let's go."

They got back in the taxi, and Marco headed up the road back toward the main road.

"Do you think they'll still be there?" said Jacob.

As if to answer his question, the two cars appeared out of nowhere. They were coming from the field opposite the market, where the dirt road was.

Marco stepped on the gas and the chase was on again.

Jacob emptied the contents of the grocery bags onto the back seat. Several bottles rolled onto the floor.

"Do you have a knife?" he asked.

The cars were gaining ground.

"No," said Marco, as he shifted lanes to avoid another car. Then he added, "Wait, there's a screwdriver in the trunk. What are you doing?"

"Trying to remember college chemistry."

Jacob leaned over the rear seat, and looked in the cargo area. Just then, shots came firing through the rear window. He ducked as glass shattered everywhere. The taxi swerved, knocking him off balance.

"Are you okay?" he yelled up front to Marco.

"Yes," said Marco. "I'm fine. Never better."

He tried to lean over the back seat again, as quickly as he could. He grabbed the screwdriver and a tire pump next to it, and fell back on the seat just as more shots were fired. The taxi shifted again as Marco got into the left lane.

"Who the hell are those guys?" said Jacob.

He frantically worked in the back seat as Marco zigzagged from lane to lane. He used the screwdriver to tear open the seat covering and pulled off a strip of cloth. He emptied half of one of the wine bottles, and then poured in a mixture of sugar, flour, butter, gasoline, and vinegar. He stuffed the cloth into the top of the bottle and took out the box of matches Max had given him. Thank God Bradley hadn't confiscated it.

"Slow down," he yelled to Marco.

"Are you crazy?"

"No, let him pull beside you. Trust me."

Marco slowed down, and the car behind them caught up and rammed them from behind. Jacob was thrown onto the floor. Marco picked up speed again.

"He's coming up beside us," said Marco.

Jacob jumped up and pushed open the side window. Dammit, it didn't open all the way. He kicked it out, just as the driver caught up beside them. As he watched the driver, a middle-aged man with a mustache, aim a gun at them, Marco swerved again, throwing him back.

"Go faster!" said Jacob.

As Marco picked up speed again, Jacob sat up to see the man next to them return his focus to his driving. This would be his one shot. Just as he was lined up with the driver, he lit the cloth and threw the bottle into the open window.

Immediately, it exploded, and he watched as the car filled up with smoke and veered off the road.

"Ha ha!" said Marco. "You're a genius!"

Just then, the other car rammed them from behind.

"No, I'm an idiot," said Jacob, as he reached into his coat pocket. He'd forgotten he still had Malcolm's gun. He leaned out the open window and aimed at the driver's front window and fired. The glass shattered, and the driver struggled to keep control of the car. Jacob kept firing until he was out of bullets, but that was apparently good enough, as the driver went off the road and right into a tree.

Exhausted, Jacob leaned back in his seat.

"Good work, my friend," said Marco.

"And we still have two bottles of wine left," said Jacob.

"My curiosity is piqued," said Marco. "What were the apples for?"

"The apples," said Jacob, holding them up, "are for us to eat."

Chapter 44
Bon Voyage

Including several stops for fuel, the unexpected altercation, and a short break in a small village for food, the trip to Hamburg had taken about eight hours. Jacob kept the disguise on, just in case they were stopped. As they approached the docks, Jacob saw a large white sign that said *HAPAG—Hamburg-Amerika*. Just beyond it was a massive steamship—the one that would take him to New York. Along the side of the vessel, he could see the ship's name, S.S. Reliance. According to Marco, the trip would take six days. He had about two hours before the huge ocean liner set sail, but there were already throngs of people waiting to board. Most of them were immigrants, although according to Marco, some of them may have been Americans visiting family in Europe.

Marco pulled alongside the ship and got out of the car. Jacob heard the trunk open and stepped outside, where Marco was awaiting with a large suitcase.

"You will need this," said Marco. "Nobody journeys across the sea without luggage. You'll find some basic belongings and twenty-five dollars in American money. It's a requirement for entry into the country. As for your passenger inspection, it was taken care of when we bought the ticket. They should give you no trouble."

"You've thought of everything," said Jacob. "I don't know what to say. You and Jacques have saved my life."

"And others have saved ours. I wish you the best, my friend. And don't forget, Brother Phillip will be waiting for you in New York. He can vouch for your identity if needed. And remember what I said earlier. You don't want to get on the immigrant barges. God be with you, my friend."

Jacob shook Marco's outstretched hand, thanked him profusely one last time, and walked toward the masses waiting to board.

Before joining the chaos, he knelt down and opened the suitcase. On top, there was a black overcoat. He looked around to make sure nobody could see what he was doing. He took off his trench coat, then took out the Kronos devices and stuck them between two layers of clothing near the bottom of the suitcase. He noticed the twenty-five dollars in cash wedged in the side, and put it in his pocket. Then he put on the black coat and quickly switched the gun to his new coat pocket. He'd have to get rid of it before boarding the ship. He certainly couldn't bring a murder weapon aboard, and especially not one from the future. The watches and cell phones were still in the other pocket, so he took those as well. Finally, he stuffed the trench coat into the suitcase and shut the latch.

He prayed they wouldn't check his luggage upon boarding. Marco didn't seem to think they would, but if they did, he'd say the devices were toy flying saucers for his nephews, and hope they bought it. The cops in Karlsruhe did. Satisfied with his plan, he picked up the suitcase and started to walk toward the mob of people ahead. Then he remembered—the gun. He had to ditch it somewhere. He noticed a small pier to his left, just before the entrance to the main docks. He walked casually onto the pier, looking around to make sure nobody was watching. Quickly, he dropped the gun into the water, followed by the two cell phones and the watches. Then he made his way to join the crowd at the docks.

After he'd spent about an hour trying to stay upright amid the hysteria, a loud horn blared, and the ship's crew began letting passengers onboard. When it was his turn, he was relieved to see there was no luggage check, only a series of questions that he could easily answer. There was also a brief medical exam, which surprised him. Luckily, they just took his temperature, checked his heart, and looked in his eyes, nose, and mouth. They didn't notice the wound. After that, he got in line with the others.

He noticed some guards up ahead checking each passenger. He wasn't sure if this was routine. He could see them looking at each passenger's ticket and then at their faces. They had a sheet of paper with them. Were they looking for him?

He tried to blend in as the guards got closer.

Before long, they were checking the old woman in front of him. He was next.

As a guard approached him, Jacob tried to look relaxed.

The man looked at his ticket, then stared at him. He hoped the mustache was on right.

"Step forward," said the guard in perfect American English, pulling him out of line.

Jacob was sweating now, and he hoped the moisture wouldn't melt the glue.

"You're in the wrong line," said the guard. "Second class is over there." He pointed to another line to the right.

"My mistake," said Jacob. He could barely contain his smile as he made his way to the other line.

When he finally got to his cabin, there was a passage regulations brochure resting on the small desk by the bed. He sat on the bed and skimmed through it. The only information of any consequence was that the ship apparently would make stops in Southampton and Cherbourg en route to New York, but that didn't bother him. Another statement caught his eye:

> *In consequence of the American prohibition laws, alcoholic drinks can only be obtained on the westbound voyage to New York on the steamers of the Hamburg-Amerika line and United American lines up to the three-mile limit.*

He wasn't planning on purchasing alcohol anyway, but the notice was one more surreal reminder of the time period he was in.

He unpacked his luggage and pulled the Kronos devices out from between the clothes, placing them in the pocket of his coat, which he laid over a chair. After checking the cabin over, he collapsed on the bed, exhausted. Before long, the loud horn sounded and the ship was off on its journey. And for the first time in a while, he slept soundly.

When he awoke, he was disoriented. He figured some air would probably help. He put on his coat and stumbled out of the cabin, making his way to the deck. Once outside, he found an isolated spot and leaned over the rails, looking out at the vast ocean in solitude. He had slept so soundly that he wasn't even sure they'd made any stops yet.

As the wind blew his hair back, he reached into his coat pocket and pulled out the two Kronos devices. He wasn't sure why he thought they might magically work all of a sudden, but he tried each one anyway, one last time. Nothing. What he wouldn't give to have never used the device to begin with, even though the first time was quite by accident. Or was it?

Things still weren't adding up—not only the trip to Dachau, but also the mysterious box with Pop's journal; Finkel and Bradley being in Paris and then pretty much running the world; and then people trying to kill him in this time period. And who the hell was the Ring of Seven? He thought back to what Malcolm had said about this being much bigger than he could ever imagine. He wondered what that could mean. Some kind of government conspiracy? Something involving aliens? Perhaps he'd never know.

He looked out at the endless sea. Then he looked down at the two Kronos devices still in his hands. With all his might, he threw the first Kronos device as far as he could. He watched as it floated for a moment and then disappeared beneath the waves. Then he threw the other one.

"Good riddance, you bastards," he said under his breath.

No sooner had he said that than he felt a hand smothering his face from behind. He struggled to breathe and felt a moist cloth against his face. It smelled like cough syrup. He tried not to inhale, and in one motion, lifted his right arm and turned around, lowering his elbow over the man's hands and up hard against his chin. He didn't recognize the man, who was burly, with short brown hair. Quickly, he pushed the man's head back against a metal pole, dazing him. For good measure, he rammed the man's skull against the pole once more, and the man fell to the wooden deck. Jacob pinned him down. The burly guy struggled, but Jacob slammed his fist into his face and grabbed his collar.

"Who the hell are you people?" said Jacob. "Why are you still after me?"

Still no response.

"Talk, damn you!"

This time, the man smiled at him with a wide bloody grin, as if out of spite. He kept struggling, but Jacob punched him again, and then got closer to his face. "Listen to me," he said, shaking him. "It's over. Hitler will live. I won't be killing him in this life or any other. It's done."

He wasn't even sure if the man understood a word he was saying, and at this point he didn't care.

All of a sudden, the man coughed and tried to speak.

"Not...over," he muttered in broken English.

So, the bastard did understand him after all.

"Wait a minute," said Jacob. "That's it! It's not over! Otherwise you wouldn't still be chasing me. You want me dead for a reason. And it's not just revenge, is it? You're afraid of me. I'm not powerless at all, am I?"

The man kept trying to get up, but Jacob slammed his fist hard against his swollen, bloody face.

"I should thank you," said Jacob. "You've given me new hope. I owe you the world, my friend."

And with that, Jacob dragged the guy to his feet, looked around to make sure nobody was around, and tossed him over the railing into the waiting sea.

Then, he returned to his cabin to write a letter—the most important letter of his life.

Chapter 45
Brotherly Love

It had been a long six days. For most people, six days at sea would have been an opportunity to socialize, read, and relax. But for Jacob, it seemed like a year. Mostly he spent the time alone, except for meals, when he made small talk with people. A few young women had approached him, but he always cut the conversation short and said he had to leave to meet someone. And when he was in his cabin, his emotions would ebb and flow, from a steadfast sense of purpose to a feeling of self-loathing to an overwhelming sense of loss for the only things in life that he loved.

But now, as he disembarked from the ship in New York, it was back to reality. The scene that greeted him was sheer chaos, as throngs of people were herded like cattle into rows. He made sure to follow Marco's advice and avoid the immigration line near the barges that led to Ellis Island. The last thing he wanted was to begin a life that would involve any interaction with people on a meaningful level. The name of the game now was to stay out of the way.

As he walked away from the immigration line toward Customs, he noticed two men in suits along the far wall staring at him. He wondered if one of them might be Brother Phillip. Just as he started to approach them, though, they turned and walked away. Strange. Perhaps their interest in him had just been his imagination.

He made his way to Customs and explained his situation to the officer. He said he'd been in Germany visiting relatives and was meeting someone here. As he was talking, a well-dressed, middle-aged man in a hat, with reddish-brown hair and a mustache, approached and said something to the officer. Then, the man in the hat motioned for Jacob to follow him.

"I'm Phillip," he said with a slight Irish accent. "You must be Brother Joseph." Jacob breathed a sigh of relief, as Phillip held out his hand and they exchanged the Masonic handshake. "My car is just outside."

When they exited the station, Jacob saw a shiny black car with wood trim and a white roof.

"Is that what I think it is?" said Jacob.

"It's a Model T," said Phillip. "I just bought it last year. They've been around forever, though; you must have been gone a while."

"Too long," said Jacob, as he climbed into the passenger seat and threw his suitcase in the back.

Phillip started the engine, which sounded like a Mack truck. "You can take off the disguise now," he said.

Jacob was surprised, but he gladly pulled off the mustache, as painful as it was. And the glasses were hurting his eyes.

"By the way," said Jacob, "I'm surprised they didn't ask for my passport."

Phillip looked at him and laughed. "You *have* been gone long," he said. "They stopped doing that three years ago."

As they drove through Manhattan, Jacob couldn't get over the hustle and bustle of the city. Even in 1924 it was built up with tall buildings, only it was much cleaner than in his time, and there were fewer cars. He looked around in awe at the scene before him. After several blocks, he noticed that a crowd was forming on the corner, everyone staring up at the sky. He stuck his head out the window and looked up to see what they were looking at. He couldn't believe his eyes. There was a giant zeppelin, floating high above them. He wondered if it was here for some kind of fair. It was quite a sight, even for him, so he could imagine how the others felt.

As he looked around, he noticed that most of the men, and even the women, wore hats—and the women all wore long dresses. Many wore gloves as well. Everyone was so well dressed. Times were certainly different.

The road out of New York was even more surprising. The turnpike hadn't been built yet, so getting places took much longer. Eventually they ended up on York Road, which Phillip mentioned was also referred to as King's Highway.

Jacob noticed the zeppelin again, flying above them on the left side. He was surprised at how fast it was moving. Then again, his perception was all relative, as they were only going about 25 miles an hour, which was about top speed in these days.

Just then, he was startled by a loud bang on the roof of the car. Then another. At first he thought it was a backfire of some sort. He looked at Phillip.

"Is that normal?"

"No," said Phillip. He looked alarmed.

Jacob looked up at the roof to see what was going on.

Suddenly, there was another deafening bang, and a small hole blew open in the roof, right where Jacob was looking.

"Someone's shooting at us!" said Phillip.

Jacob climbed to the back and looked out the left window.

"It's the zeppelin!" he said.

"Are you sure?" said Phillip.

"Go faster!"

Jacob felt the car pick up a little.

"This is as fast as it goes," said Phillip.

Another shot rang out, and Jacob darted back to the front seat and ducked down.

"Go off road," he said. "There, to the right."

He held on tight as Phillip drove into a wooded area. Jacob looked back to see the zeppelin turning their way. He was being thrown all over as Phillip plowed through the woods trying to avoid trees.

More shots rang out. Another one penetrated the vinyl roof. Jacob wished he had his gun right about now. Then another shot hit right between Jacob and Phillip.

"We need to jump out!" said Jacob. "Before we get to that clearing ahead. Put it in neutral."

"Okay," said Phillip. "On the count of three."

"One," said Jacob.

He waited until they reached a downward slope.

"Two..." he added.

Another shot fired, but missed.

"Now!"

Jacob opened the door and tumbled out onto the dirt while the car kept moving. He heard several loud bangs as the zeppelin kept shooting at the Model T.

He couldn't see if Phillip had gotten out, but he assumed so. He looked ahead to see the car rolling into the clearing—the zeppelin floating just above it.

Jacob tried to stay hidden in the trees. He noticed something small and black falling from the zeppelin, directly over the Model T. As soon as it hit the car—whatever it was—there was a huge explosion, and the car burst into flames.

He stayed down, praying Phillip had escaped, and that they were both sufficiently hidden by the trees.

Just then, he heard a noise to his left. Leaves shuffling.

"Pssst," said a voice.

It was Phillip.

"Stay down," said Jacob as quietly as he could.

Jacob peeked through the trees. The zeppelin was still there, hovering over what was left of the car. He wondered if whoever it was would try to search the forest.

After a few long minutes, the zeppelin began to move. They were in luck. It appeared to be leaving.

Phillip ran up to him.

"Stay down," said Jacob.

"That's a German zeppelin," said Phillip. "Why are they after you?"

"There was some political unrest while I was there. I'll explain later. For now, we need to stay down and listen for noises. They may circle back."

Apparently, Jacques and Marco hadn't told Phillip everything.

Jacob crawled further in, behind a large rock, and Phillip followed him.

"It'll be dark in an hour," said Jacob. "We should keep hidden and then walk back to the road under cover of night."

"Agreed," said Phillip.

Jacob wondered who these people were. He thought back to the two men who were staring at him at the train station. And to the thug who had attacked him on the ship. Somehow they must have gotten wind of his disguise. But how? Could Marco have tipped them off? That wouldn't make any sense, unless he had been tortured for the information. Then Jacob remembered the market. The two cars had resumed chasing them as soon as they had left the market. The drivers must have seen him and Marco pull into the lot. Could someone have been watching with binoculars and seen him putting on the disguise?

The more Jacob thought about it, the more this seemed the most likely scenario. The bigger question, though, was who these people were. They certainly weren't government officials, and they didn't act like secret police—not that they even existed yet.

Soon night began to fall, and it seemed that the zeppelin was long gone. Jacob motioned to Phillip, and they made their way to the road.

"We'll need to hitchhike," said Jacob.

As they approached the main road, Jacob looked around. There was no sign of the zeppelin. He held out his thumb as they walked. He heard what sounded like a wolf howling.

"Are there wolves around here?" he said.

"Plenty," said Phillip. "Coyotes, too."

Jacob shook his head and laughed. After all he'd been through, it would be just his luck to be attacked by a wolf.

Soon, an old-time vegetable truck pulled over. Jacob tried to stop thinking of everything as old-time, but it was difficult.

"Where are you headed?" said the driver. He looked like he was missing half his teeth.

"Philadelphia," said Phillip. "We're trying to get to City Hall."

"You're in luck then," said the man. "Hop back there with the carrots and potatoes and stuff. I'm headed to the docks to make a delivery."

"Docks?" said Jacob.

"Second and Walnut," the man yelled out. "Bookbinders."

"It's a seafood restaurant," said Phillip.

Jacob laughed, as he hoisted himself into the truck bed. "Yes, I know." At least one thing was familiar.

As he leaned back against the crates of vegetables, Jacob felt especially vulnerable out in the open. Even though it was dark, he wondered if they could be spotted from the air, should the zeppelin reappear. It also dawned on him that his suitcase had been in the Model T when it exploded. At least he still had the twenty-five dollars.

After several hours, having passed through Lambertville, New Hope, Lahaska, and Willow Grove, they entered North Philadelphia, and then York Road became Broad Street. It was unusual to see Temple University there in the same old spot, except in much nicer surroundings.

After another twenty minutes or so, Jacob could see the imposing gothic Masonic Temple, just ahead at 1 North Broad Street, opposite City Hall. The building looked spectacular illuminated in the night sky.

The vegetable truck pulled into an adjacent parking lot and came to a stop with a jerk.

The driver climbed out and opened the back of the truck bed.

"Will this do ya?" he said.

"Perfect," said Phillip.

Jacob and Phillip both thanked the man, and climbed down onto the street. Jacob then followed Phillip across the street and toward the grand entrance gate of the temple. The doors were huge; they had to be twenty feet high.

"If the building is anything like the doors," Jacob said, "it must be pretty impressive."

Phillip smiled. "Seeing anything in this building is like taking a crash course in architecture. The doors are Norman. They're six inches thick."

As Phillip opened the massive doors and they walked inside, Jacob felt like he had entered some grand castle. In the center of two magnificent marble staircases were two large columns and a smaller set of steps heading down toward a bronze set of doors. As they descended the steps, he noticed two huge bronze sphinxes that sat along the sides. He looked up under the grand staircase at a circular gold-framed painting and two Masonic seals.

"What's that round painting in the center?" said Jacob.

"It represents the four cardinal virtues," said Phillip. "Next to it are the Seal of the Grand Lodge and the Great Seal of Pennsylvania."

Jacob looked again at the painting and recited the virtues out loud: "Temperance, Fortitude, Prudence, and Justice."

The four virtues—the pillars of wisdom, according to scripture—were drilled into the heads of all Freemasons. Now that he looked closer, he could see each one portrayed in the painting, a sobering reminder that if he'd used a little more prudence, he might not be here in this situation. But now he'd need all four virtues in abundance.

Next, they entered through the bronze doors into a hallway that reminded him of the Hall of Mirrors in Versailles.

"This is the Grand Foyer," said Phillip. "It runs the length of the building to the museum at the far end. These portraits that line the walls are our Right Worshipful Past Grand Masters."

As he looked at the black and white diamond pattern on the floors, combined with the golden carved ceiling and the arched hallway lined with oil paintings and Grecian columns, Jacob felt as if he were in the Louvre or some priceless museum.

After a few more yards, he followed Phillip back the way they had come, up to the Grand Staircase.

"We'll stay on this floor," said Phillip. "Just ahead to the right is the office of the Worshipful Grand Master."

Jacob followed Philip toward the Grand Master's office. This was the person he needed to talk to. He didn't have many needs. He only had one simple request of his Freemason brothers.

"Do you think he's in?"

Phillip smiled. "I know he's in. He's me."

Surprised but relieved, Jacob followed Phillip into the office.

"This political unrest," said Phillip, as he sat behind the desk. "What was your involvement? What was it that caused them to hunt you even here?"

"The truth?" said Jacob.

"It would be preferable."

"Well for one, my name isn't Joseph. It's Jacob Newman. I work for the American government—an organization I'm sure you've never heard of called the Central Intelligence Agency, or CIA."

Phillip didn't bat an eye. "And what part of the government, may I ask, does this CIA belong to."

"The issue isn't what part," said Jacob. "It's when."

Jacob took an envelope out of his coat pocket. It contained the letter he had written in his cabin using the SS Reliance stationary. He handed it to Phillip.

He watched as Phillip opened the envelope, unfolded the letter, and slowly read it, digesting every last paragraph. He saw Phillip's eyes widen as he read.

"Please hold onto that," said Jacob. "It's the only thing I ask of the Brotherhood. There will be those who will try to obtain it at all costs. But it must be kept safe. The specific instructions are on the back."

Phillip continued reading. Then, when he was finished, he turned it over and read the reverse side. When he was done, he folded it back up and placed it in the envelope.

"Fine," said Phillip, matter-of-factly. "It will be done."

Jacob was astounded at Phillip's calm demeanor.

"Fine?" said Jacob. "That's it?" He thought maybe Phillip was humoring him and in reality believed that he was insane. He was waiting for the other shoe to drop.

"Yes, that's it," said Phillip. We'll do it."

"Are you sure you can keep it safe?"

Phillip smiled.

"For thousands of years," said Phillip, "the Brotherhood has kept some of the greatest treasures in antiquity safe, and, I might add, some of the world's most protected secrets. Some of them, Brother Jacob, would make even yours seem small in comparison, hard as it is to believe. You have no idea the things I've seen, even in *my* lifetime. My question to you, though, is what else you need of us. Where will you go?"

"I'll be okay," said Jacob. "I need nothing else."

"You know, you don't need to carry out what you say in the letter. We can help you."

Jacob shook his head. "No," he said. "Thank you. The instructions are all I ask."

The truth was, he couldn't afford to stay with anyone, or even interact with anyone. From now on, he would live his life on the streets as a homeless man, just doing what he needed to do to survive. The less he interfered with history, the better, even if it meant a life of hunger and solitude. He owed that to Kim, to Jessica and Ethan, to Malcolm, and all the others who deserved an unchanged life. He knew that any little interaction could have a ripple effect. He'd learned that the hard way.

After he shook Phillip's hand, he made his way up the corridor to the main entrance. And as he exited the huge doors into the night air, Jacob began his new life on the streets. He had some spare clothes and

274 EDWARD MILLER AND J. B. MANAS

twenty-five dollars to his name. That was about a week's salary in these days. He'd have to use it sparingly.

He continued up Broad Street and past Arch. Everything looked so different from the Philadelphia he remembered, and much more elegant, especially at night. For the first time, he could see how Broad Street had received its name, as he marveled at the grand boulevard that ran north and south through the city, with its gas-lit streetlights illuminating the way. He glanced at the cars passing by, engines chugging and huffing. For the first time, he could appreciate their beauty. As he walked past a black Chrysler Touring Car, a red Franklin, and a green Model T, all parked diagonally along the side of the street, it occurred to him that this experience was a car lover's dream. Except this was no dream. To him, it was more like a nightmare.

As he approached Race Street, he noticed a speakeasy on the corner. He'd almost forgotten about prohibition. He turned right and walked up Race, not exactly knowing what he was looking for. He just wanted to get familiar with the surroundings. As he passed an alley, he spotted a group of homeless people—he guessed they were called tramps in this day and age—standing around a fire of some sort.

It was at this moment, that he realized what his deepest fear was. He'd never really thought about it like this before. He'd always attributed the feeling to the tragedy of his upbringing, and to ideas he'd inherited from Pop, about needing family, and the importance of family. And maybe that was part of it. But, hidden beneath that was his fundamental and undeniable fear of being alone—and conversely, his need for camaraderie, for some kind of human connection. This from a man who spent much of his life traveling and searching for answers in the microcosms of science.

It was in this moment that he decided to walk down the alley toward the group of tramps.

As Jacob approached them, the faint smell of beef stew began to fill the air. He was starving by now. Then, something unexpected happened. One of the tramps came toward him with some kind of weapon.

He couldn't tell if it was a stick or a knife. It may have even been a cooking utensil.

"I'm not here to hurt you," said Jacob.

"That you ain't," said the raggedy-looking grey-haired man, holding up the weapon.

He was still several yards away, but Jacob could now see that it was a large carving knife he was holding.

"I only want to talk," said Jacob. "And I'm hungry. I can pay you."

"Pay us what?"

Jacob wasn't about to give up his only cash, but he had something better.

"I have a gold ring," he said.

Two other men from the group now joined the grey-haired man.

"Throw it over," said one of the other men—a tall, skinny guy with dark, curly hair.

"How do I know you won't take it and run?" said Jacob.

"Aye, you don't," said the grey-haired man.

This seemed like a good opportunity to earn their trust. Jacob pulled off his Masonic ring. He wouldn't need it anymore. He threw it on the ground ahead of him, and the tall, skinny guy picked it up.

Jacob watched as he examined it and then handed it to the other tramp—a short, fat man. Together, they looked like the number ten.

"It's real," said the fat man.

"How about the other one?" said the grey-haired man. He was pointing to Jacob's hand.

"That one's not for sale," said Jacob. "It's my wedding ring. I just lost my wife. It's all I have left of her."

At first, they all stared at him as if they were trying to make out whether he was for real. Then the grey-haired man lowered his weapon.

"I'm Billy," he said. "These here men are Clyde and Edgar. We ain't got much food, and I don't know what kinda misfortune befell ya, but the way I see it, you can join us."

As Jacob joined them to walk toward the others, the fat man, Edgar, tapped him on the shoulder.

"Here," said Edgar, handing him the Masonic ring. "We don't need your gold."

Jacob took the ring and slipped it back on. "I'll have to find another way to earn my keep," he said.

When they got to the fire, Clyde, the tall man, introduced Jacob to the others. There were about ten of them.

"This stranger is down on his luck," said Clyde, who was apparently the leader of the group. "He'll be joining us."

"We can't afford any more mouths to feed," yelled one man.

"We coulda said that when you joined us," said Billy.

The man put his head down as Clyde dipped a ladle into a large tin canister and poured the stew into a small can for Jacob.

"It smells good," said Jacob.

"It's Mulligan stew," said Clyde. "Made from whatever we can get our hands on. You're in luck today. There's meat in there."

Jacob was too hungry to respond. As he tilted the boiling hot concoction into his mouth, he savored every drop. Stew had never tasted so good, even if it did singe his throat.

Suddenly, a man came running up the alley from the same direction Jacob had come from.

"That's Herman!" said Billy.

"Roundup!" the man shouted. "Roundup!"

"He musta been nabbed and got himself free."

"Okay, men, get a wiggle on," said Clyde. "Everyone out of here!"

All at once, the whole crew began running toward the opposite end of the alley. Jacob followed them, but then turned back. There was something he had to do first, as much as he dreaded doing it.

Quickly he grabbed the large tin canister of stew that was on the fire. It was burning hot, but he forced his hands onto it, wincing, and tilted the makeshift kettle. He watched as the remaining stew poured onto the street. Then he braced himself and put his hands in the kettle, pressing them against the hot grease at the bottom as hard as he could. He'd never felt such excruciating pain, and screamed out as if that might help dull the sensation. Then he brought his greasy, melting hands to his face and pressed hard, as he continued yelling in agony. The sting was unbearable.

Just then, two policemen came running up the alley. Suddenly, Jacob felt a hand on his arm, pulling him. It was Billy!

"What in blue blazes are ya doin'?" said Billy.

Billy practically dragged him, and the two of them ran back up the alley to catch up with the others. Jacob glanced back to see the cops slowing down, but he kept running all the same. His face and hands felt like they were on fire.

Finally, he and Billy were near the end of the alley, approaching the cross street.

"They went to the right," said Billy.

He rounded the corner with Billy—right smack into two other police officers. Billy turned around and ran the other way, but just as Jacob turned to do the same, one of the officers grabbed hold of his coat. Before he could wrestle free, there was a heavy blow to the back of his head and he fell forward.

Jacob was disoriented. He must have blacked out, because when he opened his eyes, he wasn't in the alley anymore. He was lying on a bed. Everything was white. Then he felt someone shaking him.

As his eyes cleared, he could see a nurse looking down at him, and on the other side, a policeman. He was in a hospital!

"What's your name?" said the cop.

Jacob coughed. His head felt like a bowling ball. He shook his head.

"I...can't remember," he said. "How did I get here?"

"He took a strong blow to the head," said the nurse.

"He'll remember," said the cop.

"What happened?" said Jacob. His hands were all bandaged up. His face was apparently wrapped as well.

"Word has it you stuck your hands in a burning pot," said the cop. "Then you did up your face for good measure. Burnt your fingerprints too. What I want to know is why."

"I don't know what you're talking about," said Jacob. "Why would I have done that? What happened to me?"

"Officer," said the nurse, "he needs rest. Can't you question him later?"

"He's lying," said the cop. "Thirty years on the force, ma'am. I can tell these things."

"Well, after you hit him like that—"

"You were hanging with bums," said the cop, returning his attention to Jacob. "But you're not dressed like one; you're not dirty like one; and you have a wedding ring. Not only that, but a Masonic ring too, no less. My brother's a Mason. We checked with them, but of course, they said they don't know you."

"I have a wife?" said Jacob.

The cop threw up his hands. "I can do this all day," he said. "I'll tell you what. I'll get you started with a question. What kind of guy hangs with bums, wears fancy rings, and burns off his fingerprints and disfigures his face?"

"I don't know what you're talking about," said Jacob.

"Either a spy or a criminal, that's who. And I'd venture to say you're the latter. Who are you hiding from? Capone?"

Jacob shook his head. "I don't remember anything."

"Maybe he got kicked out of his house," said the nurse.

"People kicked out of houses don't burn their fingerprints and their face."

Jacob watched as the cop began pacing.

"I can't lock you up for vagrancy," said the cop. "And I can't prove any criminal activity. But you're not going to be on the streets, I can tell you that. Soon as you're able to leave, we're sending you to a shelter. And don't think about running away. You'll be easy to find."

The cop took a card out of his pocket and gave it to the nurse.

"As soon as he's healed," he said, "I want you to call me directly. My number is on the card."

After the cop had left, Jacob leaned his head back against the pillow. Everything hurt. So far, though, his ruse had worked. In a way, he wished it were true, and that he did have amnesia. But unfortunately, he remembered everything. Every little detail of his life. And now, once again, for the first time since his horrible childhood, he'd be headed to an institution in the system. But it was a necessary evil. Because he wasn't ready to die yet. There were a few things he needed to make sure of first.

Chapter 46
Helpless

The first few days in the shelter had taken some getting used to, but it wasn't as bad as Jacob had expected. The tears came at night, mostly, when he'd think of Kim and the family—reflecting on what might have been, and how he should have spent more time with them. Aside from that, his initial days there were fairly calm. He'd gotten to know a few people, and spent most of his waking hours helping with chores. He made a point, though, only to engage in small talk, and to never get too close to anyone.

Then, things got worse. Violent offenders, brought in from the streets, drunk on moonshine, would attack at random in the middle of the night. They'd steal anything they could, through force if they had to. That's how he lost his rings. Soon, weeks with little sleep turned into months—and months turned into years. It was an existence he wouldn't have wished on anyone, but it was unavoidable. When the Great Depression hit several years later, the shelter became so over-crowded that they had to move half the people to another facility. It was then that he escaped into the streets, to join with the rest of the unfortunate and downtrodden.

Over the next decade, the streets became his home, though he still ended up in and out of various shelters, some better than others. He never did find Clyde, Billy, or any of the others from that group again. He often wondered what had become of them.

It was now 1942, and as he sat on a bench looking out at the Delaware River, he thought about his life here in the past. It was hard to believe eighteen years had gone by since he'd begun his life on the streets of Philadelphia. Though he was only sixty-seven, he felt like he was eighty. And he was sure he looked at least that. Life on the streets will do that. The strange thing was, he felt much safer out here than he did in any of the institutions. He knew as long as he could stay out of trouble, he'd get by.

There was a chill in the air, but it was tolerable. He was sure it would get much colder in the evening. He'd spent many a night, by now, shivering over a steam vent, or trying to stay warm inside a subway station until someone kicked him out. He couldn't complain, though. This was the life he had chosen. Any time he felt bitter, he'd think of Kim, and Jessica and Ethan, and he'd remember he was doing this for them. And not only for them, but for the world.

Getting hungry, he looked in the trashcan next to the bench. He was in luck. Someone had thrown away a half-eaten hamburger, which was a rarity in these days of food rationing. Usually he had to dig through restaurant trash bins and look for scraps. Despite the rationing, there didn't seem to be any shortage of steaks at restaurants, and that usually meant leftovers and scraps.

The burger didn't look too old, so he grabbed it and ate it as if it were his last meal. What might have seemed disgusting to him in his old life was a delicacy now. He'd heard stories of desperate soldiers eating insects and rodents to stay alive. At least this was cooked food.

As he sat there with the crinkled hamburger wrapper, a young man with a child who looked about six or seven walked by—his daughter, no doubt. She reminded him of Jessica. As the man tossed a newspaper into the trash, the little girl whispered, "What's wrong with that man's skin?" Her father pushed her along.

Jacob glanced down at his hands. They must have looked horrible to a child, his scarred and weather-beaten face, and the rough skin where he'd burnt off his own fingerprints. That certainly wasn't something he had relished doing, but he couldn't have left anything to chance.

He reached into the trash again and pulled out the newspaper the father had thrown out. It was his only way of keeping track of the date. The paper was marked June 30th, 1942. On the front page were several reports on the war. One, a small side headline, caught his eye immediately.

Nazi Slaughter of Jews Estimated Over 1 Million

He sunk back on the bench and thought of Anna. This would have been two years after Ravensbrück, but three years before Dachau. At this very moment she was probably going through hell, either at Ravensbrück or at Auschwitz.

He clenched his fists. He couldn't save her—couldn't save any of them. He thought of Hitler, with his whip and his stories about manipulating the masses. If only he could have left him dead. But Hitler would have had his effect on the world whether he'd lived or died in 1924. Feeling helpless and unable to do anything else, Jacob slammed his fist into his knee repeatedly as a passing couple stared at him. Always staring. Wherever he went, he'd get the stares. These people knew nothing about him, but they were always quick to pass judgment. Ignoring the couple, he stretched out sideways on the bench and fell asleep.

Later—he wasn't sure what time—he was awoken by the sound of police cars. They seemed to be going in the direction of the city. He walked toward Market Street and headed west toward City Hall after them. When he finally got close to the imposing structure—which, by law, was the tallest building in the city, he could see a large crowd outside, spilling into the streets. There was some kind of protest going on.

Judging by the signs, it was an anti-Nazi demonstration. Apparently, it was threatening to turn violent, as the police were charging in to break up some arguments between the demonstrators and a pro-Nazi group of about twenty or thirty people. Among the pro-Nazi faction, he noticed a handful of posters touting the "Friends of New Germany" and "The German-American Bund."

As much as he wanted to join the fray, he thought the better of it and decided to head back to the river. This wasn't his war anymore. He had a much bigger war to fight. And he was determined to win it.

Chapter 47

A Special Day

This was a special day for Jacob. His 70th birthday had come and gone without fanfare, but today was even more important. It was May 1st, 1945, and he knew that very soon the news would arrive that Hitler had killed himself with a gunshot to the head—one more sign that Jacob had set the future back on its proper course. As he proceeded up 13th Street past Walnut, he turned left into an alley. There was a pub on the right. As he opened the door to enter, a large behemoth of a man approached.

"All right, outta here," the gorilla-like bouncer said. "You know better than that."

Jacob tried to look past the man and into the bar.

"I just want to hear something on the radio," he said. "I won't even come all the way in."

"The radio?" The man laughed. "What could the likes of you want to hear on the radio?"

Just then, everyone in the pub began to plead with one another to quiet down, and the bartender turned up the radio.

The bouncer looked at Jacob like he had two heads, then turned around to join the others.

Jacob followed him in, unnoticed.

This was the announcement he'd come to hear. It had to be.

The familiar Westminster Chimes blared from the radio. It must have been a BBC broadcast. A British female voice came on.

We are interrupting our program to bring you a news flash.

After a few seconds of silence, a male voice continued slowly and deliberately, as the pub fell into silence.

This is London calling. Here is a news flash. The German radio has just announced that Hitler is dead. I'll repeat that. The German radio has just announced that Hitler—

Suddenly, the pub erupted into cheers and Jacob couldn't hear another word. But he didn't need to. Because now he had the proof he'd been waiting for that the man he had sat with, the man he poisoned, the man he wrote essays about and lectured on, was now dead—as he was originally meant to be.

Jacob limped out of the pub, his gout beginning to hurt, and continued up 13th Street. For the first time in a long time, he smiled. Because one day, long after he'd be dead and gone, Jacob Newman would be born, and would marry Kim, who would give birth to Ethan and Jessica. And all would be right with the world, if only for a blip in time. Judgment day might still come. But at least now it would come on its own terms.

There was only one more thing he wanted to see happen while he was still alive. And that wouldn't come for many more years.

Chapter 48
Death of a Stranger

Bernie Lev was sitting in his living room watching the election results on TV. Election Day was yesterday, but the jury was still out as to whether Kennedy or Nixon had won. Nixon was now on the television, with his supporters in the background chanting, "We want Nixon, we want Nixon." To the dismay of the crowd, Nixon was acknowledging that if the trend continued, Kennedy just might win.

"I hope he does, ya bum!"

Bernie didn't know what good it did yelling at the TV, but it made him feel better. All the polls had shown the candidates dead even, and even his friends and relatives were in heated debate.

Just then his daughter Rebecca burst through the front door, looking like she'd won a million dollars.

"Guess what, Dad!"

"You're eloping," he said. He was half kidding.

"Close. Stuart wants me to marry him after he graduates. And I don't even have to move. He agreed to move to Philadelphia."

Kennedy was now on the TV, though Bernie missed what he was saying.

"Dad, did you hear me?" said Rebecca. "We're going to get married!"

"Well, that's great," he said. "I'm happy for you. But don't get too excited. Let's see if he's still serious about it in a couple years." He didn't want to burst her bubble. They still had two years before college graduation, and things change. Kids didn't seem to get that.

As the commercial came on, he turned around just in time to see her storming out of the room.

Then she came back in, her face red as a beet.

"Dad," she said, "he comes from a good family. His father is a scientist, Max Newman—he was even on TV once. What more do you want? My God, you're so negative!"

"I'm not negative, I'm just realistic." He tried to calm his tone. "I just don't want you to be disappointed, that's all."

"Why don't you let me worry about whether I'll be disappointed, and just be happy for me for once?"

"Happy? You're always happy."

"I'm not talking about me," she said. "I'm talking about you."

As they debated, the commercial ended. Bernie was half listening to Rebecca when he heard the announcement on the TV.

This just in. We have just learned that John Fitzgerald Kennedy has been declared the winner in Minnesota, making him the winner of this election. I repeat. Senator Kennedy, now President-elect Kennedy, has won the presidential election by the narrowest of margins.

"He won!" said Bernie. "Kennedy won!" He clapped his hands together, relieved at last. Apparently, Rebecca wasn't quite so happy, as she left the room again.

Though he wanted to see the upcoming speeches, Bernie went upstairs to try to make amends with his daughter. Maybe he could convince her he was just looking out for her best interests. Whenever he did that, though, it always ended up with her getting angrier with him. Women. He'd never understand them as long as he lived.

Later that evening, when everything had calmed down, he sat on the couch with Rebecca. Rose was in the kitchen cooking dinner, and he could smell the onions. She was cooking his favorite, beef stew.

The evening news was on now. They were showing a special report about the election. He was tired of seeing the same speeches over and over. Hopefully they would be getting to the sports and the weather soon. Finally, the news anchor came back on.

In other news...

"Oh, there's *other* news?" said Bernie. "Geez, I thought the election was the only thing happening in the world."

Rebecca shushed him as the newscast continued.

An unidentified man was found dead under the Benjamin Franklin Bridge, the third death this week attributed to the weather. He appeared to be a street person and is estimated to be in his eighties. No foul play is suspected, though the man's face looked to have been severely scarred, and his fingerprints had been burnt off. As temperatures dip below freezing for the third night in a row, shelters are working hard to keep up. Tomorrow, an overnight low of twenty is expected. The full weather report is next.

"You see that," Bernie yelled to nobody in particular. "The city is being invaded by those damn street people. Everyone gives them money, and all they do is use it to buy liquor. What a waste to go through life and never accomplish a damn thing. Bums. All of them."

Chapter 49
New Beginnings

As Max Newman looked down at his newborn grandson and his two-year-old granddaughter lying on the floor sound asleep, he couldn't help thinking of Anna. She had always loved children. He still missed her terribly, especially at times like this.

He also thought back to his own childhood, growing up in the orphanage. His mother was weak-willed, and suffered from depression, but that didn't mean his father had had to put her away for it. But put her away he did. And then he had the audacity to take in cousins from Russia while he and Samuel suffered in the orphanage.

This, here, was how family should be. Not in some institution.

"So what do you think, Dad?" said Stuart. "Doctor, baseball player, freedom fighter?" Stuart always managed to cheer him up.

"He'll be a scientist," said Max, "like you and me. He already told me. He wants to go to MIT. He's smart for a newborn."

"Oh, you two," Rebecca said as she walked in the room. "Let him be whatever he wants to be. I don't care if he turns out to be a plumber."

"Hey, what's wrong with plumbers?" said Bernie, from across the room. "They make damn good money!" Max had to laugh, since Bernie was a retired plumber.

"Dad!" Rebecca looked embarrassed, as she usually did around her father.

"What, I paid for most of your wedding, didn't I?"

Rebecca rolled her eyes.

Max figured he'd better create a diversion before Rebecca went into orbit. Bernie had a way of setting her off. He pointed to the kids. "Look down there. Look at our little Jacob and Ellen. That's the future of America right there!"

The funny thing was, as he looked at his grandchildren lying on the mat, the picture of innocence, he truly believed it. And it gave him hope.

Chapter 50
Déjà vu

March 15, 2024

49 Years Later

As he drove north on I-95, Jacob thought he was being followed. There was no reason anyone should be trailing him. After all, reporters wouldn't have had access to any information about his new project. His initial briefing had been given on a secure line. Nevertheless, the dark blue SUV that seemed to be weaving in and out of lanes to keep up with him was still behind him. He thought back to that time in Reykjavik when he thought he was being followed on foot by two men, only to find out they had wanted to congratulate him on his lecture at the Frontiers of Physics Conference.

After speeding up and then switching to the right lane for a few miles, he no longer saw the SUV. Either he had lost them or its seeming to follow him was just a coincidence. He took the next exit onto Route 63 and followed his usual route to the cemetery.

He loved visiting Philadelphia. He had spent his formative years here. It was hard to believe this was the thirty-fourth year he'd been coming to Pop's grave. He had visited his parents' graves first, an hour south of here, as he did every year. He was surprised to see the sad state of their plots, and made a mental note to contact the cemetery.

Before he knew it, he was pulling up to Pop's gravesite. He'd made this trip so many times, the car seemed to drive itself there. Coming from San Diego was a hell of a lot better than all those years flying in from London. This trip was a little tougher though, since he'd just returned from Paris the night before.

Getting out of the car, he glanced around. If anyone *was* following him, they didn't make it here. He walked up to the gravestone and knelt down. He spoke quietly, even though there wasn't anyone within earshot.

"You wonderful, crazy old bastard," he said. "You were right all the time, you know. They found something. Something even beyond what we imagined. All those late night talks, and now here it is on our doorstep."

Jacob paused when he heard cars coming up the road: a funeral procession. The motorcade drove past, and one by one, the cars pulled alongside a tent that had been set up nearby. He observed the growing assembly of mourners and then returned his focus downward.

"Anyway, you know you're the only one I can talk to about this. Hey, I have to tell somebody, don't I? Anyway, Pop, they need my help. Our help. I've been—"

Suddenly, he heard the crackling of dry leaves behind him and turned around to see who was approaching. He could have sworn he'd seen someone out of the corner of his eye, but as quickly as he turned around, there was nobody there. Between this and the SUV on the highway, Jacob was wondering if he was losing it. *Damn jetlag.* Scanning the crowd one last time, he took a deep breath as he knelt down again on one knee. This time he lowered his voice to a whisper.

"Pop, the military has found something—an unidentified vessel of some kind. Well, this should be no surprise to you; they think it's alien. But that's only half of it. On the ship, they found these huge display monitors—eight of them, and floating in mid-air."

Jacob stopped for a moment and glanced around, just to make sure he was still alone. A fleeting sense of déjà vu came over him. He had experienced similar bouts of déjà vu all his life, and had even seen a psychologist for it for several years, but this one seemed even stronger than usual. He shrugged off the feeling and continued.

"Now listen, Pop. Each of the viewers has a different image representing points in human history. They couldn't tell me much more, but think of what that means. Imagine what we could learn about our past. Imagine if someone, or something, has been watching us all these years—or maybe more than watching. Pop, think of it. We can finally crack all those questions we talked about."

Pausing briefly to check the time, he continued. "There's something else, Pop. I got a package in the mail with old photos and press clippings. And your journal. I never even knew you kept a journal. I don't know who sent it. I'm thinking maybe this old German guy who approached me in Paris. He said his family knew you. But why would you have given it to *him*? Anyway, I have to get to the airport, Pop, but I want you to know if it hadn't been for you, I wouldn't be here about to take part in this at all. Just from the fraction of information I know, it's—"

Just then he heard another car pull into the cemetery. As he turned to look, he got chills. It was a blue SUV. He couldn't be sure if it was the same one, but it certainly looked like it.

He stood up and watched as a thin man who looked to be in his fifties or sixties, wearing a long black overcoat and a driver's cap, slowly got out of the vehicle. The man didn't seem dangerous, but Jacob could have sworn the guy was now approaching him. As the man got closer, there was no doubt. He *was* approaching him.

The stranger walked up to Jacob and held out his hand, smiling. "Are you the Lamb of God who takes away the sins of the world?"

Jacob didn't know what to say. Was this guy off his rocker?

The man's face took on a more serious expression.

"It can be a dangerous game, Jacob." He was still holding out his hand.

Confused, Jacob reluctantly shook the man's hand and immediately recognized the handshake. He was a Freemason.

"I don't understand," said Jacob. "How do you know my name?"

The man pulled an envelope out of his coat pocket and handed it to him, smiling again. The envelope looked old and tattered.

"The letter is for you. It should explain everything. It was submitted to our lodge in Philadelphia a century ago, in 1924, with all the proper credentials. It was passed down from Grand Master to Grand Master, until it reached our current Grand Master...uh...that would be me. Seems there were specific instructions to hold it until it could be delivered to you on this date, at exactly 3:15 p.m. at Shalom Memorial Park. And, lo and behold, here you are, at the stated lot, section, and row. It even described the car you'd be driving and the license plate, which I happened to spot on the way here."

"So that was you following me," said Jacob. "Glad I wasn't going crazy. What took you so long to arrive then?"

"It wasn't 3:15 yet."

Jacob looked down at the envelope, almost afraid to open it.

"Oh, don't worry when you read it," said the Grand Master. "We're bound by our code to protect one another, as long as nothing illegal is going on—though this seems to transcend any laws I know of. From one Brother to another, my original advice still holds. You're in dangerous territory, Jacob."

Jacob was utterly and completely confused, but he opened the envelope and took out the letter. It was handwritten on several old sheets of paper, all with a letterhead that read SS Reliance. Strangely enough, the writing looked similar to his own.

He began reading.

Dear Jacob,

I'm not asking anything of you, only that you read this letter in full before deciding on any action—or not.

I'm aware that you've been transferred from the NBIC program to a new program at a secret base in Chile. I also know that your role is to examine an alien ship that seems to be able to transmit images from the past. In fact, you've already reviewed the initial briefing and are beginning to suspect that this technology might be intended for more than just observation. Perhaps even for time travel.

Jacob, I'm aware of this, yet you've shared it with no one aside from your dead grandfather, whom you've been visiting for the last thirty-four years.

Do I have your attention? Good.

You see, you don't realize it yet, but pretty soon you're going to make a terrible decision—a decision with huge repercussions for billions of people, including your own family. That's right. I didn't say millions, I said billions. You'll think it's the humanitarian thing to do—a selfless act to save the world. You couldn't be more wrong.

You are probably wondering who I am and how I know this.

I am you, Jacob.

Don't believe me? How else would I know that the briefcase in your car was given to you last night by Kim for your 49th birthday? Or that you were suspended from 5th grade for punching Billy Rosner in the nose. Nobody saw him hit you first.

Still reading? Good.

You'll be wondering how I got here—to the past, I mean. Because that's where I am as I write this letter. Of course, I'll be long dead by the time you read this.

When you found out that the technology could be used for time travel— I'll spare you the details as to how that happened—you decided to travel to the past to visit Pop and Anna. And not just to visit, but to influence Pop and dear Uncle Samuel to go ahead with their plot to kill Hitler. Oh, yes, you don't know about that yet. Read the journal that arrived in the box. It's all there, in the Landsberg section. And, no, I didn't send it, if that's what you're thinking. Maybe the old man from Paris did. By the way, his name is Abraham Finkel. And he's not to be trusted by any means.

Also, Malcolm knows more than he's letting on. Maybe you can get the truth out of him. I couldn't.

So, why did you end up trying to kill Hitler? It wasn't just out of hatred. No, you suspected that the aliens, or whoever the ship belongs to, are planning a judgment day against humanity. And that very well may be the case. But you won't address that problem by undoing Hitler. Of that, I can assure you.

Like many things, your decision seemed like a good idea at the time—as I said, the humanitarian choice, and, in your eyes, the only choice. Except the plot was much more complicated than you realized. Again, I'll spare you the details.

Oh, you succeeded in killing Hitler all right—although not without some difficulty and grave danger to everyone involved. But when you traveled forward again to 2024, that's when all hell broke loose. You returned to a much different world.

Remember how Malcolm always talked about complex systems having simple roots? Well, that one single change—the loss of Adolf Hitler— led to a series of events that were catastrophic beyond your imagination. Nuclear war. Worldwide famine, four billion people dead. Your family, gone. All because Nixon invaded Cuba during the Cuban Missile Crisis. Yes, Jacob, I said Nixon.

You may be wondering how that happened. It's irrelevant. Anything you do to the past will have subtle implications that you'd never think of in a million years.

In this case, once you saw the results, you had no choice after that but to find a way to return to 1924 to undo the deed. Once again, I'll spare you the details.

Oh, you did manage to undo it, painfully, but you were unable to return to 2024. I know; I was there, stuck in 1924 having to make my way from Germany to America. That's where I am now as I write this, in a small cabin on a ship to New York. Then it's on to Philadelphia. From this point on, I have no choice but to live a secluded and anonymous life. Somehow, I'll have to remove my fingerprints, which I can tell you I'm not looking forward to doing. But I'm determined not to interfere with history again, at least not in this life, which is all I can control.

Now it's your turn. Do you want to unleash hell, or live a good life with your family in peace? Do you want to save millions of people only to kill billions later? Let history lie, Jacob. Give yourself and the world a future. It's not ours to reason why things happen or even whether they happen for a reason. There are a million smaller ways to make a difference in the world. Aim small, Jacob. Aim small.

And next time Jessica wants to play at night, put your research aside. Spend the time. It's precious.

My request is simple. Don't do anything that will advance the team's knowledge of how the technology can be used. And most important, stay away from the alcove at the far end of the ship. In the same breath, I've given you two things—a hint and a warning. My hope is that you'll observe the warning.

An old friend of ours—someone who liked to talk about opportunities and choices—said, "Once you bite from the apple, you can't put it back." For one time, I hope he's wrong.

Yours truly,

J

Jacob was in a daze. It was hard to fathom what he had just read. How could this story be possible? At the least, it might explain the déjà vu episodes, since apparently he had lived his entire life before and didn't even know it. He didn't doubt the authenticity of the letter. He would have been foolish to. There could be no other explanation for the details it contained.

A hand on his shoulder interrupted his thoughts.

"What you do," said the Mason, "is your choice. But it's a choice I don't think any human being has had to make since Oppenheimer. And we know where that led. Choose wisely, my friend. If it helps, remember our most powerful symbol."

Jacob look at him, confused.

"The 'G,' Jacob. "Geometry and God. Reason and Faith."

With that, the Mason turned and headed toward his car.

"Where are you going?" said Jacob. If there was one time he could use someone to bounce his thoughts off, it was now, especially with someone who was sworn to secrecy.

"I'm afraid I have work to do," said the Mason. "And so do you."

As he watched the Mason get in his car and drive off, Jacob thought about what the man had said, particularly regarding Oppenheimer. He wondered how Oppenheimer felt after creating the atomic bomb, something that represented both a staggering technological achievement and an ominous potential for catastrophe. Then he remembered reading a statement by Oppenheimer about the dangers of leaving unrealized possibilities hanging over the world for some less virtuous country to discover in the future. He recalled Oppenheimer saying that if you were a scientist, then it was good to find out how the world works and to turn over to humanity the greatest possible power for controlling the world. Then all that would remain would be to figure out how to deal with its values. Not only good, Oppenheimer suggested, but almost a necessity.

It dawned on Jacob that this was the same stance he had taken at the Paris conference. Like Oppenheimer, he was a scientist, trained to be curious and to add to the advancement of human knowledge.

But Oppenheimer didn't have the benefit of hindsight, and—irony of ironies—it would be Oppenheimer's invention that would lead to global devastation if Jacob were to ignore the letter's advice.

The issue wasn't whether to travel back to change history. Knowing what would supposedly happen, he'd have to be an idiot to do so. No, the issue was whether he should help humanity understand how the technology worked, in the interest of advancing science and investigating a potential alien threat.

How could he decide? What would be worse, the threat from alien beings who'd been watching us for millennia, or the threat from human misuse of their technology?

Then he realized what the real question was. What should be *his*—Jacob Newman's—role in changing the course of the future by advancing science to the next level? Could he trust the world to show temperance and prudence? And if not, could he take part in a critical program and at the same time sabotage its success?

The risks weren't minimal. If the wrong people found out that he was interfering with a matter of national security, it could destroy his reputation in the scientific community. Worse, he could be locked up for sabotage. And how would that impact his family, especially with Kim so sick? He wondered how much leeway Malcolm would have if he needed backing.

Looking down at the gravestone, he closed his eyes for a moment and tried to take in the comfort of Pop's presence. Before long, as was usually the case when he was here, he started getting a little more clarity.

He let out a long sigh and reached into his pocket to take out the stones he'd brought with him. He knelt down, and, one by one, kissed them and placed them gently on the tombstone.

"May God be with us, Pop," he said.

Trying to gather himself after the events of the last thirty minutes, he stumbled, half-dazed, to his car. Along the way, he spotted a trashcan along the road, and wandered up to it. He took the envelope out of his pocket and pulled out the letter. He gave it one last glance and then tore it into pieces, watching as they dropped into the can.

He glanced at his watch. He had an hour and a half to get to the airport and through security.

There was no denying it. This discovery was about to change the world for better or for worse. And here he was in the middle of it.

Chapter 51

Reservations

As Jacob waited in the check-in line at Philadelphia International Airport, his mind wandered to the possibilities of time travel. He could just imagine a conversation with Benjamin Franklin, or dinner with Albert Einstein. Or maybe a visit to ancient Rome, or back even further, perhaps to see how the pyramids had been built. The possibilities were endless.

But then again, so were those ripples Malcolm liked to talk about, especially if the technology were eventually misused, as no doubt it would be.

"Next!"

He was being waved to the ticket agent.

"Do you need a boarding pass, sir?" said the agent.

"Actually, I'd like to change my reservation," he said. "I won't be going to Santiago today. Something came up. I'll be going domestic instead. San Diego."

"Thank you, sir. I can take care of that for you. It'll be a different terminal, just so you know."

"That's no problem. I can deal with that."

"I know, a small price to pay, right?"

"You might say that."

As he departed the reservation area and headed toward the monorail, he began to walk with the same confidence he had felt when he landed his first CIA job, the kind where you knew with certainty that you were meant to do something.

On the surface, his decision seemed to come down to a simple matter of percentages. The way he calculated it, he could either walk away, and leave a small chance that someone else would make all the connections necessary to exploit the technology, or he could remove all doubt and give science the tools to destroy the world. But no, the choice wasn't quite that simple.

He made his way to the departure lounge. His flight wasn't due to take off until 9 p.m., so he had about two hours to kill before boarding time. He wouldn't be arriving in San Diego until around midnight. He tried to call Kim, but she didn't answer. She was probably out running errands and, as usual, didn't have her cell phone with her—a habit that drove him crazy.

Next, he called Malcolm.

"Jake?"

"Yes, Malcolm. Listen, I'm going to be delayed a few days. I need to stop home first. Some personal stuff going on. Can't be avoided."

"I'm sorry to hear that, Jake. Is Kim okay?"

"Yes, she's doing all right. As good as can be expected. But there are some personal things I need to take care of."

There was silence on the line for a few seconds.

"You do understand why I need to stay a few days, right?" said Jacob. "If I could avoid the delay, I would."

"I understand, Jake. I can't say that Hughes will, though. He's not the sympathetic type, and especially not when it comes to national emergencies. But I'll let him know. Just get here as soon as you can."

After hanging up, Jacob went to the bar to get a drink, and sat at one of the small cocktail tables. As he nursed his dry martini and olive, trying to digest everything that happened in the last several hours, his phone buzzed. He recognized the unique sound. It was Malcolm calling on the secure line.

"Jake, I just spoke with Hughes."

"And?"

"And, as I had an idea would happen, he went ballistic. Quote: 'Come hell or high water, make sure that genius of yours gets his number crunching butt out here ASAP.'"

"Well, tell Hughes I've seen hell *and* high water, and I'm not impressed. I'll be there when I said I'd be there." As grandiose as that sounded, he realized it was probably an understatement.

He heard nothing but silence for a few seconds. Malcolm was probably rubbing his forehead about now.

"Jake, we've known each other a long time. Is there anything you want to talk about? Off the record, of course. We really need you, but if there's something going on—"

"There's nothing going on, trust me. It's—well, it's complicated, and I'm not really able to discuss it. I just need a few days."

There was a pause on the line for a few seconds.

"Fair enough, Jake. Take the time you need, but please join us as soon as you can. It's absolutely critical that you be here. I'll handle Hughes. His bark is worse than his bite."

"That's a promise. And, Malcolm?"

"Yes?"

"Thanks, from the bottom of my heart. I mean that."

"Sure, Jake."

As he hung up the phone, he was sure Malcolm was completely confused, but it was the best he could do.

He was pretty sure now what he needed to do. He went over his conclusions again. For one, after everything he'd heard about the future, about the global devastation and losing everyone he held dear, he needed to stop home for a few days. That was non-negotiable, as far as he was concerned. Then, when he returned to the program, he'd participate, but only to the extent of studying and learning. He'd stop short of anything that might reveal how the technology truly worked. And if someone did make a breakthrough, he'd be there to intervene. In the worst case, he would tell Malcolm everything. Malcolm, more than anyone else in this world, would get it.

As far as he was concerned, he wouldn't be breaking any kind of scientific code, nor would it be sabotage per se. Oh, someone might call it interference, but even if it were, so what? It would serve to prevent an even greater interference. Without a doubt, this was the right decision, for him and for mankind. And for a scientist, to do mankind a service was the utmost goal. That had to be the right answer, professional status or no. His reputation would have to take a back seat, if it came to that.

Then, something else dawned on him. What if, by interfering, he was in fact playing God? Would he be changing the future in ways he wasn't considering? Would he be building on the damage he had caused in his prior life? After all, wasn't the lesson to stay out of history's way?

It occurred to him at that moment that every act, no matter how small, changes the world in some way. And so does every failure to act. Sometimes—and this was one of them—there were no perfect solutions, only mindful ones that considered all four virtues: temperance, prudence, justice, and fortitude. In the end, all you could do was use your best judgment, knowing that the danger of making a mistake would always be there. There were no absolutes in life, even for scientists.

Wary of the time, and adequately content in his decision, Jacob glanced at the clock on the wall. He was surprised at how quickly the last hour had flown by. It was after eight—time to head to the departure gate for boarding.

Chapter 52

Judgment

The flight to San Diego was uneventful and he slept most of the way, but Jacob was exhausted nonetheless. It had been a long and taxing day, to say the least. He hadn't heard from Kim yet. As he disembarked and walked to the arrival hall, he tried once more to call her. Again, no answer.

He stepped into the restroom to splash some water on his face. It was empty, which wasn't too surprising at midnight. Just as he was washing his face, his phone buzzed. It was Kim. He grabbed for a paper towel to quickly dry his hands and face, and picked up the phone.

"Kim?"

"Jake, are you okay? I saw that you tried calling about a hundred times. I was at Susan's. I just walked in."

He looked at his watch.

"It's 12:15. That's late for you, Miss 'I have to be in bed by 10.'"

"I know," she said. "We were talking, so I stayed to chat. Ellen watched Jessica for me. Listen, Jake—"

"I just wanted to tell you," he said, "I'm here, in San Diego. I'm fine. I bought more time from Malcolm. I'll be coming home for a few more days before—"

"Jake, listen," she said. "I had my doctor's appointment today." Her voice sounded like it was cracking. "I have some news, Jake." His heart sank as he waited for her next words. He could hear that she was crying.

Just then he felt the strangest sensation. His whole body began to vibrate uncontrollably. The phone fell from his hands, and he could feel the vibrations buzz through his face, his arms, everywhere. Then, as fast as the feeling had come, it stopped, and suddenly he felt weightless as a feather. It was as if he were floating, his arms rising up to his sides. He wondered if he was having some kind of panic attack or stroke. As he hung there in suspended animation, half conscious, he felt his mind going a mile a minute, flooded with memories he vaguely recognized. The visions became crystal clear, as if he were reliving them.

In a matter of seconds, he recalled seeing his grandmother Anna's horrified face as she lay dead by the boxcars in Germany. He recalled sitting with Max and Anna in their living room in 1924. He remembered having lunch with Hitler, and narrowly escaping the fortress with his life. Then he remembered returning to the ship and being captured, and seeing all the devastation from the nuclear catastrophe he had caused. He saw Finkel and Bradley aim some kind of light beam at Malcolm, and watched Malcolm explode into tiny particles. He could see, clear as day, his time back in Karlsruhe and remembered shooting his alter ego, along with a hooded man who was about to shoot him. He recalled his time in Frankfurt, and how Jacques and Marco had helped him get to the SS Reliance in Hamburg. He remembered Clyde and Billy, and living on the streets in Philadelphia.

It all came back to him in a rush, more vivid than any dream he'd ever had. Nothing seemed real anymore. And yet *everything* seemed real.

Just then a blinding light surrounded him and he felt himself get heavier, except it was too much too fast. Way too much, as if he'd sink through the floor. He was falling now, and felt like he weighed a ton as he slid down an invisible tunnel, falling and spinning, the lights now turning into a brilliant kaleidoscope of colors. He was spinning so fast he couldn't even see. Then suddenly it all stopped. Everything. There was no thud, just a gentle touchdown as he crouched upon the ground. Only he wasn't in the restroom anymore. He knew exactly where he was. He'd been here many times, only he hadn't known it until now.

He was on the alien ship.

He wasn't in the alcove, though. He was right in the center of the cavernous vessel. He felt his hands, relieved that he still had his fingertips. He remembered burning them in the kettle. He wondered what was going on here. Where was everyone? Was there some kind of judgment about to happen? Had he, in fact, been brought here to stand trial for his actions? He had to get back to Kim, somehow.

He glanced over at the monitors. From this angle, he couldn't make out the images, so he walked closer. As he approached them, he could see that all of the images he remembered were still there. The eighth one was blank.

He walked toward the labs, but there was no longer any door there. The space where a door had been was completely sealed. Was he to die there, alone? Was that his punishment? Or maybe this was one of those alien abductions, and they were going to start experimenting on him. He walked to the opposite end of the ship, where he remembered the alcove being. It was dark, but there was just enough light coming from the monitors that he could see the alcove was still there. He approached it and felt the ground around it. He half expected to find a note from Malcolm, but there was nothing, not even on the platform inside the alcove.

Confused, he wandered back to the center of the ship toward the light of the monitors. Someone had to be watching him. He didn't know who or what, but he felt that he was being observed.

He looked up toward the slimy ceiling.

"What do you want!" he yelled, his voice echoing in the colossal chamber. "Where are the others?"

He could hear nothing but the echo of his own voice.

"Is this about me?" he called out. "Well, take me, if you want, but spare the rest of the world!"

Still no response.

"What about my daughter!" he yelled. "She's innocent. All the children are."

He shook his head. Whoever these beings were, they probably weren't worried about the children. It was the adults they feared.

"What about Jacques?" he yelled. "And Marco? Or Clyde and Billy? They were good people. There are good people everywhere—people who help others, with no benefit to themselves! And Malcolm! What about him?"

He was wondering if anyone was even listening to him, or if they understood a word he was saying. Still, he had to keep trying.

"Do I have to sacrifice my life again?" he yelled. "I did it once. I'll do it a hundred more times!"

He looked around, but there was no sign of movement or activity anywhere.

Frustrated and discouraged, he got down on his knees and prayed for God to hear his sincere thoughts. "Just let them take me," he said. "But don't let them take the others yet. Don't let them. And please take care of Jessica and Ethan, and ease Kim's pain. That's all I ask."

Just then he heard a single pair of hands clapping, off to his left.

"A very moving performance," said a familiar German-sounding voice. Jacob looked over to see two shadowy figures coming his way. As the light hit their faces he could see who it was. It was Finkel. And Bradley was walking next to him.

"How did you get here?" said Jacob. "What's going on?"

"My dear Jacob," said Finkel, "you do not understand the forces you are dealing with."

"Did you think we gave up?" said Bradley. "You only made it as far as you did because we let you. Once you dropped that letter off at the lodge, we saw it as an opportunity. And now, here we are."

"I don't get it," said Jacob. "What kind of opportunity? How could you have been there a hundred years ago?"

Finkel laughed. "My friend," he said, "you know very little about time. Past, present, future. What are these things but an illusion?"

"Well, another illusion," said Jacob, "is thinking I'd ever kill Hitler again. Is that what all this is about? Me killing Hitler?"

"Jacob, Jacob, Jacob," said Finkel, "we don't need you to kill Hitler. Not anymore. There are much more expedient ways to achieve our goal. And we have you to thank for it."

"And just what goal is that?"

Finkel smiled. "Come with us to the monitors."

Jacob followed Finkel and Bradley to the large floating monoliths.

"Behold," said Finkel. "All evidence of human capacity for violence. These monitors have captured many events over thousands of years, but these I think are the most representative. The eighth one, if you recall, showed your little journey to Dachau."

Finkel waved his hand and the boxcars with the dead bodies suddenly appeared on the eighth monitor. "But alas, that is all in the past," he said, once again waving his hand to render the image blank.

Jacob couldn't believe it. All this time, Finkel and Bradley had control over the ship. And perhaps Malcolm did too. Was this some kind of government experiment?

"I still don't understand," he said, "What does this have to do with me?"

"Oh, it has everything to do with you," said Finkel. "Because the blank monitor, you see, represents one final chance for the people of this earth, and we aim to let you be the one to help us make our case."

"What case?"

"So many questions, Jacob. Curiosity, as they say, killed the cat."

Finkel held out his hand, and Bradley handed him a handgun. Jacob recognized it as the same model Malcolm had given him, perhaps even the same gun.

The next thing Jacob knew, Finkel was aiming the gun directly at him. Finkel walked closer, then lowered the gun and held it sideways in his palm to hand it to Jacob.

"What do you want me to do with this?" said Jacob.

"Take it, please."

Jacob hesitated.

"You can take it," said Finkel. "I insist."

Jacob felt his hand involuntarily opening as Finkel placed the gun in his hand.

"You were very smart to write that letter," said Finkel. "If you hadn't, you would have been doomed to repeat the same actions over and over, killing Hitler, then undoing it, then killing Hitler again, and so on. We would have had to put a stop to it eventually. But you did write the letter, and doing that gave you a new choice. We, of course, couldn't wait for you to decide whether to kill Hitler again, and so here you are to bring about the same result."

"What, the end of Hitler?" said Jacob. "Why do you want Hitler dead? He sounds like your kind of guy."

"No, not the end of Hitler," said Finkel. "The end of humanity."

It took a few seconds for this bombshell to sink in, but once it had, Jacob felt like a train had hit him.

"So you wanted Hitler dead because you knew it would lead to global destruction," said Jacob. "I won't ask how you knew that. But then, you used me to carry out the assassination? So you sent the box! And you sent me to Dachau!"

"No," said a female voice, behind him. "I did."

Jacob turned around to see who it was, and he couldn't believe it. It was Lauren.

"You're one of them?" said Jacob. "You're in on their plan?"

Lauren smiled. "*My* plan, Jake. The plan was mine. Give credit where credit is due." She walked over to Finkel and Bradley.

"This is the end of the line, Jacob," said Bradley.

"What do you expect me to do?" said Jacob. "I won't play along, if that's what you're thinking."

He looked down at the gun in his hand.

"Yes," said Finkel. "The gun. Why don't you shoot us? You can start with me. I am but an old man. It's what you do, isn't it? You killed Hitler, and the German official—one whose wife was about to have a baby, I might add. Need I count the others?"

Jacob pointed the gun, staring at them. He knew he was being goaded. Still, his anger was flooding through his veins. He hesitated, his hand shaking.

"Maybe he needs more motivation," said Lauren.

"I trusted you," said Jacob, staring her directly in the eyes, as he aimed the gun at her.

"So did your grandmother," she said. "But she learned the hard way when I tipped off the Nazis about her escape. They caught her and brought her back, screaming her head off like a baby."

Jacob felt his muscles tense up.

"That's impossible!" he said, still pointing the gun at her. How could Lauren have even been there in 1940?

"Is it, Jake? Because it seemed pretty real when I hid her dead body, so I could leave it at Dachau for you to find. Did you really think she would have survived for five years after being caught escaping?"

"Even if that was true, why would you do that to her?" he yelled. "She did nothing wrong!" He believed her now, strange as her story sounded.

"You still don't get it, Jake. It's not about her, it's about you. It's the same reason I got to know your parents."

"What do you know about my parents?"

"Oh, they were nice people. They even invited me out to dinner one night, but I couldn't make it. Instead I went to a bar, where I picked up this really hot guy, got him drunk, and went joy riding—right into your parents' dark blue Ford Taurus."

"You're lying!!!" Jacob had never felt such rage. He was seconds from pulling the trigger, his hands shaking. He wasn't going to give her the joy of seeing him suffer, though. She was cunning. She knew what would get to him. In defiance, he put his arm down, the gun at his side, and stood firm. Finkel was laughing. Bradley was still wearing his typical stone-faced, unyielding expression.

Lauren, meanwhile, was unfazed, still smiling.

"Am I lying, Jake? I think you know the answer to that."

"Did you leave the box?"

"Of course. I even had to arrange for a photographer to chat up your grandparents and take their photo back in 1924. Then I had to leave it for you—of course, with the coordinates conveniently written on the back."

"My grandfather never kept a journal, did he?"

"I'm afraid you're right again, Jake."

"Why do all this?" he said. "Why me?"

"You can blame your grandfather for that. And his failure to kill Hitler when I asked."

Jacob shook his head, trying to piece all this together.

"So this is some kind of family vendetta?" he said.

"I don't do vendettas, Jake. Well, maybe a little. Look on the bright side, though. I didn't give your wife cancer. That was just a nice surprise. She's dying, you know."

That was it. Furious, he raised the gun again and walked directly up to Lauren, holding it to her head.

"You're all the worst form of scum I've ever seen. And you talk about *our* violence? You're all hypocrites!"

He stepped back a few feet and moved the gun from Lauren to Finkel, and then to Bradley, as they all watched, smiling. Then he thought the better of it and stepped back several yards more.

"I won't give you the satisfaction of winning," he said. "You've lost. All of you."

He lowered the gun again. Then he took a deep breath and thought of the large circular painting in the Masonic temple—the one depicting the four cardinal virtues. He recited them out loud, softly.

"Temperance," he said, "prudence, justice, and fortitude." Jacob said the words slowly and deliberately, as if they were a mantra, protecting him from doing what he so very much wanted to do.

Finkel wasn't laughing now. Jacob saw him glance over at Lauren. "Perhaps our friend," said Finkel, "would like an opportunity to undo your actions? No doubt, he would benefit from making his family whole again."

Lauren smiled. "Of course," she said. She pulled out the Kronos device and tossed it on the floor in front of Jacob.

"Go ahead," said Finkel. "Take it. You can warn your beloved grandmother. You can even save your parents. Or maybe your goals are, shall we say, bigger. Think of all the violence you can undo in the world, Jacob. That *is* what you want to do, is it not? Save the world?"

"Not this way, I don't," said Jacob.

"But I'm offering you a chance to be master of time. Time heals all wounds, Jacob—especially when you are master of it. This may be your only chance."

Lauren held up a hand, as if to say it was her turn now. Jacob watched as she approached him slowly, like a cat stalking its prey.

He stood still as she pressed close to him. He felt unable to move. As much as he hated her with all his energy, her soft scent almost held him captive.

"I know what you want," she whispered in his ear. "You want your wife back. You want her healthy." He felt her lips close on his ear-lobe, as her hand worked down his chest to his stomach. "I can make that happen, Jake. All you have to do is say the word."

Her hand moved lower, over the front of his pants. "You can have me, too, Jake," she said, her fingers tracing circles. "Any time you want. Think of it. Everything you wanted can be yours. I know you want me, Jake." She got closer to his ear again and whispered, "I can tell."

Something inside him shook him loose from her spell. He couldn't do this. There would be no deals. They were using Kim to get to him. But the choice was his. It had to be or they wouldn't have been trying to convince him so strongly.

He pushed Lauren back with all his might, and watched her shocked expression as she fell back toward the others.

"Don't flatter yourself, bitch," he said.

With that, he pointed the gun straight at Lauren, then at Bradley and Finkel, who was once again smiling. Then he aimed it at the Kronos device and fired. He kept firing, one shot after the other, until, to his surprise, the device vanished into thin air.

Finkel, Lauren, and Bradley all looked at him in horror. The next thing Jacob knew, Lauren had raised her hands toward him, and he felt an intense pain, like nothing he'd ever experienced. He could see beams of light firing toward him out of her hands, and immediately he thought of what they had done to Malcolm. It felt like his skin was on fire, and he was being jabbed with a hundred knives. In the midst of his pain, he thought of Kim. And he saw Jessica's innocent face. He wanted to be with his family. To comfort them. He wasn't ready to die yet. And at that moment, something happened. He felt the pain being distributed throughout his body, slowly decreasing to a dull throbbing. He forced himself to stand up straight, despite the beams firing at him. He held out his arms, and the light beams projected out of his arms and dissipated.

Finkel and Lauren looked like they couldn't believe what was going on. Bradley had a blank expression, somewhere between confusion and curiosity.

Then Finkel raised his arms and fired light at Jacob. This time, the initial pain was duller. Again, Jacob disbursed the beams harmlessly.

"You have no power over him," a voice said from behind.

Jacob turned around.

It was Malcolm!

Malcolm walked closer and put a hand on Jacob's shoulder.

"In your arrogance," said Malcolm, looking at Finkel and the others, "you've defeated yourselves. You thought you'd merge his memories so he'd succumb to his anger, but you did the opposite. You gave him all the benefits of hindsight, and all the courage and perseverance from every ordeal you put him through."

Finkel laughed and looked at Jacob. "You think he is on your side, Jacob, but I am afraid it is not so simple. You see, your friend Malcolm was one of us."

"That's a lie!" said Jacob.

"Oh, is it?" said Finkel. "Think, Jacob. You are a wise scientist. It should not be difficult to deduce. Who brought you to this project? Surely, it was not I. It was your friend Malcolm. Why would he do that? Why would he put you in harm's way?"

"Don't listen to him, Jake," said Malcolm. "I had no choice but to bring you here."

Jacob was confused now. Why *would* Malcolm have brought him here?

"Did you know?" he asked Malcolm.

Malcolm hesitated.

"You knew?" said Jacob.

"I knew they were going to try something," said Malcolm. "I just didn't know what at first. I had to set the bait for Lauren."

"Liar!" said Lauren.

"The hell he is!" said another voice from behind. Jacob turned around again.

It was Beeze!

"So, it turns out," said Beeze, "that you really *are* the bitch from hell."

Lauren sneered at him.

Beeze stepped forward beside Malcolm and dropped a large, poster-size photograph in Jacob's hands. Jacob looked at the photo. It was a close-up of Hitler making a speech. He recognized it as a cropped shot from the monitor image, blown up in detail. Only, there was a red circle around a face several people to the left of Hitler. There was no doubt whose face it was. Standing on the very stage with Adolf Hitler was Lauren.

"You see, Jake," said Beeze, "we ain't supposed to interfere directly in human affairs, but our friends here didn't get that memo. Not only that, but they bragged about it, plantin' people with rings in all their photos, like they was damn garden gnomes."

"Rings," said Jacob. "Is that related to the Ring of Seven?"

"Sure as hell is," said Beeze.

"A mere signature," said Finkel. "Something to show that we were there to observe. But always, it was to observe—nothing more. Your accusations are insulting."

"The photographic evidence suggests otherwise," said Malcolm.

"Yeah," said Beeze, "and so does our contact in Frankfurt. Were your thugs observers too? The dude in the hood? He did a real good job observing. So did those lackeys in the car. And that bozo on the ship? Man, he's doin' some good observing, right down there at the bottom of the ocean."

"Those were not sentinels," said Finkel. "They were mere humans, acting on the power of suggestion."

"Yeah, a damn strong suggestion."

"Wait a minute," said Jacob. "What contact in Frankfurt? What are sentinels?"

"It seems we are forgetting," said Finkel, "that we have a judgment that is due. And while our friend Jacob's efforts have been quite remarkable, so have been his crimes and his arrogance."

"Y'all should talk about arrogance," said Beeze.

"What crimes?" said Jacob. "The crime of receiving a box of manufactured items meant to lure me to my grandparents? Or the crime of being sent to Dachau to see my dead grandmother, who wasn't even supposed to be there in the first place? Or was it the crime of seeing your images of violence on those monitors and thinking I had a chance to undo one of them? Or maybe it was killing the lowlifes you sent after me, after they tried to kill me. Maybe those are the crimes you're talking about."

He walked closer to Finkel. Beeze put a hand on his shoulder to stop him, but Jacob held a hand up to say it's okay.

"On the arrogance, though," said Jacob, "you got me. I've been guilty of the worst kind of arrogance. Of putting more focus on the advancement of humankind than humankind itself, starting with my family. And thinking that science was separate from ethics, and that the morality of it should be left to some bureaucrats to debate. And also, of thinking that it was okay to tamper with unknown powers without fully understanding the implications. Of all of these things, I'm guilty as charged."

"Then we're agreed," said Finkel.

"But let me be arrogant one last time," said Jacob, cutting him off. "You need me, you crinkled old bastard. Yes, that's right. You can't do squat to our planet without me for some reason. Otherwise you wouldn't have gone through all this. I don't know why, but you need me to prove your case. Well, let me tell you this. You'll have to kill me before I help you prove one damn thing."

"You're wrong, my friend," said Finkel. "So very wrong. Oh, you will die, but not by our hands. You'll die very shortly, with the rest of your failed species. I've already arranged for the outcome, based on the evidence we've accumulated. And my request has been granted by one far greater than us all."

Finkel held up both his hands. "I call upon the great arbiter to let the judgment begin!"

Jacob looked back at Malcolm. Just then, the entire ship began rumbling. Beeze was looking around to see what was going on, but Malcolm held his hand out to calm him.

"Oh, and Jacob," said Finkel, "Your precious little daughter might have lived if you had cooperated with us."

The noise grew louder as the monitor images glowed brighter. Jacob felt the gun still in his hand. This was one of those defining moments. Should he wait for a judgment to wipe out his family and the rest of the world? Or should he try to shoot Finkel in the hope of buying more time. The way he looked at the choices, he had nothing to lose.

He lifted the gun and aimed it at Finkel's chest. He pressed his hand lightly on the trigger.

"Jake, no!" yelled Beeze.

He pulled the trigger and fired. Then he aimed at Lauren and fired again. Then Bradley.

Finkel began laughing, as the rumbling grew even louder. Lauren fell back clutching her chest. Finkel looked at her. He looked surprised. Then he, too, began feeling his chest. Jacob watched as Finkel collapsed on the ground next to Lauren. Bradley was still standing, looking down at them in disbelief.

Jacob aimed his gun at Bradley as the general bent down to check their bodies. The rumbling stopped.

"Jake," said Malcolm, "it's over."

Bradley got up and started walking toward him. Jacob aimed the gun, but Malcolm grabbed his arm.

"Jake, it's okay," he said. "He's with us. He's on our side."

"How did that happen?" said Bradley.

"I'll explain in a minute," said Malcolm. "Look."

He was pointing to the bodies. They appeared to be fading. Then, in a matter of seconds, they had completely disintegrated.

"Where the hell did they go?" said Jacob.

"Exactly," said a familiar voice coming from the direction of the monitors.

Jacob looked over to see if his ears were deceiving him. But no, there he was—Jacques—alive and well, and wearing a long white robe.

Jacques' sudden appearance took a minute to register. Then, Jacob began to put two and two together.

"Wait a minute," he said. "Are you—"

"I'm Jacques," said the Frenchman. "We met in Frankfurt."

"No, said Jacob, "I mean besides being Jacques, are you who I think you are?"

"But I do not know who you think I am," said Jacques, who appeared as mystified as Jacob.

"He's one of us," said Malcolm. "A sentinel. He was sent to watch over you in Frankfurt."

"Yes," said Jacques. "And I fear our friend in the Masonic library there was one of *them*. I told you he was not to be trusted."

"It sure took you long enough to get here," said Beeze.

"But I did as we agreed and presented all the evidence to the arbiter."

"The arbiter?" said Jacob.

Jacques looked up at the monitors. "Voilà," he said, pointing to the eighth monitor.

Jacob watched as a new image began appearing. Slowly, he could begin to make it out. It was a bridge of some sort.

Then, as the image cleared, he could see that it was a picture of him, as an old man, lying dead under the Benjamin Franklin Bridge in Philadelphia. He remembered that bitter, cold night, trying to stay alive to hear the election results. He never did hear them. But he knew from this life that Kennedy had won. How strange to have the memories of both lives.

"I don't understand," he said. "What does it mean?"

"It means," said Malcolm, "that your sacrifice has given humanity another chance, Jake. Finkel requested a judgment from the arbiter. And he got one. Except once we brought our evidence forward of their tampering, the judgment was against them."

Jacob felt a hand on his shoulder.

"You did good, Jake." It was Bradley. "I'm sorry for all the turmoil I put you through, but it was necessary. One of my guards was one of *them*."

"It's okay," said Jacob.

Jacob looked over to the floor where Finkel and Lauren had disappeared. "Why were my bullets able to kill them?" he said. "But not you."

"Ah," said Jacques, "the arbiter's judgment rendered them mortal. And, so they were at your mercy. Only they did not know it yet. But they are not dead. It is unfortunate, but they were taken just before they disappeared. By the evil one. Now there will be no doubt about their allegiance."

"Who took them? What evil one?"

Just then, the rumbling sounds began again. Jacob looked up to see another monitor rising up beside the others—a ninth. When it reached the height of the other monitors, the noises stopped. It was blank. Jacob watched anxiously, waiting to see what the image would be. But it never came.

"There will be another judgment," said Malcolm. "It could be years from now, or centuries. Meanwhile, our task is to set things right again. But there are other, powerful forces working against us."

Malcolm waved his arm and a giant holographic screen appeared.

"You have many questions, Jake, I know," said Malcolm. "Including your part in all this, and why you were chosen as the subject of this particular judgment. Watch. I'll explain who we are, who the arbiter is, and tell you the truth about your involvement."

Chapter 53
The Ring of Seven

Jacob stared at the massive holographic display. A series of egg-shaped clusters of stars and celestial bodies was appearing on the screen.

"Jake," said Malcolm, "as the scientific community has theorized for years, there are many universes. And each of these clusters represents a separate universe. There are many more than this image shows. What you see is just a graphical representation."

Malcolm waved his hand, and a large circle appeared, surrounding all the clusters.

"Together," he said, "they make up what scientists have come to call the *multiverse*. As you know, this mega-universe is often described as constantly expanding, and yet space and distance are purely human concepts, as is time. I won't get into the physics, nor the errors that scientists have made for decades trying to reconcile the theory of everything. And CMB radiation is a red herring."

"I don't quite follow," said Jacob.

"And you won't. Not that part, anyway."

Jacob watched as a series of small dots now appeared around each egg-shaped cluster.

"Each universe," said Malcolm, "is overseen by two hundred sentinels, or watchers. Their role—or I should say *our* role—is to maintain and evolve the species, with the ultimate goal of reproducing sentinel-level beings, a process which, I might add, can take millions of your years. The earth is pretty unique in that regard. It's one of the only places in the entire multiverse with the right conditions for evolutionary life."

"Are there others?" said Jacob.

"Of course." Malcolm looked surprised that he'd even ask.

Jacob watched in awe as a hand-like symbol appeared next to each cluster. The pictogram looked similar to the Hamsa symbol, used by both Jews and Muslims to represent the hand of God—though, from what he remembered, its origins predated both religions.

"For each universe," said Malcolm, "there is an arbiter. Think of it as sort of a cosmic judge. But all of the arbiters—like every single entity in the multiverse—are bound to a single, cosmic force. It might help to think of the arbiters as mirrors of that force."

"So the arbiters are all-seeing?" said Jacob.

"We don't know for sure. It's an energy force. We can make requests, and we can sense the response. But the arbiter doesn't act independently. Even we don't know its true nature. There's much more, but you need to trust me that you wouldn't even begin to comprehend it."

Jacob was amazed. He felt as if he had some private entrée to the secrets of the world. And yet, in a way, he knew as little as he had before, perhaps even less.

"So now, said Malcolm, "I guess you want to know about all of us—the sentinels."

"Yes," said Jacob. "I mean I've known you most of my life. And yet there are only two hundred of you in the entire universe? Where are all the others?"

Malcolm smiled, as Bradley walked up beside him.

"Jake," said Bradley, "the sentinels are all over the place. We wander the earth in human form. In the early days, we were more hands-on, so to speak. It was sentinels who first taught the world about gardening, and tools. And everything from astrology to cosmetics, weapons, writing, the signs of the sun and moon, you name it."

"Hey," said Beeze, "you forgot about me."

Bradley laughed, "Oh yes, and stories. That was Beeze's role. He's a relatively new sentinel of some five millennia, the baby of the group. Anyway, we used stories to impart wisdom, and then it was up to the human tribes to pass it down."

"Yeah, and you know how that goes," said Beeze. "Damn fools changed everything around."

"Jake," said Malcolm, "through the years, we've appeared to prophets, philosophers, pacifists, and anyone we felt would be influential. In the old days, some called us gods, and in the western religions, we were thought to be angels or messengers. That's when we were more obvious in our appearance and speech. Now, we blend in."

Bradley looked at Beeze. "Some more than others," he said.

"So the Greek and Roman myths," said Jacob, "and the Egyptian beliefs, all those gods and goddesses—"

"All based on manifestations of the same cosmic force," said Malcolm. "And mostly inspired by us. And yet, you all still fight over your various belief systems."

"Separateness," said Jacques, "is the greatest illusion of mankind."

This was a revelation to Jacob. All his life, he had struggled to understand how the many religions, each firm in their own beliefs, could hold fast to the idea that theirs was the right way. Everything he was now hearing was validating what he truly believed, that everyone was connected somehow.

"So, I have to ask," said Jacob. "Are there good sentinels and bad sentinels?" The whole idea of good and evil was something he'd always wondered about.

Malcolm, Beeze, Jacques, and Bradley all looked at each other, as if they weren't sure how to answer the question.

"Do we tell him?" said Beeze.

Malcolm nodded.

Jacques spoke first.

"After monitoring humans in the early days," he said, "it became obvious that the human experiment was at risk. The species did not appear to be evolving as it should. As you may imagine, this development was very disturbing to us. After all, this was our fifth try—three of them on Earth and two on the planet you call Mars. This, so far, was our best hope."

"Mars?" said Jacob. "And when were the other attempts on Earth?"

"Before you were born," said Beeze.

"Anyway," said Jacques, "the Order of Sentinels decided to watch and wait. But some of us grew impatient. We argued over whether to get involved once again, but we could not come to an agreement. This is when Monsieur Finkel began calling for a restart."

"What's a restart?" said Jacob.

It's a relaunch of the species," said Malcolm. "A fresh start, in hopes it might evolve differently. Think of the earth as a garden. If the seeds don't take, you change some things around, change the soil a little, and try again. This is what Finkel and six other sentinels were trying to justify."

"Is that the Ring of Seven?" said Jacob.

"Yes," said Malcolm, "and I was one of them. We each wore a ring with a doomsday symbol to signify our commitment."

Malcolm pointed to the screen and an image of a ring appeared, showing a strange symbol that looked like a three-pronged ladder.

"It didn't take long, though," said Malcolm, "before I started to become suspicious of their motives. Originally, their intentions were sincere. But then it became obvious they were being influenced by a much darker force, especially when they began discussing ways to influence history in their favor."

"You mean by interfering with human events?" said Jacob.

"Indirectly, but yes," said Malcolm. "That's when I alerted Cole here. We were both going to leave the group, but I convinced him to stay, to keep an eye on things. I did leave though, and I've been watching them ever since. They replaced me with another member. It's thanks to Cole that we got wind of their devious plan."

"And what was their plan?" said Jacob.

"I watched it all unfold," said Bradley. "The initial idea was Finkel's. If Hitler would die before his rise to power, the intricate web of changes would lead to a global nuclear catastrophe, just as you witnessed."

"But how did Finkel know that would happen?" said Jacob.

"How can I put this?" said Bradley. "We see more...broadly than you do. That doesn't mean we know every event that will happen; but we can quickly see all the possibilities, probabilities, and interconnecting waterways, so to speak. Anyway, the next thing they had to figure out was how to get Hitler to die without killing him directly, since it's a cardinal sin for us to do that."

"Wait a minute," said Jacob. "I thought Finkel was the one who negotiated peace in the Middle East. Why would he do that?"

"Like I said," said Malcolm, "Finkel was a wolf in sheep's clothing. A small population of peaceful, unarmed people would be an easy mark for a takeover by someone who could be groomed into a position of power. It might have taken a few years, or maybe decades, but it would have happened. You see, Jake, Finkel wasn't aiming for peace; he was aiming for control. I could see it in his eyes at the conference in DC. He was no longer the Finkel I knew. He was being guided by a much darker force—one that we've learned over the years to recognize. And when he told you that maybe it was God's plan for you to change the world, I'd had enough."

"Yeah," said Beeze, "but Finkel was easy compared to our buddy Lauren."

"It was Lauren," said Bradley, "who led the effort to kill Hitler. You see, there's something you need to know about Lauren. She's the ultimate temptress, able to get anyone to give in to her seductive ways without the blink of an eye."

"I can vouch for that," said Jacob.

"Well, you ain't the only one," said Beeze. "She's been doin' that to folks since antiquity. She's been known by a shitload of names, too. Lilith. Isis. Ishtar. Aphrodite. Venus. And when people stopped believing in gods and goddesses, that's when she became even more dangerous. So, I'd say, all things considered, you did pretty damn good. You pulled some magic outta your ass. Like Twain said, 'It's important to give it all you have while you have the chance.' And you came through when it counted."

"Beeze," said Malcolm, "I'm impressed. I didn't even know Mark Twain said that."

"He didn't," said Beeze. "That was *Shania* Twain."

"You'll have to excuse Monsieur Beeze," said Jacques. "He is, as we said, newer than the rest of us."

"Yeah, and after all these millennia, I finally earned my wings!" said Beeze.

"Wait a minute," said Jacob. "You mean, you guys have w—"

"Nah," said Beeze. "I'm kiddin' about the wings. It'd be cool, though!"

Malcolm was shaking his head, chuckling.

"Jake," said Bradley, taking a more serious tone, "it was Lauren who sent all those people after you. As she usually does, she manipulated them indirectly. Typically, these groups operate through a barely traceable series of connections, generally under a leader who's been lied to and manipulated. The people who attacked you probably never even met her."

Jacob shook his head. "So, how did she come to use me to kill Hitler? How did I get involved in all this?"

Bradley glanced at Malcolm.

"Lauren tried all sorts of things," said Malcolm. "And if she couldn't bring about Hitler's death, she'd try to bring about his insanity, or I should say expedite it. She started by possessing Eva Braun, leading her to engage in wild partying, nude sunbathing, anything to taunt Hitler."

"Nowadays, she'd be in Hollywood in her own reality show," said Beeze.

Jacob couldn't help laughing.

"The more Eva taunted," said Malcolm, "the angrier Hitler got. He was consumed by his own visions of grandeur. But as it turned out, the one being tortured to madness was Eva, not Hitler. She tried a number of times to kill herself. She eventually did, with Hitler no less, but by that time, the damage was done."

"That's incomprehensible!" said Jacob.

"It gets worse," said Beeze.

"Next," said Malcolm, "she moved on to Hitler's niece. Lauren possessed her too, luring her to make efforts to seduce her own uncle. Hitler rejected her, and, like Eva Braun, she killed herself. She wasn't much older than a child."

"Gotta hand it to Hitler," said Beeze. "The man had morals."

Jacob shook his head in disgust.

"Lauren was secretly influential in seventeen known attempts to kill Hitler," said Malcolm, and a dozen or so others that were never discovered. They all went wrong for various reasons. Some we were able to avert indirectly. But, Lauren doesn't take well to failure. In every case, she gets even."

"So, where do I come in?" said Jacob.

Malcolm looked at him and took a breath. The others were looking back and forth at Malcolm and Jacob.

"Lauren's very first attempt to kill Hitler," said Malcolm, "was with your grandfather."

Malcolm paused.

"Tell me," said Jacob. "I want to know everything."

He was trying to keep calm, but, inside, his blood was boiling.

"It was Lauren," said Bradley, "who orchestrated your grandfather and uncle's plot. She took the role of a local prostitute in Munich. She introduced her favorite client, Müller, to the bartender, Joseph. She even arranged for Hitler's regular psychiatrist to be out of the country. Then, she seduced and slept with Samuel to put the ideas in his head. But they never went through with the plot. Max didn't want to involve Anna and felt it was too risky overall. Samuel agreed."

"So she wanted to get even," said Jacob. "How, by killing Anna? By killing my parents?"

"Yes," said Malcolm. "Indirectly, of course. One of the Nazi officers who caught your grandmother was a member of the Ring of Seven. Alexander Kurtz."

"You think the others are bad," said Beeze. "Wait till you see that scar-faced bastard."

"Wait a minute," said Jacob. "Did you say scar-faced?"

"Yeah," said Beeze. "Big ole' scar running down the side of his face. Given to him by Lauren, too. The only good thing she ever did."

"I met him," said Jacob."

"Yes," said Bradley. "He was at the conference in Paris."

"I remember now," said Jacob. "The reporter in the audience who kept giving me a hard time. But why were they there? Why was Finkel there?"

"That's exactly what I was trying to figure out," said Bradley. "It was me who pulled you out of the mob afterward, so you could get to the taxi."

Jacob thought back to the conference, trying to piece things together. It still wasn't making sense.

"So, with all this," said Jacob, "where do I come in? How did I get on this project? And what is this ship, anyway?"

"Jake," said Malcolm, "it's complicated, but I'll explain. After all the failed attempts on Hitler's life, Lauren came up with an ingenious plan. If she couldn't convince someone to kill Hitler, she'd groom someone to do it. Not only that, but she could exact her revenge on your grandfather in the process. You see, all of her actions—killing Anna, killing your parents, and everything that followed—would eventually feed your anger."

"But that took generations."

"It's all relative. Generations to you go by like minutes to her. Anyway, thanks to Cole, I got wind that she was targeting you for something, but we didn't know what. All the things I've told you so far, I know in hindsight, and wasn't aware of at the time. Anyway, when your grandfather died, I volunteered at the detention center where you were living, to keep an eye on you. But for years, nothing else happened. It wasn't until I saw that an Ab Ovo unit was exposed that I knew something was up."

"A what?"

"Ab Ovo unit. That's what you've been referring to as the ship."

"So it's not a ship? Then what is it?"

At that moment, Jacob was almost knocked off his feet when the ship—or whatever it was—began shaking again.

"I'll tell you what it is," said Beeze. "It's something we shouldn't be in right now!"

Jacob tried to stay upright as the vibrations grew stronger. This episode seemed more powerful than any of the others. As he looked around, it now appeared that the monitors, and even the walls, were fading.

He felt Malcolm grab his arm.

"What's going on?" said Jacob.

He could feel the vibrations run through his body, to the point where he couldn't tell his own flesh apart from what was happening around him. Everything was a blur, and he felt as if he were stuck in the middle of a huge earthquake. Then he felt his body lifting slowly. He knew what was coming next. He'd be taking that grueling thrill ride once again—though to where, he didn't know.

Chapter 54

Answers

When he finally stopped falling, Jacob found himself kneeling on soft grass. He stood up and looked around. He was on some kind of grassy plateau atop a high mountain. He saw Malcolm standing at the edge of the plateau, staring out at a vast green valley. He didn't see Beeze, Jacques, or Bradley anywhere.

"Where are the others?" said Jacob.

"Oh, they're around," said Malcolm. "It's a big planet," he added, smiling.

"Where the hell are we, anyway?"

"Someplace Earth-like, where you can breathe oxygen. Let's leave it at that. Beautiful, isn't it?"

"Yes," said Jacob. That was an understatement. Everything was pristine, with perfectly green grass and purple, yellow, and red flowers. He felt like he was in a Monet painting. "What happened to all the lab techs and the crew?" he added.

"They were evacuated safely before you arrived," said Malcolm. "We had to arrange an event that warranted evacuation. A bit of a fire."

"So what was all that violent shaking? What just happened? And what did you call that thing?"

"An Ab Ovo unit," said Malcolm. "The arbiter rendered it invisible again, as it was supposed to be."

"And just what is an Ab Ovo unit?"

"It's a womb of sorts. It means 'from the egg' in Latin. There are many around the world. They're usually invisible to the human eye. That's why it's organic. It's used to generate all life forms on earth. Even humans, in fact, began as an aquatic life form. The full evolutionary process takes quite a long time. If you really want to know about the origins of human evolution, Jake, study the seas. Anyway, the Ab Ovo units are where new human life would come from in the event of a true restart."

"A restart?"

"Like I mentioned earlier, a new attempt at the species. This isn't the first one, you know, and it may not be the last. Anyway, as soon as this particular unit was exposed, I knew Finkel and Lauren had to be up to something. They knew it would be discovered by the U.S. Navy, and that you, as the world's foremost expert on image transfer and communication, might be sought out. But more important, the Ring knew I'd bring you in as bait. You see, they weren't only getting even with your grandfather; they were getting even with me. Like a fool, I played right into their hands. Their plan was absolutely ingenious."

"So they used the Ab Ovo unit to lure me to the ship through you. And then what? They planted time travel devices?"

"Exactly. They carried out their plan to use you to kill Hitler, right under my eyes."

"But the images on the monitors—"

"Put there by the Ring of Seven for three reasons. To build a case for the arbiter; to lure you to the ship; and mostly, to keep Beeze and me busy while Lauren carried out her plan."

"How about the Kronos device?"

"The device, the sphere, the alcove, all of it was manifested by them as a puzzle to allow you to figure out how to traverse universal boundaries."

"Travel through time."

"Well, not really, but you can think of it that way. The fact is, the truth would blow your mind, and don't ask because I'm not about to explain it. Either way, I brought Beeze in to shadow Lauren. But neither of us knew exactly what that equipment was for, or what she was up to. Along with the images, the Kronos device was the perfect distraction."

"Yes, about the Kronos device: when I shot it, it disappeared."

"That's because it was no longer needed. You made the wise decision to reject it. You didn't notice, but at the same time, the sphere disappeared too. So did the alcove."

Jacob thought about all this. Something was still puzzling him.

"When you rescued me when our plane was about to crash," he said, "you were using the Kronos device."

"You only thought I was using it. I had to give that illusion at the time. The fact is, I have no clue how that thing works. You transported to the Ab Ovo unit because I brought you there, not because of the device."

"But then I saw you explode into a million pieces of light!"

"Again, looks can be deceiving, Jake. It was a distraction, that's all. I set up a field to hold Finkel at bay as long as I could, then I transported away."

"I was worried," said Jacob. "I thought you were dead. So what now? Where do I go from here? Do we still have a project?"

Malcolm smiled.

"Well, Jake, the Kronos Project is finished. It'll be filed away and labeled unsolvable. The Ab Ovo unit will be gone, as far as human perception is concerned. But we'll have other needs for your services, both in your world, and ours."

"Yours?" said Jacob. "I'm human. What good could I do in your world? I'm not even sure how to act in mine."

"Jake, when Finkel and Lauren attacked you with their energy beams, you withstood them. What you don't understand is that they weren't trying to kill you. Even they wouldn't dare kill a human. They were trying to use your own negative energy—fear, and anger, and revenge—and turn it back on you tenfold, until you had no choice but to react with violence. But you rejected those emotions. You knew that you can't put out a fire with another fire. Instead you chose love. You thought of your wife, and your daughter, and the negative energy was gone. You couldn't have done that without the memories of all you'd been through, and the strength from already having sacrificed your life once. That's a powerful thing, Jake. Lauren was dead set on using you to make a case to the arbiter. The Ring could have used a million other cases of human violence, and on a much grander scale, but she wanted you. And if they had gotten you to attack them, they might have made a grand case—the creature attacks its creator. But you didn't."

"Actually, I did," said Jacob. "I shot them."

"By then," said Malcolm, "the arbiter's judgment had been made. Like I said, Finkel called for a judgment, and he got one. And besides, you shot them to protect humanity, and this time it was an imminent threat, not a hunch. Jake, I think you came to the conclusion yourself earlier. There are no absolutes in life. Only opportunities, and choices. Do you understand that now?"

Jacob nodded. For the first time, he really did understand. He thought more about Finkel, and Lauren, and the others. Finkel and Lauren were gone now. But what about the rest of them?

"Malcolm," he said, "what about the others?"

"I don't follow," said Malcolm.

"The rest of the Ring of Seven. Besides Finkel and Lauren, there was Cole Bradley and one of his guards, and that guy Alex Kurtz. So that leaves two more."

"Don't forget about the librarian at the lodge in Frankfurt," said Malcolm.

"Okay, so that still leaves one. Not to mention that Kurtz is still running around somewhere."

Malcolm took a deep breath.

"Jake," he said, "we won this round. Thanks to you, humanity has a chance to redeem itself. But the war is far from over. Finkel and Lauren are aligned with a powerful and much darker force now, and you can be sure they'll be in contact with Kurtz. As for the seventh member of the Ring, let's just say it's a situation we're keeping a very close eye on. You're right to be concerned. You have some unique powers of your own though, Jake, which is good. They'll be a new weapon in our fight. Still, those powers will be put to the test. The Ring can't kill you or they'd be breaking a universal law, but they can try to get at you in other ways. But you won't be alone, I can assure you."

Just then, Jacob heard a faint hum, and saw a pillar of swirling, colored lights forming in the distance, in mid-air. It was coming closer.

"What is that?" he said.

"Your ride home," said Malcolm.

"Aren't you coming?"

"Not quite yet. But you haven't seen the last of me by a long shot. I'll be calling you for your next project. Meanwhile, be with your family. You've earned it."

The pillar of light touched down onto the grass, several yards in front of them. Jacob walked toward it and turned around.

"How can I reach you?" he said.

"I'll be in touch. And you have my cell." Malcolm was smiling.

"Will anything be different when I go back?"

"Everything will be the same," said Malcolm, "except for your new outlook on life, and one other thing, but I'll let you figure out what that is when you get there."

Jacob was curious, but he didn't ask. There was one thing, though.

"One last question," he said, "and you don't have to answer it if you don't want to."

"Shoot," said Malcolm.

"Which came first, the chicken or the egg?"

Malcolm smiled, then he turned and walked away, vanishing into thin air. Jacob saw a million lights in his place. Then the lights dissipated.

Jacob shook his head and turned again toward the pillar of light. He stepped into it and felt the vibrations extend throughout his body. He froze in place, anticipating that floating feeling, when suddenly, he felt a hand on his shoulder. He couldn't turn around, but then the figure moved around to his front.

It was Beeze.

Jacob could feel himself lifting high into the air.

"The chicken!" yelled Beeze, looking up at him. "It's always the chicken!"

At that second, he felt himself falling and spinning, practically losing consciousness, as he took the grueling trip through time and space. It seemed to go on forever, much longer than any of his other trips.

When he finally landed, he shook off the cobwebs to see where he was. To his surprise, he was back in the airport restroom, where he'd been talking to Kim. His cell phone was still on the floor where he'd dropped it.

He picked it up.

"Kim?"

"Jake, what was that noise?" she said.

"Nothing. I just dropped the phone. How long was I gone?"

"Just for a second, but I heard a bang. Are you okay?"

Her voice sounded shaky still.

"Am I okay?" he said. "Yes, but how about you?"

"The doctor," she said. Then she broke off crying again. "The cancer..."

His heart was in his throat.

"The cancer's gone," she said. "It's gone." Then she started crying uncontrollably again.

"What do you mean, it's gone?" he said. He was choked up, and could barely get the words out.

"I mean gone," she said, "as in no sign of it. They said it's like a miracle. Come home, Jake. Please come home."

"I'm coming home now," he said.

Just then, Jess's tiny voice came on the phone.

"I love you, Daddy," she said.

Her voice had never sounded so precious.

"I love you too, peanut," he said. "More than you will ever know. I'm coming home now."

"Yay!" she said.

After hanging up, he couldn't help thinking of the Beatles song. Maybe they were right. Maybe all you need is love. That, and friends in high places.

Chapter 55

Return

As the taxi pulled up to his house, Jacob felt a combination of complete joy, utter fatigue, and a tremendous weight on his shoulders. A million thoughts were floating in his head as he absent-mindedly paid the driver.

He unlocked the door quietly, as it was late, and Kim and Jessica would be asleep. He entered without making a sound. It was dark, as he expected, save for a light near the kitchen that Kim always left on. There was a note on the kitchen table from Kim.

Love you, honey.
Welcome back! Talk in the AM.
Your two sweeties

Jacob smiled. Part of him felt like he'd been away for a hundred years, though he knew it had only been a day. He'd have to get used to the combined memories of two lives. Next time he had déjà vu, at least he'd know where it was coming from.

As late as it was, he knew he couldn't just lie down and go to sleep. He was too wired. Instead, he poured a glass of milk and sat in the armchair in the family room. His mind wandered to the day before in Paris. He thought about what Bradley had said, how it was strange that Finkel and Kurtz would be there for no apparent reason, except perhaps to meet the subject of their devious plans. Then, he thought perhaps there was more to it. It was quite a coincidence that the video he had presented from the dead brain was taken from a World War II soldier. Could it, too, have been staged, in an attempt to get him thinking about Hitler?

Curious, he turned on the hologram player, keeping the sound down, and popped in the video transmission card. The video began. He watched as the title came on:

NBIC—Program 4233, File Q1240, Sample #12.

Then the video started. The Jewish prisoner was running away toward an open field. Jacob could see only the back of the man.

"Shoot him," said the offscreen voice to the right.

Jacob watched as the soldier's trembling hand appeared, aiming a gun. The soldier hesitated.

The voice again said, "Shoot him!"

Jacob looked carefully as the prisoner reached the trees in the distance and started heading back with a handful of fruit.

He paused the image to see if he could make out the man's face, but he couldn't.

He pressed *Play* again, and the video continued.

"Look," said the soldier. "He was only going for fruit. He's coming back."

The man offscreen, no doubt a Nazi official, grabbed the gun out of the soldier's hand and shot the prisoner. Jacob paused the image, then put it in reverse, clicking to move frame by frame. He wanted to see the Nazi's hand.

As he clicked back to where the Nazi was grabbing the gun away, he could make out a ring on the man's finger. He zoomed in on the image, and his heart started pounding. Sure enough, it was the same doomsday symbol Malcolm had shown him from the Ring of Seven!

Jacob clicked back a few more frames until he could see the back of the Nazi officer's head. After a few more clicks, he could see the man turning his head ever so slightly, just enough for Jacob to make out the long scar that ran down the side of the man's face. It was Kurtz!

"Gotcha!" said Jacob. Then he realized something. At first, it didn't dawn on him. He was so excited that he'd made the discovery that he didn't realize its full implications. But now he did. He now had video evidence of a member of the Ring of Seven directly murdering a human being. This had to be worth something.

Immediately, Jacob ran to his secure phone and tried calling Malcolm. The phone rang multiple times, but there was no answer. Malcolm was probably beyond reach somewhere. Jacob half expected a voice mail message that said, "I'm in another universe at the moment, but please leave a message at the beep." But there was no message at all, as usual.

After hanging up the phone, Jacob went back to turn off the hologram player and took out the video card. He'd have to keep it secure until he could get it to Malcolm. He walked down to the basement, where he kept a hidden safe for top secret scientific information. He entered the passcode, held his hand on the fingerprint scanner, and opened the safe. Then he slipped the video card in and locked it up.

Finally exhausted enough for sleep, he headed upstairs to bed.

He felt like he had been asleep for five minutes, when he was awoken by Jess jumping on him. The light was shining in through the bedroom window. It was morning already.

"Daddy, Daddy!" she said.

He was groggy, but held her tight. He held onto her and smelled her soft hair. He never wanted to let go. He'd lost her once, albeit in another life, and would never lose her again.

"I'm here," he said. "I'm here."

He could smell coffee. Kim must have already gone downstairs.

"Let's go see Mommy," he said.

He climbed out of bed, picked Jessica up and carried her downstairs.

When he saw Kim and she rushed up to him and hugged him, he felt like all was right with the world, if only for this moment. He wanted to bottle the experience so he could take it with him anywhere he went. He was so glad to have her alive, and healthy, and cancer-free. She even looked more vibrant. The old glow was back, and her smile was brighter than ever. He held Jessica, and the three of them embraced. Malcolm was right. Something *had* changed.

"The project was canceled," he said. "Looks like I'll be home for a while. Remember my promise—we'd have all the time in the world?"

"I didn't think you'd keep it," she said. "And I *really* didn't think I could. I guess somebody was on our side."

He had to laugh. "Yes," he said. "I think somebody was."

"Oh, I almost forgot," she said. "Malcolm called this morning."

"Malcolm? He did? Damn, I was hoping to reach him. Did you talk to him?"

"Yes, he was very nice as usual. He said he'd be out of town for a few days, but would call you when he returned. His exact words were to tell you to sit tight."

A few days. Crap. He was dying to talk to Malcolm, but as long as the video card was secure, he supposed a few days wouldn't matter. After all, what was done was done.

"Okay," he said. "Sit tight I will."

He glanced over at all the items on the kitchen counter: flour, butter, eggs, sugar. He couldn't help thinking of the market on the road to Hamburg.

"I'm making pancakes," Kim said. "I'll call you when they're ready."

"Can't wait," he said.

He went into the family room and turned on the TV.

The president was boarding Air Force One. He was heading to the Middle East for peace talks. Relations were at an all-time low between Israel and the Arab countries. Each side was blaming the other, as they always did, but there didn't seem to be any room for negotiation, and violence was escalating. The situation made him think of Finkel, negotiating peace in the Middle East. Except Finkel was negotiating a false peace in a war-ravaged world. The world could use someone to bring about a real peace, but with better intentions—and without a nuclear

Armageddon. Already though, the nukes were heating up again among Russia, China, and the U.S.

As the president was waving, Jacob noticed the sunlight flashing off his ring. He had to laugh. After all the events of the last twenty-four hours, he'd be looking at anyone and everyone with a ring, and thinking they were some demonic entity. Luckily, there was only one more Ring of Seven member to be found, and, like Malcolm had said, it was a situation they were watching closely.

Just for shits and giggles, he decided to back the image up and watch again as the president waved. As soon as the light hit the ring, he froze the frame. Then he zoomed in.

As he looked closer, the ring at first looked suspiciously like the one Malcolm had showed him. It had to be a coincidence, though. Then he zoomed more and waited for the image to clear.

As it sharpened, pixel by pixel, he felt the hair on his arms stand up. A chill ran down his spine.

It *was* the doomsday ring, down to every last goddamn detail!

He sunk back in his armchair and looked up.

"You have got to be fucking kidding me!"

"Hey, you know Jess is in here," Kim yelled from the kitchen.

Just then, Jessica came running in to see him.

"Daddy," she said, "God made Mommy better, and He hears everything."

He smiled and held her hands in his.

"You're right, Jess," he said. "He'll forgive me though. You see, He and I have an understanding."

He unpaused the image and watched as the president boarded the plane. He shook his head and looked up again. "Really?" he said.

"Pancakes are ready!" yelled Kim.

"Come on, Daddy," said Jessica.

He took a deep breath, held up the remote, and turned off the TV.

When he walked into the kitchen with Jessica, Kim was looking at him with a crooked smile.

"So," she said, "you and God have an understanding? This I'd like to hear."

Jacob put his arm around Jessica and looked at Kim. It was hard to believe he'd almost lost them both.

"He understands," said Jacob, "that I couldn't live without either of you."

"You don't have to," said Kim. She embraced him, and they both held Jessica close.

Just then, he looked up, and saw Ethan standing at the kitchen entrance! He must have gotten the good news about Kim.

As Ethan joined them, Jacob could barely contain himself. For the first time in what seemed like a very long time, he had his whole family back. And he knew, no matter what happened next, he wasn't about to lose them again.

About the Authors

Edward Miller

As chief editor for a sci-fi gaming website for over fifteen years, Edward Miller has crafted hundreds of stories designed to take readers to new places and immerse them in mind-bending situations. This is his first full-length novel.

In a former life as a musician, Edward toured the United States with such acts as Foghat, The Allman Brothers Band, Edgar Winter, 38 Special, and others. Edward resides in Willow Grove, Pennsylvania with his wife and family, along with their dog, Lady.

J. B. Manas

J. B. Manas is a Philadelphia native whose world travels and passion for science, history, and the arts have led some to call him the consummate Renaissance Man. He's an avid movie buff, a wine collector, a songwriter and guitarist, a technology geek, and an armchair philosopher—all of which make their way into his writing at one time or another.

A senior editor by day and a leading expert on organizational ethics and lessons from history, his bestselling non-fiction works have received critical acclaim for being extensively researched, yet entertaining and accessible. This is his debut leap into fiction.

Visit the authors' blog at www.MillerandManas.wordpress.com

Like us on Facebook at www.facebook.com/MillerandManas

For more books from Pop Culture Zoo Press, visit www.popculturezoopress.com

Made in the USA
Lexington, KY
21 August 2012